Praise for DANIEL

"*Warrior Witch* felt like a roller coaster to me, in the best way possible. I loved how Jensen managed to throw me off still by revealing aspects about certain characters. How she managed to change my mind on characters I felt very strongly about. In my opinion, this is a great example of a final book done right."
The Fictional Reader

"*Warrior Witch* is the ending that this amazing series deserves. The ending that completely destroys you and then fixes you. The ending that your heart will never forget."
The Reader & the Chef

"From all the endings of series I've loved before, *Warrior Witch* has got to be the most painfully beautiful I've read."
The Nocturnal Fey

"*Stolen Songbird* is a fantastic debut. The book had an amazing cast of developed characters, an intriguing plot, a swoon-worthy romance and an ending that'll have you itching for the next book. I'd definitely recommend it."
YA Midnight Reads

"*Stolen Songbird* is an absolutely wonderful edition to the fantasy genre. The book is full of magic, adventure, outlandish creatures, and at its heart is one of the most touching love stories I have ever read... This novel takes a very old fairytale cliché, and turns it into a stunningly original and beautiful story... So obviously I really like this book and I am going to go ahead and give it a 9/10. This is the highest rating so far!"
Avid Reviews

"*Stolen Songbird* is an enticing beginning to a magical new trilogy. The passion between Cécile and Tristan simmers tantalizingly beneath the surface, anticipating the slightest of sparks that will fully ignite it. Jensen has created a vivid and complex world that readers will be eager to explore further in the next two instalments."

Teen Reads

"*Hidden Huntress* opens up the world, simply put. It felt bigger and more encompassing, upping the ante for all involved. The pull of the story was irresistible, given how so much more now rests on the success of our protagonists. Everything that the first book set us up for comes to fruition, complete with welcome twists and unexpected surprises... that incredible ending sure has me eager for book three."

The Bibliosanctum

"Overall, *Hidden Huntress* undeniably surpasses as a sequel to *Stolen Songbird*. I was blown away by the ending and cannot wait for book three! Danielle L Jensen has shaped an underground city of magical creatures into one of my most valued book worlds – and that makes me extremely excited for future works."

Life Writings of a Reader

"With all kinds of magic and witchery, this book embodies the title of *Hidden Huntress*. Danielle L Jensen has shaped an underground city of magical creatures into one of my most valued book worlds – and that makes me extremely excited for future works."

Adriyanna K Zimmerman

"Without any doubt, I can already say that *Stolen Songbird* will end up on my and many other lists of best novels for young adults published this year. *Stolen Songbird* is an example is how it looks when a team of professionals works on a book: great writing, editing and design too. What did I like? The list is mile long."

YA Books Central

DANIELLE L JENSEN

Warrior Witch

THE MALEDICTION TRILOGY III

ANGRY
ROBOT

ANGRY ROBOT
An imprint of Watkins Media Ltd

Lace Market House,
54-56 High Pavement,
Nottingham,
NG1 1HW
UK

www.angryrobotbooks.com
twitter.com/angryrobotbooks
Ever after

An Angry Robot paperback original 2016

Cover by Steve Stone
Set in Sabon by Epub Services

Distributed in the United States by Penguin Random House, Inc., New York.

ISBN 978 0 85766 469 3
Ebook ISBN 978 0 85766 470 9

Printed in the United States of America

9 8 7 6 5 4 3 2 1

*For KG, who allowed me just enough sleep
to finish this novel.*

CHAPTER 1
Cécile

My voice, the one thing about me that had always been valued, suddenly seemed inconsequential in the cacophony of voices filling the courtyard. Questions and demands fought with the cries of those whose nerves had collapsed in the face of this unknown adversary, their collective onslaught driving me back step by step until I stood apart in the snow.

Tristan raised one hand, silencing the din. "Your questions will be answered, but not here and not now." To the grim-faced Regent, he added, "Assemble your counsel. We've plans to make and time is short."

"You presume to give orders to me, boy?" the Regent replied, his tone as chilly as the air. He alone seemed calm, and I *almost* admired him for it, given that he must have known what, if not who, Tristan was. *Almost,* because I knew his scorn was directed at the one *boy* capable of saving us all.

Tristan's flash of frustration made my teeth clench, and a prickle of unease burned between my shoulders, causing me to glance in the direction of Trollus. *How soon would they come? And what would they do when they arrived?* They were questions that likely sat heavily in Tristan's mind, and both of us knew we didn't have time to stand in a courtyard arguing.

"Presume?" There was almost no inflection in Tristan's voice, but tension sang through the crowd. "Have you forgotten why you, and all those before you, have styled yourselves as 'regents'? Or perhaps you're unaware of what the title means?"

"I've forgotten nothing," the Regent snapped. "I know our history."

"Then you know it is no presumption," Tristan said. "You owe your allegiance to my family and our crown; and if you do not offer it freely, it is within my right, and certainly within my power, to take it by force."

He was silent for a moment, and I held my breath, uncertain of what he'd say next or why he believed that threatening this man was the right path to take. We needed him on our side.

"But instead I offer you a choice," Tristan continued. "Side with me and fight for the freedom of your race."

"Or?" The Regent wasn't a weak man – was as born and bred to politics as Tristan. But I did not miss the unsteadiness in his voice.

"Or don't. And I will walk away and leave you to fight this war on your own with no doubt in my mind that it will be over by morning. And all that your people will have lost – lives and loved ones and liberty – will be on your hands. That is, if my father allows you to live long enough for you to see the outcome of your choice."

All the world's blood will be on your hands... My mother's, no, Anushka's words, echoed through my thoughts, and I bit my lip.

The Regent's eyes tracked to my brother, who remained disguised as Lord Aiden. "You knew this was coming, and yet said nothing?"

Wise enough to know the man would recognize that Fred's voice was not his son's, my brother only nodded and hung his head.

The horns of Trollus ceased their call, yet, in their absence, somehow seemed more present. More ominous.

"Choose," Tristan said, and only our bond gave away his apprehension.

The Regent let out a ragged breath and inclined his head, the cords in his neck standing out as though his body itself fought the gesture of subservience. "Very well." He turned his head to a man standing to his left. "Assemble the council."

The crowd parted to make a path to the entrance of the castle, but the Regent stepped to one side. "After you, Your Highness."

Tristan started forward, Fred and the Regent falling in behind him, and none of them looked back. I raised a foot to follow, then lowered it back into the puddle that the magic coating my skin had melted into the snow. I was not needed in this, nor, I thought, glancing down at my tattered and bloodstained costume, welcome.

The crowd of nobles dispersed, some calling desperately for their carriages so they might escape to the dubious safety of their homes, while others went to peer through the lowered portcullis, the wind having eroded away the dragon's shape, leaving behind only a mound of snow. Many of them cast suspicious glances my way, understanding that I was somehow involved, but none of them guessing in what capacity. That I was responsible. That in the space of a few heartbeats, I had determined the fate of us all.

Almost from the moment I'd known the trolls existed, my purpose had been set. My goal known. Kill the witch. End the curse. Rescue Tristan. Free my friends. All of which I had accomplished.

And now?

I'd unleashed the trolls and worse upon the world with a vague certainty that it could be made to work, that we would triumph and peace would be had; but not once had I considered what role I would play. What part Tristan would play, yes. The innate decency of most of the trolls, yes. The ability of my friends to overthrow the wicked, yes. But of myself...

I swallowed hard, panic creeping in around the edges of my thoughts. Tristan had walked away without acknowledging who I was or what I'd done. Without so much as a backward glance. Logically, I knew that he would not have done so without reason. Good reason. But the dreadful grasping claws of doubt whispered something else.

The gazes of those left outside no longer seemed suspicious; they seemed full of accusation and blame. The urge to run filled me, but to where? The home of the woman I'd murdered? The hotel room filled with memories? There was nowhere and no one in Trianon that I could turn to for guidance. Except...

My feet moved, and I flew up the steps into the castle. Faster and faster I ran, through the dim corridors until I found the door I was looking for. Flinging it open, I stumbled inside. "Sabine?"

And slid to a stop. Julian knelt on the floor, his face streaked with tears and my mother's corpse in his arms. His eyes blazed with anger, and with one hand, he fumbled for the pistol at his waist and pointed it at my chest. "Murderer," he hissed.

He was not wrong.

"I laughed, I ranted, I cried twice. It was a bit of an emotional rollercoaster for me but I thoroughly enjoyed it and look forward to reading the next book in the trilogy."

Leanne Crabtree

"The writing-style was superb. I was transported to the world of Trollus and I walked side-by-side with Cécile. The setting was magical and I was sucked into the story, which has a very interesting and complex plot without being overwhelming."

The Daily Prophecy

"I would recommend this book in a heartbeat. It's a wonderful fantasy book filled with tons of magic that will leave you wanting more. I am very much looking forward to the next instalment."

The Nightly Book Owl

"If you're looking for a YA fantasy full of magic and mystery and intrigue and romance and wonderful, heartfelt characters that you could easily accept to be trapped under a mountain with, then don't just read *Stolen Songbird* – inhale it. I didn't want to wake up – and neither will you."

Jet Black Ink

"If you love fantasies, romance, and political intrigue, then you really need to add this book to your wishlist and tell all your friends you want it for your birthday, because Oh my gosh, it is my new favourite book of this year."

Book Marks the Spot

"*Hidden Huntress* definitely does not suffer 'Middle Book Syndrome'. It is full of action and gives us what we long for too. I am even more in love with the series than after finishing the first book!"

The Reading Nook NZ

CHAPTER 2
Tristan

Do not look at her! I screamed the order at myself, but keeping my back turned and taking those first few steps seemed almost impossible.

But so very necessary.

They could not learn that it was Cécile who'd killed Anushka. Bad enough that she was clearly complicit, but if the humans learned she'd wielded the knife, they'd blame her for what was to come. And already her death was sought by too many. Better that they believed it was me and have all the violence and vitriol cast at my feet.

Yet knowing it was the right choice did little to ease the sting of leaving her standing alone in the snow, hands stained with blood. It was Anushka's blood, not her mother's – for Genevieve had been dead many long years – but I doubted very much that she was yet capable of disassociating the two.

Unbidden, the memory of her lashing out with the knife crossed my vision, the blow shallow and clumsy, and yet filled with uncharacteristic violence. The second strike: more certain and deep enough to kill. And the reasons she'd given me for doing it... They'd been good and just – motivations I'd expect, knowing her as I did. Yet I couldn't help but question what had really driven her hand. She'd been under compulsion, and now, having delivered on her promise, was no longer. Did she regret what she had done?

Did I?

I shoved the thoughts from my mind. What was done was done, and my focus needed to be on formulating a plan to prevent my people – and the fey – from wreaking havoc on the Isle. And on the world. Wresting control from my father. Putting an end to Angoulême, and... *managing* Roland.

I resisted the urge to glance at Fred; that bit of deception was bound to bite me on the ass sooner rather than later, because Aiden had freed himself while I was cut off from my power. It was my fault for not tying off the magic binding him. That he hadn't shown up yet made me very uneasy. He was under my father's compulsion, but how that would manifest was yet unknown. There were too many players, too many moving parts, and I didn't feel well-enough informed to make a move one way or another.

But doing nothing would only ensure our defeat. Our enemies were almost certainly on the move – schemes months, if not years in the making, were unfolding as I scrambled to catch up.

Ahead, the doors to a chamber opened, the guards standing at either side eyeing me nervously as I passed. Ignoring the massive table surrounded by chairs, I went to the stone staircase on the far side of the room. "This leads to the tower?" I asked no one in particular.

"Yes," Fred replied, and I didn't miss the sharp glance the Regent shot his direction, silently willing Fred to keep his mouth shut until I could manage his revealing appropriately.

Taking the steps three at a time, I shoved open the iron-bound oak door at the top and stepped out into the bitter cold of winter. From this height, all of Trianon was spread out before me, the walls marked in intervals with burning torches and the better parts of the city glowing faintly from the gaslights lining the streets. It was eerily quiet, but the tension seeping out from every household was palpable, even from my lofty perch. The humans were afraid, and as much as I hated to admit it, the Winter Queen had done me a favor in that. Fear could be a unifying force, and if I could harness it, so much the better.

Shifting my gaze in the direction of Trollus, I leaned my elbows against the stone parapet, only vaguely aware of those who'd followed. My father had told Cécile of his intention to take the Isle peaceably, and to a certain extent I believed him. To that end, I knew his target would be Trianon, because whoever held the capital and its leaders controlled the Isle. Right now, *I* held the city, and it had to stay that way.

A vision of what I needed formed in my mind, and I let magic drift out and away, shaping it with willpower and practice. The walls surrounding Trianon began to glow with silver light until they appeared more magic than stone. And then I made them higher. Up and up the wall of light climbed, curving inward until the city was encased in a massive dome of magic.

"Is that to keep your kind out or us in?"

I turned. Fred, the Regent, and one other man, whom I presumed was his advisor, stood with their faces turned to the sky. Lady Marie shivered beside them, lips drawn into a thin line as she waited for an answer to her question.

"Both," I said, neglecting to add that my father and a handful of others had enough power to break through, should they feel inclined. The purpose was not to stop a frontal attack, but to keep anyone from sneaking up on me unawares. My father didn't want a war – he wanted to pull strings until everything fell into place. But that didn't mean he wouldn't resort to force if necessary. "It will buy us time to plan."

"Us?" she snarled. "If your interests were so aligned with ours, why didn't you let Anushka be? If she was still alive, none of this would be happening."

And Cécile would be dead, with me along with her. And my people would remain at the mercy of my enemies. "The costs were too high." I hesitated. "I've come to believe there's a better way."

"Is that what you told Cécile to convince her to help you kill her mother?"

It had been very much the other way around, but I was content to let her believe I was the instigator. The Regent was staring at his wife as though she were a stranger, confirming he'd had no idea that Marie was harboring the witch he'd been hunting on our behalf.

"Genevieve de Troyes was one of the many aliases Anushka used over the years," I said.

"And you knew?" the Regent demanded of his wife. "You harbored her? Do you have any idea what they would have done to us if they'd discovered your betrayal?" It dawned on him then that one of *them* stood less than two paces away. "I didn't know."

"Clearly," I said, wondering how well he was going to take the revelation of his son's betrayal. "But no longer relevant. What matters now is the defense of Trianon."

They stepped aside for me as I made my way back to the heavy door. Cécile was moving through the castle, her distress biting at my concentration. I wanted to talk to her, to find out what was going on in her head, but what I needed was to focus on discovering the plans of both my father and Angoulême. And Winter.

"What about those flying creatures? Will your dome keep them out?" Marie demanded, following me down the stairs.

Considering the fey could tear a path between worlds nearly anywhere they chose, I highly doubted it, but the question was good. She alone seemed to understand the urgency of the situation. "Only iron–" I broke off when a slice of fear lanced through me. *Cécile.*

"Iron?" she asked. "What of it?"

Where was she? Had my father's minions reached us before

I'd cut them off? Or Angoulême's?

"Marie, be silent," the Regent hissed. "He isn't interested in listening to the questions of a woman."

Pain.

I bolted down the last few stairs and across the room, passing Aiden-Fred as I ran. Only as my hands slammed against the door did it occur to me that his presence didn't make sense. Fred had been up in the tower with us. Had been silently shadowing the Regent on the stairs. Which meant the man who'd just passed me wasn't Cécile's brother.

Marie screamed, and I turned around in time to see Aiden du Chastelier plunge the point of a sword through his father's heart.

CHAPTER 3
Cécile

My first instinct was to dive out into the corridor, but sensing my intentions, Julian's finger tightened on the trigger and I froze. No amount of luck would allow me to dodge a bullet at this range: I was no troll.

"Julian, don't." I forced as much power as I could into the command, but he only sneered and flicked the sprig of rowan pinned to his collar, the expression grotesque on his tear-stained face.

"Do you think I'd leave myself vulnerable to your tricks?"

I swallowed the bile rising from my stomach. "I'm sorry, Julian. If you knew the truth then you'd understand that I–"

"Shut. Up." The words were barely louder than a whisper, but they silenced me more thoroughly than any shout.

"I know everything," he continued, voice shaking but pistol steady. "You might be little more than a back-country twit, but you were right when you said she trusted me more than you with her secrets. Her greatest secret. I know who she was, who you are, what he is, and more about *them* than you could even dream of." He wiped his face with his free hand. "Most of all, I know that you are the one who was supposed to die, but instead…" His eyes flickered down to my mother's corpse, then back to me. "All I have left is revenge."

He gripped the pistol with both hands, leveling it at my face. *It couldn't end now. Not after everything. Not like this.* "Please."

He bared his teeth. "Not so brave without your troll to protect you?"

"She doesn't need a troll for protection from the likes of you." Sabine stepped out of the bedroom and pressed my mother's gun against the back of his head. "A human is plenty good enough."

Julian was quiet for one heartbeat. Two. Three. Then he smiled. "When you've lost your reason for living, much becomes worth dying for."

The retort of the pistol shattered my ears, and pain sliced across my face. I staggered sideways, my head ringing and hot trickles of blood coating my fingers as I pressed them to my cheek. But it was nothing in comparison to the gore pooling at Sabine's feet.

"Idiot," she said, lowering the still smoking gun. "What good is dying for the dead? They are past caring."

Lifting her head, Sabine's eyes landed on me. She dropped the gun and clapped a hand over her mouth. "Oh, Cécile. Your face!"

"It's fine," I said, even though my cheek burned, the line the bullet had scored across my skin deep enough to mark me permanently. A fraction of an inch closer, and I would've been dead, and no amount of vanity could undermine that fact.

We both stumbled forward, collapsing into each other's arms. "I knew he would do it," she said. "I knew from the moment you came in that I was going to have to kill him. He was never one to think beyond the moment."

Much the same could be said about me. The world still shook from what *I* had decided in a moment. The implications of my actions had begun to descend with leaden wings the moment that dragon's scream had shattered the night air, filtering through the rush of adrenaline-fueled fear to brush against me in the courtyard when Tristan had left me alone in the snow.

Now they settled their full weight upon my shoulders, and I found I could not think. I could barely breathe.

"She's dead? Your mother, I mean, Anushka?"

I squeezed my fingers together. They were tacky with my blood. *Her blood.*

"And the trolls? They're free?"

And what power in this world could stop them?

"Where's Tristan?"

He walked away.

"Cécile? Cécile!"

My head snapped sideways with the force of her slap. I stared at her, and she shook her head. "I'm sorry for that, but this is the wrong time for you to lose your nerve."

Taking in a few shaking breaths, I squared my shoulders. "You're right."

Letting Sabine lead me into the other room, I let the story spill out while she examined my cheek, finishing with, "I was so consumed with finding Anushka and breaking the curse that I never stopped to think about what we'd do if we succeeded." I pressed a handkerchief to my injury, using the pain to clear my head. "They could be here right now."

My skin prickled as I imagined Lessa or Roland creeping through the streets of Trianon. Now that the trolls were free, there was nothing to stop them from coming after Tristan. Or me.

"I'm not sure that's the case." Sabine walked to the window, and gestured to the faintly glowing dome encasing the city. "I saw it form while I was hiding from Julian. It's Tristan's doing, isn't it? He's keeping them out?"

I nodded, feeling only a modicum of relief, because the dome was only a stopgap measure. Tristan couldn't take the crown from his father or put an end to Angoulême by hiding behind walls, and I knew he couldn't protect the whole city from an outright attack. And the dome did nothing to help those outside of Trianon. "Our families are out there," I said. "The trolls know who they are. They know where to find them."

Sabine pressed a hand against the bloody shoulder of her gown, rubbing it as one does an old injury. "Tristan sent Chris back to the Hollow with instructions. They won't be caught unaware." But the expression on her face told me we were of a like mind, both wondering what possible preparations they could undertake to protect themselves.

I blew a breath out, watching it mist against the glass. "We can't afford to wait around to see what they intend to do. We need to act first. Find out what they're up to."

"How?" Sabine asked. "I'm not guessing they'll make it easy to spy on them, and if whoever we sent got caught–"

"The trolls will kill them," I finished. But the Regent and Tristan would send them anyway, because what other option was there? The trouble was, I didn't think that even if the spies made it there and back that they'd have anything useful to tell us. Counting numbers and establishing positions as one might do in a battle between human armies would do us no good, because the trolls wouldn't fight that way. What we needed was to learn where allegiances lay amongst the trolls and the half-bloods, where the balance of power sat between the Duke and the King, and above all, what was going on in the mind of Thibault himself.

I exhaled another breath against the glass, watching as the mist formed into an elaborate pattern of frost even as a plan began to form in my mind. We needed to *see*, and for that, we needed the help of someone who saw *all*. "I have an idea," I said. "But to put it into play, we're going to have to go into the city."

CHAPTER 4
Tristan

The wave of relief I felt from Cécile was little comfort; the distraction had been momentary, but it had certainly been damning. I forced her out of my thoughts, taking in the scene before me.

The Regent was dead.

Aiden stood frozen, sword slipping from his fingers to clatter against the stone floor. "What have I done?" he whispered. "What have I done?"

What he'd promised my father he'd do.

I slammed him to the floor with more force than was necessary, knocking him out. Then I blocked the doors and, most importantly, muffled the sounds of Lady Marie's wails. Already, her dress was soaked with her husband's blood, and she rocked back and forth, his corpse clutched to her chest.

"How is this possible?" the advisor asked, his eyes going back and forth between the unconscious Aiden and Fred wearing his Aiden mask. "What devilry is this?" He pulled a sword that appeared more decorative than useful, but before he could decide which man to attack, Marie wrenched it out of his hands.

"Monster," she screamed, jabbing the point at the prone Aiden. "Take off my son's face, you wretch."

The tip of the blade thudded against my magic, and she screamed, attacking it over and over as though by sheer strength of will she could force the weapon through. I let her do it, taking the moment to come to grip with how quickly circumstances had devolved. How quickly I'd lost control.

Aiden was regaining consciousness, his face wet with tears. His stifled sobs tickled at my magic, and I had to curb the urge to grind his bones to dust for what he'd done. For whatever weakness that had caused him to make a deal with my father, and for the lack of strength that saw him caving in the space of an hour to the will of the troll Cécile had resisted for weeks.

The Regent had been a capable ruler, well liked by the people. I didn't have time to win the islanders over, if such a thing was even possible. I'd needed him, because the humans would have followed him. And now I was left with this: a man who had committed patricide and regicide, and in doing so, had ensured no one in their right mind would follow him.

"Do something." Marie's voice pulled me from my thoughts. She'd dropped the sword and was crawling through the pooled blood toward Fred, her hand outstretched. "Aiden, do something. Avenge your father."

Fred took a step back, eyes going to mine for directive. "Tristan?"

Marie froze. "You are not my son."

Someone pounded on the door. I had only minutes to decide what to do, how to salvage the situation. I removed the magic disguising Fred. "No, he isn't."

Her skin went deathly pale, eyes going back to Aiden. The realization that her own son had killed his father marched across her face, and as angry as I was with Aiden, it struck a chord in my heart. Would I see the same expression on my own mother's face when the time came? Would my justifications matter to her, or would she only see a cold-blooded killer who'd murdered his own father?

"He's not in control of his own mind," I said, not sure how much of a difference knowing would make. "He's made some sort of promise to cede the Isle to my father, and he's under compulsion to fulfill his word."

"Why would you do such a thing?" Her voice shook.

For a moment, I didn't think Aiden would answer, wondered if he even *could*. Then he said, "I never thought it would come to this. I never believed they'd be freed."

It was an excuse, not an answer, and to her credit, Marie understood that as well. "Why agree to it at all?"

Before Aiden could speak, something heavy hit the door. They were trying to break in, no doubt believing I'd dispatched their entire ruling family. And when they saw the bloody scene in the council chambers, it wouldn't be Aiden they turned on first.

I dropped to one knee in front of Marie and caught hold of her shoulders. "There isn't time for explanations. We've only a matter of hours to prepare our defense against my father, and I do not think your soldiers will follow Aiden after what he has done." I glanced at the weeping lord. "And even if they will, we can't risk it while he remains under compulsion."

Crack! The wood of the door splintered. They wouldn't be able to break through my magic, but as soon as they were through the door, they'd know it was me keeping them out. I gave Marie's shoulders a little shake. "Will your soldiers follow your orders?"

"You can't be serious?" The lord whose weapon Marie had taken had been inching toward the door through our exchange, but my words had stopped him in his tracks. "She's a woman!"

Marie ignored him. "How do I get my son free of this compulsion?"

Crack! I grimaced. "The only way is to kill my father."

"And then Aiden will be himself once again?"

There was no way to predict how Aiden would fare, whether his sanity would survive, whether he'd revert to man he was before. "He will control his own will, his own self."

She went very still.

"Marie, there is no time for this." My heart threatened to beat out of my chest, and it was all I could do to keep from looking toward the shattering door. "Will they follow you?"

"Get your hands off me, troll," she whispered.

I exhaled, letting my hands drop to my sides as the awareness that I was going to have to take control of Trianon by force settled onto my mind.

"Step back," she said, reaching for the sword next to her.

I did what she asked.

Her eyes went to the lord who was now clawing futilely at my magic. "My Lord Lachance, attend to me. Help me away from this creature." She held out a beseeching hand.

Lachance stiffened, and with palpable reluctance, edged his way toward Marie. "Stay back, fiend," he said, and under other circumstances, I might have laughed.

"My lady." He reached a hand to her without removing his eyes from me.

She stabbed the point of the sword through his throat.

I gaped as the dying man collapsed, entirely unsure of what I was witnessing.

Marie placed the hilt of the sword next to his hand, then climbed to her feet. "Lachance was a traitor," she said. "A spy and assassin in the employ of the troll king. He killed my husband, and would've killed me if not for the quick actions of my son." Walking to Fred, she extracted the blade from his hand, dipped it in the pool of blood, then replaced it. "Put his disguise back in place."

I complied, seeing the beginnings of her plan.

"If anyone learns what Aiden's done," she said, "they'll see him hanged. I've already lost my husband to you creatures – I'll not lose my son. We'll keep him hidden away until we've won this war, and then you–" she leveled a finger at Aiden, "–you will spend the rest of your life atoning."

She turned to me. "Bind him. Hide him. And then let them in."

CHAPTER 5
Cécile

"I've never known such cold," Sabine said, wrapping her cloak more snugly around her shoulders only to have it torn open again by the freezing wind as we crossed the bridge. "And this snow… It's not natural."

Given I was wading through white powder well above my knees and couldn't see more than a few paces in either direction, I was inclined to agree.

"It's the fairies," I shouted over the gale. "This is their doing." Or, at the very least, *her* doing. In my opinion, one did not claim to be the queen of a season without having a certain degree of power over the weather.

"Why?" she demanded. "If they can go to worlds beyond number, what makes ours so special? What do they want?"

Something. The foretelling had come from the fey, which meant they had wanted the curse broken. I sincerely doubted it was for the freedom of coming and going from this particular world, and it hadn't been for the sake of the trolls. The fey didn't do favors. The Summer King, at any rate, had something to gain from their freedom, but what, I couldn't say.

"Maybe we should go back." Sabine stopped in her tracks, dropping the skirts of her elaborate gown so that it pooled around her knees. "Tristan said the fairies cannot pass the steel in the walls encircling the castle – that we'd be safe within them."

I shoved my hands into my armpits, eyeing the grey haze blocking the Regent's castle from our view. I didn't want to go much further into the city in case we needed to make a hasty retreat. "Well, clearly they don't keep trolls out, so *safe* is a relative term. The trolls are the immediate threat, and if we are to have any hope of winning this war, we need to know their plans. And we can't talk to the fairies unless we're somewhere they can reach us." I started walking again, forcing her to follow. "We're doing the right thing."

"Which is why you *didn't* tell Tristan where we were going?"

I stumbled over something hidden beneath the snow and fell, swearing as my borrowed skirts caught and tore. "He's got his hands full with the Regent." And judging from the emotions coming from him, it wasn't going well.

"Time is of the essence," I said, thrashing around in the snow in an attempt to free myself. "We can't be sitting around waiting for Tristan's *permission* for every move we make."

"For goodness sake, what are you doing?" Sabine grabbed me under the armpits and heaved.

"My skirt is stuck on something," I said, kicking my feet.

She pulled harder, and both of us inhaled sharply as a frozen corpse appeared from beneath the snow. Half of a corpse.

"The dragon," I said, tugging my skirt free from where it was caught on the shattered ribcage, my plan suddenly seeming far more risky as we glanced skyward.

What felt like icy fingers brushed my brow and the world seemed to shudder. The sensation faded in an instant, but Sabine was also shaking her head as though to clear it. My spine prickled with unease. "Maybe we should go back."

Sabine's fingers tightened on my arms. "I'm not sure we can."

I looked back and my stomach tightened. Shadows dragged themselves out from under the bridge, consuming the light from the gas lamps on either side of it until the route back to the castle became a yawning mouth of blackness. And over the wind, the skittering sound of things with claws filled the night.

"We'll go into the city. Someone will give us shelter." Sabine grabbed my hand and hauled me toward a café, but before we'd gone more than a pace, a gale-force wind blasted from above, driving the snow into drifts that blocked all the doors and windows from sight, leaving the center of the street bare. A pathway.

"I should never be allowed to come up with plans," I breathed, trying to keep my fear in check.

"Maybe you should summon Tristan?" Sabine was digging at the snow bank, but the wind only pushed her efforts back in place, seeming to mock her with its little teasing gusts.

"No." I needed to prove that my worth hadn't ended the moment Anushka drew her last breath. Not to Tristan, but to myself. I'd unleashed the trolls, which meant I was responsible for everything that happened as a result. "If they'd wanted to harm us, they would have. This is… This is something else."

Holding tight to each other's hands, we followed the path through the streets, Trianon growing steadily less recognizable as we progressed. The drifts of snow blocking the buildings rose higher, turning to walls of transparent ice, swirling whorls and patterns forming before our eyes as though an invisible hand were scoring whimsical designs.

"It's leading me home," I said, averting my eyes from a woman standing utterly still behind the wall, her mouth open and fixed mid-sentence. There were dozens of others like her – men and women who appeared to have been frozen in place.

"Look."

I followed Sabine's pointed finger and gasped. Faintly illuminated by Tristan's dome of magic, a palace of ice was rising up from the earth. Tower after tower materialized, each decorated with elaborate frozen cornices, delicate balconies, and transparent spires. And inside the frozen rooms, winged creatures danced, their motions jerking and strange. The walled street rounded a bend to where my mother's townhouse was.

Or used to be.

The whole block formed the base of the palace, the row of stone townhouses coated in a thick layer of ice, doors and windows frozen shut. All except the door to my home, which was flung wide, barely recognizable beneath the icy ornamentation. I navigated my way around the fountains that formed out of nothingness, snow spewing from the mouths of fanged creatures whose frosted eyes seemed to follow us as we walked.

Sabine broke away from me, going up the steps to one of the doorways. The entrance was covered with a wall of transparent ice, but beyond, one of my neighbors appeared to have been frozen on her way out the door. "She looks alive," Sabine said, resting a hand against the ice.

I peered through, watching the woman's chest intently. "She's not breathing."

"You can't tell that for sure." Sabine picked up a brick and smashed it against the ice. Cracks radiated out from the impact, but seconds later, they retreated as though the ice were healing itself. She hit it again and again, but the result was the same. I caught her wrist and shook my head.

From our position on the steps, we could see that the ice walls filled with darkness snaked through Trianon to the castle, but that was not the limit of the city's transformation. It was now a fantasyland of glittering towers and spires that defied logic and the laws of nature in their height and design. It was beautiful, but utterly horrifying, because it was entirely devoid of life.

"Everyone in the castle was alive when we left." As always, Tristan was present in my mind, but as I concentrated on him, I noticed a strangeness to his emotions. They seemed static... Frozen.

"If he was frozen, he'd be dead and you'd know it," I muttered at myself, and then to Sabine, "If we're alive, then there's no reason to believe others aren't, too." I shook my head. "Either way, we've come this far…" I didn't finish the statement, because if everyone on the Isle was dead, hadn't we already lost?

Hand in hand, we made our way down the steps and over to those leading up to the open door of my home. "Hello?" My breath made little misty clouds as I stepped inside. "Is anyone here?"

Brushing snow off the lamp that mysteriously still burned on the front table, I tried to turn up the flame, but my efforts were ineffective. It remained static. Unchanged. Strange. "Hello?"

We inched our way into the great room, both of us instinctively going to the fireplace where the banked coals glowed cherry red. Sabine held her hands out to them, then jerked her fingers back. "No heat," she said, bending and blowing on the charred wood in a failed attempt to draw up the flames. "Something about this isn't right." She reached a gloved hand for an iron poker, seeming intent on rectifying this one trivial thing in the face of all the many things that *weren't right*. I turned my back on the process and called out again. "Hello?"

No response. Nothing but silence.

I shouted, "Well? We're here. And given you owe your freedom to me, perhaps you might show somewhat more courtesy."

An unearthly chuckle filled the room, and I stumbled into Sabine as the air in front of me tore like a panel of silk. The opening spread wide, revealing a throne carved of solid ice, which would've been unremarkable if not for countless eyes of all shapes and colors frozen into its depths. Eyes, which judging from the bloody veins and tissue tangling from them, had been torn from their owners' heads by force. To either side of the throne sat two immense lupine creatures, fangs as long as my hand protruding from black lips. But it was the creature sitting on the throne that stole my attention.

I'd seen her before.

"Owe?" The sound of her voice made my head ache, and I pressed a gloved hand to my temple, trying and failing to relieve the pressure. "I recall making no deals with *you*, human. Nor do I recall you doing me any *favors.*"

"Maybe not," I conceded, dropping my hand from my head. "But you've benefited from my actions." She was the woman – fairy – that I'd seen in my dream. The one the Summer King had called wife; and sure enough, there were bonding marks across one of her hands. Only in my dream, in that land of endless summer, she'd seemed... passive. And what sat before me was anything but. This was the Winter Queen.

"Have I? Are you so sure about that?"

I hesitated. "You're here, aren't you? A day ago, that wasn't possible."

She shrugged one elegant shoulder, long black hair brushing against a gown made of mist and stars that shifted and moved in a way that made it dizzying to look upon. "Do not look for gratitude from me, mortal. I've walked through worlds beyond number; what does the loss or gain of one filthy bit of earth matter to me?"

I opened my mouth to retort that it mattered enough for her to turn it into her own winter palace, but then clamped my lips shut. Not *listening* had caught me more times than I cared to count with the trolls and, immortal or not, she was of the same ilk. There was a reason why she was bothering with this "filthy bit of earth", and it would be something worth knowing. "You tell me."

She smiled, pale pink lips pulling back to reveal a mouthful of fangs. My heart skipped and I blinked. The fangs were gone, replaced by pearly white human teeth. "You wished to ask a favor of me, Cécile de Troyes." She tapped a long fingernail against her throne, and I swallowed hard as the eye beneath twitched, rolling to look up at her.

I remembered her words to the Summer King. *A favor given is a favor owed...* "No," I said. "But I do wish to bargain."

Her verdelite eyes narrowed. "What makes you believe *you* have anything *I* want?"

I thought about the massive ice walls that had formed for the express purpose of herding us toward this meeting; the grandstanding and showmanship that was obviously intended to intimidate and impress. "I do not think," I murmured, dropping into a deep curtsey, "that the Queen of all of Winter would condescend to meet with a mortal such as I if there were nothing I could do for her."

Her laughter sounded like the shattering of glass, and I fought the urge to clap my hands over my ears. "Perhaps it is only that an *immortal such as I*," she said the words in a perfect mimicry of my voice, "becomes easily bored."

She rose to her feet, and two winged creatures scuttled over to the dais to offer their hands as she walked down the steps. It made me wonder who – and what – else was present in her icy throne room. As if in answer to my question, clawed hands folded around the tear between our worlds, drawing the edges back.

"And besides–" she stopped just before the tear "–you are no mere mortal, but one who is bonded to the prince of the trolls." She cocked her head to one side and peered through the opening. "He is not with you."

Her voice was toneless, nothing in her expression telling me whether she considered Tristan's absence a good or bad thing, or whether she cared at all. And before I could so much as blink, she had stepped into our world. Although *stepped* wasn't the right word – one moment she was *there* and the next moment *here*. And while *there* she'd seemed as solid as Sabine or me, *here* she appeared like a mist that had coalesced into the shape of a woman, fluid, shifting, and changing. Her eyes met mine, and I swore they delved into the depths of my soul, flipping through my memories like pages of a book. Tristan had told me that the trolls' magic had been corrupted by iron and mortality, that it was nothing like that of their immortal ancestors. But he'd never told me what they *could* do, and I was starting to fear what it would mean to find out.

"What is it you want, Princess?" The Queen's voice was mocking, but that concerned me far less than my growing suspicion that she had plans for me. Plans that I wouldn't like. That she'd ask me for something I didn't want to give. But I'd come too far to come away with nothing.

"You can *see* anywhere you want?" I asked. "Anyone?"

"What will you give me for the answer?" The settee was coated with ice, but it gave beneath her as she settled as though it were stuffed with down.

I nibbled on my lip. "Nothing. I already know you can. What I want is to see… and hear what our enemy is up to. What they're planning. Where they are now."

She tapped a claw – no, a fingernail – against one tooth. "What will you give me in return?"

"What do you want?" I countered.

Her lips pursed, and she drifted one hand through the air as though conducting an orchestra. "A song."

I blinked, more stunned by the odd request than I would have been if she'd asked for my life. "A song?"

She held up one finger. "Your *favorite* song."

I glanced sideways at Sabine, who had been silent through the exchange thus far. Her back was pressed against the wall. Despite the chill, her cheeks were leached of color, the whites of her eyes gleaming in the lamplight. Without taking her gaze off the fairy, she shook her head.

I ground my teeth, and glanced back at the queen. Looking at her gave me a headache – I kept seeing one thing and then another, and I didn't know what was real. "How is it even possible for me to give you a song?"

"Agree to the bargain. Sing the song. Then it will be mine."

It couldn't be as easy as that, but try as I might, I couldn't think of any consequences worth declining the bargain. "And if I do this, you'll give me what I asked for? Right now," I added, remembering the importance of specificity.

She smiled, and Sabine made a soft choking noise. "Yes."

"All right, then," I said. "I agree."

The air flashed frigid, the bare skin of my face burning and my bones aching, and I felt the weight of the bargain clamp down on me like pinchers on the back of my neck. While I'd had some small ability to resist the troll king's compulsion, resisting *her* was impossible. I was a feather and she a hurricane, and I was more likely to cut out my own heart than resist her power. I began to sing.

My song was no half-hearted means to an end. The ballad tore from my lips, filled with all the passion, heartbreak, and joy that I associated with the lyrics. And it felt like each word, each note, was being excised by a straight razor. I wanted to cry, to scream, to throw myself on the floor and claw at my skull, but I did none of those things for they would have stolen some of what I owed. When it was over, I clenched my eyes shut and fell to my knees, so taxed that all I could do was breathe.

"That was lovely."

The voice was too close. Opening my eyes revealed the Winter Queen's face only inches from my own, her breath smelling like a midwinter's night, and it was all I could do not to cringe.

"Lovely," she repeated, her head tipping back and forth as though she were listening to my voice inside her head. "A treasure."

"Your turn." My voice rasped against my aching throat.

"But of course." She straightened and turned, the misty apparition that was her gown passing through my arms, entirely intangible. She made her way to a mirror hanging on the wall, and with one careless gesture, she tore an opening in the world.

"Come, come," she said, glancing over her shoulder. "And behold your enemy."

Rising on shaking knees, I walked over and looked through the opening.

CHAPTER 6
Tristan

Two-dozen soldiers poured through the shattered doors, half going to the defense of the heir and his mother, the rest turning on the apparent threat.

Me.

I winced against the thunderous echoes of firing pistols, allowing the bullets to sink into a wall of magic lest they ricochet and kill someone else.

"Cease fire!" Fred's bellow cut through the noise, and the confused soldiers slowly lowered their pistols.

"It wasn't him." Marie wisely took control of the moment of duplicity, Fred bowing his head over the Regent in apparent grief. "Lachance killed my husband. He was a traitor – a spy and assassin for the troll king." Her voice shook with real emotion as she plucked at her blood soaked gown with hands stained red. "Get that wretch's body out of my sight."

Three of the soldiers moved to comply, but one approached me, reaching out a hand to touch one of the dozens of bullets suspended in midair. "Can all of you... trolls do this?"

"To a greater or lesser extent." I released the magic, bits of metal clattering against the stone floor.

He lifted the hand still holding his pistol and stared at the weapon, then let his arm fall limply to his side. "How can we hope to fight against such power?"

"I'll show you." As unplanned as it was, this display of magic would do much to prepare the humans for what they were about to face.

Walking past him, I went to where Fred knelt next to the Regent's body. "We need as many eyes as can be spared on the walls and scouts between here and Trollus. Choose a handful of your best to see what information they can gather. I need to know if my father is on the move."

Fred nodded. "I'll send riders."

I shook my head. "Tell them to approach on foot. Stealth will be the only thing that keeps them safe – any troll worth his salt will be able to outrun a horse in the dark."

Fred's eyes widened, but he nodded and climbed to his feet. "I'll give the orders."

Catching his arm before he could leave, I murmured, "Can you do this?"

"Doesn't look like I have much choice." His eyes flicked to Marie, who had returned to her knees next to her dead husband, cheeks wet with tears.

I could not help but admire her quick thinking in what was undoubtedly the worst moment of her life. My father's plan to push Aiden into murdering the Regent was good, because either way it fell saw my father gain control. The people would either accept Aiden – whose will was under my father's control – as their leader, or they'd hang him for his actions, leaving the Isle leaderless. But in one decisive moment, Marie had sabotaged my father's plans. The people would see the troll king as the culprit behind the murder of their beloved Regent and unify against him, rallying to our impostor Aiden. And she'd only had to murder an innocent man to accomplish it.

My eyes went to the puddle of blood left behind by Lachance's corpse and then to the illusion of a wall, behind which the real Aiden sat slumped. No part of me believed Marie's actions were driven by a desire to see me triumph – they'd been to save her son. To give him a chance at a future. And I'd do well to remember that.

"Send guards to find Cécile and Sabine," I said. "Make sure they are safe."

Cécile was at the far end of the castle, my sense of her faded, as though she were sleeping. Which was just as well – she needed the rest. But given the ruthlessness Marie had just displayed, I needed Cécile aware of the danger she was in. Marie alone knew her importance, and I would not put it past her to use Cécile against me.

I twitched, feeling something slam against the magic of the dome with enough force that I knew it had been no human. But before I could raise the alarm, I felt another series of thuds. A pattern. One I hadn't heard since the days when I held secret meetings in the Dregs.

"Do you know where she is?" Fred's voice pulled me back to the council chambers, and I focused on Cécile.

"Far end of the castle," I said, then hesitated. She seemed further than that, if not by much. Which if she was sleeping, made no sense at all. "Something's not right." I said, then a wave of dizziness sent me staggering. A sudden wakefulness accompanied by pain and panic.

"Stones and sky, Cécile," I swore, righting myself. "What have you done?"

CHAPTER 7
Cécile

Roland sat straight-backed in a chair before an easel in Angoulême's parlor. His brow was softer than usual, cheeks rounded with a smile as he dipped a brush in a dollop of crimson paint and began adding deft little touches to the piece. He was strikingly talented, his subject represented in exquisite detail. Unfortunately.

"Macabre," the Queen murmured over my shoulder. "But the boy is naught but a tool in your enemy's arsenal." The view shifted, Roland relegated to the periphery in favor of Angoulême and Lessa, who stood bent over a map covered in what appeared to be golden Guerre pieces. He was dressed as was his custom, but she wore what I could only describe as armor: dull black leather reinforced with crimson scales. A sword hung at her side and she awkwardly touched the pommel from time to time in a way Anaïs never would've. How Angoulême had not recognized she was an impostor was beyond me.

"You'll take him and the rest of your party down the Ocean Road while my mother sets our plans into action in Courville," he said, tracing a finger along the map. "Don't waste your time on the smaller hamlets – we have others who will manage those."

"Not even to make a point?" she asked. "His Highness might enjoy that."

Out of the corner of my eye, I saw Roland smile.

Angoulême shook his head. "Make a point of those who refuse to swear allegiance to him. To him," he repeated, turning to Lessa. "Tristan has shown an unwillingness to harm his brother in the past, and we can use that to our advantage. The sooner we swell our ranks, the sooner we can set humans to fighting humans. Tristan will be distracted with the task of keeping them from slaughtering each other, and then we'll make our first move."

Lessa scowled. "I want him–"

"In time," Angoulême said, cutting her off and casting a meaningful glance in Roland's direction. "Not even he can take them both on at the same time, and the boy has shown some reticence. We must be strategic."

Several other trolls I recognized as aristocrats loyal to Angoulême came into the room, all dressed similarly to Lessa, the Dowager Duchesse Damia among them.

"We need to move now, Your Grace," one of them said. "Thibault's soldiers have the River Road and labyrinth gates secured and are enforcing curfew. Unless you want to fight your way through, we need to break open one of the old sluag tunnels and make our way through the labyrinth."

"No fighting," Angoulême said. "I want Trollus intact when His Highness takes the throne. We'll be along in a moment. Wait outside."

The trolls departed. "They'll guide you to the outskirts of the rock fall," Angoulême said. "Keep you safe from any sluag you come across. Are you ready for this?"

"All my life," Lessa said in perfect mimicry of Anaïs's voice. "Your Highness, it is time for us to go."

A flash of annoyance crossed the boy's face, but he got to his feet. "I would wear my new sword," he announced, and left the room.

The mood in the room shifted as soon as Roland departed, and Angoulême rested a hand on the small of Lessa's back. "I've instructed him to follow your council," he said. "But make no mistakes. He snaps at his fetters like a rabid dog, and I won't be there to protect you if he sees through our deception."

"I don't make mistakes," Lessa said, and she tried to pull out of his grip, but Angoulême caught her wrist.

"When this is over, you'll be queen," he said. "*I* will make you queen."

She smiled, her face full of naked adoration. Then she turned back to the map, her fingers resting on the edge of the paper. "A shame I couldn't go with you – I would've liked to see the faces of my ancestors."

Before the Duke could respond, Roland came back into the room. "You said it was time."

Neither acknowledged him. Instead, Lessa leaned over and kissed the Duke's cheek. "Victory will be ours," she said. "And it will be thanks to you… Father."

The three of them departed.

The tear slowly began to heal from top to bottom, edges folding in until it was gone. I glanced up at the Queen, who cocked both eyebrows. "Well?"

"I was expecting to see the troll King."

Her eyes glittered. "You didn't ask to see him."

I opened my mouth to argue, then shut it again. I'd asked to see my enemy, and she'd shown me Angoulême, which meant that was who she believed it to be. Given she saw all, that was no small thing. Now we knew the Duke was leaving Trollus, that he intended to recruit humans – unwillingly – to his cause, and that Roland was giving them some trouble. Best of all, Lessa had given away where we were to find him. *I would've liked to see the faces of my ancestors…*

"Of course, if you'd like to see your… father-in-law, it is easily done." The Queen's smile revealed a maw full of razor sharp teeth. I blinked, and they were gone. "For a small price."

My stomach clenched at the memory of the pain that had

come from her *taking* my song, but it hadn't lasted long and it had been worth it to see what the Duke was planning. I could go through it again if it meant learning as much about Thibault. "What sort of small price? Another song?"

The Queen stared into the depths of the mirror on the wall. "No," she said. "Something else. A meeting, I think."

"With Tristan." It wasn't a question. "Why?"

"I desire to renew our acquaintance."

A sour taste filled my mouth, and I turned away from her so she couldn't see my face while I thought. She had something to gain from meeting with Tristan, that much was certain. But was her gain our sacrifice? "I'd have to go back to the castle to ask if he'd be willing," I said. "I don't speak for him."

"Of course not." Her tongue ran over her lips. "But why make the trek back through the cold when you can ask him from here? It is within your power."

She meant that I should use his *name*. It was a simple enough thing to do, and although I knew he wouldn't appreciate me using it, he might deem it worth it in the end.

"Cécile." Sabine's voice interrupted my thoughts. "Sing that song again."

"Why?" I asked at the same time the Queen said, "You are not part of this negotiation, girl."

It was the first time she'd so much as acknowledged Sabine's presence, and that, more than the dismissiveness of her tone, made me wary.

"Please."

As strange as the request was, she wouldn't ask without reason. So I drew in a deep breath and… nothing came out. I couldn't remember the words. I couldn't remember ever even *knowing* them. It was as though the song had been… *taken* from me. Stripped from my thoughts. And if she could take a song, how hard would it be to take something like a *name*.

Silently thanking Sabine, I turned back to the Queen. "He

made me promise never to use it," I lied. "He may well agree to a meeting, but I'll have to ask him in person."

The Queen went very still. Could she tell I was lying? "We'll go straight away," I said, bobbing a quick curtsey and then inching toward the door after Sabine. "It was a pleasure meeting you, and you really were most helpful." I was babbling. "He'll be wondering where I am. We really should get back."

"I think not," the Queen said, and wind whipped through the room, little bits of ice flying through the air and biting at my skin. Walls of packed snow formed, blocking our exit. The lupine creatures watching from her winter palace crept closer to the tear, snarls filling the air.

"Call him here," she ordered, the mist forming her ebony hair rising and falling on the blizzard of her own making.

If she wanted Tristan here so badly, it could only be to our detriment. "No."

The pupils of her eyes elongated like a cat's, then snapped back into a round, human shape. And before I could think to move, her misty outline solidified and she snatched hold of my arm. Cold unlike anything I'd felt before burned through my skin, my muscle, and into my bone. I screamed, the sound like a rabbit caught in a trap.

Then my ears rang with a loud report, and it was the Queen screaming. She let go of my arm and I scrambled back, my eyes going to Sabine, who had a firm grip on Anushka's still smoking pistol. The ice coating everything in the room exploded, and the ground shook as the icy palace collapsed around us. The world shuddered. Everywhere I looked I saw layers of the same. A dozen sofas. A hundred Sabines. I lost my balance and fell, my empty stomach heaving.

The fairy hissed at us once, then staggered through the opening between worlds, the tear gone as quickly as it had appeared.

We were outside in the snow, not a hundred yards from the bridge over the river to the castle, which was obscured by the raging blizzard. I pulled up my sleeve to see what sort of injury she'd dealt me, but my skin was unmarked, only a memory of pain remaining. The fairy had caught us in an illusion or a dream, but not for a second did I doubt what had happened. Or the danger to Tristan if he stepped outside those walls. And he was coming this way.

Closing my eyes, I focused. *Tristanthysium, do not leave the castle walls until we have the chance to talk.* His outrage was immediate and fierce, but it was worth it to keep him safe.

"How did you know to do that?" I asked, letting Sabine help me to my feet.

"Tristan told Chris and me all sorts of things about them," she replied. "That they could be harmed by iron or steel, but only if they were corpor… solid." She made a face. "And that if we stood inside a steel circle or kept the metal against our skin, that we'd be able to see through their glamour, because their magic couldn't affect us. When she started getting angry, I took hold of my gun, and the illusion fell away, and I saw you standing in the snow talking not to a woman, but a monster."

Sabine scrubbed a hand across her eyes as though to wipe away the memory, and I could understand why. If those glimpses I'd had of fangs and claws were real, I could only imagine what she'd looked like in her entirety.

As if on cue, a chilling howl filled the air. Then another. And another. Those lupine creatures that had flanked her throne, with fangs as long as my hand. I'd only seen the pair of them, but judging from the howls, there were more. We needed to get behind the castle walls.

I met Sabine's terrified gaze. "Run."

CHAPTER 8
Cécile

Before we could take a step, three pony-sized wolves stepped out of the blizzard, blocking our path. Their white fur was misty and insubstantial, but their snarls were real enough.

"Back, back," I hissed, dragging Sabine with me until we were up against an ironwork fence, her hands fumbling with the gun as she reloaded. Leveling the weapon, she fired at one of the creatures, but it passed through with no effect.

"What do we do?" she hissed.

I clenched my teeth, wishing I had an answer. The Queen knew Tristan and I were bonded and what that meant. If she'd wanted to kill him, I wouldn't still be standing. She wanted to lure him out, which meant her monsters wouldn't kill me. But there was nothing to stop them from slaughtering Sabine.

"They have to be solid," Sabine whispered. "I can't shoot them if they're not solid."

"If they aren't solid, they can't bite." Spotting a coal shovel leaning against a wall, I snatched it up and took a step forward.

One of the creatures sprung, solidifying mid-air, but my shovel caught it in the shoulder. It yelped and staggered, but was back at me in an instant, teeth snapping just out of reach of my weapon. I attacked again, but out of the corner of my eye, I saw the others creeping around me. Trying to get at Sabine.

I stumbled back, pressing her against the protection of the fence, brandishing my shovel. "Help," I shouted. "Someone help us." But the streets were empty, everyone hiding from the danger in the skies.

Sabine gasped, and I whirled around. One of the creatures had caught hold of her dress through the bars of the fence, and it had her pinned against the metal. She fired her gun, and the wolf exploded into snow and ice, but before she could reload one of the other creatures swiped a paw at the weapon, knocking it from her hand. It hissed, paw smoking where it had impacted the steel, but now there was nothing to keep it from attacking her. I lunged toward my friend, but a massive weight hit me between the shoulders and I went face first into the snow.

"No!" I jammed the handle of the shovel into the slavering maw behind my shoulder, and was rewarded with a sizzle and a cry of pain. Scrambling on my hands and knees, I swung at the haunches of the creatures stalking toward Sabine, but claws sank into my skirts, dragging me away. I rolled onto my back, jabbing the shovel at the paws holding me down. But I was losing the battle. I couldn't get free and Sabine wouldn't be able to hold them off. They were going to kill her.

From this distance, Tristan could help Sabine. Could pluck her out of the danger I put her in. But with the snow blinding his view, he'd need my guidance. And to do that, I'd have to use his name.

"Don't do it, Cécile," Sabine shouted as though sensing my thoughts. "She's watching!"

I shrieked every expletive I knew at the opening between worlds and the queen standing just beyond, her face twisted with pain and expectation. Teeth closed on the heel of my boot, dragging me her direction. I swiped at the tear, but the shovel passed through as though it were empty air. Letting Sabine die wasn't an option – I wouldn't let it happen. I started to pull Tristan's name from the depths of my mind, when the sharp squeal and the stench of burning fur and flesh pulled me back into the moment.

One of the fairy wolves was pressed against the iron fence by some invisible force, while another two were dashed against the wall of a building. There was a flurry of motion, and three shapes descended on the scene, two tall and one cloaked in shadow. Steel blades sliced through the air, the wolves exploding into sprays of snow and ice. The shadowed figure strode toward me, and the pressure on my heel released. When I looked back over my shoulder, the creatures that had been restraining me were gone.

Warm tendrils of magic lifted me to my feet, but I brushed them away and flung myself at my friend. "Marc!" The fine wool of his cloak was blissfully warm against my frozen cheek, and I let the shovel fall from my numb fingers with a clatter. "What are you doing here?"

"Saving your scrawny behind," Vincent answered for him, picking up my shovel and examining it. "Your choice of weapon is somewhat suspect, Cécile. It's a good thing Marc has heard your shrieks for help before and recognized them."

"Don't I know it." I squeezed Marc tighter. "Stones and sky, am I glad to see you three."

"Perhaps we might delay this little reunion until we're behind the castle walls." We all turned to Sabine, who had retrieved her gun, the skirts of her gown shredded. Not waiting for a response, she turned on her heel and started walking.

The twins both cocked amused eyebrows, but Marc gave me a gentle push between the shoulders to set me walking. "She's right." Then, falling into stride next to me, he murmured, "Thibault sent us."

"Why?"

"To deliver a message."

"But…" I frowned, shaking my head. "That doesn't make any sense. Why send you when he could send someone whose allegiance he is sure of?"

"That is a very good question."

Show me our enemy. Our enemy. Enemy.

I gave my weary head a little shake. No, that the Queen had shown me Angoulême did not mean the King was on our side – it only meant that our enemies were many. She'd known Thibault was the troll I'd wanted to see – it was all just a trick for her to gain control over Tristan.

But...

We were in no position to fight a war on two fronts – three, if I counted the Winter Queen, which I did. And if we had to ally with someone... Thibault hated Angoulême as much as we did, and maybe there was something to be said for putting aside our animosities for a time for the sake of destroying the greater evil.

The problem was, even if that was the correct strategy, I wasn't sure Tristan would be able to put aside his hatred of his father long enough to see it.

CHAPTER 9
Tristan

I paced back and forth across the council room chambers, barely hearing the reports being given to me by the city's administrators.

"You're making people nervous," Fred said, after the last messenger exited the room, leaving us alone.

"Blame your sister," I muttered, throwing myself into the chair across from him with enough force that the wood creaked. I'd been almost to the gates when she'd stopped me in my tracks, leaving me to stare helplessly at the blizzard while she negotiated whatever disaster she'd stumbled upon. Or instigated.

It smacked of fey magic – powerful fey magic – and their involvement couldn't be good. My uncle hadn't provided the foretelling that had ultimately freed us out of the goodness of his heart – there was something in it for him. And if there were something in it for him, the Winter Queen would be doing her damnedest to counter him. The question was, and had always been, what did Summer have to gain from the curse being broken? And, conversely, what did Winter stand to lose?

"Cécile will have reasons for what she did," Fred replied, interrupting my speculation before walking over to the illusion boxing Aiden away from the world. The man had been scratching and picking at my magic, and I wished Marie would hurry up with finding a place to lock him away. "She'll probably even think they are good ones," he added.

"I would have thought Sabine would temper her recklessness."

Fred laughed as though my comment were ludicrous, then knocked a fist against the illusion. "What's he doing in there?"

"A good question." Marie stalked into the room. "And you might have more care, gentlemen. I should not like for our plan to fall apart because you were not mindful of who is listening."

I'd spent the better part of my life being mindful about who was listening, but I let the comment slide. Blocking the doorway, I let the barrier holding Aiden turn transparent. And swore at what I saw.

My magic was streaked with blood and bits of fingernail; and though the tips of his fingers looked worn down to the bone, the wild-eyed Aiden continued to claw away, mouth open in muted screams.

"God in heaven, let him out," Marie shrieked.

The second the barrier dropped, Marie flung herself at her son, but instead of welcoming her comfort, he snapped at her like some wild animal, a string of violent expletives streaming from his lips.

She recoiled, then rounded on me. "You said he'd be fine."

"I said no such thing." Pinning Aiden to the floor, I kneeled next to him, searching for any sign of sanity in his mad gaze. "He's desperate to fulfill his word and we're preventing him. He's losing his mind." And I'd never seen anything like this before. At least, not in a human. Did my father know his peon had been rendered useless and this was his way of disposing of him? Or...

"Help him." Marie's fingernails dug into my arm.

"I can't. The only way to end this is to kill my father." *Or to let my father win.*

"If he dies, I'll make you pay." Her voice was a whisper, but the threat was clear. And I didn't think it mattered to her that the world might pay along with me. I needed to think of a solution, and quickly.

"We could drug him." Fred was leaning over my shoulder, his breath coming in short little whistles past my ear. "Can't harm himself or anyone else if he's out cold."

"Do you have something?"

"I've a sleeping draught in my chambers," Marie answered, but she didn't move.

"Go get it," I snapped. "And Fred, linger in the corridor and keep everyone out. The last thing we need is an interruption."

Both leapt into action, leaving me alone with the ailing lord. I watched his labored breathing for a long moment before asking, "Is there anything of you left in there, Aiden du Chastelier?"

There was power in a name – even in a human one, and he slowly turned his head, some level of sanity returning to his gaze. "Yes."

"Good." I sat back on my heels. "If you endeavor to hold on to that, I'll endeavor to see you freed of this foolish promise you made."

"Do I have your word on that, Your Highness?" He cackled softly, throat convulsing.

"No." I tilted my head, listening to the frantic beat of his heart. "I've made a few foolish promises of my own of late, and I'm finding them quite taxing."

"Wise." He rested his forehead against the stone. "I was young. I didn't know what I was doing when I made those promises to your father."

"I'm not interested in your excuses," I said, wishing Marie would hurry up. "And blaming one's poor choices on youth is a derivative excuse most often employed by the old."

"Not excuses," he said. "Just an explanation. And I might never have another chance to voice it."

Talking seemed to have improved his lucidity, if nothing else, so I shrugged. "Confess away."

"I promised to cede the Isle to him peaceably should the trolls ever be freed of the curse."

"I'd gathered that much," I said, then bit my tongue to keep any further sarcasm from passing my lips. "Why?"

"I was young. Foolish. Desperate. And the curse had held for centuries, so what were the chances of my debt being called?" He twitched against the magic binding his wrists. "And I didn't realize what giving my word to him really meant."

"You mean you didn't think you'd have to keep it," I said, not bothering to keep the sourness from my tone. "What did he give you in return?"

"Gold." His color was high, but no longer from madness, I thought. It was shame. "I'd been running wild. Gambling, drinking, women – and my father did not approve. He cut me off completely. I was angry, and I knew... I knew bargains could be made under the mountain. Your father met with me personally. Feasted me and plied me with wine and listened to me complain about my father. Then he offered to pay my debts, and all he asked was for my word to come back and visit him again."

I winced, knowing full well that my father could be jovial and charming when he was inclined. It was in those moments one should worry most.

"I paid my debts, but went straight back to the same behavior. When my creditors came calling, I returned again to Trollus and he offered me the same bargain."

"And on the third time?" *It is always threes.*

"He told me that he would provide an endless supply of gold, but in exchange, he wanted my word that I'd cede control of the Isle should he ever be freed. My word that I'd always come when he called me. That I'd do his bidding." Aiden's hands flexed as though they wanted to make fists but couldn't. "I thought he was the fool, gambling so much wealth on a hope with less substance than smoke on the wind. I... I didn't realize it would be binding."

"You were wrong." The greedy ones were always the easiest to catch.

"Do you think I haven't learned that lesson a thousand times since?" His eyes went to the bloodstain on the floor that had been hastily wiped up. "I would have put a bullet in my skull months ago, but…" A shudder ran through him, his desire to end his own life running counter to my father's orders. He began to thrash as Marie came back into the room, and I swore as blood ran from the corners of his mouth.

"What did you do to him?" she demanded, clutching at the vial in her hand.

I ignored her accusation and pried Aiden's jaw open, wedging magic between his teeth to keep him from biting off his tongue entirely. "Whatever it is you have, give it to him now!"

Her hands shook as she measured drops into his bloody mouth. He gurgled and hissed, trying to spit it back at her, but I pinched his nose until he had to swallow. "How long will it take to work?" I asked.

"Moments." A bead of sweat dribbled down her cheek.

Moments passed with no results, and his heart labored to keep its frantic pace. "Give him more."

She spilled more of the tonic than she got in his mouth while he swore and screamed that he'd maim and kill us both for thwarting him.

"It's not working," I said, grabbing Aiden's shoulders and pinning him to the floor. He fought back with incredible strength, but it was coming at great cost, capillaries in his skin bursting, joints popping, and muscles straining.

"Any more will kill him." She let the bottle slip through her fingers to smash against the floor.

"Then he's a dead man," I said. "His heart will fail under the strain."

"Not if I have anything to say about it."

I jumped at the sound of Cécile's voice, so caught up with Aiden that I hadn't felt her approach. There was a streak of red across her cheek – an injury that had only just begun to scab over – but otherwise, she seemed fine. Marc stood behind her, face hidden within the shadows of his hood.

"The twins have gone with Sabine to retrieve my moth – Anushka's – supplies." She dropped to her knees between Marie and me. "What did he promise?"

"To cede the Isle to my father," I said. "Among other things."

Cécile's brow furrowed, and she tucked a stray curl behind one ear. "This is not his way," she murmured, but before I could question her meaning, Sabine and the twins rushed in, a large chest floating ahead of them.

"The book," Cécile ordered, and Victoria plucked the grimoire from the chest and tossed it to her. She flipped swiftly through the pages, then stopped on one, scanning the contents. "This will do."

"Don't you dare hurt him," Marie said, but Cécile ignored her. "Nettle leaf and camphor," she said.

Victoria frowned, and Sabine elbowed past her, leaning in to the chest and rummaging through the glass bottles. Cécile listed the rest of the ingredients for the spell, then set the book aside and began dropping bits of this and that into a bowl. "I need a stone."

The twins looked around, then Vincent heaved one of the flagstones out of the floor. "This do?"

She nodded and he set it in front of her. "Fire."

Sabine handed her a candle, and she muttered, "Sleep," lit the contents of the bowl on fire, then poured the mixture over the stone. Instead of a chunky mess of plants and bones, the mixture was liquid flame. It hit the stone, then, defying gravity, circled back up to pool in the bottom of the overturned basin. Cécile muttered, "Sleep," once again, and turned the basin over, revealing what looked like water.

"Cup."

Victoria handed her a dirty wine glass that had been sitting on the table, and Cécile dunked it into her potion. "Hold him steady." She looked up then, blue eyes meeting mine, and I saw the uncertainty that I'd been feeling. She didn't know if it would work.

"What is this supposed to do?" I asked.

"Put him into a deep sleep." She licked her lips once. Then again.

"We tried that with a tonic," I said, more for Marie's benefit than Cécile's. Better her expectations be low.

"But this is magic," Cécile said, and then she poured the potion into the lord's mouth. "Sleep," she repeated, and all the candles in the room flared bright, then guttered out.

Three balls of troll-light filled the room, none of them mine.

"Is he... dead?" Marie looked like she was about to be sick.

"He's asleep." I tilted my head, listening to the slow but steady beat of the other man's heart. "How long will it last?"

Cécile sighed. "We'll have to give him more of the potion in a few days. And figure out a way to keep him fed. All this will be for nothing if he starves to death." Climbing to her feet, she surveyed the room, eyes widening at the bloodstains covering the floor. "What has happened?"

Letting Aiden's head drop to the floor with a thud, I got to my feet as well. "Compulsion drove him to kill his father."

She covered her mouth with one hand, and I felt the stab of empathetic grief as she turned to Marie. "My lady, I am so sorry."

"As you should be." Marie extracted a handkerchief and wiped the mess from her son's face. "It's your fault."

The retort that formed in my mind died on my lips as Cécile gave a slight shake of her head. She could defend herself, but had chosen not to.

"You've a place to keep him?" I didn't wait for Marie's nod, before continuing, "Take him there now." To Vincent, I said, "Make sure no one sees him."

I waited for my friend to leave with Aiden and Marie before saying more, purposefully refraining from looking Cécile's direction. I could sense the anticipation on her – that there was something she wanted to tell me or needed to say, but whatever it was could wait. And if she thought otherwise, she could bloody well order me to listen to her, since she clearly had no compunctions against doing so.

Marc stood next to Sabine – an unlikely pair, though neither appeared discomforted. "How long do we have?" I asked him, not wasting time on pleasantries. He and the twins must have broken out of Trollus moments after the curse was lifted, then come to Trianon at full sprint with whatever warnings they had for me. If they were here, then I'd no doubt that the frontrunners of my father's soldiers were right behind them.

Marc didn't answer, only extracted a letter from a pocket and handed it over. I recognized the seal as my father's, the wax smeared as though applied with great haste. "What is this?"

"I don't know." He rocked slightly on his heels. "All he said was that it was to be brought to you with no delays."

My fingers hesitated over the seal, the paper feeling heavy in my hands.

"Tristan–"

"Later." I cut Cécile off before she could say more, and then snapped the seal.

Tristan,

   You have succeeded where five centuries of rulers have failed, as I knew you would. All is forgiven. Return post-haste to Trollus with Cécile so that you can be reinstated as heir. Your people need you here. As do I.

   T

Everything in the room fell away as I read and reread the lines, the paper in my hand trembling.

"Tristan, what does it say?" Marc's question filled my ears, though I sensed he'd had to repeat it more than once. I cleared my throat, but the words caught, so I cleared it again and read the note. As I did, I could hear my father's voice and see his gloating face, and all I could think of was that iron-rimmed square on my aunt's Guerre set where the onyx piece with my face sat. How my father considered me a puppet to be played as he saw fit. How he believed he could pull my strings until I'd accomplished what *he* wanted, never once caring about the cost, then call me back to heel.

I hated him.

I hated him.

I hated him.

"Tristan." I felt Cécile's hand on my sleeve. "Tristan, listen to me. Your father isn't the enemy."

The paper in my hands exploded into fire.

CHAPTER 10
Cécile

The moment I said it, I knew it was a mistake. Not because I was wrong, but because Tristan wasn't ready to hear it. I should've explained the facts and given him the chance to come to the conclusion himself, because when it came to his father, he was not logical. He was not reasonable. He wasn't himself.

The letter from his father exploded into silvery fire, and I dropped my hand from Tristan's sleeve and took a step back from the heat.

He went very still in the way only trolls could manage, then slowly turned his head to fix me with an unblinking stare. That strange and alien gaze that seemed entirely without emotion. Almost without... life. A lie of an expression, because the sense of betrayal I felt from him twisted my guts. The silence stretched for what seemed like painful minutes before he exhaled and said, "Explain."

"We went to talk to the fairies," I started to say, then stopped, realizing that it sounded like I'd deliberately courted disaster. "We needed to know what was going on in Trollus – what our enemies were planning." I glanced at Sabine, and she nodded once in encouragement. "I knew you'd send scouts to spy, but even if they evaded capture – which isn't likely – they wouldn't know what to look for. They wouldn't understand the dynamics like we would. And I knew the fairies could open a hole that would allow me to see what's happening in Trollus without risk of capture."

"Without risk?" Tristan's voice was toneless, but somehow managed to be filled with incredulity and admonition.

Ignoring the comment, I continued, "She came when I called, and bargained with me. In exchange for a song, she agreed to show me our enemy." I dragged my gaze up from the floor to meet Tristan's eyes. "She showed me Angoulême, Roland, and Lessa."

"She?"

I nodded. "The Winter Queen."

Victoria whistled through her teeth, but I barely heard it through the jolt of trepidation I felt from Tristan. "And?" he asked.

An explanation of what I'd seen poured from my lips, but as valuable as the information was, I was more interested in his reaction to the Queen's comments about his father. I repeated the conversation word for word, and then held my breath, waiting.

Nothing.

"She thinks Angoulême is the enemy we should focus on."

Tristan let out a humorless laugh. "No, she withheld what you really wanted so that she could get what she really wanted. Which was?"

I swallowed, my chest feeling tight. "She wanted me to arrange a meeting with you. She wanted to trick me into getting you outside these walls. But ultimately, what she wanted was your name."

Everyone in the room went quiet.

"Obviously I declined that bargain," I said.

"I suppose we can consider that a win," Tristan said, and my spine stiffened.

"Don't you take that tone with her." Sabine stormed up and

inserted herself between Tristan and me. "We might have taken a risk in talking to those creatures, but at least we accomplished something. We know which of our enemies is most worth our attention and at least part of their plan, including a hint as to where the Duke might be hiding. And we know that monster who styles herself as a Queen has an interest in getting you out into the open. What have *you* done?" She waved her hand at the bloodstains. "Let Aiden run willy-nilly through the castle despite knowing he was under your father's control. Let him kill the Regent. Glassed us in with magic that so far hasn't protected us from *anything*. Stones and sky, you should be thanking Cécile for arriving when she did or Aiden would be dead and Marie, the only ruler you could expect the soldiers to follow, would hate your miserable guts."

"If you two hadn't provided such a timely distraction, the Regent wouldn't be dead," Tristan retorted. "And your clue to Angoulême's intended hiding place is hardly helpful. 'The faces of Anaïs's ancestors?'" He shook his head sharply. "It could be the ruins of one of their old properties or a stockpile of artwork and possessions. She might not even have meant her family specifically, but rather something related to the fey. Nor need it be on the Isle: for all we know, he intends to catch a ship to the continent and run things from there. Distance means little when one has a name."

It was then that I tuned them out, their bickering nothing but a drone of noise in the background. My cheek stung and I was exhausted from days without sleep, but I knew if I closed my eyes, all I would see was Roland walking across the Isle and slaughtering as he went. Tristan and I had unleashed him on the world, and what were we doing to stop him? Fighting amongst ourselves.

"Well?"

I blinked, realizing that everyone was staring at me. "Pardon?"

Tristan's face darkened further. "What do *you* suggest we do?"

I swallowed into the empty pit that was my stomach. "We can't hope to fight a war on two fronts and win. Your father is the lesser evil. For now, we need to join forces with him to stop Angoulême and Roland."

I swayed against the wave of emotion that smashed into me, and it was an effort to meet Tristan's eyes. The room became uncomfortably hot, the itchy tingle of too much magic in too small of a space marching across my skin.

"No." His voice was barely more than a whisper, but everyone heard it. Stepping around Sabine, he walked out of the room.

I tried to go after him, but Marc stepped into my path. "Let him go." He nodded once at Victoria, and she swiftly departed. "She'll calm him down."

"How many people will have to die before he realizes he's making a mistake?" I asked, rubbing a hand across my face. It came away coated in gold glitter – remnants of my costume from a performance that seemed a lifetime ago.

Marc caught hold of my elbow and led me over to the table. "Sit." To Sabine, he said, "She needs to eat something – can you arrange for that?"

She didn't answer, but her shoes made soft little thuds as she crossed the room. Marc sat next to me, and though he was silent, his presence was as much a comfort as it had always been.

"It is hard for any of us to imagine Thibault as an ally," he eventually said. "But for Tristan…"

"I understand that." I rested both elbows on the table. "I hate him, too. He's hurt me. Hurt those I care about."

"*Do* you understand?"

I lifted my head, surprised.

"I do not wish to marginalize the harm Thibault has caused you," he said, gloved finger tracing a knot in the wood of the table. "But you've been under his thumb for a matter of months, whereas we've been there our entire lives, Tristan especially. Almost his entire life has been predicated upon the belief that his father is the enemy – the man he needed to defeat at whatever cost. To set that aside – even if it is the correct choice – is no small thing."

"Do *you* think it's the correct choice?" I asked.

Marc leaned back in his chair, troll-light moving with him so that his face remained in shadows, and from the corner of my eye, I saw Sabine standing at the door, expression intent. "I think it would certainly be the swiftest and surest way to put a stop to Angoulême, Roland, and their followers. That in the short term, it would mean less loss of life. And," he held up a hand to forestall my interjection, "that is worth something. But it would come at a cost."

I chewed on my thumbnail. "Because it would put the King back in control?"

"Worse," Marc replied. "It would *cement* his power to the point we might never be able to wrest it from him again." He leaned toward me, elbows on his knees. "Tristan has worked for a very long time to create an alternative to the way his father rules Trollus. At first, it was covert, appealing only to the half-bloods and a few token sympathizers. But that's changed. The city is ready to follow him, ready to fight for a new way of life, and if he were to bend knee to his father now…" Marc sighed. "It would be a betrayal I'm not sure he'd ever be able to overcome. And it would mean the Isle would be subject to Thibault's rule for the rest of his life."

I had no stomach for this: for the weighing of strategies when lives were at stake. I'd always take the path that would save lives *now* versus saving lives *later*, because I believed that time would provide a solution that would see *all* lives saved. Some – Tristan included – would say that it was a lack of foresight on my part, but I couldn't stand by and watch people die because it was the strategically correct thing to do.

"He wouldn't really be bending knee to his father," I protested. "It would only be until we've dealt with Angoulême, and then Tristan can rid Trollus and the world of his father."

"And do you think Thibault wouldn't be ready for that?"

I jumped to my feet, chair tipping over with a clatter. "So you think I'm wrong? That we should just sit back and let Roland slaughter our friends and families while we figure out a way to assassinate the King?"

"I didn't say you were wrong, Cécile," Marc said. "Only that the solution might not be as clear cut as you might wish."

"And both of you are forgetting one big problem," Sabine said, bringing a tray of food to the table. "The fairy queen."

I took a bowl of soup from the tray and began spooning it into my mouth as I considered Sabine's words. "She did something to our bond so that Tristan didn't know I'd left the castle," I said.

Marc shook his head. "She couldn't affect that. What she did was catch you in an illusion within your own mind – one that you and Sabine shared."

I blinked once and Sabine lifted her eyebrows.

"She wanted you to believe you were across the city from Tristan," Marc said. "But she knew he would sense the distance, so instead she used illusion to deceive you. Time flows differently in the mind, but it would have been taxing, even for her."

My mind couldn't even begin to wrap itself around the concept, so I set that part of his explanation aside and focused on the last. "If it was so taxing, why did she do it?"

"Because she wanted to talk to you without his interference." Marc rubbed his chin. "She didn't care to risk a direct confrontation with him. It's well within his power to do her a great deal of harm."

And here I'd thought it was the other way around. I let my spoon fall against the lip of the bowl with a clatter. "Then why is he afraid of her?"

"He should be wary, yes. Her power is immense, and she commands an enormous host of deadly creatures. But her magic isn't a weapon in the way a troll's is."

"I didn't say wary." My skin burned with my rising anger. "I said afraid."

Marc hesitated, his stillness betraying his unease. "I don't know."

I desire to renew our acquaintance... The fairy queen's words danced through my head and I swore. "They've met before." Shoving a roll in my pocket, I started toward the door.

"Cécile–"

I stopped without turning around. "No, Marc. I know you're trying to protect him, but if he's keeping things from us then he doesn't deserve it. We're at war, and there's no place for us keeping secrets from each other. Not for Tristan. Not for any of us."

I left the room and he didn't try to stop me.

CHAPTER 11
Cécile

I climbed the stairs of the other tower, wrapping my cloak around me before I shoved open the heavy oak door. The chill made my arm ache in memory of Winter's touch, but I shoved aside the pain as I scanned the darkness for Tristan.

He stood in the shadows, elbows resting on the weatherworn parapet. Though he knew I was there, he didn't turn and, after a moment, I went to stand next to him. Casting my eyes out over the city, I noticed the light of the dome was gone, its presence apparent only through the slight distortion in the air. The blizzard had ceased, but the cloud cover had thickened, blocking out all light from the stars and moon. The Isle should have been pitch black in the hour before dawn.

But it wasn't.

In the distance rose an orange glow. Fire, fierce and bright, and not just burning in one location. It burned in many. And even as I watched, a massive gout of silvery troll fire exploded into the night sky, rising higher and higher before fading into the colors of natural flames. "Roland," I whispered. "It's him, isn't it?"

"Yes." Tristan's voice was barely audible over the wind.

"Can you tell where he is?"

"Just beyond Trollus." His fingers dug into the stone, little bits of it crumbling to fall into the darkness below.

"The Hollow?" I was shaking, my teeth clattering together even as my skin burned hot. "My family? Chris?"

"I can't tell for certain." He shifted, snow crunching beneath his weight. "I think he's keeping to the Ocean Road, but he isn't the only troll out there."

Tears dribbled down my cheeks, the names of all the small villages and hamlets along the road rising up in my mind. All those people dead or enslaved. And if he was going that direction, Courville would be next. Turning my head, I looked out over the ocean to see if I could glimpse the glow of the city on the far side of the bay, but the mist hanging over the water blocked it from sight. Other than Trianon and Trollus, Courville was the only other city on the Isle. Thousands of people lived there. Thousands of soon to be victims.

"And why is it," I asked, scrubbing the tears from my face, "that you haven't gone to stop him?"

Tristan was silent for so long that I wondered if he'd answer me at all. Then he said, "I made a bargain with Winter to save my life. That's how I survived the sluag sting. Its venom is a sort of magic. She controls them, and therefore she controls their magic and its effects. I owe her a life-debt. There is almost nothing she cannot ask of me." He scrubbed a hand through his hair. "I told Victoria, and she will explain the circumstances to your brother. They'll come up with a reasonable excuse for why I'm hiding behind the walls while my brother destroys every town and village he comes across."

I said nothing while I mastered my temper, then, "It's been months since you were stung, and you never once mentioned this little detail."

"Actually, I did," he said, and my mind prickled with a half-recalled memory. The scent of frost. I focused hard, and the forgotten conversation slowly moved to the forefront of my thoughts. *Someone with a great deal of power did me a favor. I owe her a very great debt.*

"She made me forget," I said. "How is that possible?"

"More of a strong suggestion that our conversation wasn't worth remembering," he said. "She couldn't take something without giving up something in return."

"Why didn't you remind me?"

Tristan sighed. "I gave her my word not to speak of the conversation that happened between the two of us, and... And as long as the curse was in place, I didn't have to worry about the debt."

And he'd believed he never would, as I'd yet to convince him that the trolls deserved to be freed.

"Do you know what she wants?" I asked. *Could he tell me if he did?*

He shook his head. "No, but it will be something I don't want to give. She wouldn't waste the debt on anything I'd sacrifice freely."

I leaned over the edge, fighting the urge to rid myself of the small amount of soup I'd eaten. "I didn't think things could get worse."

"I've warned you about the dangers of optimism."

I laughed, but it had a strange, almost hysterical edge to it. "Does she need to see you face to face to call in this debt?"

He gave a small nod. "Which is why she was using you to try to lure me out. But a debt can only be called once. A name, though... You know as well as anyone what an effective tool that is. Be thankful it's the one thing she can't ask me for."

His words sound like a barb, but they didn't feel that way. He was past anger, slumped into the depths of indecision and regret.

"You couldn't have known it would come to this," I said, resting my hand on top of his, feeling the heat of his skin through the leather of his glove.

"Don't try to give me absolution in this, Cécile," he said. "I knew it would cost me, but with my life on the line – and yours – it was a risk I was willing to take. There wasn't anything I wouldn't have given her."

He leaned against the wall, keen eyes delving into the darkness. "I should be out there stopping him. He's my responsibility. But what if I step outside these walls and she calls my debt? What if whatever she asks of me not only keeps me from stopping Roland, it prevents me from protecting those in Trianon? But if I don't... I don't know what to do."

Another tower of silver flame lit the night sky and I squeezed Tristan's hand. Now wasn't the time to push an alliance with Thibault, so instead I asked, "Why hasn't your father moved?"

"Because he knows I won't attack him while he's in Trollus," Tristan said. "There's too much of a chance of one of us bringing the mountain down on the city. And, likely, he's using Angoulême's actions as a way to force me into an alliance. As a way of bringing me to heel. If only he knew that I've already effectively been caged."

I racked my brain for a solution, for a way to find out what the Queen intended. "What about your uncle?" I asked. "Could he stop her?"

"He can't prevent her from claiming what's owed to her any more than she could keep him from doing the same." He gave me a meaningful glance that I chose to ignore.

Closing my eyes, I remembered the being I'd met in that land of endless summer. How he had seemed to glow golden like the sun. It was hard to imagine him subjugated, and it also didn't make sense. "But he called her his wife?"

A ghost of a smile drifted across Tristan's face. "They would've framed themselves in a way you'd understand. Spoken your language. Appeared in a form they believed you'd find pleasing. The higher fey are..." He paused, seeming to flounder for an explanation, "they're not solid, static creatures populated by a soul in the way a human is. They are sentient entities that appear as they wish, and the lesser fey are their creations. Splinters of themselves that they've shaped into certain forms then abandoned to their own devices. When the higher fey came to this world, they formed themselves as humans to blend in with those living on the Isle. Perfect humans. And when the iron eventually bound them here, they found themselves imprisoned in their human forms."

I remembered Anushka's words: *that's what they are. Base. To the human eye, they are so very lovely, but to their ancestors, the immortal fey, they are wretched, ugly, and colorless things. Trolls.*

"The rulers of Summer and Winter are bonded," he continued. "But they hate each other. They're continually at odds, their warriors constantly warring against each other. And with the ebb and flow of battle, so do the seasons shift in all the many worlds they touch upon." He opened his hand and let the snow blow off into the night. "Winter is at the height of her power."

I frowned, a thought occurring to me as I remembered my conversation with the fairy queen.

"What?"

I pursed my lips. "Is it possible she didn't want the curse broken?" I replayed the conversation over to him as best as I could remember.

Tristan's brow furrowed, and he absently brushed snow off the parapet so he could rest his elbows as he thought. Reaching into my pocket, I handed him the bun I'd stuffed in there prior to abandoning Marc and Sabine.

"My aunt has long believed her prophesies came from the Summer Court," he took a bite, chewing slowly. "If my uncle wanted us freed, it would be because it benefited him in some way, so it would make sense that it would be to Winter's detriment."

"Any guesses as to what that benefit might be?" I asked.

"We are technically part of his court," he replied. "All my

aunt's prophesies have been information that has helped my people, warned us about trouble." He shrugged. "Maybe he's not done with us yet." He turned to look at me. "We know for certain he's not done with you. You owe him for my name."

My mouth went dry, less for the reminder of the debt I owed than for the reminder of the name I possessed. I'd been on the cusp of using it today to save Sabine, and as much as it made me sick, I knew that doing so would've been a mistake. "Is there a way to unknow it?"

"Unknowing it wouldn't cancel your debt." He tilted his head. "But that isn't your reason for asking, is it?"

I shook my head. "It's too great a weapon. I'm afraid of misusing it."

"What if you need it?"

"That's what I'm afraid of," I whispered.

The hinges of the door creaked, and we both turned. "We'll talk about this later," Tristan murmured.

Fred appeared in the entrance. "The scouts have all departed, and I've sent ships out to see if they can pinpoint your brother's progress as well as to warn Courville. Lady Victoria indicated that he'd have no difficulty sinking the ships from shore, so they know to be out of sight by dawn."

"Good." Tristan exhaled. "And you've sent riders with warnings?"

"Already gone. Hopefully the islanders listen and take refuge in the mountains where they'll be harder to find, although it will be difficult with the snow and the cold. We've begun loading what ships are in the harbor with those who can't fight, but they'll need to set sail soon if they are to be out of range before full light. The winds aren't in our favor."

"Marc can help push them out of the harbor," Tristan said. "I'll send him straight away."

My brother's eyes widened, and it occurred to me that he really hadn't seen the scope of a troll's power. "Right," he said, then looked away and scratched his chin, giving away his discomfort. "Lady Victoria explained your predicament. I think if we tell those in Trianon that you must remain in the city to keep it protected that none of them will protest too heartily about you not venturing out. For now, anyway."

"It's not far from the truth," Tristan said, eyes going to fires in the distance. "His power has grown."

Doubt twisted my guts, and I knew it was doing the same to Tristan's. Roland was testing his powers, seeing how far he could push them now that he was freed of the confines of Trollus. And for the first time ever, I wondered who the most powerful troll on the Isle really was.

CHAPTER 12
Tristan

Dawn came far too soon.

While Cécile disappeared to check on Aiden, I spent the first hours of the morning listening to the tallies of soldiers, arms, and supplies. To strategies put forth by men who had no real concept of what they were facing. Even with my little demonstration, the idea that Roland could stand in the face of an army's worth of artillery and laugh was inconceivable to them. And though the Regent's council remained uneasy in my and Victoria's presence, it didn't take long for them to start talking over us. Fred they included in the conversation – given Aiden was only a ceremony away from becoming Regent – but the volume of his voice suggested he was no less frustrated.

"They really are quite dense," Victoria said, sliding her chair back a couple paces and settling her booted heels on the table with a thud. Several of the men shot her appalled glances, but she ignored them. "Maybe we should have sent them down to watch Marc push boats out to sea."

"I believe they are called ships," I said, the conversation around us stalling, just as she had intended.

"Semantics," she declared, and began pruning her fingernails with a razor sharp filament of magic. When all twelve pairs of eyes at the table were on her, she asked, "Are you lot of armchair generals ready to listen or must I sit through another hour of your abysmal strategies?"

Eyes bulged and jaws twitched, but before anyone could speak, the door opened and Marc came in, an out-of-breath man trailing at his heels. "First ships have returned," my cousin said. "But not all of them will make it back." He nudged the man. "Tell them."

The sailor peered up at Marc, trying to get a glimpse within the depths of his hood, then seemed to think better of it. "We went up the coast, but kept lights out and silence on the deck as she directed," he nodded at Victoria. "There's some coastal villages that seem untouched – could see folk moving about with torches and lanterns – but others..." He swallowed hard, Adam's apple bobbing. "They're nothing but glowing pits of char."

The councilmen broke out in exclamations of dismay, but I held up a hand to silence them. "How many?"

"Four, by my count."

"And how far down the coast has he reached?" I gestured to the map on the table, watching as he tapped a finger against a hamlet located on the Ocean Road. "This is where we saw him."

"Not that far from Trollus," I muttered to Victoria.

She nodded, tapping her bottom lip. "They could be much further if all they cared about is destruction."

The look in her eyes told me we were thinking the same thing: that just as Cécile had said, Roland was taking oaths of loyalty from those who surrendered. What he might choose to do with those oaths made my stomach clench. Then the sailor's words finally settled. "You *saw* him?"

The sailor nodded, face pale. "Was hard to make out anything in the dark, so we stayed until dawn, but retreated away from the coast so we needed a scope to see." He blew out a long breath. "Came down onto the beach, and he was just a boy. Just a boy."

How many times had the same sentiment stayed my hand?

"He waded in – didn't seem to care a wit about the cold – and then he started splashing his hands in the water like a child. Laughing like a child. But the ocean *moved*."

"It does that, I hear," Victoria said, but there was little levity in her voice.

"It was like a giant was playing in the water. Or a god. All my life has been spent at sea, and I've never experienced waves like that."

There was nothing heavier than the ocean. A bead of sweat ran down my spine.

"Then the ship closest to the coast disappeared under the surface, only to reappear and be plunged down again." His eyes went distant. "Like a toy in a bathtub. But the men were screaming…" He shook his head sharply to dispel the memory. "Thought we were all done for, but an ice fog came in fast and no one could see more than a few feet either way. Not even him."

She'd interfered to save the ships. But why? I left Victoria to continue questioning the sailor as I considered the Winter Queen's motivations. First her showing Cécile Angoulême's plans and now this? It seemed almost as though she were siding with us against him, but it couldn't be that simple. She wasn't trying to rid the world of my brother out of the goodness of her heart – there wasn't a benevolent bone in her body. There had to be something in it for her.

"He's telling the truth," Marc said. "I was on the docks when the waves came in. I did what I could, but…" He lifted one shoulder. "Most of the harbor was destroyed, lower reaches of the city flooded. Those living there will need help."

"So much for your protection," one of the councilmen muttered, but I ignored him, giving the command to evacuate those whose homes had been damaged to higher ground as my mind turned to my father and Angoulême.

Both of them were banking on my refusal to harm my brother. Cécile had heard Angoulême say as much, and even if she hadn't, the fact that the Duke was allowing his puppet prince to roam in plain view made it abundantly clear. If he truly believed Roland was at risk from me, he'd be taking more care. And my father? I toyed with the cuff of my sleeve, wishing I had any such certainty about his strategy. He had the capacity to stop Roland, but he hadn't done so. He had the ability to pull Trianon out from under me, but hadn't so much as stirred from Trollus. And the Winter Queen? I scrubbed a hand across my eyes, the questions Cécile had raised making me wonder if her actions were part of a larger game than I realized.

"Your Highness?" I heard one of the advisors speak, but I ignored him. This was as complex a game of Guerre as I had ever played, but there was far more at stake than tiny gold figurines. People were dying as I sat safely behind castle walls trying to unpack the plots of a multi-headed enemy, and I knew that if I sat here another month I still might not understand every motivation, every plan. And even if I did, at that point, would there be anything left to save?

I stood up, the humans flinching and Marc squaring his shoulders, seeming to sense my plan of action before I'd uttered a word.

"My brother cannot be allowed to continue unchecked," I said. "Ready your ship, Captain. We move against him tonight."

CHAPTER 13
Cécile

"You should rest," I said to Lady Marie as I entered the cell, holding up my hands to the brazier. I'd expected her to put her son in a sumptuous suite of rooms, but even in her grief, Marie was pragmatic. The dungeons, dank from the river that ran to either side of the castle, were rarely used (as far as I knew) since the construction of the Bastille, but they had been maintained, the iron bars on the windowless cells strong and secure. The heavy stone assured no sound would pass into the upper levels, and the singular entrance made it easy for the trolls to keep anyone unwanted out. Most importantly, in my mind, should Aiden become unmanageable, then the dungeon would serve its intended purpose.

She shifted on the stool next to the cot on which Aiden lay, pulling her shawl tighter around her shoulders. "Do you truly believe I'm going to leave my son alone with you, witch?"

She said "witch", but I heard another word. Judging from the scowl that appeared on Vincent's face, he heard the same. I gave a slight shake of my head. "What precisely do you think I'll do to him?"

Marie's jaw tightened and she turned bloodshot eyes on me.

"He needs to be watched at all times," I said. "There are only a handful of individuals we can trust with the task, and most of them are needed for more important ventures." I sat on the edge of the bed. "And that includes you. My brother is bright and capable, but he was raised on a pig farm and you've abandoned him to impersonate a man raised with all the power and privilege the Isle has to offer. This is your plan, motivated by your desire for your son to have a chance at life after we triumph, but if there is to be any hope of it succeeding, you must remain present and involved."

Her eyelid twitched. "There was a time I felt sorry for you – believed you were naught but an innocent victim. Of the trolls. Of Anushka. Of fate and chance." She rose to her feet and dropped into a deep curtsey. "As you wish, so shall it be, Your Highness."

Vincent let out an explosive sigh after she left. "Stones and sky, Cécile. You couldn't have come sooner? Cursed woman has been staring at me as though I were a rabid dog."

"Have you ever seen a rabid dog?" I asked, leaning down to listen to the lord's breathing. Even in sleep, it seemed unsteady. Afraid.

"No." He pushed away from the wall, coming to stand next to me. "But it's a turn of phrase that I've always wanted to use."

"The trouble with a rabid dog," I said, resting my hand against Aiden's forehead and frowning as he flinched, "is that no matter how much you care for it, you still have to put it down." I straightened. "I'm afraid that when he wakes, there won't be anything human left."

It was several hours later when Vincent roused me from where I'd fallen asleep with my head resting on the edge of Aiden's cot. Sabine stood just beyond, a lamp full of troll-light in one of her hands.

"Tristan give you that?" I asked, rubbing my eyes.

"No…" She hesitated, then shook her head. "But Tristan does want to see you – both of you. I'll stay with Lord Aiden."

•••

We found Tristan in the council chamber in the company of Victoria, Marc, and my brother. I wanted to go to him, but there was an agitation in his movements that warned me to keep my distance.

"We need to act now," he said with no preamble. "Allowing Roland to continue as he has will cost us more than we can hope to gain by waiting."

"Tristan–"

"I know, Cécile." His eyes ran over me, then he turned away as though what he saw was physically painful. "I'm not going anywhere."

"Then who–"

Fred slammed his cup down on the table, interrupting me. "I've things to take care of, and my opinion on this venture has counted for nothing." He stomped from the room.

"Marc, Vincent, and Victoria will go," Tristan said, his voice steady. "They are trained in combat, whereas Lessa and Roland are not. It might give them the advantage they need to take them down."

"Might?" I was on my feet, though I couldn't remember standing. "You can't be serious, Tristan? You're sending them to an almost certain death!"

"So little faith," Victoria said, an unfamiliar smile crossing her face. "Lessa and I have a score to settle, and it's not one I intend for her to walk away from."

"Only if I don't get to her first," Vincent said, crossing his arms behind his head and leaning back until his chair creaked dangerously. "Marc, you can take Roland."

"Thank you for that." Marc leaned forward, dropping the magic that hid his face so that I could see him. "Cécile, it's the only option. We cannot allow Roland and Lessa to continue unchecked, and we dare not send Tristan out with the power Winter has over him unless there is no other choice."

"You mean if you're dead." My eyes burned.

Marc sat back. "Yes."

I sank my teeth into my bottom lip. "Then we need to even the odds." I turned to Tristan. "I'm going with them."

I expected a knee-jerk reaction from him. An instantaneous no. But he had expected this. "You're in the same circumstance as I am, Cécile. *She* wants to get her hands on you, so she can get to me. They'll be watching for you, and not just the fey, but the trolls as well. You're too recognizable."

I pulled the knife from my belt. "I can remedy that." I sliced the blade across my braid, as close to my head as I could get without risking my neck. Then I dropped the slowly unraveling crimson plait on the table. "I'm going with them. End of story."

"Oh, Cécile." Sabine stood back to inspect her handiwork, giving a slight shake of her head.

"It's just hair." I said the words, but as I tugged the black locks hanging just above my shoulders, I knew I was lying. It was vain and foolish, but my hair had meant a lot. "It will grow back."

"And the black will come out, I promise." She hugged me, the long plait of my hair falling over her shoulder. It would be the other part of our deception: Sabine, disguised as me, going out onto the towers with Tristan.

I rubbed the dark that had transferred from my hair to her shoulder, and took one final glance in the hand mirror, confirming that the cosmetics she'd applied had satisfactory darkened my lashes and brows. I wore trousers and a coat that had been hastily altered to fit, and the scarf Sabine handed me completed my disguise. It wasn't as good as troll magic, but unlike magic, it was firmly in place.

"Sabine, I need to speak with Cécile."

I'd felt Tristan enter the room, but I took my time turning around, not entirely desirous of him seeing me like this.

"You look dreadful," he said, stepping aside so that Sabine

could leave the room, seemingly oblivious to the dark glare she cast his direction.

"I didn't realize your feelings were so dependent on my appearance," I said, crossing my arms.

"They aren't." And before I could blink, he was across the room, lifting me up and against him. "But I'm tired of disguising you and sending you off while I wait to see if you'll return."

"I always come back," I murmured, gently kissing his forehead, the heat of his skin against my lips making me burn hot in other places. "I *will* always come back. And besides, you *aren't* sending me. I..." Frowning, I straightened so I could meet his gaze, seeing his self-satisfaction even as I felt it. "You knew I'd insist on going."

"Of course I knew," he said. "Why do you think your brother was in such a foul temper?"

"Am I so predictable?"

"Predictable? No." He buried his face in my neck, teeth catching at the skin of my throat. "Steadfast and constant? Yes. Brave? Always."

He walked backwards, then fell onto the bed so that my knees rested on either side of him on the coverlet. One gloved hand gripped my waist, then slid over the curve of my hip, while the other cupped the nape of my neck, gently tugging me downward. The feel of leather against my skin irritated me for reasons I could not quite articulate, and I resisted, bracing my arm against his shoulder. "Then why the pretense?"

He turned his head, cheek pressing against the bed as he stared into the fire burning in the hearth. "In case I was wrong."

His doubt gnawed at me, and I sensed it was for reasons other than the subject at hand. And also that he had no intention of talking about them. Sighing, I relaxed my arm and lowered myself to his chest, listening to the measured thud of his heart. I wanted to stay like this for as long as I could, content in his arms, the warm glow of the fire in my eyes. But there was no time. For us, there was never time. "Tell me."

Tristan's hand dropped from my waist. Lifting me up slightly, he extracted something from his coat pocket. I blinked and focused, then frowned as I saw it was Anushka's grimoire, the latch unfastened. "You left it open after you helped Aiden," he said. "I found it when I went back to the council chambers. There's a spell in here that I think we could use."

Rolling me over so we were facing each other, our legs tangled together, he held up the grimoire and illuminated the text with a ball of light. "It's near the back," he muttered.

Flip, flip. His gloved thumb turned the pages, and my head felt light as though I were about to faint as I waited to see where he would stop. Because somehow, I knew what page he was looking for.

CHAPTER 14
Tristan

"Does this spell work?" I asked her, wishing that I didn't have to. Wishing that I'd never picked up the grimoire and flipped through the pages. Hating the pragmatic and logical part of myself that had seen the spell and immediately considered how it could be used for my benefit.

The shot of anguish was immediate and fierce. Cécile's eyes shut, but tears squeezed out of the corners and dripped down her cheek. "Why?"

I let the book slip out of my grasp to fall with a soft thud on the bed behind me. Pulling off my glove with my teeth, I wiped away one tear, then kissed away another before pulling her close so that her head rested under my chin.

The words stuck in my throat, coming out as a slight exhalation of air. "I…"

Her shoulders were shaking, a damp spot growing on the front of my shirt where her face was pressed against it. Was it even worth it, given the grief it would cause her? The grief it would cause me? Closing my eyes, I remembered my argument with Marc deep in the mines. If I backed away from this, I'd be nothing more than a coward and a hypocrite.

"If something happens," I said, brushing a stray lock of hair from her face, "it can't happen to both of us. We broke the curse believing we could make a better world, and if one of us falls, the other must see our dream through to the end, whatever that end might be."

One ragged breath, and the tears stopped. "You're planning for me to die."

"That's not–" I broke off, tugging at the collar of my shirt in an attempt to relieve the tightness in my throat. "I'm sorry."

A slender arm wedged between us, and she pushed away. I let her. "Cécile…"

Her blue eyes were bloodshot. Weary. Resigned. She pressed a cold finger to my lips. "No, it's smart. It's a good plan. I hate it, but it's a good plan. We need to function with autonomy, which is hard when we can feel what each other is feeling–" Her voice cracked.

Catching her hand with mine, I held it to my chest. There were things I should've said, explanations and justifications. Words to make her understand that in a perfect world, I'd never consider asking her for this. That in a perfect world, she would always come first, and I'd spend every waking moment proving it to her.

But ours was an imperfect world. Flawed and cruel.

"Will it work?" I asked.

She closed her eyes for a long moment, then nodded. "I think it might."

Cécile worked quickly, brow furrowed as she rummaged through Anushka's chest, coming out with a vial filled with dried petals. "*Passiflora*," she muttered. "Truthfully, I'm not sure the herbs are necessary. The iron I understand, but…" She sniffed the contents. "Might be that they are only to focus the witch on her objective. I just don't know."

She wasn't talking to me, so I didn't respond, instead going to the window and drawing back the shade. Dusk was settling on Trianon, the sun backlighting the mountains in shades of red and orange. The ship would soon be ready in what remained of the harbor, and in the darkest hour of the night, I'd send my wife and closest friends to kill my brother.

"I need blood, but only a little."

Pulling back my sleeve, I sliced the back of my arm with magic. Blood dribbled down my wrist, crimson lines in contrast to veins still blackened with the scars of iron rot. As soon as Cécile withdrew the basin, I jerked my sleeve down to cover the mess, turning my gaze back to the window.

Soon, I'd feel nothing.

Cécile murmured an incantation, and I felt the invasive pull on my magic as she drew on it, shaping it to her own purpose. "It's done," she said, and I turned back to her.

On the palm of her hand rested three black balls the size of marbles. They fluxed and shifted like globs of oil in water, and Cécile's fingers curled and twitched as though she desired nothing more than to fling them to the floor. "You're supposed to eat them," she said.

"That's unfortunate. How long will it last?"

"I don't know." She bit her lower lip. "The magic doesn't affect the bond – it affects you. You won't feel what I'm feeling, because you won't feel anything at all. You'll be able to make decisions logically, not because of what may or may not be happening to me." She held out her hand. "I suppose you should try one while I'm still here."

I picked up an empty glass and tipped the contents of her palm into it. Setting it aside, I said, "Not yet."

"Tristan."

Shaking my head once to silence her, I eased the coat off her shoulders, letting it drop to the ground. Beneath, she wore a boy's shirt that covered far more than any of her dresses, yet concealed nothing as her body reacted to my touch. The lids of her eyes stayed heavy, but the weariness was washed away by a heat far more to my liking. Catching hold of the laces at her throat, I tugged them loose, her soft exhalation making me ache in a way that bordered on pain.

She caught hold of my hands, lowering them to her hips. "Let me." Her eyes fixed on mine, holding me in place as she pulled loose my cravat, letting the fabric drift to the floor. She unfastened one button, then the next, her fingers sliding under my shirt to brush against my chest, my stomach, before stopping just above my belt, which she used to pull me closer.

My breath was loud in my ears, quick and ragged, and beyond my control. Her hands drifted back up to my shoulders, pushing my shirt and coat down until they caught on my wrists, binding my arms in place until I was willing to let her go. Which I wasn't.

Only then did her gaze break from mine, eyes running over me even as her fingers traced feather-light lines of fire down my arms, across my ribs, up my back. She'd touched me before, but it seemed like it had been a thousand years ago. Like I'd been dying of thirst, but hadn't known it until handed a glass of icy water. She was in my head and in my hands, desire ricocheting back and forth between us. There was nothing like it. There never would be anything like it.

Cécile stood on her tiptoes, the linen of her shirt rough against my skin, her arms wrapping around my neck. Fingers tangling in my hair. She kissed me – barely more than a brush of her lips against mine – but it sent a shudder through me. Pushing my control to the very limits.

Her breath was warm. Sweet. "We don't have much time."

Prophetic words.

I let go of control.

It was not slow or sweet or gentle. Seams on clothing strained and tore. Kisses were desperate and edged with teeth. Caresses seared, fingernails scraping across naked skin. I needed to know every inch of her. Every taste. Every sound.

Just in case.

Because it could be the last time I ever held her. Ever kissed her. Ever heard her voice. And whether an hour or a lifetime passed, I needed to be able to close my eyes and have it be her who filled them.

CHAPTER 15
Cécile

Our friends waited in the council chambers, all four of them staring at the row of perfume bottles Sabine had tracked down. "Will these do?" she asked, eyes running over my face and making me doubt how well I'd fixed my cosmetics.

"As well as anything," I replied, picking one up. It smelled overpoweringly floral, and I wrinkled my nose. "All that matters is that they break at the right time. The blood must come in contact with their skin."

"Not a problem." Vincent hefted one of the perfume bottles and pretended to throw it at Marc's head. Marc didn't so much as flinch. "How close do you need to be, Cécile?"

"Closer than I'd like." I nibbled on my thumbnail, watching Tristan go to the far side of the table. The seeds of magic had disappeared into one of his pockets, but I felt their presence acutely. *When would he take one? What would it do?* "We'll only get one chance to attack them." And I wasn't entirely confident I could take down more than one troll at a time. Roland had to be first, because at least my friends could handle Lessa and the others if they had to. But what if Angoulême's plans had changed? What if there were more trolls with them than we expected?

"Perhaps we might have a contest to see how many we can hit

Lessa with before Cécile finishes her spell," Victoria suggested, interrupting my thoughts.

Tristan coughed. "As the donor supplying your projectiles, I'm going to veto that plan."

"Does it need to be you?" Marc asked. "You're taxed as it is with this dome you've created. The last thing we need to be doing is bleeding you dry."

Tristan sat down at the table and rested his chin on his hands, eyes thoughtful. "When Anushka used the spell on me, it was as though I were bound by my own power. Cécile will be manipulating the magic of whomever's blood she uses, which suggests the more powerful the donor, the better."

"But Anaïs was able to stop your father," I reminded him.

"I know." He frowned. "But better not to take chances." And before anyone could argue with him, he pulled a knife out of his boot, pushed up his sleeve, and sliced the blade across his forearm where the earlier laceration had long since faded. Angling the tip of the weapon, he watched expressionless as rivulets of crimson ran down the steel and into one of the bottles.

"That'll do," I said after the third bottle was full. "The last thing we need is you fainting and Trianon falling while we're gone."

Tristan gave a slight roll of his eyes, but didn't argue as I tied a handkerchief around his arm. As he fussed with the sleeve of his shirt, I caught Sabine's attention and held it. *Watch him for me.*

She nodded.

Carefully wrapping the bottles in a scarf, I put them in my satchel. "Night is upon us. It's time we set sail."

The sails of the ship snapped tight with a gust of wind, the masts creaking, and water slapping against the hull. With each sound, I flinched, certain that Roland stood on the beach under the cover of night, his sharp ears marking our progress, waiting for the right moment to strike. The sailors seemed of a like mind, the tension rolling off them palpable even in the darkness.

"This is as far as we take you," the captain said, and I curbed the urge to shush him. "You'll need to row yourselves to shore." The tiny boat in question hit the water with a splash, and a squeak of fear forced its way out of my throat.

"Thank you," Marc replied. "But we'll walk. Please hold your position until we signal."

I heard the rustle of his cloak and a sliver of moonlight peeked through the clouds to illuminate him standing on the railing, one hand held out to me. "Mademoiselle?"

Though we'd agreed no one would use my name lest they draw the attention of the Winter Queen, it still jarred in my ears to be called anything but. Swallowing hard, I took hold and allowed him to pull me up, his steady grip the only thing keeping me from falling into the black waters below. "Ready?"

"For what?" I spluttered.

Marc stepped off the rail.

I gasped, but instead of plunging down, he stood suspended in thin air. I cautiously edged the tip of my boot out, my heart slowing not in the slightest as I felt the firm plank of magic beneath my foot. "I can't see," I whispered. "I don't know where to step."

"Just follow my lead," he said, tugging me forward. I took a hesitant step, but spray from the ocean had already coated the magic, and my boots slid on the slick surface. The ship rocked on a wave, and the invisible plank bobbed up and down wildly. I ripped my hand from Marc's grip and dropped to my stomach, grasping about until my fingers closed over the edges of the magic. Then I pressed my face against it, trying and failing not to think about what it would feel like to plunge into the icy waters below.

"Want me to carry you?" Victoria asked.

"No." Taking a few measured breaths, I added, "I'm fine."

The plank took that opportunity to buck like an untrained horse, and I slid to one side, spray soaking into my clothing. Lingering in this position wasn't doing me any favors.

I crawled forward, keeping a tight grip on the edges and the faint shadows of Marc's boots directly in front of my nose. I made it perhaps the equivalent of ten paces before magic looped around my waist and flung me over Victoria's shoulder.

Holding onto the end of her braid with one hand, I clenched my teeth and held my breath as the three of them moved at reckless speed over the open water, inhaling only when I felt Victoria's boots sink into the deep sand of the beach. She sat me on my feet, but I immediately sank to my haunches, waiting for the world to quit spinning. Acutely aware that the three of them were watching, I asked, "Did you signal the captain?"

"He's been trying to sail away since we stepped off the ship," Marc replied. "His signal is that I let him." The debris covering the beach crunched beneath his boots. "We need to get out of the open. There are only a few hours left until dawn."

We found the first destroyed village by smell more than anything else. Wood smoke, wet ash, and, worst of all, burned meat.

"He's not there," Marc said, catching my arm as I veered off the Ocean Road and up the less trafficked one leading to Nomeny. I knew it was so, because there was a sign at the crossroads, the top of it singed black.

"I need to know," was all I said, my boots crunching as I strode across the ice – snow that had been melted, then frozen again in a sheet as far as the eye could see. At first the trees were only scorched, but as we drew closer to the village, they became blackened, burned, then nothing more than ash on the ground. And scattered amongst them were bodies, heat and fire having rendered them unrecognizable, but every one of them face down. They'd been fleeing. Running for their lives.

There was nothing left of the village but a faintly glowing pit in the ground. I stumbled toward it, my boots sliding in the grey slush, until I stood on the edge. There was nothing. Nothing but rock that had melted and hardened, still hot hours after the attack. And ash. Dozens of lives reduced to ash.

If the world burns, its blood will be on your hands.

Turning, I made my way back to where my friends stood next to what remained of the tree line. The dawn rose as I reached them, and as it did, my sense of Tristan went flat. I stopped with one foot raised mid-stride.

Victoria bent down, her eyes squinting in the glowing brightness of the sun. "Are you well?"

"Yes," I said, then stumbled over to a charred trunk and spilled my guts onto the grey ice. I'd known he would use the seed, had known what it would do to him, but the reality was so much worse.

"I made one of Anushka's potions for Tristan," I said. "It's meant to mute our bond, but it works by suppressing his emotions."

"Why?" Victoria demanded.

"So that if something happens to her, he'll be able to carry on," Marc said, then slowly shook his head as though he had more to say on the matter but was choosing not to. "Can you tell if it worked?"

My throat convulsed as I swallowed. "Yes. Maybe a little too well."

No one spoke, the only sound the wind and the hiss of snowflakes falling into the pit.

And the tread of many feet.

I lifted my head, the trolls already facing back to the Ocean Road, heads cocked as they listened.

"At least a dozen," Vincent murmured. "Perhaps more."

We crept back through the blackened trees, magic blocking us from sight but our silence dependent on stealth. Reaching the

Ocean Road, we stopped, groups of islanders trudging past us, many of them bearing signs of injury, and all under guard. But not troll guards.

Human.

"Black, white, and red," Marc muttered as one of the guards passed close to us. "Roland's new colors?"

"How is this possible?" I asked, turning to spit in the snow, the taste of vomit still sour on my tongue. "How could he have recruited so many in so little time?"

"He didn't," Marc replied. "This plan has been years in the making."

There was nothing else to do but follow them.

We took the hour's walk to the village of Colombey as an opportunity to discover information, the four of us ranging up and down in pairs to listen to the guards and prisoners. But we learned little other than that the islanders had been roused from their hamlets and told they'd either swear fealty to the rightful ruler of the Isle or find themselves on the sharp end of a sword. Most had capitulated. Some had not. Those who had not hadn't survived long.

The village had a thousand times its usual population, many milling about aimlessly, while others sat in the mud, their eyes distant. The armed men bullied townsfolk, farmers, and fishermen into a ragged line leading into the tavern. Men and women. Children, some so young they had to be carried by a parent or older sibling. The only people I saw none of were the elderly and infirm, and a sickening suspicion filled my gut that it was because Lessa had already ordered them killed.

They shoved a woman holding a child wrapped in blankets toward the line, but she resisted, asking, "Who is he? And why does he need the oaths of children barely old enough to speak? My boy's sick – he can't be out in the cold like this."

"He's Prince Roland de Montigny," one of the men replied,

hand drifting to the blade strapped to his waist. "Heir to the throne and soon to be King of the Isle of Light."

"What of the Regent?" She looked bewildered, and I wanted to warn her, to tell her to be silent. "The Isle has no King."

"It does now," the man replied. "And His Highness has been wont to take off the heads of those who say otherwise, so best you keep those pretty lips of yours sealed unless it's to swear allegiance to him. As for your boy…" He ran a finger down the edge of his sword. "He swears or he dies, so he'd best muster up his strength while you wait."

The woman paled and pulled the blanket-wrapped form closer. Then she stepped into line.

There were too many people for us to risk going closer, the chances of one of them stumbling through Marc's illusion growing by the second.

"It's too bright! Shut the door!" Roland's voice cut through the noise of the crowd, and I instinctively edged closer to Marc. "Can you see him?" I whispered. "What's he doing?"

"He's taking their oaths." Marc drew me backwards, and we retreated into the barn where the twins waited.

"No sign of Lessa, but Roland is inside with two of Angoulême's lackeys," he told them. "Roland, it would seem, has developed an intense dislike for the sun."

"And here I thought I'd never find common ground with the boy," Vincent replied, rubbing at one eye. "No doubt Lessa has the place warded, and even if she doesn't, we get that close and one of them is going to sense our power."

"Agreed." Marc rested his elbows on the door of a stall, eyes on the horse within, though I doubted he was giving it much thought. "They'll have to come out eventually, though it will likely be after dark. We'll ambush them then."

"When they're expecting it." The words were out of my mouth before the thought was fully formed. "They might think Tristan won't attack his brother, but they aren't fools. They'll have taken precautions, and they know he'll be more likely to make his move when Roland isn't surrounded by innocents."

Taking a moment to organize my thoughts, I sat on a bale of hay. "It's the core of their strategy: they're building an army of humans not because they're a threat to Tristan, but because he won't harm them. They're forming a human shield."

"What do you propose?" Marc asked. "*Our* entire strategy is predicated on us catching him unaware, which is impossible with them closeted inside that building."

"What about through the window?" Victoria asked. "A quick burst of magic and–"

"He's flanked by the other trolls and the line of sight isn't good," Marc said, shaking his head. "You'd have to be only a few paces away to have a clear shot, and he'd sense the magic. None of us can get close enough, and if we take out the entire building, there'll be countless human casualties."

I coughed once, and waited.

Three sets of silver eyes turned on me. "No," Marc said. "Absolutely not."

"Why?" I asked. "He's letting the humans right up close to him. What better chance do I have to cut him off from his magic?"

"Probably none," Marc said.

"Well then?"

"Cutting him off from his power is only half the battle," he replied. "Unfortunately for you and for us, he doesn't need magic to rip out your throat. Which is exactly what he'll do if you walk in, curtsey, and then throw a perfume bottle full of blood at his face."

"I wasn't planning to get that close," I muttered. "I've a good arm."

"And what about the other two? Three, if Lessa is close by, which we should assume she is. Is your aim good enough to take out all of them?"

"You three can take out those two, and if Lessa is there, I won't act."

"But you will come out oath-sworn to Roland, which is problematic," Marc said. "It's a bad plan."

"It's humans who are enforcing the lines," I countered. "It's nothing for me to compel my way out."

"Not without drawing attention to yourself, which runs the risk of Roland or Lessa seeing through your disguise."

"How long do you think they'll argue if we don't interrupt?"

I heard Victoria's comment, but I ignored her, my irritation at Marc commanding my attention. He was as bad as Tristan – refusing to put me at risk even when it was worth the reward.

"The better part of an hour, I expect," Vincent replied, and I shot him a dark look, but not before Victoria countered with, "Care to make a wager?"

"Enough!" I rounded on my friend and plucked out the piece of hay she had stuck between her teeth. "Unless you have something to contribute *other* than jests, I don't want to hear a peep from you. Understood?"

She nodded, then took the piece of hay back and replaced it between her teeth. "Peep."

CHAPTER 16
Tristan

"Are they even watching?" Sabine stomped her feet, the snow crunching beneath her boots. The wind caught at the hood of her cloak, and I reached up to keep it in place, but her hand was already there. "I've got it," she snapped, and adjusted Cécile's long braid of hair to ensure it remained visible.

Her sour temper was grinding on my nerves. I'd thought her animosity toward me had eased over the days we'd spent in and out of each other's company, but she'd apparently been storing it up. "If you'd quit complaining and listen, then you'd answer your own question."

She stiffened, but remained silent, and moments later, the faint thump-thump of wings reached our ears. I tracked the sound, and when the dragon circled east, I pointed at the shape outlined by the coming dawn. "There. It's been circling outside the dome all night."

"Why?"

I resisted the urge to slam a fist against the stone of the tower, her tone testing my patience. "Because they are watching. Obviously."

"I know that," she snarled. "I meant why hasn't it come inside the dome? She knows you're hiding behind these walls, so it isn't because it's afraid of you."

I frowned at the dragon, forgetting my annoyance. "That's a good question."

"Shocking," she muttered under her breath, then added, "There hasn't been a single report of a fairy within the city since you erected that dome, with the exception of those wolves she sent after me and Cécile. And that, I think, was a fit of temper on her part. Why? Why is she leaving Trianon alone?"

A rooster crowed from somewhere in the city, and already there were people out in the streets going about their business. "They feel safe," I said. "They think they're protected."

"And they have their new ruler to thank for it."

It seemed like madness to even consider it, but the Winter Queen appeared to be aiding our cause. First, sending the dragon to attack the city, then making it seem as though my protection was keeping them away. While Roland was terrorizing the countryside, Trianon appeared a bastion of safety. She was giving the humans a reason to fight for me.

"I should have you on my council rather than those nitwits the Regent employed," I said. "You ask all the right questions and you never mince words."

But there was another reason why the Winter fey hadn't descended on the Isle; only I couldn't speak of it to anyone, because it had come from that fateful conversation where my debt had been incurred. Winter wouldn't have forbidden me to reveal what I'd learned if the information wasn't important, but as yet, I wasn't sure how it factored into her game.

"Those men on the council were born to the position, they didn't earn it," Sabine replied, then hissed in irritation, catching at her hood as the wind threatened to take it again. "Can we go inside?"

"Soon." I'd told Cécile I'd take one of the seeds at dawn. Which would be any minute now.

She was quiet for a few moments. "What if what the Queen wants to talk to you about is an alliance? Would you consider it?"

"Even if that's what she's offering," I said, choosing not to answer her query, "it begs the question of why? What's in it for her, and what would she want in return?"

"Might it be worth it?"

Though my ancestors had been trapped in this world millennia ago, that fact remained that we were Summer creatures, and the idea of allying with Winter felt traitorous to the core. And misguided. We were the descendants of her adversary.

To Sabine, I said, "Just because she'd help us defeat our enemy doesn't mean we'd win in the end." Too easily, I remembered the gleam in her verdelite eyes as we'd struck the bargain that had allowed me to keep my life. We were nothing more than pieces on their Guerre board, and I couldn't even begin to guess how we'd be played.

It was time. Reaching into my pocket, I extracted the folded handkerchief holding the seeds.

Sabine leaned over my arm. "Stones and sky, what are those?"

"They are the product of one of Anushka's spells." I swiftly explained what they did as the sun crested the horizon.

"And you don't know exactly what they will do or how long the effects will last?" She caught hold of my wrist. "Tristan, this doesn't feel right. Please don't take them."

"And if something happens to Cécile? I..." Breaking off, I chewed on the insides of my cheeks, thinking of how the Regent would be alive if I hadn't gone running her direction. If I'd kept my head. "It's easy to stand here now and say that I wouldn't go to her the moment she was hurt or afraid, but history has proven otherwise. It's my weakness, and this... this is a solution."

Sunlight fell upon her face, turning her skin golden. Her lips parted in mute appeal, then she shook her head and let go of my wrist.

I wished she'd argued with me harder.

Plucking up one of the seeds, I stared into its swirling depths. And before I could lose my nerve, I swallowed it whole.

CHAPTER 17
Cécile

I kept my head down, doing my best not to think about how our fates were reliant on the success of a single prank even as I balanced the tray containing the means of its delivery.

"It'll work," Victoria had insisted. "We pulled it on Tristan once, and his mouth was stained purple for the better part of the day."

"Would've been longer, but he insisted on washing his own mouth out with soap." Vincent had smiled. "So vain. Would've been better if it had been Anaïs, though."

"I'm not sure you would've survived if it had," Marc had said. Then he'd sighed. "But it did work. And using the ploy eliminates much of the risk, so best we find ourselves some sugar."

And so I found myself approaching the rear door of the tavern, not with a weapon, but with two desserts.

"What's this?" One of the guards stepped into my path.

"Confections for His Highness," I said, hoping he wouldn't notice the trembling of the tray. "We heard he was partial to sweets."

The guard leaned closer, and it was a struggle not to recoil from the sourness of his breath. "How do we know it's not poison?"

I wanted to retort that it wouldn't matter if it was, but instead I handed him the decoy. "Spun sugar and cherry cordial."

He held it up to the light, then bit off a piece of the sugar lattice work, the candy crunching beneath his teeth.

"Avenge me if I drop dead," he declared to his fellows, then bit into the globe. Cherry cordial poured out of his mouth and down his chin. "S'good," he said, wiping his lips with the back of his grimy hand, then licking the cordial off. "I'll take another."

I stepped back. "I've heard His Highness handles disappointment poorly. And already it's a shame there isn't one for his female companion."

Their eyes took on a lascivious gleam and I had my confirmation that Lessa was present. "You'll bring them to His Highness yourself," I said, filling my words with power. "And you'll be sure to tell him how much you enjoyed the one you ate." It was malicious and cruel of me, because I knew how Roland would react to a human taking his sweets. But I found I didn't care. They were traitors to their kind.

"I will." He took the tray, and the globe trembled on its candy legs. "Careful, now," I murmured, watching his arms steady under my command. When he'd disappeared inside, I nodded once at his companions. "You never saw me."

Their eyes glazed, and I scuttled around the corner before they could take notice of me again. Then I got in line.

With weapons and threats, the guards herded us in single file toward the tavern, the guard at the door allowing one person in for every one who left. All their attention was for those who had yet to swear, and those who had just done so seemed confused by their newfound liberty as they exited the building.

"Where do I go?" one of them asked. "What do I do?"

"Don't rightly care," the guard responded, cracking a staff across the man's shoulders. "Move."

The man stumbled away, mouth opening and closing like a fish. "Where do I go? Where do I go?" He looked right at me, and I averted my eyes, but not before I noticed that his clothing was singed, his hands red with burns.

"Next!"

There was no one left in front of me. I stepped inside.

My eyes took a moment to adjust to the dimness, sunspots dancing across my vision as I moved forward, bumping into the woman in front of me.

A platform had been constructed where I expected the bar had once stood, and, on it, Roland perched atop a large overstuffed chair, his feet swinging back and forth just above the floor. There was a man on his knees in front of the platform, and Lessa stood next to him, mostly hidden by the crowd. "Repeat exactly what I say," she ordered. "I, your name, swear fealty to Prince Roland de Montigny, and promise to obey his summons and commands for as long as I live."

"I, your name," the man whispered, and Lessa kicked him in the ribs.

"Say your name, you idiot."

Weeping, the man complied, and when he'd finished, Roland reached over to pat him on the head like a dog.

The next person was shoved forward, but before Lessa could speak, the guard I'd compelled approached. Bowing, he set the tray on the table next to the young troll. Roland seemed so innocent from afar, cheeks curving with delight at the sight of Victoria's sugar creation. He plucked the dessert from the tray and snapped off piece of the lattice, popping it in his mouth.

Crunch, crunch, crunch. I imagined the sound of his perfect white teeth chewing the sugar, and I tensed, drawing magic up from the earth even though I wouldn't use it – all the power I needed was in that little crimson globe clutched in Roland's pale fingers.

He snapped off another piece of lattice. *Crunch, crunch, crunch.*

My breath was coming in short little gasps, my heart pounding so loud I was surprised those around me couldn't hear it.

Was I close enough?

Would it work?

Roland lifted the globe to his lips, licking the smooth sugary surface.

Then the guard spoke and Roland froze, all semblance of innocence falling away as the monster peered out, eyes flicking to the man who had stolen one of his treats. I clenched my teeth together, my skin burning hot and cold as I desperately wished I could undo what I'd said. That I could take it back.

Snap. The man's head twisted in a full circle, and for a moment, he stood as he was. If not for the peculiar cant of his neck and the blankness in his eyes, it would have seemed as nothing had happened, for no one had moved. Then Roland smiled and blew a whimsical puff of air his direction, and the guard collapsed.

Someone screamed, but other than a collective flinch, no one in the room stirred. They were too stunned, too afraid, to move.

You killed him. I stared at the guard's body knowing that I'd set him up to die, but unable to comprehend that it had actually happened. *Murderer.*

I dragged my eyes from the corpse in time to see Lessa shake her head, expression sour. She said something to Roland that looked like an admonition, but he ignored her, his attention back on the sweet in his hand. I took a deep breath, trying to regain my focus. There would be just one chance, and I couldn't miss it.

My pulse roaring in my ears, I watched Roland lick the sugared globe once. Twice. Then he opened his mouth wide...

Something flashed past in my peripheral vision. Roland started, candy slipping from his hand to smash against the ground at his feet.

"No," I breathed. "No, no." Embedded in magic not more than a foot in front the boy's face was an arrow, the fletching still shuddering from the impact.

"Who did that?" he screamed, and I silently asked the same question as I watched our plan fall apart before my eyes.

He lunged, but Lessa reached up from where she was kneeling on the ground and jerked him back. As I struggled to hold my ground against a crowd that had reached its breaking point, she held up gloved fingers smeared with crimson from the broken candy globe, one word on her lips. One name.

Mine.

I fell in with the crowd, trying to keep my feet as men and women jostled against each other, fighting to get through the narrow doors, glass shattering as some turned to the windows for escape. People were going down, others clambering over their backs, heedless of the screams. I was caught up in the flow, the press of bodies so tight I couldn't breathe. I lifted my arms, trying and failing to protect my head from elbows and fists.

Then I was through.

I fell once, agony lancing through the back of my legs as they were stomped on, but I caught hold of the cloak of a man ahead and clambered up.

"Cécile!"

Roland's voice filled the air, drowning out the cries of the terrified and injured.

Then the tavern exploded. The force of it must have thrown me forward, because the next thing I knew, I was face down in the slush and mud, my ears ringing. All around were people in the same position: some dazed, some clutching at wounds the explosion had inflicted, some not moving at all.

The air contracted with a massive flux of magic, and I closed my eyes, waiting for whatever was to come. Again and again the air pulsed with enormous concussions, but the blow I expected never landed. Turning my head slowly, I looked behind me.

Roland was writhing in the rubble that had been the tavern, one arm pressed against his face. Lessa and the other two crouched a few paces away from him, backs to me.

"Stop it, stop it," Roland screeched, his voice tiny and distant against my rattled eardrums. "I'll kill you. I'll end you. I'll rend your heart!" His free hand was flailing above him, each gesture accompanied by an enormous outpouring of magic. But the motions were random and strange, seemingly directed at nothing.

No, not nothing. The sun.

Lessa rose on unsteady legs and lifted her arms to the sky. Clouds of black magic furled out from her palms, rising and spreading until the sun was obscured, a dark shadow cast across half the town. "Roland, stop!"

The concussions ceased, the only sound the weeping of the injured and the ringing in my ears.

I didn't know what to do. The last thing I wanted was draw their attention, but lying on the ground waiting didn't seem much better. Stones and sky, where were Marc and the twins? Why weren't they doing anything?

A whistle pierced the air, and the trolls turned in the direction of the sound. Taking advantage of the distraction, I pushed up onto my elbows. A man sat on a black horse in the center of the road leading out of the village. He was too far away for me to recognize his face, but I didn't miss the bow slung across his shoulder. He'd been the one to take the shot at Roland. The one who'd ruined our plans.

"All hail Prince Tristan," the man shouted. "True heir to Trollus and the Isle of Light."

My shoulders twitched with shock, and not because of his words. I recognized his voice.

CHAPTER 18
Cécile

"Damn you, Chris," I whispered. "What are you thinking?"

Roland rose to his feet. "I. Will. Be. King!" The ground shuddered, and he slashed his hand sideways, the air shimmering with a lethal blade of magic.

"No," I gasped, but Chris was already moving, his black horse galloping flat out toward the nearby woods. Clenching my fists, I watched, waiting for the magic to catch up, to slice through both horse and rider. But it fell short.

A string of oaths poured from Roland's lips, but before he could go after him, Lessa closed her hands over his shoulders. "It's a trap." Her eyes panned the surroundings. "Cécile is here, which means Tristan likely is too. They're trying to draw you out."

"Tristan?" The anger fell away from Roland's face, and he rose up on his tiptoes as though the extra few inches would give him the vantage he needed.

"Don't be a fool," she snarled. "He just tried to have you killed, can't you see that?"

Roland's face fell, but his half-sister ignored him. "Go after the rider," she ordered the other two trolls. "Bring him back alive – he might have information about their plans."

Both inclined their head, then they were running. I bit my

lip as I watched them disappear down the road. I'd known trolls were fast – had seen the way they moved. But Trollus had kept them contained in more ways than one, so I'd never seen one in an all-out sprint. Chris's horse wouldn't outpace them for long.

A hand closed around my arm, and I would've yelped, but another covered my mouth. "Shh," Marc murmured in my ear. "We need to move while they're distracted."

Surrounded by illusion, Marc led me through the still forms scattered across the square, not speaking until we were tucked behind another building where the twins were waiting.

"They know I'm here," I said.

"Oh, was that why Roland was shouting your name?" Vincent crossed his arms. "You weren't supposed to let them see you."

Plucking a piece of debris from my ebony locks, I frowned at him. "I didn't. Lessa's seen me work that spell before – she put two and two together." I swiftly explained what happened. "I don't know what we should do now. We aren't going to get a second chance."

"Which is why we're going after Lessa's lackeys," Marc replied. "It may be that they know where Angoulême is hiding, and ultimately, it's the Duke who Tristan wants us to catch. If your friend Chris survives his little stunt, I'll have to thank him."

"For what?" I snapped. "Ruining our plan?"

"Did he? Or did you with that stunt with the guard?" Marc didn't wait to see his jab land, his cloaked form going to the corner of the building. "They're starting to search the town. We need to be gone."

I didn't argue. If I hadn't taken that extra step – a step that had been both unnecessary and cruel – Roland would've bitten into the candy, spilled the blood, and I would have performed the spell just in time for Chris's arrow to find its way into his skull. All those corpses in the town square? Their deaths were as much my fault as his. More. I felt sick with guilt and grief. They'd been innocent.

And I knew they wouldn't be the last.

Slipping out of the village was no trouble. For one, people, oath-sworn or not, were fleeing in all directions. Two, while Lessa had set her human soldiers to patrolling the town in search of a girl of my description, they were woefully unprepared for dealing with my friends. As was Lessa herself.

"How anyone can believe she's Anaïs is beyond me," Victoria muttered for the tenth time. "She doesn't know a thing about setting up a perimeter or organizing troops or…" The list went on, but I stopped listening, because it didn't matter if Lessa had a talent for any of these things. All she needed to do was keep Roland in check and corral as many humans into swearing fealty to him as she possibly could, and so far she seemed to be succeeding.

With Vincent carrying me for the sake of speed, we'd reached the tree line some time ago, following the tracks Chris's horse had left in the snow, as well as the boot prints of the trolls in pursuit.

"Be quiet, Victoria," Marc said from his position in the lead. "If they were going to catch him, they'd have done it by now and will be coming back this way. I'd rather not give them advance warning of our presence." Then he stopped.

"Put me down," I said to Vincent, and once my feet were firmly on the path I made my way over to where Marc stood at a fork.

"Two sets of tracks," he said. "The trolls split up to follow both trails."

"I see that." I pointed to the right. "Chris went that way. His horse is shod, the other isn't." I took in the churned up snow and horse dung. "The second rider was waiting here for him. They knew there would be more than one and they wanted to split the trolls up." I kicked a clump of snow. "Chris never intended to kill Roland with that shot – he knew they'd be shielded. He wanted the trolls to follow him."

I started down the path Chris had taken, but not before casting a backward glance at my friends. "Keep your wits about you."

We moved at a more measured pace, Marc in front, Victoria at my arm, and Vincent holding up the rear. All three of them had weapons in their hands, heads turning at the slightest sound, and eyes scanning our surroundings for any sign of motion. Or scanning them as well as they could. The sun was directly overhead, and even though the forest with its thick evergreens blocked most of the brightness, I still caught all three of them wiping their eyes with the back of their hands.

A scream echoed through the woods, and we stopped, waiting for another. "From the other trail, I think," Marc said. "But hard to say whether it was human or troll. Let's keep moving."

We stepped into a clearing, and the sun beat off the pristine snow, making even my eyes sting.

"Stones and sky," Vincent hissed. "Never thought I'd miss being stuck underground, but I do."

They were walking blind, so I tried to look every which way for them. Despite the chill in the air, sweat dribbled down my back, and every bird chirp or crack of a branch made me jump. I rotated in a circle, peering into the depths of the forest as I turned. Though we were almost through the clearing, I rotated again. Then something caught my eye.

"Stop."

Marc froze. I circled around him, noting the way the hoof prints moved up the side of the path, whereas the troll's boot prints just... disappeared. "Give me your sword," I said, then, taking the blade, I poked the ground in front of the last footprint.

Solid.

I shuffled forward a pace, and poked the ground. Nothing.

A thought occurred to me, and I snapped my head up so hard my neck clicked. But there was no troll hiding in the branches above. Frowning, I took another step, and the ground fell out from under my foot.

I shrieked and threw my weight back, sprawling in the snow.

"Well I'll be damned," Victoria said, even as Marc added, "And the mice discover a way to kill the lions."

Rolling onto my hands and knees, I stared into the hole that had nearly claimed me as its next victim. It was deep, and the bottom was covered in sharpened steel spikes. Impaled on one of them was a troll.

"Is he dead?" I asked, hardly willing to believe it was possible.

"Quite." Marc dropped the edge of the white sheet of canvas that, along with a fresh dusting of snow, had been used to conceal the opening. Keen eyes would have seen the trap, but those of a running troll half blind from the sun? Not likely.

A grouse called from the woods, and I stiffened. "They're watching us," I said under my breath. If they were with Chris, then they were my friends, but I was in disguise and none but he would know Marc and the twins were allies. Lifting my hands to my mouth, I repeated the bird call.

Silence. And too much of it. "Companions of Chris will know who I am," I whispered to Marc. He nodded once, and held out an arm to help me to my feet.

Taking a deep breath, I called out, "We're no threat to you. I'm a friend of Christophe Girard."

For several long and painful moments, no one responded, then the bushes rustled and Chris's face emerged. "Cécile? What did you do to your hair?"

I winced at his use of my name, hoping the fairies weren't watching. "Long story." I gestured at the pit. "What's going on here?"

He emerged from the bushes, and with a wave of his hand, four other faces appeared from the woods – all folk from

Goshawk's Hollow. "Tristan gave me a few ideas before I left," he said. "The rest... Well, I remembered how blinded he was those first few days after he left Trollus, and I figured we could take advantage of that."

"And you decided Roland should be your first target?" I balled my hands into fists, curbing the urge to lay into him for ruining our plans. What was done was done.

Chris shook his head. "We've been watching them. Roland refuses to come out into the sun, and besides, Lessa seems to control his every move. Didn't seem likely she'd let him chase after us into the woods." Scrubbing his fingers through his hair, he glanced into the pit. "The other two were our targets. Figured we'd take out as many as we could so Tristan'd have a clear shot at his brother. Speaking of which..."

"He's protecting Trianon," I said. "That's why we're here – he sent us to put a stop to Roland."

Chris's gaze shot back to me, his brow furrowing. "And judging from your tone, we muddied up your plans."

I crossed my arms. "You're supposed to be helping people to safety."

"That's already done," he replied. "Your gran personally set to dragging everyone out of their homes and into the mountains, but..." He nodded at the four who'd overcome their fear of Marc and the twins and finally approached. "There's plenty who'd rather fight than hide, and I'm one of them."

I bristled at the implied accusation, but before I could respond, Marc asked, "How many have you killed?"

"Six." Chris jerked his chin at the body in the pit. "If that scream was his friend, it will be seven. Cocky bastards are easy to separate, and they've not yet figured out our game."

"That won't last." Magic pried one of the stakes out the ground, and Marc examined it thoughtfully as it floated in front of him. "All it takes is one getting out of a trap alive, or another coming along before you've reset it."

The air filled with the thud of hooves, and a cloaked rider came through the trees, horse blowing hard in the frosty air. "We caught him! Worked like a charm."

"Josette?" Her name came out of my mouth more as an accusation than a greeting, and my sister pulled her horse up hard. "Cécile? What happened to your hair?"

"Stones and sky! You're supposed to be hiding in the mountains, not… not…" Lost for words, I gestured at the scene around us.

"I'm not hiding while some child-monster destroys my home," she snapped. "I'll leave that to his older brother."

My jaw dropped and Chris stepped between us. "Good riding, Joss. Now get rid of the body and pull up the stakes. We'll need them for the next trap we set."

My sister winced. "There's a problem with that."

Chris frowned. "How so?"

She cast a sideways glance at Marc and the twins. "There's some concern about getting too close to it."

"Why?" Chris demanded. "You aren't getting squeamish on me now, are you?"

"Hardly." She sat up a bit straighter in the saddle. "But neither have I got stupid. No way I'm getting too close while the damn thing's still alive."

CHAPTER 19
Cécile

"Albert, Albert, Albert," Marc said, stopping at the edge of the pit. "And here I believed your loyalty was to His Majesty. When did you turn traitor?"

I crept up next to him, leaning over the edge to see the troll who had once chased me through the streets of Trollus and been shamed by Tristan for it. He hung suspended on one side, spikes skewering both legs, his torso, and one arm. Though nothing vital appeared hit, the blood pooling beneath him told me it was only a matter of time before he succumbed to his injuries.

He spat a bloodstained glob. "Should've guessed it would be you three idiots helping the humans."

"Says the one who met his end by falling into a hole," Victoria said. She and Vincent had flanked the other side of the pit in case the captive tried anything creative. "Did the humans dangle a pastry as bait over their trap, or were you just too stupid to watch where you were going?"

He swore at her, but she only kicked snow in his face.

"You didn't answer my question," Marc said.

Albert laughed, then ground his teeth together against the pain. "Months. Since Thibault showed his true colors and wed his human-lover of a son to that red-haired whore. Weaklings like that don't belong on the throne. Guillaume and I both recognized that it was time to switch sides."

I frowned, realizing that he didn't recognize me through my disguise.

"I knew it," he gasped out. "Knew it the moment Tristan stopped me from killing *him*," his eyes went to Chris, "And then humiliated me for the sake of that stupid girl: the Duke was right about him being a sympathizer. Worse than a sympathizer, he was willingly bedding that nasty little creature. Was in love with *it*. And Thibault *knew*. Put up with Tristan's proclivities and forgave his treason. That says something." He coughed. "That *means* something."

Marc didn't react. "Where is the Duke?"

Albert grinned. "Somewhere you'll never find him."

"He doesn't know," Vincent said. "Angoulême wouldn't trust his plans to a turncoat commoner. Those human recruits bending knee to Roland probably know as much."

"Maybe they do and maybe they don't," Albert responded. "But if you think to get the information by torturing it out of me, you're wrong. I. Won't. Tell. I'm a dead man as it is."

Whether he'd given an oath to the Duke or was that convinced of his own fortitude in the face of torture, he meant what he said. He was as bound to tell the truth as any of them. Part of me wanted to tell them to let him die, but the cost of my earlier cruelty was fresh in my mind. Such a slippery slope it was to become cavalier with life just because the life in question was that of my enemy. It was the attitude of Thibault and Angoulême, and if I was no different, how could I claim to be better?

My hand went to the two remaining perfume bottles in my satchel, and with a sigh, I gave Marc a little nudge with my elbow. "What about for the chance to live?"

The injured troll's eyes bulged with recognition. "You." His face contorted with effort. But Albert was not Anaïs or Tristan, and the iron piercing his body kept him in check.

"That's the offer," I said. "Tell us where the Duke is hiding, and I'll save your life." I'd save it anyway, even if was for only as long as it took for him to go to trial for his actions. "I'll even heal you first as a token of goodwill."

Hope flashed across his face and I knew I'd offered the one thing that would cause him to betray the Duke. But my elation lasted only for a second, then he lifted his head and drove it down on the spike beneath it.

I clapped a hand over my mouth, wanting to turn away from the sight but forcing myself to bear witness to this latest victim of my actions.

"Angoulême wouldn't have taken a traitor into the fold without oaths that ensured his loyalty," Marc said, resting a hand on my shoulder. "He was a dead man regardless."

I turned out of his grip and walked some distance away before resting my forehead against a tree, the frozen sap digging into my skin. Chris's orders to remove the spikes and bury the body in the pit reached my ears but barely registered.

Snow crunched behind me. "Did you know him?" Joss asked.

I gave a slight nod.

"Was he a… friend?"

"No." I turned my head, watching her squish a little pattern into the snow with the toe of her boot, her cheeks pinched in from where she was biting them with her teeth. "You were the other rider."

Joss nodded without lifting her head. "They needed someone light who could ride fast, and after we saw what he'd done to Nomeny, everyone else was too afraid."

Everyone but my little sister. The folk around us were all men and women grown – they should've been the ones to take the risk. Not a child. But she wouldn't like being protected while her friends were in danger any more than I would. "It was well done," I said.

Her eyes met mine. "Why hasn't Tristan stopped him? Why

isn't he helping us?"

"He's protecting Trianon." My voice cracked as I gave the excuse, and I realized for the first time how terrible it sounded. How worthless it made those not in the capital feel, especially my sister, who had met him. Who was family to him. And pragmatically, I saw how swiftly we were losing our chance to convince the people of the Isle to rally to our cause.

"He can't," I whispered, and shivered as a cold wind brushed against my neck. "Is there somewhere safe we can talk?"

"Camp's got a cabin circled with steel," she said. "You can ride with me."

I followed her to where her horse was tethered to a branch. She slipped the bit back in the gelding's mouth, checked the girth, then fiddled with the buckle of her stirrup. "Cécile?"

My skin prickled. "Yes?"

"Is mother all right?"

CHAPTER 20
Tristan

I shifted one of the pieces on the Guerre board I'd made out of light and illusion, then turned to Fred, who'd insisted on standing and watching while I considered my next move. "Yes?"

"There are refugees outside the gates," Fred said, his face flushed. "They managed to escape the Duke's militiamen."

"Tell them to seek refuge in the mountains." I shifted several of the Duke's human players closer to my own.

"They have no supplies. Even if they don't freeze to death, they'll surely starve."

"A certain number of casualties are inevitable." I took a sip of mulled wine and circled the game, nudging Fred out of my way. He huffed out a breath, one hand balling into a fist.

"What is it that you want?" I asked.

"For you to pay attention to me, for starts," he snapped.

"I am paying attention to you," I said. "I'm not so simple-minded that I can't manage two things at once." Although it would've been my preference that he left so that I could focus on puzzling through our enemy's strategies, which, in my opinion, was a far better use of my time. I told him as much, and his scowl deepened.

"You need to let them into Trianon."

I shook my head. "They might claim to have escaped my

brother, but it's just as likely they are lying. They could be spies, or worse, insurgents with orders to stir up what chaos they can."

"Insurgents? There are children amongst them. Stones and sky, there are babies still in their mothers' arms!"

"Roland is a child."

Fred threw the jug of wine across the room, where it splattered against the wall, the air filling with the smell of cinnamon and cloves. Souris promptly ran over to the mess and began licking it up.

"A child can point a pistol as well as any man," I explained. "Letting them in Trianon would put all those whom we know to be loyal at risk, which would be a disservice to them."

"I'm not turning them away."

I sighed, and sipped at my drink only to find my cup was empty. "I don't recall giving you a choice in the matter."

Expletives fountained from his mouth, and I catalogued a few away for future use.

"You can't turn them away, Your Highness." Sabine came into the room wearing a gown that was too elaborate and costly to be hers, and judging from the sheen of her hair, she'd heeded my earlier advice and bathed. "It is a strategically poor decision in the long run," she continued. "The people of the Isle will see you as callous and cruel, and they will hate you for it and seek to betray you."

"Don't they understand–"

She held up a hand. "No. They don't. You must think of another solution."

I set my cup down and extracted a map of the city from a pile, spreading it out smooth. "Is there room at the Bastille?"

"Putting famers and their families in a prison lousy with vermin and disease is no better."

Frowning, I traced a finger over the map. "The opera house, then. It is easily secured, and it's likely more comfortable than any residence these farmers have ever known."

Sabine closed her eyes and muttered something I couldn't make out before saying, "It will do."

"Provide what they need," I said to Fred. "They're your responsibility."

He turned and left without acknowledging the order, and Sabine gave me a black look as she sat, crossing her ankles beneath her chair.

We'd been through this earlier, her explaining that my reactions were inappropriate, hurtful, and offensive. That Cécile's magic had wiped away not only the emotions I felt from her, but also my own. I believed her; knew, logically, that my mind was altered from its normal state. But I felt no displeasure or discomfort with the change – quite the opposite, as my ability to focus on a singular problem for hours at a time could only be an advantage.

"Is Cécile alive?" she asked.

"Yes."

"What if she's hurt? Would you know?"

I shrugged. "Likely."

"What if she needs your help?"

It seemed to me that Sabine was missing the logic behind why Cécile had created the seeds in the first place. "If it is dire, she can always use my name." I refrained from adding that if there were a way to eliminate that particular avenue, I'd do it. Cécile had all but offered to promise never to use my name, but I hadn't taken her up on it. That had been a mistake.

"I'm going up into the tower," she said. "Are you coming?"

I shook my head. With Fred gone and Sabine lingering outside, I'd have a rare moment alone to think, and I intended to use it. Ignoring her exasperated snort, I waited until I heard the click of the door latch shutting, and then sat on a chair and let myself slip into my thoughts.

Nearly everything I knew about the fey was information I'd been told or read. Nearly all, because, for a brief moment at the height of summer, I'd been in Arcadia and met the Winter Queen. It was into that memory that I delved.

It had hurt. The moment when my heart had stopped and I'd felt the bond between Cécile and me sever almost completely, the few frayed threads doing nothing to combat the feeling of loss. The empty void in my mind where my sense of her, and all her kaleidoscope of emotions, had lived.

Darkness.

Then the scent of grass and flowers and rain had filled my nose, and I'd opened my eyes to meet the verdelite gaze of a woman, her breath icy against my cheek. "Greetings, mortal."

I'd tried to scramble back, but my wrists and ankles had been bound to the earth with ice, which, inexplicably, I couldn't break. I reached for my power, but it wasn't there.

"The last fleeting moment of consciousness of a soulless thing has no magic, mortal." She smiled, revealing a mouth full of fangs. "You've little time – *she* has little time – and we've much to discuss."

Cécile. If I was dead, then she... "Who are you," I demanded, though I already knew. This was Arcadia. We were in a meadow, and all around things grew lush and fragrant. Alive. Except, where her hands rested, the grass was brown. Death snaked out and away from her, leaves changing color and falling from the trees, petals withering into dried little husks. Which should not be possible. Not at the height of summer, in the depths of my uncle's court.

Winter.

"What do you want?" I demanded, trying to maintain focus. But it was hard, because I was dead and I had not been through with life. There had been so much left to do, and Cécile...

Winter ran one clawed finger down my cheek, and I felt the burning cut of cold. The silver lace of bonding marks covered her knuckles, the back of her hand, her wrist. "It is a cruel thing," she whispered, "to be tied to the one whom you hate.

To battle and war for eternity while knowing you will never see your enemy's demise, for it would also be your own."

"That's not an answer," I snarled. But the bravado was false, because I could feel myself fading. Soon I would be nothing, and Cécile... *Please live,* I silently pleaded. *Please try.*

Amusement filled the fairy queen's gaze, and she said, "Summer was in the bloom of its power those many millennia ago when *He* allowed his brother, and his brother's warriors, to wander in your world unchecked. *He* was so convinced of his invulnerability with me quelled and chained to his throne that he did not see the danger. But *I* did. And it was a sweet thing indeed to watch him lose so much out of his own arrogance."

Her eyes were bright and vicious, and I wanted to tell her to get on with it. To tell me what it was that she wanted, because she would not be wasting her time on this conversation if moments later I'd cease to exist.

"There was a reason no fey of ice and snow were trapped in your miserable world," she said. "I protect my people. I keep them safe." Bending over, she kissed my forehead, and it was all I could do not to scream in pain. "And now, Winter is once again in power."

"What. Do. You. Want." I said the words between my teeth. *Please don't let me be too late.*

"I can send you back." She sat on her heels, the ice disappearing from my wrists and ankles. "The sluag are mine. Their power is my power. I can bring you back to life." She licked her lips, her tongue silvery and forked. "For a price."

I'd give her anything. I knew it. She knew it. "Name it."

"A life-debt," she said, rising to her feet and drawing me to mine. "To be called at a time of my choosing."

If it ever came to pass that she and I stood face to face once more, she could ask anything of me, even to take my own life. But what choice did I have? "Done."

"And one more thing," she purred. "You will agree never to

speak of what I have told you. To anyone."

"Fine," I said, knowing that somehow, I was getting the worst of this bargain. "Now bring me back to life."

"It will be done."

And before I could say another word, I fell back into blackness the only sound her voice. "Goodbye, mortal prince. For now."

"Tristan!"

I blinked, Sabine's face inches from mine, her eyes wild with panic. "They're here," she screamed, and with impressive strength, dragged me towards the stairs.

Up and up we went, then out the door and she was pointing out over the city.

My eyes tracked that direction, and there was no mistaking the cause of her fright. The streets of Trianon were full of troll-lights. Hundreds of them. And they were coming this way.

CHAPTER 21
Cécile

"She's dead."

The answer fell out of my mouth, and I immediately wished I could take it back and deliver it in a way that wouldn't cause my sister's eyes to fill with tears, her chin to tremble. As if there were such a way. Joss had disliked Genevieve, but she'd still been her mother.

"How? Was it the witch? Anushka?"

I swallowed hard. "She *was* Anushka."

Silence.

"*You* killed her."

"I had to. It wasn't her. Our real mother was already dead." I was babbling. None of what I said made any sense, but I couldn't seem to piece together a sentence that would do what I intended. "It was the only way."

"To free them?"

"Yes."

She shoved me, and I landed hard on my bottom.

"You don't understand," I said. "Let me explain."

"What's there to explain?" she shouted, blind to the panicked expressions on the others' faces. "This is your fault. You killed our mother and you set these monsters free to slaughter innocent people. And all for some stupid boy who can't be bothered to

122

come out from behind his castle walls to undo the damage that he's caused."

"Joss–"

"I wish you'd stayed dead," she spat, then swung onto her horse and galloped up the trail.

Everyone was staring, silent, with hands in pockets or resting on hips.

Chris stepped up next to me. "You can explain what happened when we get back to camp. It's not safe for us to linger here any longer."

It took us the rest of the day and into the evening to reach camp, a set of cabins on the edge of Moraine Lake that hunters used and maintained. They sat in the midst of at least two dozen tents, and though it was too dark for me to see the faces of those moving between them, I recognized most of the voices.

"That's Joss's horse," Chris said, helping me off the back of his animal. "So you can quit fretting."

"I somehow doubt that."

He shrugged. "This way."

As I followed Chris toward one of the cabins, Marc and the twins fell into step next to me, and the world fell silent as we were enveloped in magic.

"What do you intend to tell them?" Marc asked.

"The truth."

I could all but feel the silent conversation taking place over my head. "These are my people," I snapped. "They deserve to know."

"Perhaps they do," Marc replied. "But will they understand what you tell them? Will knowing the truth about why Tristan remains in Trianon help or hinder them? Will it help or hinder us?"

I chewed the inside of my cheeks, considering how I might explain to people who knew little or nothing about trolls why

Tristan remained hidden while the people of the Isle suffered at his brother's hand. How to explain the weight of a promise. The value of a name. It would sound like nonsense in their ears, a ridiculous excuse.

"We need them," Marc said, slowing his pace to buy us more time to talk. "We cannot hope to win this war without the support of the humans, but to have that, we need to give them a reason to fight for us. You need to give them that reason."

"I'm not a leader, Marc," I said, my skin prickling as I counted down the steps to the doorway of the cabin. "And even if I was, I'm the one who unleashed Roland. What could I possibly say that would make up for that?"

"You made that choice based on the belief that we would prevail over our enemies. That we could build a world where your kind and mine lived in harmony." He caught hold of my arm, pulling me around to face him. "Did you think that it would happen easily?"

I mutely shook my head.

"You're a princess, Cécile. The future Queen. Start acting like it."

The crackling of the fires and the whistle of the wind through the mountains filled my ears once more.

"You coming in, or we having this meeting out in the cold?" Chris stood in the entrance to the cabin, beyond him those men and women who were respected in our community, Jérôme, my gran, and my father included.

"Give me a minute alone with them," I said to Marc and the twins, and then I stepped through the door.

There were ten people crammed inside the small building, the fire at the center of the lone room more for light than heat, the press of human flesh enough to put beads of sweat on the brows of all present.

"How much do they know?" I asked under my breath.

"As much as I do. I've explained about Roland, Angoulême,

and the King – they understand the factions," he said. "And this building is ringed with steel, so you don't need to worry about anyone listening in."

I lifted one eyebrow.

"Tristan prepared me as best he could in the time he had. How to protect ourselves, and how to fight." Chris jerked his chin at the group. "They know that much, too."

I licked my lips, tasting sweat. Tristan had laid the groundwork for building an army, and this was the moment when I'd either build upon that foundation or burn it to the ground. I coughed to clear my throat, then my father stepped in front of me.

"Cécile, is it true what your sister says you've done?" he asked, and the anguish in his voice was like a knife to my heart.

I opened my mouth, but nothing came out. Of course Joss had told them. How could I possibly have expected otherwise? My eyes raced around the room, taking in the crossed arms and mouths fixed in unbending lines.

"Did you kill your mother?"

Be a queen.

I lifted my chin. "No. I killed her murderer. I killed the witch who'd stolen my mother's body and used it as her own. I killed the woman who intended to do the exact same thing to me."

"You slaughtered the only thing that stood between us and these monsters," Sabine's father said. "And where is my girl? Is she well?"

"Sabine is in Trianon," I said. "She's staying in the Regent's castle, and is under the protection of my husband. There is no safer place."

A flurry of whispers filled the room, and I held my hand up to silence them. "Among trolls, as among humans, there are villains. Individuals who are corrupt, selfish, and cruel. The Duke d'Angoulême is one such troll. He controls my husband's younger brother, Prince Roland, who is a child graced with incredible power, but also afflicted with violent madness. While it is the Prince who has been delivering wrath and ruin upon the Isle these past days, it is the Duke who is the mind behind the violence, his every move intended to bring him one step closer to his goal: taking the crown. We came to Colombey today to kill Roland."

"And yet he's still alive," Sabine's father snapped.

Chris coughed. "I'm afraid that's our doing. Our stunt interrupted their plans, and…" He shrugged. "There was no way to know."

"If this Duke's the problem, why not go after him?"

"Because he's gone into hiding," I answered. "And by the time we found him, the war would be over."

Or so my friends believed. Between Tristan, Marc, and the twins, they'd come up with dozens of places related to the Angoulême family, which was almost as unhelpful as coming up with none. They were convinced they wouldn't find him that way, although I was not so sure. There had been something about the way Lessa had said it. Something about the entire exchange between her and the Duke…

"Why'd Tristan send you to do his dirty work?" Everyone turned to my father, who stood with his hands shoved in his pockets, shoulders tensed.

I hesitated. They were owed the truth, but was Marc right? Would telling them do more harm than good? "The Duke is building an army of humans. That's why all the islanders are being rounded up – so that they can be made to swear fealty to Roland. An oath to a troll is binding," I said. "And if you don't believe me, ask Chris or Jérôme what it feels like for a troll to hold you to your word."

Both of them nodded.

"My husband, Prince Tristan de Montigny, remains in Trianon to protect it. To keep it as a safe haven for all who seek refuge. To come and put an end to Roland himself would mean leaving those many thousands of people undefended, and," I swallowed hard, "there are other villains who would take advantage."

"The troll king, you mean," my father said.

I nodded. "We are fighting a two-sided war, and if we lose…"
If the world burns, its blood will be on your hands.

"And if you win?" Sabine's father demanded. "If *this* Tristan
defeats his brother, this Duke, and his own father, will he be able
to control his people?"

"Yes," I said, uncertain whether it was the truth or a lie.

Mutters and whispers filled the cabin, people turning to those
closest to them to voice their opinions.

"But we cannot win without your help," I said, sensing this
was the moment I'd either win them or lose them for good. The
door opened behind me, but I didn't turn around. "You might
be safe hiding in the mountains for now, but if the Duke takes
the crown, he'll hunt you down one by one. Now, he is at his
weakest, which means now is the time for us to strike."

"What exactly do you suggest we do?" Jérôme demanded.
"Pick them off individually? That's no way to win a war."

"He's right." Marc stepped up next to me. "Which is why we
aren't going to limit ourselves to a few trolls – we're going to
take away his army."

CHAPTER 22
Tristan

"I don't understand how they got past my wards," I said to no one in particular, peering through the lowered portcullis at the silvery glow moving through Trianon. My first thought was that Cécile's brother had let in several hundred of what he'd believed were humans, but were actually trolls in disguise. Only the lights weren't coming from the direction of the gate, so I'd swiftly rejected the notion.

"What difference does it make?" Sabine snapped. "They're in. What matters now is what we're going to do to stop them."

Turning from the portcullis, I stood unmoving in the snow as human soldiers raced through the courtyard and outbuildings, arms loaded with weapons, eyes wide and mouths drawn into straight lines. Fred, having arrived only moments before on a winded horse, stood amongst them, shouting orders. Despite the chill, the sharp scent of sweat drifted on the breeze, and, from time to time, I heard a muttered prayer from one of the men.

I patted the pocket of my coat, feeling the bulge of the handkerchief holding my magic seeds. Fear made them act like fools, all logic lost upon them, whereas I saw clearly. Cécile would need to recast the spell for me when she returned. *If she returns,* I reminded myself, tucking away the idea that I should find another witch.

Just in case.

The thought scratched at me, but only for a moment. "They are wasting their time. Against so many, all of this," I waved my hand at the chaos of soldiers, "will do nothing."

Sabine's hands balled into fists. I watched with interest to see if she'd actually go so far to use them, but she only inhaled and exhaled, then said, "Do *you* intend to do something to stop them?"

"Obviously." I snapped my fingers at Fred, motioning for him to follow us up the stairs into one of the guard towers. "I'll need them to get closer so that I can identify who is amongst them," I said. "I'll pick off the strongest, but I'll need you and your men to distract the rest. You'll be like a swarm of flies to a bear, but you should be able to give me the time I need. Once the most powerful are dead, it will be no trouble for me to kill the rest."

Both Sabine and Fred were staring at me. "Well?" I said. "Go prepare yourselves for my signal."

Turning my back on them, I rested one hand in the narrow arrow slit. I needed to capture at least one alive to ascertain how they had passed my wards. Though why I was bothering with the wards at all was a mystery to me. They were a drain on my magic, and their sole purpose was to protect the humans in Trianon.

Which was no longer important. So I let the wards drop, raising them up around the castle walls instead.

The city was silent, the river muffled by the heavy sheet of ice resting on its surface. The haze of troll-light came closer without spreading out, almost like a procession through the street. A peculiar tactic, and not one I'd expect from my father. He was a strategic master, but it had been a long time since I'd played against him so directly.

A very long time.

I'd been ten years old, and it had been a timed game of Guerre played before most of our court. Though the hourglass had only allowed us a minute per move, we'd been at the game for hours and I'd been bored. Partially because losing to my father was inevitable, and partially because I'd intended to go swimming in the lake with my friends.

Anaïs sat in the first row behind my father and, despite my best efforts, my gaze kept tracking to her. Her grandmother, the Dowager Duchesse, had forced her to wear a dress, and Anaïs was twitching irritably, casting the occasional sideways glance at her sister, who was deep in conversation with Marc. The twins had been forbidden from the throne room after the last prank they'd played, but I knew they'd be waiting for us at the boat. Anaïs caught my gaze and then crossed her eyes, and I bit my lip to keep from grinning.

"Tristan."

My attention snapped back to my father, then to the timer, the last few grains of sand falling to the tiny white peak below. I shoved a piece onto a different square, my stomach clenching a second later as I saw the error. My skin prickled as my father's magic manifested with his anger, but I kept my eyes on the board, too afraid to look up.

In one swift move, he snatched up my piece and hurled it across the throne room where it shattered against the wall. "Everyone out," he bellowed, and the court fled, Anaïs the only one brave enough to hesitate, but even then, it was only for a second.

The doors to the throne room slammed shut, and my father backhanded the Guerre boards, sending pieces tumbling across the floor. "You said he was improving," he demanded of my aunt, whose hand rested on my shoulder.

"He is," she replied. "It's not a matter of his intelligence or aptitude, Thibault, it's a matter of interest. His heart is not in the game."

I felt his eyes burning into me, but I refused to look up. "And how," he asked, "do you expect to rule without these skills?"

"It's just a stupid game," I muttered. "It's not real."

My aunt's grip tightened, not that I needed her signal to know that I was pushing my luck.

"'Just a stupid game,'" my father repeated, then, "It's not a game, you fool; it's a tool. A way to train the mind and develop focus, and to be King of Trollus, you must master it. You must be the best at it."

I fought the urge to take my mother's hand. With her here, his temper would remain in check. "If you're the best–" I lifted my face "–then why aren't you teaching me?"

His jaw worked from side to side, and for the first and only time, he looked away before I did. *It was a stupid question,* I told myself. *He doesn't have time for you.*

"Because," he finally replied, "how will you ever beat me if I know all of your moves?"

My heart sank, and though it was childish, I reached for my mother's hand, squeezing it tightly.

"He needs motivation to play the game, Thibault," my aunt said over my head. "And you must be the one to provide it."

I listened to him sigh, wishing I wasn't such a disappointment to him. Wishing he had time for me as he once had. But he only turned and walked out of the room, never once looking back.

Blinking, I pulled myself from the memory and focused on the troll-lights filtering through Trianon. Why was I doing this? Defending these humans, fighting this thankless battle, and for what? What did I have to gain?

Nothing.

It was all a waste of my time – time that should be spent solving my conundrum with Winter, because until I did, I was trapped.

The procession stopped, two figures breaking away from the pack and walking onto the bridge. The girl's grey hood swept back to reveal long dark hair, and the man walked with the aid of a wooden crutch. "Let them in," I called out, and trotted down the steps to await Zoé and Tips.

The portcullis creaked upwards, the half-bloods ducking underneath and approaching me. "Stones and sky, but it's good to see you." A grin spread across Tips's face. "You did it, you and Cécile." He lifted his face to the sky. "Never believed–"

"How did you get past my wards?" I asked, interrupting him. He blinked. "Pardon?"

"My wards. The dome," I added for clarity. "How did you get past them?"

"Mostly miners with me," he said. "We went under."

"Ah," I said. Then I turned my back on the lot of them and went into the castle.

CHAPTER 23
Cécile

"He's not going to be happy about this." Marc kicked the base of a tree in a rare display of frustration, muttering what I suspected was profanity as a heap of snow landed on his head. "All three of us were to remain with you, and we were to return as soon as the deed was done."

"The deed's not done," I said, rubbing my hands together and casting a longing glance at the glowing fire.

"You're splitting hairs."

I smiled. "How very trollish of me." My levity felt out of place, given that our plan to kill Roland was ruined, but I felt better than I had since I'd plunged that knife into Anushka's chest. I had a plan. A place. A purpose. Even if it did mean remaining parted from Tristan.

"Of a surety, she's seen through your disguise," he said, trying a different tactic. "Dozens of people have called you by name, and if she can separate you from the twins, she'll use you to get to Tristan. Those wretched seeds you two concocted won't last forever, and a millennium of experience has no doubt developed her skills of extracting information she wants."

"Can't extract what's not there," I said. "I've thought this through, so you can quit trying to convince me to run back to Trianon and hide."

"And if I say no?"

I considered the question before responding. "As you said, Marc, I'm a princess of Trollus. Your future queen. And this isn't a request – it's a command."

Part of me expected him to retaliate, to push back. But I should've known better.

He bowed with somewhat more flair than was typical of him. "As you command, Your Highness, so shall it be."

I shuffled about in the snow. "I'd keep you here, if I could. Better to have all three of you taking down Angoulême's forces, but I can't leave Tristan alone in Trianon with only Sabine to watch his back. Especially given she's more likely than most to stick a knife in it."

"Queens don't explain themselves."

"I know," I said. "I'd send one of the twins, but it seems wrong to separate them after everything they've been through. And Tristan is more likely to listen to you than them, anyway. Someone needs to keep him behind those walls, and there's no one better suited to the task than you."

"Cécile…"

"You need to make him understand that one of us needs to be out here visible and fighting. If we both stay hidden within the safety of Trianon's walls, we'll lose the support of the rest of the Isle. And out here, there are things that I can–" I broke off, hugging my arms around my ribs. "You're sure you can make it back to Trianon in the dark?"

"Better in the dark than that cursed sun." I couldn't see his face in the shadows, but I didn't need to to know that he was smiling. "I'll manage. Stay safe, Cécile."

Inclining his head, he turned to go, but I caught his arm. "Tell Tristan that…" *I love him.* I bit down on the words. Queens didn't send sentimental messages, and with what I'd been feeling from Tristan since dawn, I didn't think he'd care anyway. "Tell him to think of a way to find Angoulême.

Now that our plans are awry, it's our best chance of stopping Roland."

He nodded once, then disappeared into the dark.

"Gran?"

She looked up from the supplies she was organizing into neat piles on the cabin shelves. "What's wrong, dear?"

"I can't find Joss." I'd spent the last half hour searching the camp for my sister, but no one had seen her since dusk.

My gran jerked her head up. "Is her horse gone?"

I shook my head.

"Then like as much she's avoiding you." She set a jar on a shelf, but her hand remained on the lid as though she'd forgotten what she intended to do next. "I'll find her and explain the full truth of what happened to Genevieve. She'll come around."

If that had been the only thing Joss was upset about, I might have agreed. But it wasn't. "I'm sorry," I said. "I know that all of this is horrible, and that it's my fault."

"From what Christophe told us, it sounds as though it was inevitable." She withdrew her hand from the jar. "If you've come for absolution, you're wasting your breath, child. You made your decision, and now is not the time to beg for forgiveness, it's time to make things right."

"I'm trying." I sighed and sat down on a cot, my body so very weary. "I need a favor."

"Oh?"

"There's a spell I need cast." Pulling a scrap of paper from my pocket, I fiddled with the corners.

My gran sniffed. "From what I've heard, you're more than capable of doing your own casting. And more than willing to delve into magics that you shouldn't."

"This isn't anything like that," I said. "And I need your help because the spell is for me."

She eyed me up and down. "What is it you need done?"

I'd been thinking about this since I made the decision not to go back to Trianon. Staying was a risk, because of a surety, the Winter Queen would figure out I was here, if she hadn't already. My name had been used, and she would know these were my family members. My people. I couldn't trust that Vincent and Victoria would always be there to watch over me.

"I need you to help me forget something," I said, my heart heavy as I focused on Tristan. Cold. Emotionless. "I need to forget a name."

I was staggering on exhausted feet back to the cabin to get some sleep when my sister stepped into my path. "Cécile? Can I talk to you for a minute?"

Nodding, I motioned for Vincent to give us a moment, then closed the distance between us. "You look frozen," I said, taking her hands, which felt like icicles, between mine and squeezing them. Her blonde hair was so coated with frost it appeared white, and her cheeks and nose were cherry red. "Come inside with me to warm up at the fire."

"In a bit." Her teeth chattered. "I wanted to say sorry for how I acted. I should've heard you out before reacting the way I did."

"It's all right," I said, wrapping my arms around her in an attempt to ward away the chill. "I don't blame you for being upset. No matter how you look at it, our mother is dead." My eyes burned. "And I'm so sorry for how you found out."

Her arms tightened around me. "I'm afraid," she whispered. "I don't see how we can win without help." Her voice took on a desperate edge. "Why won't Tristan leave Trianon to fight his brother?"

Stones and sky, but I was too tired for this conversation. I could barely think straight, and I was wary of saying the wrong thing and setting her off again. "He can't, Joss. At least, not yet."

"Can't you make him?"

How did she know about that? I rubbed one temple. *Chris must have told her.*

"Not anymore," I said. "I had Gran do a spell on me earlier – his name is gone from my mind forever." *I hope you heard that,* I silently told the Winter Queen. *Good luck getting it out of me now.*

"I see." Joss took a step back, her eyes fixed on her feet. "I'm going to leave in the morning to join the rest of the Hollow folk. I… I don't have the stomach for this."

Her words surprised me, because the last thing my sister was, was a coward. But in truth, keeping her away from the fighting would be an immense relief, so I didn't argue. "If that's what you want."

"It is." Her smile was strained. "I'll say goodbye before I leave in the morning."

A gentle hand shook me awake. "What time is it?" I asked, trying to get my bearings in the windowless cabin. I'd been ordered off to bed after I'd started dropping off mid-sentence, and I'd slept curled up next to my gran on the floor. She'd been asleep when I arrived, so I hadn't a chance to thank her for speaking to Joss on my behalf. My back ached, but I felt alert. Ready.

"An hour or so before dawn." Victoria faintly illuminated the room, then pressed a bowl of porridge into my hands. "Eat this. It's dreadfully bland, but it appears no one thought to pack sugar. Or raisins. A life without raisins is barely a life at all."

Laughing softly so as not to disturb those still sleeping in the cabin, I followed her outside, spooning the hot oats into my mouth as we walked. "What's the plan?"

"I'll show you." Bending low, she went inside the other cabin.

Chris broke off his conversation with Vincent and nodded at me, but my eyes were all for the magical miniature town suspended above the cold firepit at the center of the room. "What is this?"

"A map, of sorts." My father handed me a tin cup of weak tea. "Jérôme and I have been working with the, uh, Baron Vincent to construct a replica of Revigny and its surroundings."

"It's only Lord Vincent at the moment," Vincent replied. "But I hope to rectify that shortly."

My father frowned, then shrugged. "It's been a world of help with planning, given that not everyone has ventured so far out of the Hollow. Chris?"

"Right." My friend cleared his throat, and I watched how the eyes of everyone in the room went to him. He was, I realized, their leader.

"We received word from our scouts that Roland and Lessa took control of Triaucourt in the night," he said. "If he holds to his pattern – and I think he will – they'll remain under cover, taking oaths from those his militiamen round up, and then move on again tonight."

"Then why aren't we looking at Triaucourt?" I asked.

"Because the same gambit isn't going to work twice, and we don't have the clout," he gave an apologetic look to the twins, "to take them on directly."

He picked up a map and laid it out in front of me, and I noted the marks indicating the villages Roland had either destroyed or taken over. "This process of taking oaths eats up time," Chris said. "Time that people could use to flee their homes and seek refuge in the mountains. The militiamen are rounding up those in the smaller hamlets, but Angoulême has groups of two or three trolls capturing and holding the more middling size villages until Roland has time to reach them. Revigny is one of them."

I traced a finger over the little dots on the map. "Why bother?" I muttered. "These places can't have more than a hundred people living in them. I hate to say it, but they're hardly worth the effort. Why doesn't he just attack Courville? In one fell swoop he'd have the human army he needs."

"Maybe, maybe not," Chris replied. "If he attacked Courville, Tristan would likely intervene before Roland could take control of the city, and he'd be risking a direct confrontation with his elder brother, which he wouldn't win."

I wasn't so sure about that, but I kept my doubts to myself.

"But by doing it this way, building his army in small attacks, the risk of Tristan leaving Trianon unprotected – especially with their father's plans remaining unknown – are much less."

"And once he has this army, then what?" My mind filled with the image of families driven to take up pitchforks and shovels, rusty swords, and pistols that hadn't been fired in years, and then to attack their countrymen. Not because they wanted to, but because they had no choice.

"When he's ready, we think he'll have them march en masse on Courville," Vincent replied. "Tristan would have to leave Trianon unprotected to save the other city from his brother's army."

"While Roland and Lessa backtrack to Trianon and take it while it's undefended," I said, not waiting for him to finish. "They have to know he won't fall for such a strategy."

"True." Chris set the map aside. "So Tristan sees through their game and remains in Trianon. Roland's army takes Courville. Not only is the death toll likely to be catastrophic, he'll now have control over nearly half the Isle's population, none of whom will hold Tristan in particularly high regard given he's remained holed up behind castle walls the entire time."

And none of them would care that he hadn't had a choice. I exhaled softly. "Then Roland can march his army against Trianon, or even Trollus, at his pleasure. It won't matter to him or Angoulême how many humans die, because keeping them alive has never been their plan. It was ours." The porridge soured in my stomach. "How do we stop him?"

"By taking away his army, bit by bit, village by village," Chris replied. "By forcing Roland to meet Tristan on a level playing field and making the battle between them alone. Watch." He gestured at the faintly glowing miniature.

Two figures appeared in the model, tiny replicas of Vincent and Victoria. They were both standing on their hands, wobbling back and forth. Victoria's figure toppled over, and I heard her grumble softly over my shoulder. Vincent smiled, and a dozen tiny figures bearing our faces appeared. "This," he said, "is how it will go."

CHAPTER 24
Cécile

"Stones and sky, but they're cocky," Victoria muttered, kneeling next to me in the snow.

Revigny sat between two mountains, a cluster of houses and one general store, with a population that was far outnumbered by the goats they raised on the grassy southern slopes. And by my reckoning, every one of them was locked behind the invisible wall encasing the village. Goats included.

Their troll captors relaxed in a pavilion that looked like it had been plucked from the glass gardens, only this version was an illusion with the sole purpose of blocking out the brilliant sun from overhead. Two of them sat on rough wooden chairs plucked from someone's kitchen, while a third twirled about half-naked in the snow, hands raised up to the sun.

"Do you recognize them?" I asked. That had been one of the bigger unknowns. Victoria and Vincent had an idea of which trolls the Duke had recruited to his cause, but there was no way to know who had been sent to each village. Or how much power they had.

"The woman is Comtesse Báthory," Victoria whispered. "Don't be fooled by her performance – she's the only member of the peerage the King's ever banned from owning half-bloods."

"Why?"

"You don't want to know. But it's probably the reason she's sided with Angoulême – he's unlikely to stand in the way of her pastime. She's not particularly lucid, but she's powerful. Very powerful. The other two are minor lords – cousins to more important members of the aristocracy who are likely hoping a change in rule will put them in power."

We watched them for another few minutes, then Victoria huffed out a frustrated breath, pointing a finger at Báthory. "It's no good. They've been warned about you – look at the size of her footprints versus the size of her feet. She's shielded herself against everything, not just steel."

We'd expected that, given Revigny's proximity to Roland's current position, but I couldn't help but feel a flicker of nerves. Taking out the most powerful of the trio with my spells had been the original, and far less risky, plan. Now we had to try to get rid of Báthory another way. "I suppose that leaves us with plan B."

Victoria patted my hand. "It'll work. And perhaps Roland will take care of her for us – he does not handle disappointment well."

I was less concerned about that, and infinitely more concerned about the friend I was about to put at risk.

A flicker of light caught my eye, and I squinted at the opposite side of the pass. "Vincent's in position."

Victoria returned the signal, then said, "Time to send out the bait." She rested her chin on her forearms, and we hunkered down to wait.

It didn't take long. Chris emerged from the trees on horseback, the armband bearing Roland's modified colors of black, white, and red visible even from where we watched. He stopped, waiting for the three trolls to acknowledge him. Báthory had ceased dancing the moment she'd seem him, and with a lazy hand gesture, she beckoned him.

My heart was in my throat as he trotted forward, knowing there'd be no chance for him to escape if our plan went awry. Even if she fell for the trick, she was dangerous and unpredictable, and if she decided to harm him out of hand, there was little we could do to stop her. Not without revealing we had trolls helping us.

Chris dismounted in front of the woman, bowed low, and passed her the sealed letter. She plucked it out of his hand, strode a few paces away and scanned the contents. This was the moment of reckoning.

The twins, it had turned out, were fine forgers, and it was no difficulty for them to draft a letter in Anaïs's hand, finished off with Roland's looping signature – the key to our backup plan. The letter requested Báthory's presence in Triaucourt immediately for a task that Roland felt required her particular skill set. "She won't be able to resist," Vincent had said, signing the document with a flourish, his magical pen disappearing the moment he was done. "She'll be cautious in her journey, of course. She's delusional, not stupid. But given that we *want* her to reach Roland, it hardly matters."

"But she'll have proof," I said, pointing at the letter. "They'll know we're up to something."

Vincent shook his head. "The ink's magic – an illusion. By the time she reaches Roland, it will be nothing more than a blank sheet of paper. She can claim it says all she wants to – they'll think it's another one of her delusions. And when they send someone back to the village…" He winked. "Báthory herself will start to question what she's seen."

"She's smiling," Victoria whispered pulling me back to the moment. I tensed, watching the troll roll our forged letter and tap it thoughtfully against her chin. Then in a smooth motion, she pulled up the bodice of her dress and stowed the document in her cleavage.

"Watch over the prisoners, my lords," she called to the pair watching from their gazebo. "His Highness is desirous of my presence."

She took several quick steps toward the path Chris had come from, then stopped, eyeing him for a long moment. "I should make you run ahead of me lest I step on something I might wish I had not."

Chris rolled his shoulders, twisting the reins in his hands. Anyone, including the Comtesse, could see he was nervous, and I prayed she'd think his reaction was nothing more than wariness of the creature in front of him. "If that is what you wish, my lady. But I have these left to deliver," he pulled two more letters from his coat pocket, shaking fingers dropping them to the snow. "And His Highness…" He bent down, fumbling twice before he managed to pick them up. "His Highness–"

"Yes, yes." Báthory smirked. "You are right to be afraid, human. And brighter than most to have allied with the winning side early."

Not waiting for Chris's response, she sprinted toward the dense forest, magic carving a path as she made her way down to the coast. The crack and thud of falling trees echoed between the mountains, and we watched her progress until she was out of earshot. "Time to move," Victoria said.

Holding onto the back of her coat, I followed my friend down toward the village, trusting that her brother had his illusion in place. The people watching through the walls of their magical prison backed away at our approach, but I held up a calming hand even as Victoria created a faintly glowing set of stairs overtop of the wall.

"We're here to rescue you," I said. "Gather everyone at the center of town."

"They'll see us," one of the men exclaimed. "They told us they'd kill anyone who tried to escape before their prince arrived."

"They won't see." I pointed to the oblivious trolls speaking to Chris some hundred yards away. "And if you wait for Prince Roland to arrive, the only freedom you'll ever know is death."

The man blanched, but it was the herding gestures my overly tall companion was making that got them moving. "Gather the animals, too," Victoria said to the villagers. "Tell them we've goats to go." She grinned and I shook my head at the pun.

"Are you sure you can do this?" I asked.

"Don't undermine my confidence with your doubts. Go dose the people with your potion – the last thing we need is them all running about like frightened chickens."

The villagers peppered me with questions as I ushered them to the largest building, the general store. "For courage," I said, handing a flask topped off with magic to one of the men and watching it pass from mouth to mouth as those in terrifying circumstances were wont to do, aided by a bit of compulsion on my part for those reluctant to partake. For the children, I handed out tiny potion-laced candies that Victoria had helped me make, which they gobbled down, growing silent and still the moment the sweets hit their bellies.

Victoria leaned in the front door, and I nodded once, going to stand in front of the only window. *Ready.*

"Everyone be calm," I whispered, hearing the wind howl down the mountainside. "We're going to get you out of here."

In hindsight, the potion might not have been necessary, so smooth was Victoria's magic as she lifted the tiny village off the ground, her actions hidden by her brother's illusion. But I could see the ground moving away, and I found myself swallowing down a wave of dizziness as the building, and all those around us, rose on a platform of magic to a dozen or more feet off the ground before beginning the long journey deeper into the mountains.

I held my breath, waiting for one of the trolls to see something, or hear something, but they lounged contently in their gazebo, watching with disinterest as Chris pushed his horse through the snow, fighting to get to safety before the second part of our plan took place.

The crack was deafening, like a hundred pistols firing simultaneously, but for a second, it seemed a sound without cause. Then one of the mountain slopes began moving.

At first it appeared a single sheet of snow was sliding, then it tumbled and crumbled, clouds of white rising up into the air as it roared down with deadly force. The gazebo blinked out of sight and the trolls raced toward the opposite slope, one significantly faster than the other.

The avalanche slammed into the barrier that had surrounded the town, destroying or burying it, I couldn't tell which, and then it overtook the slower troll. Snow burst up high as he tried to shield himself, but the earth's might battered his efforts and he disappeared from sight. The faster troll made it partially up the opposing slope before turning. I imagined how he felt: the moment of relief when he believed he had cheated death. Then a tall figure stepped out of nothingness and clamped a hand on the smaller troll's shoulders.

We had our prisoner.

It took several hours for Victoria and me to deliver Revigny to its new location, explain the situation to the villagers, and secure their cooperation. The journey to the rallying point took far less time – all of which I spent with my eyes squeezed shut – thanks to Victoria's fearlessness and a magic sled.

"Any luck?" I asked Chris, accepting his offer of an arm to steady my still wobbly knees.

He shook his head. "Not sure if he's not talking because he can't or he won't, but Vincent hasn't been able to get a word out of him."

Given what had happened with Albert, I wasn't entirely surprised, but part of me had still hoped that we might have gained at least a clue as to where Angoulême was hiding. "I want to try something."

Along with Anushka's grimoire, I'd packed small amounts

of the herbs required to perform certain spells, and I took out several of those now, setting them on the snow next to our troll captive. He eyed them nervously, muscles flexing as he tested the magic binding him.

"I need a bit of your blood," I said. "This will sting." Pushing up the sleeve of his coat, I cut across his forearm, ignoring his sharp intake of breath as I held a clay bowl under the stream of blood. Picking up a handful of snow, I tossed it in where it melted instantly, then added the herbs.

"Fire?" Victoria asked.

"No." Dipping a finger into the mixture, I marked his forehead and then my own. Then I tossed the rest of the bowl's contents up in the air. Little droplets hung suspended like a cloud of rubies, then they began to swirl between me and the troll. I closed my eyes.

His thoughts came in little flashes. A troll woman smiling. A sword. The waterfall in Trollus.

"She's in my mind," the troll screamed, but I tuned him out and focused. *Roland.*

The troll prince appeared, himself, but twisted, as though the troll's mind saw him for the monster he was. "I will rule," he screamed. "I will rule."

Other trolls were on their knees in front of him, and one of them said, "Death to Thibault! Death to Tristan!"

Roland leapt to his feet, spittle flying from his mouth. "You do not touch my brother!"

The offending troll exploded into bloody mist, and I recoiled, unable to separate the remembered screams from the screams happening outside my shuttered eyes. *Angoulême.*

The Duke appeared, cane balanced between both hands. "Those who serve our cause will be rewarded. Lands, titles, power – it will all be yours. Will you swear?"

"Yes."

I pulled away from the thought, afraid of triggering one of

the Duke's oaths. *Where is he?*

Anaïs. Lessa appeared, dressed in her armor, arms crossed. "All contact with my father will happen through me, do you understand?"

I pressed harder. *Where is he?*

Mountains flashed across my vision, their white peaks glittering in the sun.

"Cécile, stop!" Someone was shaking me, but I ignored them. I had to find where the Duke was hiding. Lives depended on it.

What are his plans?

The light of the mountainscape turned to darkness. But I could hear the Duke's voice, "Thibault dies first, then..."

Pain lanced through my skull and I severed the connection, falling back into Victoria's arms. "What happened?"

"He's dead."

"How?" I struggled forward, taking in the dead troll and Vincent sitting on the ground next to him, hair drenched with sweat and face drawn.

"Burned out his light trying to get free," he responded. "Stones and sky, what did you do?"

"I dug through his thoughts to find Angoulême," I said. "He's in the mountains." I rubbed my temples, the pain in my head fierce. "Lessa knows where he is. I think she might be the only one who does."

No one responded, and when I lifted my face, everyone had drawn away, leaving me alone in a circle of space. "What?"

Chris twisted his horse's reins, jaw working back and forth. "Did you learn anything else?"

"That Roland doesn't want anyone to harm Tristan – he must want to do the deed himself," I said, the boy's rage briefly filling my vision. "And that Angoulême intends to go after Thibault first."

"I suppose that's one less troll for *us* to kill," Victoria said, but when I turned her direction, she was staring at the snow, and I found I didn't know how to respond. I wanted to be ruthless, to pretend that I didn't care that I'd caused the death of the troll on the ground in front of us. But I did. Just because he was caught up in the Duke's schemes didn't mean he'd deserved this fate.

"This is why we need to find Angoulême and stop him," I said. "He doesn't even care about the lives of his own followers."

They all made sounds of agreement, but I could feel their judgment. And I deserved it. With one swift motion, I reached down to close the lids of the troll's unseeing eyes. "Where is our next target?"

CHAPTER 25
Tristan

The only thing I cared about, the only thing I thought about, was discovering what Winter wanted and how to thwart her.

Nothing else mattered.

I surrounded myself with the pieces of the puzzle. What I could accomplish for Winter that she couldn't do herself. How Cécile's powers might be manipulated. What I knew of the fey and what I knew of the conflict between courts, because that would be the heart of her motivation. All the foretellings given my aunt over the years, their phrasing, and how we'd benefited. How Summer had benefited. The moves Winter had made since her return; the words she'd said. All these things turned and twisted around me as I contemplated how they fit together.

I spoke to no one but Souris, who was the ideal companion, as he listened well and said nothing at all, his only demand the scraps from the plates of food Sabine brought at regular intervals.

They all came and went, talking at me or to each other, and I stored the things they said in the back of my mind in case I required them later.

Marc returned to Trianon.

"All he does is play with his imaginary games and jabber at the dog," Sabine said, slamming my dinner down on the table in front of me. "We don't even know what he's doing other than abandoning us."

"He's thinking," Marc said, wandering through my puzzle while I picked at the roast chicken, setting the greens on the floor for the dog. He didn't want them either. "And he hasn't abandoned us – he's merely focused on the most central problem."

"You'll excuse me if I see it differently," she said. "He's left us undefended, and even from here, we can see his cursed brother burning his way through the countryside. There's nothing to stop Roland from attacking Trianon at his leisure. Pigalle was destroyed when the waves swamped the harbor, plus we have hundreds of refugees who fled Roland's attack looking for succor. We have to feed them, keep them warm, and he won't so much as stir from this room."

"The situation is dire," Marc agreed. "But we cannot reasonably expect him to be a solution to every problem."

"So what do you suggest? That we leave him to sit here and do nothing."

"It's not nothing," Marc said, "if he comes up with a solution. But in the meantime, we must hold up our end until he is himself again."

"When will that be?" Sabine demanded. "He's still got two more of those wretched bits of magic."

"That might need to be rectified."

I patted the pocket containing my seeds, the lump of the handkerchief containing them chasing away the momentary pang of unease.

"We need to assemble our council," Marc said. "Fred, Marie, Tips, and whatever half-bloods he feels should be present. They need to be informed that our plan to take down Roland failed, but that Cécile, the twins, and Chris's followers are working to get as many to safety as possible. We need to keep Trianon secure for those who are here and for those who will come."

Sabine nodded. "I'll fetch them here."

As she turned to leave, Marc caught her arm. "You aren't helpless in this, Sabine. Circumstance has put you in a position to make a difference, if you are willing."

"I am," she said. When she reached the door, she hesitated. "I'm very glad to have you back with us, Marc."

My cousin waited until the door shut before turning to me. "Think faster, Tristan. We don't have much time."

I nodded once, then turned back to my puzzle.

They met in the council chambers – five of them, for Tips had brought Zoé. All of them glared at me until Marc came into the room. "Ignore him," he said. "Tristan isn't the reason why we are here."

"Then I don't have time for this." Marie stood.

"My lady," Marc said. "I'd ask that you reconsider how your time is best spent. Trianon is bursting at the seams with those who have lost their homes."

She crossed her arms. "Do you think I don't know that?"

Marc inclined his head. "I've no doubt that you do. But the fact remains that they need shelter, and you are in the best position to manage that process. The peerage, I expect, have empty rooms they could fill."

"Then order them to open their doors."

Marc leaned back in his chair. "You have a more deft touch. Better for them to delight in their own charity than resent being ordered about." His gaze shifted. "Zoé will watch over your son."

"I'm not leaving Aiden in the care of one of you creatures."

Both Zoé and Tips stiffened, but Marc raised a calming hand. "Zoé's power is formidable. If Trianon is attacked, she is capable of taking Aiden to safety. Can you claim as much?"

Marie's jaw tightened.

"My lady, your grievance is with King Thibault. Please don't allow your hatred of him to color the rest of us with the same brush. We are not him, and even if we were, you have a duty to your people."

"I'll see what I can do," she said, then left the room.

"Fred," Marc continued. "I need you to send men out to bring back what grain and supplies you can in order to keep the city fed."

"I'm not leaving Trianon's walls undefended," Cécile's brother said, glancing my direction.

"Tips and his half-bloods will hold the wall," Marc replied. "With my help."

"Not happening," Fred said. "I'm not delegating the defense of the city to a bunch of miners and chambermaids, never mind that they might just decide to abandon their posts halfway through the battle."

That comment, I was quite certain, was directed at me.

"Then don't," Tips snapped. "Try defending yourselves if Angoulême's followers come calling, and see how long you last."

"Enough," Sabine said. "Fred, *you* wanted these people in the city, so it's your responsibility to take care of them. And you, sir," she glared at Tips, "don't forget that you came here looking for salvation as much as any of them."

There were glares all around, but eventually all departed but for Marc and Sabine. There was an unexpected level of comfort between the two, as though they'd engaged in far more conversation than I'd been privy to. "What would you have me do?" she asked him.

"You're doing it," he said. "We need to have a unified front if we are to have any hope of making it through this war. They need to see that they are on the same side, and I think you can make that happen."

"He's not helping the cause," she said, coming over to stand in front of me. I handed her my empty plate and walked away.

"This isn't him," Marc said. "You know that. They all know that."

"It is so him," she said. "It's just a him that isn't tempered by empathy."

My cousin didn't argue.

"I respect Tristan," Sabine continued. "Sometimes I even like him. And I truly believe he loves Cécile, and for that, I can forgive his faults." Staring at the plate, she set it on the table. "But damned if he isn't the most entitled creature I've ever met."

Marc laughed softly. "It's a common trait amongst the nobility, human and troll alike."

Her eyes flicked to him. "Not you."

"Yes, well…" He turned, tugging his hood forward so that his face was obscured. "He had some advantages I did not."

She touched his sleeve; and though they looked nothing alike, for a moment, she reminded me of Pénélope. "I think you are the better man for it."

The room was silent for the first time in far too long, but unfortunately, it didn't last. A knock sounded on the door, and one of Tips's miners leaned into the room. "Got a girl here who claims to be Cécile's sister."

"Let her in," Marc said, and both of them straightened in surprise as Josette de Troyes entered the room, setting Souris off into a flurry of barking.

CHAPTER 26
Cécile

Three days and six villages later, and we were all exhausted. As was the twins' supply of tricks. The only strategy we had left was direct conflict between them and Angoulême's followers, and given their drawn faces and sluggish steps, I was desperately afraid of how that would go. The thought of losing one of them terrified me, not only because they were dear friends, but because together, they represented half of the trolls we had on our side.

I rested my shoulders against the rough wood of the cabin and closed my eyes, wishing Tristan was here. Or that I was in Trianon. It was strange that we'd fought so hard to get back together, to be physically in each other's presence, and almost as soon as we'd managed it, I'd left.

You could go back.

I bit the insides of my cheeks, knowing that if I returned to Trianon, it would be for my own selfish reasons. I hated the effects of the spell I'd cast on Tristan, hated the flat, toneless intensity of his presence in my head. It wasn't him. Was like being bonded to a stranger. The purpose of the spell had been to allow me to leave the safety of the city, and if I went back, it would no longer be required.

But what good would I do once I was there?

The solution to our troubles was not in Trianon, but neither was it in this camp. We weren't going to win this way. It was a stopgap, but the fact remained that Tristan was the only one capable of defeating Roland, and he was as much caged within the Regent's steel-rimmed castle walls as he ever had been in Trollus. By the time we found a solution to his debt to the Winter Queen – if there even was one – all the folk we'd hidden in the mountains would either have starved to death or sworn oaths to our enemies in a desperate attempt to save themselves. We needed to find Angoulême, capture him, and use him to bring Roland to heel, and I knew we weren't going to discover his hiding spot through any of his followers. I'd already lost count of how many had fallen dead at my feet as I tried every trick I could think of to extricate the information on their leader's whereabouts. But he'd been too clever – had been planning his strategy for far too long. The only information I'd gleaned was that Lessa was the only one who knew his location.

Lessa.

The more I thought about it, the more convinced I became that the key was the statement Tristan's half-sister had made to the Duke. *A shame I can't go with you – I would've liked to see the faces of my ancestors.* Yes, Anaïs's ancestors were famous and powerful trolls – there were countless portraits of them in Trollus. Probably dozens of places on the Isle where others still hung, but what would be so special about them?

Nothing.

Which meant that was the wrong track, because there had been reverence in her tone. This place was somewhere special, somewhere unique. And just because Tristan and my friends didn't know about it didn't mean no one did.

I chewed on my bottom lip, knowing that it would be risky. But we were running out of options and out of time, so maybe it was time to take a chance. I needed to go back to where the answers to my questions always seemed to be.

Back to Trollus.

•••

There was no time to make preparations, nor any real need, given that I'd be going alone. It was reckless, I knew, but there was no other option. Victoria and Vincent were the only two holding back Roland's growing army, Tristan was stuck in Trianon, and he needed Marc to help him hold the city. It had to be me.

But convincing my friends to let me go without them would be next to impossible. They'd argue that my life shouldn't be put in danger, because I'd also be putting Tristan at risk. Except that was why we'd created the seeds – so that I *could* do what needed to be done. And judging from his ceaselessly neutral emotional state, the magic was still in effect.

I waited until the darkest part of the night, when everyone except those on watch would be fast asleep. Gran stirred as I stood, and I bent down to murmur, "Nature calls," before edging the door open wide enough for me to sneak outside.

The twins had a tent next to my cabin, but only one of them would be sleeping in it, the other patrolling our camp until it was time to be relieved. I lingered in the shadows, watching the horses on the picket line until, almost as one, they turned their heads and stared off into the darkness. It was something I'd noticed with all animals around the trolls, especially Souris: they *watched* them. And they *listened*. The twins had only shrugged when I'd asked why, but now the observation would serve me well.

Marking the direction the animals were staring, I eventually picked out the faint crunch of snow beneath the boots of an invisible troll. Waiting until whichever twin it was moved on, I crept over to the horses, compelling them to be silent as I slipped a saddle and bridle on my mount and led him into the trees, walking slowly as I searched for the wards I knew were in place.

The twins disdained the tall fences Angoulême's followers used to surround their camps, preferring to use a series of what could only be described as triplines. They used so little magic that they were virtually undetectable, but would instantly warn either of them if they were triggered. Fortunately, I knew where they were and how to get by them. The first set were about knee height, and I set a branch across two rocks so that my horse would step over it. The second would cut across my waist, and it took me several minutes to build a jump in front of it. Mounting my horse, I walked back until I was almost at the first tripline, then dug in my heels and cantered toward the jump, praying the wind would drown out the sound of hoof beats.

I leaned forward as the horse leapt, my gut clenching as I heard his hoof clip one of the branches. *Don't fall, don't fall,* I prayed, pulling the animal up on the far side and listening for alarm in the camp.

Nothing. I'd made it out, but I only had a few hours until my absence was noted. I needed to put them to good use.

The wind howled, and I scanned the blackness of the forest, praying I wouldn't run afoul of a mountain cat or pack of wolves. I'd brought a bow and handful of arrows, but they were unlikely to do me much good. I watched my horse's ears, trusting the animal's instincts to warn me if danger lurked in the darkness.

The river flowed in near silence, the winter so cold that even the roughest rapids now rushed beneath a frozen surface. I guided my horse down the trail flanking the fall, watching for the pond that marked the entrance to the labyrinth.

I almost missed it.

The pond was frozen over and then blanketed with snow, the marks that Angoulême's party had made when they ventured out long since buried. If not for the rough paddock the traders had built, I would have bypassed it entirely. Slipping off my horse, I led him through the gate before removing the saddle and bridle and turning him loose. The fence was enough to keep him here for a time, but should something happen to me, he'd have no trouble breaking free if he put his mind to it.

Shouldering my satchel, I held up the lantern and stepped onto the ice, the light trembling as I ascertained whether the way was passable or if the cavern was frozen over for the winter.

It was open. But barely.

The ice groaned as I crept toward the rocks, the sound so loud that I was sure anyone within miles would hear it. Reaching the overhang, I dropped to my knees and set the lantern aside so I could shovel snow out of the way.

It would be tight.

Even with the snow cleared down to the ice, there was less than a foot between pond and rock. Easing the lantern under the ledge, I shoved my bag after it, then lay on my back, tipping my head to the side so I could pull myself through. The ice bit and scraped at my cheek, and the rock caught at the front of my cloak, making me glad I wasn't busty. My breath was deafeningly loud, pulse racing as I considered how exposed I was: head and shoulders in one world and feet thrashing for traction in another. I kept waiting for someone or something to grab me from either end, the cruel press of teeth or the bite of steel, and I wriggled harder.

Then I was through.

The ice creaked as I rose to my hands and knees, the sound echoing through the small cavern. With the lantern flame as high as it would go, I scanned the darkness to ensure nothing was lying in wait before crawling deeper inside.

Though I'd been in this place only twice and never lingered, it was deeply familiar to me, the jagged rocks of the ceiling and sharp embankment leading down to the pond featured often in my dreams. It was the beginning and end of my time in Trollus – the pathway to a world I'd never imagined, a life I'd never dreamed possible.

And it was a pathway that had seen a great deal of traffic in recent days.

Muddy footprints marred the surface of the ice, and there were signs that several trolls had tarried here for some time: remnants of meals, a discarded wineskin, and the less than pleasant smell of urine. Angoulême and his followers had come this way; had others as well? How many had snuck out of Trollus before the King had locked the city down, and where had they gone? Were they inflicting their own form of destruction on the Isle or were they only trying to flee the war between three powers?

But such thoughts were only procrastination on my part. Right up until this moment, I'd felt confident that I could brave the labyrinth once again, yet looking into that yawning black tunnel, I was tempted to slide under the rocky overhang and scuttle back to camp. And maybe that was the right thing to do.

I stood frozen in place, second-guessing my decision, which, frankly, had the potential to be the latest in a series of less than wonderful choices. Except, try as I might, I couldn't think of another way to find the answers we needed. So I started forward.

It seemed impossible for the labyrinth to become any more treacherous, but it had. The dank wet of spring and summer had made the rocks slippery enough; now there were patches of ice hidden in the shadows to contend with, and my numb fingers were reluctant allies in my attempts to keep my balance.

The only aspect that was no longer a challenge was finding the correct path. Where the traders' markings had once been were now arrows slapped onto the stone in red paint, and even without them, there were obvious signs of traffic. Boot prints and discarded bits of food. Smells that were a different sort of rank than what the sluag left behind. It added another level of fear, because while before the labyrinth had been empty with the exception of sluag and the occasional trader, now I was at risk of coming across a troll at every turn. So I kept my lantern turned as low as I dared and stopped often to listen.

"Only a few left, and you can get back to standing in front of the gate."

The sour voice bounced off the walls, and I squeezed into a crack between the rocks, snapping the shield closed on my lantern and tucking it behind my cloak for good measure. A boot scraped against stone, and though I was a few paces away from the path, I held my breath.

Silver light illuminated the blackness and, seconds later, an orb floated past my hiding spot. Then an armored guard carrying a sluag spear, followed by what looked like a troll in a miner's guild uniform, then another guard. They were moving in the same direction as I had been, which meant they'd either been outside or somewhere else within the labyrinth.

"Here."

Steel clinked against rock and feet shuffled. I wanted to see what they were doing, but I didn't dare move. Trolls had exceptional hearing, and my luck wasn't good. Either way, they didn't linger, footsteps falling away. I waited until I was sure they were gone, then squeezed out of my hiding spot. Looking both ways to make sure I saw no trace of silver light, I turned up my lantern and proceeded forward, passing a bright red X.

I paused. It wasn't the first such marking I'd seen, but I hadn't been able to make heads or tails of what they indicated, so I'd ignored them. Only this was where the group had lingered, so it must mean something. The X was above a fissure in the rock; otherwise, I could see nothing remarkable about the location. Pulling off my glove, I tentatively lifted my hand to the crack, then froze as heat warmed my fingers.

Magic.

But for what purpose, I couldn't say. My skin prickled, but standing here staring seemed unlikely to provide answers, so I kept walking.

I passed several more X markings as I made my way toward Trollus, but no other parties of trolls. Other than tired feet, a skinned knee, and a bruised elbow, I'd escaped the labyrinth unscathed. Rather than filling me with confidence, my skin prickled with gooseflesh and my mouth felt dry no matter how many sips I took from my water skin. *Something's not right. Something's not right.*

Trailing one hand along the wall, I walked across the cracked cobbles of the parts of Trollus that had been destroyed by rock, hearing the first echoes of the waterfall and remembering when I'd come this way with Marc and Luc. How it had been terrifying and magical and unknown, and now... I swallowed down the pang in my heart. Now it felt almost like coming home.

Voices. I closed the shield on my lantern, pressing a hand against the crushed buildings. I rounded a slight bend, and stopped, a group of a dozen trolls standing next to the closed gate. I'd suspected it would be guarded, and I swiftly retreated back until I found an open street branching off the main. Angoulême and his followers hadn't come through the gate – they'd used a hole in the upper reaches to gain access to the labyrinth. And it was that entrance I sought.

What I found was the slime and the stench of sluag, and judging from the slick mess beneath my feet, more than one.

"Stones and sky," I whispered, covering my mouth and nose with one hand while the other held the lantern up so I could see.

I instantly regretted it.

The street was filled with bones. It was impossible to say how many bodies there were, because the remains were all mixed together in pools of offal. Dozens. Maybe more. The sluag had carved their way into some of the crushed buildings to create dank warrens from which smell and darkness poured, and my heart escalated into a staccato beat as I crept past the openings, my legs wanting to run even as my mind knew it would only draw their attention.

The bones didn't crunch beneath my feet so much as they bent, giving way beneath my weight as though they were made of rubber. Scraps of fabric, buttons, weapons, and bits of simple jewelry were scattered amongst them, but I couldn't tell if they'd come from trolls, half-bloods, humans, or a mixture of all three.

Barooom. The sluag's call was faint, but I flinched. It was time to be gone from this place.

Barooom. My nerves cracked and I broke into a run, leaping over piles of bones, sludge splashing up on my trouser legs. The ceiling of the tunnel dropped, and I bent lower and lower until I had to rest one hand on the ground for balance.

Barooom. Was it getting closer? I almost wished the space would get smaller so that the creature wouldn't be able to follow, and, caught up in my wishing, I almost fell into a hole that yawned up in the ground in front of me.

It was the odor I recognized more than anything else, a damp and faintly musty scent that I associated with Trollus. Setting my lantern aside, I leaned down into the hole and was rewarded with a faint glimmer of silver light.

I'd found a route into the city.

CHAPTER 27
Tristan

Josette informed them that her sister had sent her to Trianon for her own safety, which was absolute lunacy, in my opinion. Trianon was a target, not a safe haven. But Sabine and Marc were clearly both too distracted to question her claim, and I was more interested in what the spy who'd just landed in our midst intended to do than I was in outing her.

They left Joss alone with me.

I pretended to ignore her.

"Cécile sends her love," she said, skirting around the growling dog. "She misses you."

I highly doubted Cécile had sent along those sentiments, but my chest tightened nonetheless. She'd been worming her way into my thoughts for the past several hours. I'd told myself it was because she was relevant to my problem with the Winter Queen, but it was more than that. She was up to something, and whatever it was had her nerves stretched tight. I patted my pocket, thinking it might be time to take another dose.

"Is my sister all right?" Joss asked. "I've been worried about her since I left."

I didn't answer. This was Winter trying to ascertain how affective Cécile's spell was; whether she could use her to lure me out. But the fact of the matter was that I knew Winter wouldn't risk killing Cécile, so it was a failed gambit. And if the direness of Cécile's situation came from another source, it wasn't as though she couldn't drag me out of the castle whether I willed it or not.

"Cécile got Gran to do a spell to make her forget your name."

That caught my attention, although I didn't let her know it. Was it the truth? Maybe. Cécile had been clear in her desire to unknow it, but I'd quietly refused to entertain that option. I'd wanted her to have the failsafe, because while it was one thing to curb my urge to go running to her whenever *I* believed she was in danger, it was quite another to ignore her call for my help. That, I'd never intended to do. No matter what the risk. But now there was no way for me to know the difference.

Unless Joss was lying.

"That's fascinating, but I'm rather busy at the moment," I said. "Perhaps you might find another place to linger."

"I see," she said, her face turning bright red. "I'll leave you to it."

Waiting until she was out of earshot, I turned to Souris. "Care to go for a walk?"

The dog stayed close to my heels as we trailed Josette through the castle. She continually cast furtive glances over her shoulder, confirming my suspicion she was up to no good. Exiting through a door in the kitchen, she meandered through the outbuildings in the direction of the wall, which Marc and Fred appeared to have manned with half the soldiers at their disposal.

She paused next to the narrow stairs leading to the battlements, but instead of going up, scurried beneath them. The space was full of building material – blocks of stone and sacks of sand – that, judging from the layer of dust coating them, had languished there for some time. Josette squeezed between them, her feet briefly sticking out, and then she disappeared from sight.

Curious, I ducked under the stairs, shifting the materials

slightly to reveal a small opening that had been eroded under the wall, probably by the river flooding. Even if I'd been inclined to do so, it was too small for me to fit through. But Josette's slender frame had clearly managed the task. "The rat has found a hole," I said. Or more accurately, had been told where to find the hole, given that, to my knowledge, she'd never been to this place.

Souris growled and wove between my feet, lips pulled back to reveal his fangs.

Dropping to my hands and knees, I lowered my head into the opening – careful not to pass the iron barrier above me – and I listened.

"He's still under the spell," Joss whispered, and I motioned Souris to be silent so that I could better hear. "From what I've heard, all he does is sit in the council chambers with his game and that dog. He speaks to no one, and that the entire city hasn't fallen into chaos is all thanks to Marc arriving when he did."

"It will not last," a woman said, her voice melodious and soothing. "Magic fades. It is the way of these things."

"But what if it doesn't fade in time?" Joss's voice cracked. "You showed me what Roland's done so far. All those people dead. How many more will die while we sit around waiting?"

"A valid fear." The Winter Queen's voice was morose. "Mortal lives are already brief – to see them cut short is no doubt heart-wrenching."

I shook my head at Joss's inability to see through the fairy's false sentiments.

"Isn't there anything you can do to stop Roland?" Joss asked. "You're a queen, an immortal. Surely…"

A heavy sigh. "Not alone, I'm afraid. The trolls are an abomination, Josette. An unintended outcome that should never have been allowed to live. They are too powerful, and far, far too dangerous. I fear humanity is in grave danger."

"All because of my sister."

The Queen made a tutting noise. "Now, now. Amongst the three powers, Tristan alone desires to protect your kind, and your sister knows that. But he has colored her mind against an alliance."

"But why?"

"An ancient animosity exists between his family's court and mine," she said. "One he seems unable to set aside. One that keeps him from seeing that my assistance will secure his victory over his enemies, and that will ensure the survival of humanity."

"Couldn't you just tell me where the Duke is?" Joss asked, her tone pleading. "Maybe then he'd see your intentions were good."

"I've told you why." Winter's voice was chilly, her patience for providing explanations to a sixteen year-old human, I suspected, growing thin. "If I give him the information he desires, with what will I negotiate for the safety of my court? I wish to see humanity triumph, but above all, I must protect my kind from his. Do you understand?"

"Ah," I murmured, patting Souris on the head, the pieces of the puzzle falling into place. Since the mountain had fallen and Anushka had cursed the trolls, my uncle, the Summer King, had been working to keep us alive, especially in recent years. Winter, on the other hand, had been content to see us contained, sending the sluag to our world to trouble us, though it meant they'd be as trapped as we were. As mortal as we were. She wanted the trolls destroyed, because she believed, if freed, we'd be a threat to her court. How that was the case, I did not know, but what mattered was that now I understood why she wanted an alliance.

She wanted to use my magic to destroy my kind once and for all.

My guts twisted as I pictured how she would do it, helping me kill my father, my brother, Angoulême, and everyone else with the power to stand in my way. Then she'd use my debt to force me to slaughter every other troll alive.

"I understand, my lady," Joss whispered, pulling me from my thoughts. "What do you want me to do?"

"We must lure him out," Winter said. "And there is only one way to do that. He must believe your sister's life is in danger."

"I don't want Cécile hurt." There was an edge to Joss's voice.

"Of course you don't," Winter replied, her voice soothing. "She needn't be in true jeopardy – it's her fear that will lure him out. Her life will be in no danger from me."

"But will he care?"

"If we time it correctly. You must watch him, look for signs the magic is fading. Then I will move."

I listened to their plan until one of the guards heard voices and called down, sending Joss scampering back through her hole and into the castle.

Tucking my shivering dog inside my coat, I watched her go, breathing in the cool night air as I thought. Knowing what she intended, there were ways to protect myself. Ways to prevent her from using me to slaughter my people. But that would mean my debt remained, and I was tired of it hanging over my head. I wanted it called due, but on my terms.

I turned in the direction of Trollus, letting the game expand in my mind. I'd set aside the problem of my father in the belief I could do nothing about him until I'd dealt with Winter, but I might have been wrong about that. She was trying to use me, but if I played this right, I might be able to turn the tables. Controlling my magic was Winter's goal.

And maybe it was time to give her what she wanted.

CHAPTER 28
Cécile

Turning the lantern down so that barely a flicker of flame remained, I set it in a rocky alcove to wait for my return; then, clinging to what handholds I could find, I crept lower. With every move, bits of rock and debris broke free to pour out the tunnel, but at least the sound covered up my labored breathing and the racket of my heart.

"Almost there, almost there," I whispered, then I heard voices.

"Curses! There's another one!"

I froze. Several trolls were approaching the tunnel opening.

"Go report that there's another sluag in the city," one of them said, and boots thudded rapidly against the ground as another went to do his bidding.

"Blasted creatures. Never known them to be so aggressive about trying to get in."

A ball of light floated past me, and I swallowed a gasp of panic. Shifting my position, I wedged into a bend and held my breath. Seconds later, a head and shoulders appeared beneath me as one of the trolls climbed into the tunnel. My arms and legs trembled from the effort of holding myself up, and I was certain he'd hear my heart hammering, turn his head, and see me. But he swiftly retreated.

"Came through recently," he said to his companion. "Reeks."

"Close it up – last thing we need is to make it easier for them to get their next meal."

My heart leapt out of my chest, and I desperately tried to inch my way back up the tunnel before one of them brought it down on my head. Then bells began to ring.

"The miners will deal with it later. Go, go!" Boots pounded away, and not a second too soon. The narrow ledge I was balanced on collapsed beneath me, and I skidded down the rest of the tunnel and tumbled out into Trollus.

My trousers were torn and my knees bleeding, but I didn't pause to examine my injuries. I ran. The sluag's tunnel had let me out in the Elysium quarter, not far from where Tristan had set me down when I'd come in through the moon hole. Bearings in check, I sprinted through the streets, not worrying about anyone recognizing me in the chaos.

"Sluag, sluag!" Trolls were running in every direction, some carrying heavy spears, while others seemed more interested in taking cover. Troll-lights flickered, then went out, and screams filled the air.

I skidded down one flight of stairs and then the next, less concerned about taking the most direct route to the library than I was of staying ahead of the darkness biting at my heels.

And the sluag in Elysium wasn't alone. Across the river, there were three more pools of blackness moving through the streets. How many sluag were in Trollus, and why had they all of a sudden become so aggressive?

"Move!"

I stumbled sideways, nearly falling into a fountain as four guards stormed up the steps, spears in hand. Seconds later, the screams of a sluag filled the air. *So close. Too close.* I couldn't help but wonder if the creatures knew I was here. Whether they were hunting me in particular.

The great columns of the library reared up ahead, troll-light burning comfortingly in the crystal sconces to either side of the entrance. But I couldn't go in that way. The librarians were not typically confrontational, but neither did they allow just anyone to wander their stacks. Instead, I crept around to a small entrance at the rear that I'd used in the past.

It was locked.

Swearing a streak that would've made Tristan proud, I reached up to retrieve a hairpin, realizing only as my fingers brushed my newly shortened curls that there were none to be had. I touched the dagger at my belt, debating whether I could use it to break the lock. Bells were still echoing through the cavern, which in combination with the waterfall, would surely drown out the noise.

Extracting the blade, I slid the tip into the mechanism and then slammed my weight against it. Metal ground against metal, but when I tried to turn the knife, nothing happened.

The sound of voices drifted toward me. It was another patrol. Grabbing hold of the hilt with both hands, I tried to remove the blade, but it was stuck.

I heaved and hauled for all I was worth, but I was out of time. Just as the patrol rounded the corner, I dived off the side of the staircase and into the shadows.

"It's as though the blasted things knew what we were planning," one of the guards said, spitting into the gutter. "Has to be a dozen of them in the city, if not more."

"They'll all be in the city if the miners guild doesn't speed along the process," another replied.

"It's not the miners, it's the builders," a third chimed in. "Seems there's some concern about the strain it'll put on the tree, and half of them are tied up with finishing the construction."

"Waste of time, that," the first said. "No point to it other than to free Tristan from that folly of a promise. Looks like the old devil has a soft spot for his son, after all."

They all laughed, then one added, "Wouldn't be our problem if the King would open the gates. Five centuries of captivity and we finally get our freedom only to have to hide in the same old hole for the sake of a feud between royals."

"Do you want to be caught between Tristan and Roland?" the first asked, but however the other two responded was drowned out by a series of booms.

I cowered next to the steps, eyes on the darkness above as I waited for the rocks to start falling. For Trollus to be destroyed, everyone killed, and me along with them.

But other than a shower of tiny pebbles and dust, nothing happened.

"Hope no one was still in the labyrinth," one of the guards laughed, but there was a slight shake to his voice. "Will be strange not to see the occasional trader coming through that gate. End of an era."

"End of an era," the others repeated, and then they moved on.

It hit me then what had happened. Whether it had been to stop the sluag or prevent anyone from leaving, the trolls had collapsed the labyrinth. And I'd lost my escape route.

My stomach hollowed and I struggled to keep the sharp edges of panic from cutting too deep. I'd find another way, and if not, I still had friends in Trollus. If I needed to, I could hide in the city while we figured out a way for me to escape. But in the meantime, I'd risked everything coming here for information, and I refused to leave empty-handed.

Cautiously sticking my head out from the shadows, I checked to make sure the guards were gone, and then I turned my attention to my dagger, which was still jammed in the door. Getting in the library that way wasn't going to happen. Neither, frankly, was getting anywhere other than the shadows I was crouched in. Trollus had been locked down, everyone but the King's guards and those tasked with hunting down the sluag was hidden behind doors.

I shifted my weight on the sewer grate beneath me, cursing

the sluag, Angoulême, the King, and most of all myself. I was going to be stuck here until curfew was lifted.

Water sloshed beneath me, a foul smell rising, and I buried my face in my sleeve. *Could things get any worse?* Then an idea occurred to me, and I looked down.

An elaborate network of sewers ran beneath Trollus; every structure – even those in the Dregs – connected to the system. The trolls had little tolerance for filth, and, as such, the crown had a small army of half-bloods that kept the system clean and in working order, living their lives in the tunnels that their betters barely acknowledged existed. And if they could move around down there, so could I.

Easing open the latch holding the grate shut, I lifted the metal bars, silently thanking whoever had recently oiled the hinges. Then I lay on my stomach and peered inside.

The sewer was perhaps six feet in diameter, a stream of water and waste running down the center of it. But while I'd expected total blackness, the space was dimly lit by lamps fastened to the ceiling. Holding onto the edge of the hole, I lowered myself in, dropping the last bit to land with my feet on either side of the malodorous stream. The library latrine was located at the rear of the building, and sure enough, I only had to go a few dozen paces before I encountered a shaft leading upwards.

As I suspected, it was large enough, albeit barely, for me to fit, and I could see the trap door covering the top. Unfortunately, the shaft was coated with filth.

Until this moment, I'd have said that growing up on a pig farm had stripped away any squeamishness I'd been born with, but staring into that foul space, I was sorely tempted to go back the way I'd came. But lives depended on me finding out where Angoulême was hidden, and if saving them meant wallowing in troll shit, then I'd do it.

Pulling off my cloak, I used it to wipe away as much of the waste as I could reach; then, taking a deep a breath that nearly turned into a retch, I wriggled into the shaft.

It was awful, and for every six inches of progress, I slid an inch back, my boots scraping against the slimy stone. The smell made me dizzy, my heart pounding as I contemplated what would happen if I became stuck. But after what seemed an eternity, my fingers knocked against the trap, flipping it open. Fresh air filtered down, and I gasped in a few mouthfuls before taking a firm grip on the edge and pulling myself out. I landed with a soft thud on the polished floor, and I fumbled around in the darkness until I found the basin of wash water and toweling, using them to wipe the worst of the filth off my hands and face.

Inching open the door, I checked to make sure there was no one nearby, then hurried into the depths of the stacks. From the time I'd spent here searching for information on Anushka, I was vaguely familiar with the layout, and I trotted in the direction of the estate histories, hoping to find something on the Angoulême lands dating back before the curse. Keeping my smelly fingers to myself, I walked up and down the rows, taking in title after title even as my heart sank. The information might well be here, but it would take me days, if not weeks, to find it by myself.

"I know you're here, you cursed creature."

I leapt at the muttered words, spinning in a circle as I tried to figure out where they were coming from.

"I can smell you. And if you think you can dine on my books, you are sorely mistaken. Ah hah!" A troll leapt out from behind a stack, sluag spear in hand.

I stumbled backward, holding up my hands. "Martin, stop!"

The spear froze in midair, only a few inches from my face.

"Who are you?" Light blossomed, and I heard his sharp intake of breath. "Princess? What are you doing here? And why do you smell like–"

"I sneaked in through the sewer."

His jaw dropped. "And you've been touching the books?"

"I cleaned my hands," I said. "Martin, you mustn't tell

anyone I'm here. If the King were to capture me, it would be disastrous." Even as the words poured out, I realized that I'd no idea where the librarian's loyalties lay, or if he even looked up from his books enough to care.

"And you've come here with an interest in estates?" His voice was hard. "Looking to settle down already?"

I shook my head. "We're trying to find Angoulême. We know he's…" I trailed off, the expression on his face making me step back. Timid and bookish he might be, but Martin was still a troll. It was well within his power to harm me. And in his mind, I might deserve it, given what had happened to the girl he loved.

"I'm so sorry about Élise," I whispered. "She was my friend, and she died saving my life."

Silence.

"Do you know what he did to her?" Each word was torn from his throat. "He locked her in a box, then paraded it though the city so we could all hear her screams. Until we couldn't any more." His hand went to a shelf for balance, knocking several volumes to the floor. "I tried to help her, but I wasn't strong enough. Duchesse Sylvie and the Queen did nothing. The King did nothing."

Tears ran down my cheeks. "I can't bring her back, but I can offer you a chance for revenge against the Duke, because as soon as we find him, we're going to kill him."

He stared at his feet for long enough that I wondered if he were waiting for me to leave. Wondered if maybe my promises seemed empty, because they were powerless to undo the hurt he'd endured. When he finally moved, I flinched, but he only reached inside his robes to pull out a slender vial hanging from a silver chain. The contents glowed a faint blue, and I immediately knew what it was: Élixir de la Lune.

"Tristan promised her that once he was king that he'd allow anyone to be bonded, not just full-bloods," Martin said. "But I didn't want to take the chance that he'd…"

I wondered what had been his concern. That Tristan would find a way around his promise or that he wouldn't become king?

Before I could ask he added, "So I sneaked into the garden and stole a vial of the Élixir. I convinced Élise to use it on next full moon–" his eyes flicked to mine "–the night you broke the curse. But she was dead by then."

I opened my mouth to apologize, but no sound came out.

"Even if Tristan wins and delivers on his word," he said, "it's too late for us. I should get rid of this blasted potion." He tugged on the chain. "It's useless now."

Before he could break the links, I caught his hand in mine and squeezed it tight. "It's not. Please keep it. It meant something to her, and it would've broken her heart to see you throw it away."

"It's useless," he repeated. "Angoulême took her away before I had the chance to know her – to truly know her."

"I understand, but maybe one day–" I started to say that he might one day meet another girl he loved just as much, but instead said, "Maybe one day it will give someone else a chance."

"Maybe." He was silent for a long moment, then he tucked the vial back in his robes. "I'll do whatever it takes to see that monster of a duke bleed out, just as his daughter did. How can I help? What do you need to know?"

I explained to him the only clue we had, and he swiftly moved amongst the shelves, withdrawing several books that he laid open on a table. "These were the Angoulême lands," he said, tracing the outline of an area on the other side of the Isle. "Their estate was here, but the castle and all the surrounding property was destroyed after the Fall." He shook his head. "Everything was. The humans wanted no part of our legacy to remain, and while there might be ruins of some of the larger structures, of a surety, no portraiture would have survived intact."

I dug my nails into the table, trying not to let my frustration get the better of me. "Is there nothing of the trolls that survived? No place left on the Isle that would have meaning?"

"None that I know of, except..." He hesitated. "But no, none of the Angoulême ancestors were entombed there. The Montignys married with every other great family, but never them."

"What are you talking about?"

"The Montigny tomb in the mountains." Martin went back to the stacks and retrieved another volume, this one filled with drawings embellished with beautiful color. "Until the Fall rendered it impossible to do so, every Montigny was interred in a mountain tomb. And when a king or queen died..." He stopped flipping through the book and spread it flat.

I stared at the drawing. "They carved their faces into the rock."

Martin nodded. "The sculptures were too large for the humans to destroy, if they even knew they were there."

This was the place where Angoulême was hiding, I knew it. And in the knowing, all the other pieces fell into place: the way Angoulême seemed oblivious to the flaws in Lessa's disguise. His inappropriate familiarity with the girl who was supposed to be his daughter. Angoulême knew it was Lessa beneath Anaïs's face, and had for some time.

"Where is this place?" I asked.

Martin flipped to a map, then went very still, his eyes wide.

"If my memory serves me correctly," a deep voice said. "It's right about here." A hand that matched the voice reached over my shoulder, a thick index finger tapping a spot deep within the mountains.

A shuddering breath exited my lips, and I slowly turned around, my eyes tracking up until they met the silver gaze of King Thibault de Montigny.

CHAPTER 29
Cécile

"I must confess," the King said, resting the butt of his sluag spear on the ground, "that I did not think it was possible for you to look worse than you did when you first came to us." He flicked at a soiled lock of my hair, and I flinched. "You've proven me wrong."

"How did you know I was here?" It hardly mattered, but it was the only thing I could think of to say.

"I didn't. A runner brought word of a foul smell in the library, which the librarians feared was a sluag." He glanced around at the stacks. "I've spent many a long hour in these hallowed halls, so I took it upon myself to personally deal with the problem." One eyebrow rose. "Imagine my surprise when I discovered it was my dear daughter-in-law who was the source of the stink."

"Sewers." My mind raced, trying and failing to come up with some way to extricate myself from his clutches.

"Hmm." He frowned. "They have been neglected in recent days, I'm afraid."

"Why?" I asked. "Did you kill off all the half-bloods that cleaned them for you?"

"No, they abandoned me for my son." His eyes went to Martin. "I do not feel you need to be privy to this conversation."

Launching myself off the stool I'd perched on, I stepped between the librarian and the King. "Don't you dare hurt him."

Something that looked almost like hurt flickered through his eyes, but was gone in an instant. "Why would I? Good librarians are hard to come by."

Martin said nothing, and when I turned my head, I saw that the King had encased him in an opaque box, effectively removing him from either hearing or witnessing the conversation. "What are you doing here?" he asked.

"Trying to figure out where the Duke is hiding so that we can capture him and stop Roland," I said, sticking with the truth and saving my lies for when I needed them.

"Tristan is quite capable of stopping his brother," he replied. "Why hasn't he?"

"Why haven't you?" I countered. "What happened to your plan to take the Isle peaceably?"

"You happened." His eyes narrowed. "I've been informed the Regent is dead, killed by a lord allegedly under my control. Lord Aiden, under the directive of my son, has taken his father's position, and together, they have formed an alliance against me, and against Roland and Angoulême."

"That is correct," I said, holding his gaze. "You are well informed."

"I am." He tilted his head. "And you, Cécile, are a liar. Aiden du Chastelier, having failed to deliver on his word to me, is likely little more than a drooling mess of madness at this point. Tristan has taken a page from my book, and has someone else masquerading as the lord. Is Aiden still alive?"

"And well," I lied. "I worked a spell to temper your compulsion. It troubles him still, but not so much so that we cannot keep him in check."

"If you knew of such a spell, you would've used it for yourself."

"Yes, I would've," I said. "But I didn't know of it until after I was past needing it. Anushka showed me a good many things before she died."

"As any mother should."

Of course he knew. Was there anything he didn't know?

"Why are you here, Cécile?" he asked. "Why did Tristan send you and his friends to dispatch Roland? And when you failed, why did he take the risk of sending you here in an attempt to discover Angoulême's location? Why has he not dealt with Roland himself?"

With each question, he leaned closer, until the final one brought us almost nose to nose.

"He's protecting Trianon," I said. "We are going after the Duke because he's an easier target."

"Folly," the King snarled. "Kill the Duke and Roland will be free to slaughter at will, which he is sure to do. Capture the Duke, and he will only order the boy to rescue him. This plan of yours is rife with flaws, and not one my son would ever agree to without more cause and justification than you've provided."

"The Winter Queen sent a dragon to attack Trianon – the city needs to be protected."

He grimaced as though my words were utter lunacy. "Tristan's two clowns are quite capable of managing whatever that meddlesome trickster sends their way, and he knows it. Winter is…"

I shifted uneasily, and the King noticed, hissing out a breath between his teeth.

"Ah. Winter is the problem. That's why he remains within the iron ring of the Regent's castle." He stared through me, eyes shifting as he thought. "What has she done to him?"

"Nothing." I was afraid to say more, knowing he'd pick the truth out of whatever lies I spun. He was too intelligent. Too experienced with deception. A true mastermind of manipulation.

His gaze shifted to the spear in his hand. "The sluag." His fist clenched around the steel. "A life-debt."

I tensed and then swore silently for giving myself away. Not that it mattered – he knew.

"And what does that thrice-damned frigid bitch want from my son?"

His jaw tightened and the metal of the spear groaned, bending under his grip. I'd seen him irritated before. Angry, even. But nothing like this.

"We don't know." My voice shook. "She told me she wanted to meet with him to discuss an alliance. It's why I'm disguised."

Thibault's jaw tightened. "No. No, he must not agree to that. You need to go back to Trianon. Tell Tristan to stay put behind those walls. I'll…" He grimaced. "I'll deal with Roland."

"Do you know what it is she wants?"

"I have my suspicions."

But before he could elaborate, a slithering sound reached our ears, and the troll-lights at the end of the row flickered, then went out. I went very still like a rabbit that's scented a fox; but the King straightened, eyes searching and head cocked, listening. Hunting.

"Three," he murmured. "No, four."

Four sluag. My hands and feet went cold, my pulse thundering in my ears. I'd never heard of sluag hunting together, but why else would they converge like this? Unless someone had sent them…

The magic encasing Martin dissolved, and I mouthed, "Sluag," at him. He nodded once, and picked up his discarded spear. The tip of the weapon trembled.

Barooom. One of the sluag called out; then another answered, *Barooom.*

"I hear you," the King said, then he lifted his arms. The bookcases around us shot back, row after row sliding away as though they weighed nothing, their momentum carrying them even as the sluag's power melted away the King's. Several of them toppled, and a squeal of pain rang in my ears as one of the creatures was crushed.

We stood in the middle of a large empty space, devoid of

anything but the books that had fallen off the shelves, the only light that which hovered over the two trolls. But it was flickering.

The King picked up a volume and glanced at the title. "Tax law." He smiled, and the book burst into flame, first the silver of magic, but then the yellow and red of natural fire took over. A shadow moved between two fallen shelves, and their balls of light winked out.

Martin stepped closer to me, twitching with every shiver of motion in the shadows, but the King seemed unaffected. Unafraid. Lighting several more books on fire, he tossed them in a circle around us, creating a perimeter of flame.

A stinger flashed out from the darkness, whipping toward the King's face, but he batted it aside with his spear and laughed. "You'll have to do better than that, vermin."

The sluag shrieked and lunged, its white bulk surging toward the troll even as I sensed motion behind us. I screamed a warning, but the King was already moving.

With impossible speed, he launched the spear in his hands at the first sluag, the force of the blow driving the point through its maw and out the other side. Whirling, he snatched the weapon Martin clutched, and slammed it into the body of the creature attacking from the rear, catching the fleshly stalk of its stinger and wrenching it from its throat.

The sluag writhed, slimy body slamming back and forth in its death throes, but he calmly approached it and pulled the weapon from its flesh with a nauseating slurp.

The flames were burning low, their paper fuel nearly exhausted, and I watched their glow diminish with growing trepidation. There was a third – I could hear it moving through the stacks – and not even the King of the trolls could see in the dark. The building shuddered, and a cloud of dust rolled over us as part of a wall tumbled in, the calls of at least two more sluag audible over the smash of rock hitting the marble floor.

"When I give the word, Martin," Thibault murmured, gaze tracking the sluag's progress, "I want you to take Cécile and run."

"Where, Your Grace?" The librarian's voice was surprisingly steady considering how tight his grip was on my arm.

"Out of Trollus and back to Trianon." He lifted his spear. "Go to Tristan's favorite place to contemplate his woes; there is a passage leading to the surface."

The lake.

"Tristan told me of no such passage." Even now, I found it impossible to trust Thibault.

"My son doesn't know half as much as he thinks." He took a few steps toward the stacks. "Lessa needn't have left if she'd wanted to see the faces of her ancestors, and neither did her puppet master."

He was speaking in code, which meant he believed that Winter was watching. And that she'd try to stop me.

"Run!"

Martin didn't hesitate. Hauling on my arm, he dragged me across the room. We leapt over piles of books, climbing over the fallen shelves until we reached the side door.

"It's stuck!" he hissed, hand scrabbling at the handle.

My dagger.

"Break it down!" One of the sluag screamed, and I cast a backward glance toward Tristan's father. He stood at the center of the dying flames, powerful, brilliant, and fearless, and for an instant, I saw the ruler he might have been.

As though sensing my scrutiny, he turned his head. "Run," he commanded.

And I obeyed.

The door lay in splinters on the street, and Martin stood staring at it as though it was the first time he'd ever used his formidable strength. I grabbed his hand and dragged him toward the palace grounds. But as we rounded the corner of the library, we ran up against four guards.

"Sluag in the library," I shouted. "His Majesty is fighting them alone. Go!"

For a moment, I wondered if I had erred. Whether they'd see it as an opportunity to rid themselves of their King once and for all. But not one of them hesitated.

The librarian seemed at a loss of how to make his way unseen through the city, so I took the lead, scampering down back alleys and through courtyards, always keeping to the shadowy routes my friends had shown me.

But that could only take us so far.

The gate to the River Road was closed, and several armored trolls stood before it, silver eyes watchful. The right branch of the river and the narrow path running next to it were undefended, but there was no way to reach it without the guards seeing us.

"Will they stop us?" I whispered even as I recognized Guillaume amongst them and knew I couldn't risk him spotting me. He was as much Angoulême's as Albert had been.

"They'll do more than stop us." Martin rested one hand against the building. "Curfew is in effect, and even if it wasn't, there's no reason for us to go to the lake. It was Prince Tristan's haunt, and his father's before him.

"Then we'll have to rely on illusion," I muttered. "Once we're by them, there won't be anything between us and the outside."

Martin's shoulders shook, and I realized he was laughing. "As if that were some small thing," he said. "You've been fraternizing with the nobility – the most powerful amongst us. What they can do… The detail. The concentration." He shook his head. "The guards will see right through my attempt and then question our duplicity."

"You're something of a defeatist, Martin." I chewed on my bottom lip, considering our options. Which, near as I could tell, were none. "It's not a good trait."

"I prefer the term realist."

"I'd prefer you thought of a solution." The city had gone mostly silent, but there was no way of knowing whether it was because the King and his men had killed all the sluag, or whether the sluag had killed them and were now hunting for us.

"How long can you hold your breath?"

All thoughts vacated my head, and I turned to stare at him. "Why?"

"A human once came in through the falls in a barrel. He survived the impact. It's possible," he said, cringing as though the speculation were physically painful, "that I could replicate a barrel with magic."

"Possible." All too clearly I remembered how I'd almost killed myself leaping into the river, saved only by the quick thinking of Élise. The rapids were as deadly now as they'd been then – more so, given the freezing temperature, chunks of ice smashing against the bars blocking the river's path to the sea. If Martin misjudged his capability, it would be us smashing against those bars. He might survive it. I certainly wouldn't.

He licked his lips. "Maintaining the structure itself will be simple enough, but I'd need to render it opaque so we wouldn't be seen, which makes any form of navigation a challenge. And there would be a limited amount of air to breathe, so..."

If he passed out, his magic would lose its form quickly, and we'd be bodies in the water.

Leaning out of the building's shadows, I peered at the tiered streets lining the valley walls. Here and there, lights flickered, and I knew we were running out of time. "You don't have to do this," I said. "You could hide. It's me they're after."

"I want Angoulême to pay for what he did to Élise," Martin said, rising into a crouch. "That won't happen if you're dead. And besides," he added, taking my arm and drawing me through the shadows toward a bridge embankment. "The King does not take kindly to those who disobey his orders."

"He might be dead."

"I don't deal in mights." He pulled me close, wrapping an arm around my ribs, his fingers digging into my side. "Deep breath."

I sucked one in, but it didn't seem like enough. There wasn't a chance for another. Magic closed around us, blocking out sight and sound, but not the sensation of falling. We hit the water on our sides, and my elbow slammed painfully against the magic. Up and down we plunged, rolling and rotating like a log in the frothing rapids. Dizziness and nausea swept through me, and no matter how hard I tried not to, I gasped in little breaths with each jarring bounce.

But nothing could've prepared me for the impact of us hitting the rock that split the river in two. My teeth rattled together, and I cried out in pain as my head slammed against our magical container. We rolled, caught up against the rock, and I heard Martin curse, his body quivering with effort, and then we were moving again. I waited for us to smash up against the bars and begin the endless tumble that would be our doom, but it never came.

The worst of the bouncing ceased. Then the magic disappeared and icy cold water closed over my head. My heels jarred against the riverbed, and I kicked up, spluttering and gasping as I broke the surface.

The darkness was absolute, the current tugging me through the winding tunnel, but I knew it eventually spilled down what had once been the steps of the stadium, and I needed to get out before then.

"Martin?" I hissed, turning in the water so my feet would take the brunt of anything I ran up against. "Where are you?"

The only response was my wildly chattering teeth. "Martin?" What if he'd hit his head? What if he couldn't swim? What if yet another friend had died trying to help me?

Ahead, I heard the rush of the water pouring down into the lake. I had to get free of the current. Kicking my feet, I swam toward the bank. My fingers brushed against the rock, and I reached up, trying to catch hold of the lip. But all I found was rock worn smooth by centuries of flowing water.

I was so cold. Already, my limbs felt sluggish and heavy, and I kicked futilely, no longer certain where the edge was. *Get out! You have to get out!* Stretching my arm, I found the bank again, and drawing on what little reserves of energy were left in my body, I lunged up.

And magic closed around my wrist.

My body flew out of the river and was dropped like a sack of potatoes on the bank. Curling up into a ball, I blinked at the light in front of my face, ready to castigate Martin the moment I'd recovered my breath.

But I never got a chance, because the troll kneeing in front of me wasn't the librarian.

CHAPTER 30
Cécile

"I'm not sure how your half-blood friends managed to sneak their way out of the city," the guard said, nudging me with the butt of her spear, "but I can assure you that none of them swam out."

I curled in on myself, trying to hide my face. Not that it would do me much good in the long run.

She dropped to one knee. "There's not a one of us who doesn't want to see the outside, girl, but it isn't safe. Especially not for those like you. Prince Roland is roaming the Isle with none but the Duke to keep him in check, and he holds no love for half-bloods. Do you want to run afoul of him?"

I shook my head.

"Trollus is safe," the guard said, patting me on the shoulder. "Here, you are under the King's protection. Be grateful for that. Now get up."

Even if I'd wanted to, I wasn't sure if I could. My body felt numb, and though I could move my arms and legs, they didn't feel like my own.

"Stones and sky," the troll grumbled. "You're not going to make me drag you back, are you?"

Thud.

I opened my eyes just in time to see the guard drop to the

ground next to me, eyes blank and unseeing. Martin stood behind her, robes dripping with river water. "She won't be unconscious for long," he said. "And when she comes after us, she won't come alone."

With Martin half carrying me, we ran to the end of the tunnel and down the endless steps to the lake. It gleamed like polished onyx, and it wasn't until I tried to push the boat into it that I realized the water was frozen.

"Will it hold our weight?" I asked, wrapping one of the blankets from the boat around my shoulders as best I could. I was dizzy, adrenaline and exertion barely holding back hypothermia.

"I don't feel in a position to…"

Not waiting for him to finish, I stomped past him, then eased onto the lake, sliding my boots across the slick surface. "Keep your distance," I muttered. "We don't both want to fall through."

The ice groaned and creaked as we made our way out over the black depths, keeping close to the walls of the stadium. But we hadn't gone more than fifty yards before the tunnel filled with the sound of running feet. Martin extinguished his already faint light, and we plunged into darkness.

"She's not alone." The female guard's voice drifted across the void, all traces of kindness gone. She was plainly visible where she stood on the bank with three others, and the moment they moved their lights out over the lake, we'd be just as exposed.

"You're sure they came this way?" one of the others asked. "It's a dead end."

"It was either this way, or back out underneath your noses, so you tell me." Another light formed over her head, then began a slow progress across the lake.

Dropping to my elbows and knees, I scuttled toward the shadow of one of the ancient pillars, using its bulk to hide from view. Seconds later, Martin joined me, the ice protesting against our combined weight. Cracks spidered out from beneath us as the guard's light passed by, searching. Hunting.

"This is a waste of time," one of the guards muttered. "Cursed city is full of sluag and worse, and you've got us chasing after some half-blood who's decided to take up skating."

"Catching the fool who assaulted me is an excellent use of my time," she responded. "Go back and stand in front of the gate – I'll deal with them myself."

The ice moaned, and I risked peeking around the corner of the pillar. The light from the three other guards was retreating into the tunnel, but the female was making her way out toward the center of the lake. Martin plucked at my sleeve. I ignored him, suspecting that his martial talents had been exhausted in the singular blow he'd dealt to the guard's head. But he insistently tugged at my sleeve again.

"What?" I whispered.

He pointed down through the glassy surface, and seconds later, something moved.

I could not say what the creature was – only that it was a great leviathan. Its serpentine form moved lazily beneath the ice, opalescent scales gleaming as though it were lit from within. The guard hadn't noticed it yet, and she moved with a measured stride across the lake, her eyes roving for someone that hid above, not something that hunted beneath.

"Don't move," Martin whispered. "Maybe it won't notice us."

"We can't stay here forever." Already, my lack of motion was allowing the cold to take over, but I dared not ask Martin to use magic to warm me lest it draw the attention of either the troll or what I strongly suspected was a Winter creature.

A voice echoed through the cavern, a song both lovely and eerily familiar. A song being sung with my voice.

My skin prickled with tension, and I realized then that it wasn't just my own. My spell had worn off Tristan at the worst

She filled both wine glasses to the brim, walking carefully back to the table and depositing one next to the plate containing the remains of my meal. I ignored it in favor of picking at a loose thread on my shirt, and as predicted, Souris leapt onto the table, knocking the wine glass as he went for the scraps of food. The red liquid sloshed over my trousers, and I swore.

"Damn it, Souris!" I shouted at him, then picked up the empty glass and hurled it across the room where it smashed against a particularly ugly tapestry. He barked once, then scuttled under the table where he eyed me with a toothy grin.

"Tristan," Joss said, her face pale. "I think Cécile's spell is wearing off."

I stood staring at her for a long moment, then I dived toward my discarded coat, ripping the pocket as I extracted the handkerchief the seeds – and, more recently, the marbles – had been wrapped in.

"They're gone," I hissed, the scrap of fabric disappearing in a burst of flame.

The room trembled, magic compounding the heat of the fire.

"Are you sure?" Josette was shaking, her wine a pool of red on the tabletop.

I turned and gave her black glare.

"Maybe they're in your other coat," she whispered.

Taking a deep breath, I said, "I need them."

And it was the truth. It was taking every ounce of willpower I had not to react to Cécile's terror. *It's not real,* I told myself. *It's all part of Winter's plan.*

But what if it was real? What if Cécile needed me and this plan was a mistake? The back of the chair cracked and splintered beneath my grip, and I shoved it aside.

Moving with speed no human possessed, I was around the table, catching hold of Joss's sleeve and dragging her close. "Your sister is in danger, but if I leave…" I stared intently at her, as though she possessed the solution to my dilemma.

She cracked. "Please help my sister, Tristan. Please don't let anything happen to her."

It was either the finest bit of acting she'd managed, or she was genuinely afraid for Cécile's wellbeing. Suspecting the latter, I bit the inside of my cheeks. Something wasn't right, but I didn't dare stop now.

"I need those seeds," I said. "Who took them?"

"I don't know," she whispered, and I knew this wasn't going as she had planned. She'd expected me to go running straight out the castle gates and into Winter's clutches, and now she didn't know what to do.

"Sabine," I hissed. "She was against me using the magic, and she's had the opportunity. She took them from me."

Josette blanched. "Surely not. She wouldn't steal from you. Sabine is loyal."

"Don't protect her." I shoved past, moving out into the corridor, doors exploding open as I passed. "Do you know what I do to thieves?"

Her eyes were bright with panic as she clutched at my arm, her fear for the innocent Sabine warring with her desire to trick me, and with her terror of just what I'd do if she admitted to having thrown them in the flames. "You need to help Cécile," she pleaded, but I shrugged her off.

Catching hold of one of the half-bloods hurrying down the hall, I jerked him close. "Where is Sabine?"

"The gatehouse, Your Highness," he replied. "With Lord Marc."

Joss took off running, and I strode after her, winding my way through the corridors and out into the open air.

"Sabine," Josette screamed. "Run. You need to run."

Cécile's blonde friend twisted around, her eyes widening at the sight of us. Then Marc stepped in the line of fire. "Stones and sky, Tristan, what's going on?"

"My seeds," I shouted, and then I leveled a finger at her.

"Where. Are. They?"

Sabine took a step back. Then another.

"Tristan, she hasn't done anything wrong," Marc said, throwing up a shield to block my path. I shattered it with a single blow and demanded, "Where are they?"

"They were a mistake, Tristan," Sabine shouted, her voice echoing through the air. "Even if I had them, you don't need them."

"Give them back!"

Marc raised another shield and stepped between us. "Sabine, run!"

She didn't hesitate, swinging up onto the back of Cécile's horse and laying the ends of her reins to the mare's haunches. In a matter of seconds, she was across the bridge and into the city.

Marc backed up until he stood just outside the iron barrier. "Tristan, you can't step outside the walls."

"Then bring her back! The seeds are mine."

Marc took a deep breath. "You don't need them."

But I did need them. *Cécile…* "You know what the punishment is for a human who steals from a troll," I snarled. "Death."

I smashed through his shield and knocked him out of the way. I hesitated only for a second before stepping across the circle protecting me, and then I broke into a run.

With every stride, I was sure the world would tear open and Winter would step out, stopping me in my tracks. That this plan was folly and would never work, but I saw no sign of her or any of her minions.

But of a surety, they were watching.

I chased the sound of the hooves through Trianon, gaining ground by cutting across yards and going over walls. But Sabine was riding at reckless speed, and I didn't catch sight of her until she was galloping up the street toward Bouchard's residence, bent low over the horse's back, hair whipping out behind her.

"Give them back, Sabine!" I howled, and tore her off the back of the horse.

I let her dangle in the air for an instant, then dropped her in a pile of snow next to the open gate to the property.

Watching her scramble back, I slowly stalked forward. "Give them to me."

"Please, Tristan, please," she sobbed. "I don't have them."

"The law is the law," I said, then the air charged with magic and she collapsed in the snow, unmoving.

I dug into her pockets, discretely pulling out the seeds, relief filling me at the sight of them even as I pantomimed the frustration of one thwarted. But before I could do anything more the world tore, and Winter stepped out.

CHAPTER 32
Tristan

The tear folded back on itself like the pages of book, stretching from the ground to the upper reaches of the sky to reveal desolate fields of snow and ice, wind howling across the great expanse like some tortured beast.

"Highness." The Winter Queen inclined her head, black hair falling over her shoulder like a silken curtain of mist, the tear closing behind her. "We meet again." Her eyes went to the unmoving Sabine. "This pleases me. She was a wicked creature."

Which is why she'd been happy to let me chase Sabine down and kill her.

"I have no patience for thieves," I snapped, readying my magic.

"Let's not be so hasty," she said. A small tear appeared, and through it, I could see Cécile underwater, trying desperately to make her way to the surface. But a sheet of ice blocked her path. My blood ran cold. This wasn't how it was supposed to go. Winter had told Josette that she'd only scare her sister, that she wouldn't put her in real danger.

She wouldn't put… I swore silently, desperately, and the tear closed.

She clucked softly. "Your situation has grown dire indeed. I can help with that."

I spat at her feet, trying to keep my thoughts straight with Cécile fading by the second. I had not planned for this, but I could not stop now. Could not give up now. I squeezed the seeds tightly, keeping them at the ready.

Winter sighed, the misty folds of her gown drifting and flowing. "Cécile went into Trollus in search of information on the whereabouts of your enemy, he who calls himself the Duke d'Angoulême. I'm afraid she ran afoul of your father." Her eyes met mine. "I can help her. I can help you."

"In exchange for what?" She'd known when she'd spoken to Joss that Cécile was walking into trouble.

"An alliance. I will save Cécile and do all I can to help you see your enemies dead. In exchange, you will give your word to protect my court from yours."

Given we were bound to this world, and given she had no intention of allowing her kind to linger here for fear of losing them to the iron, I failed to see how we were a threat to the Winter fey. But that wasn't important in this precise moment. All that mattered was that she believed we were.

I hesitated, then said, "No. On my word, I'll never ally with you or your court. Nor will I harm a living soul for your benefit."

The air shivered as my promise bound me, and her pupils elongated as fury fractured her glamour. She could use my debt to order me to do it anyway, but the combination would drive me mad in moments. I was gambling that her plan didn't include me losing my mind.

"You will regret that choice, mortal."

I stared her down, praying that Cécile wouldn't pay the price of me forcing the fairy queen's hand.

"I call your debt due, mortal prince. Bequeath me your power," she said. "I would possess the greatest weapon in this world and the next."

I lowered my head, keeping my eyes on the snow so she would not see my expression. Not that it mattered: she had cemented her half of the bargain, and she would have her due. I closed the distance between us, the icy scent of winter tickling my nostrils as I leaned down.

"Done," I said, and the moment the words crossed my lips, my magic was gone. Her form turned as solid as my own, lips parting with a silent shriek of pain as my iron-corrupted power burned into her. I slammed my palm against her mouth, forcing one of the seeds between her teeth, driving her backwards, knowing it would only take a second for the spell to work even as we fell into Bouchard's property and Sabine leapt to her feet and slammed the iron gates behind us.

Before Winter could react, I rolled backward, vaulting over the fence and into a pile of snow.

Crouched next to Sabine, I watched as the creature who was as old as time came to the realization she'd been tricked. No emotion came with the understanding, but I suspected she'd shake the spell quickly, and that her wrath would be formidable.

Boots pounded up behind us as Marc raced onto the scene. "Are you all right?" he asked, helping Sabine to her feet, while I watched Winter circle the property, testing out her new set of powers, which, as I'd suspected, were as bound as she was by the iron circle.

Cécile.

I opened my palm to reveal the remaining black orb. It shifted and swirled, repulsive, yet incredibly alluring at the same time. *It was easier not to feel.*

But when had I ever chosen the easier path?

Dropping the seed on the ground, I crushed it with the heel of my boot. "Hold the city," I said. "Give me a few hours head start, then you know what to do."

"What if she won't deal?" Marc asked, his arm steadying Sabine. She'd taken a huge risk stepping outside the castle walls and tempting Winter's wrath, but it had paid off.

I cast a backward glance at Winter – who was watching us

with a gaze so alien and strange, it almost made me feel human – and wondered how long it would take her to figure out just how trapped she was. "I don't think you need to worry about that," I said, then I started toward Trollus.

CHAPTER 33
Cécile

Water closed over my head and, when I kicked upwards, my hands hit a glassy sheet. I needed air. Needed to breath, but I couldn't find a way up. The satchel strapped to my back was weighing me down, but it had Anushka's grimoire, the perfume bottles full of blood.

They won't do you any good if you're dead.

Slipping off the strap, I kicked hard, desperation giving me strength. Then magic wrapped around my waist, jerking me up into the air. "I've got you," Martin said, then there was rock beneath my bottom as he pulled me through the illusion and into the tunnel.

"Wait," I choked. "The guard."

We leaned back through the opening, but there was only blackness and silence. Martin sent a wisp of light over the surface of the lake and it reflected off the glossy surface. The water was frozen solid, all trace of both guard and leviathan gone.

Winter had accomplished what she intended.

At the far end, lights from the other guards bobbed into view, drawn by the noise.

"We need to go," Martin said, and he dragged me through the narrow passage in the rocks, and out into the open. We were on the rock fall, but beneath the wooden bridge that ran over top. Despite the cover the planks provided, Martin had one arm pressed against his eyes, the other raised as though he could ward off the midday sun.

"I'm going to freeze to death if you don't do something," I stuttered out through my clattering teeth, unable to move from where I lay. Everything was numb, the act of breathing all I could manage.

Magic enveloped me like a warm blanket, and with it came a wave of sleepiness that I knew I needed to fight. But it was so hard. Too hard, and before I knew it, I'd drifted off.

I awoke to find myself suspended in the air, my body warm from the press of magic. "Where are we?" I muttered.

"On the way to Trianon," Martin said, squinting at me with teary bloodshot eyes. "I've been avoiding the road, just in case."

"Put me down." My clothes were mostly dry and, though I was exhausted, I no longer felt on the brink of death. I retied the lace on one of my boots, then started walking. We needed to get to Trianon with the information on Angoulême's location. And I needed to tell Tristan that his father had defended me from the sluag, had let me go. That he was going to help with the Winter Queen. That Tristan needed to stay where he was.

"Wrong way," Martin said, tugging on my arm.

I blinked and looked around, feeling disoriented. "But Tristan…"

Wasn't in Trianon.

"Oh, no," I whispered. "He's on his way to Trollus." But he had to have passed us on his way, and I could think of no good reason why he wouldn't have stopped when he knew I was all right. Unless it wasn't his choice.

"We have to go back," I said, dragging on Martin's arm.

"But Thibault told us to go to Trianon."

I fixed him with a glare that made clear exactly what I thought of that proposition, and then I broke into a run.

CHAPTER 34

Tristan

I'd seen Martin carrying Cécile in the direction of Trianon, but hadn't stopped. There wasn't time, and I trusted the librarian as much as anyone to get her to the relative safety of the city. Or at least I would have, if she'd remained unconscious. Now she was backtracking toward Trollus, and I didn't have time to do anything about it.

Slipping under the overhang, I made my way up the River Road until I heard the sound of voices. "Searched the lake from back to front," someone said. "No sign of her or the half-bloods she was going on about."

"Maybe she snuck out for a nap," replied another, and I recognized the voice as Guilluame's.

"But you heard the noise!"

"Could've just been rocks falling into the lake. Tree's been neglected of late."

"But the lake was frozen solid."

I coughed, interrupting the guards' conversation. Not a one of the four had sensed my approach. "Excuse me."

"Another blasted human," one said, resting his elbows on the bars. "Go! If you seek shelter, you'll find it in Trianon with Prince Tristan."

"I'm afraid that's no longer the case." I pulled back the hood of my cloak, readying to duck and run if one of them attacked.

To their credit, none of them turned tail. The air went scalding hot as they linked their magic, the gate going cherry red and the surrounding rocks smoldering from the intensity of their shield. "I need to speak to my father."

"Something's not right," said the female amongst them. "I can't feel his power. We should've known he was coming a mile off."

"It's a trick," Guilluame replied. "He's a human disguised as Tristan."

"That's easy enough for you to check," I snapped. There was only so much time, and I couldn't afford a delay. "Either let me pass or send someone to fetch the King."

The heat remained, their faces unconvinced.

"I've been deprived of my magic," I said, sweat trickling down my back. "One of you should be more than sufficient to keep me in line, if that is your concern."

"Go to the palace," the female ordered the youngest of them. To the others, she said, "Let him in. We'll keep him here until we have our orders."

The glowing gate swung outward, and I gave it wide berth as I passed, not wishing to be burned. My skin stung from the radiant heat as it was, healing mortal slow without my magic. So strange to fear something so insignificant.

When I was through, the female pulled off her gauntlet and slapped a hand against my cheek, feeling for the presence of a disguise. "Nothing," she said, her voice curious. "It's him."

"Deprived of your magic, you say." Guillaume pulled off his helmet. "How'd that come to pass?"

"That's a conversation I'll have with my father and none other."

"Of course." He grinned, revealing a piece of something green stuck between his two front teeth. "I wonder how well His Grace will reward me for putting you down." Then he attacked, not me, but his fellows, sending the female flying through the air and then slicing the remaining guard in two.

I turned to run, but his magic caught my ankle, then slammed me against the cobbles. "Some things are better done by hand," he said, and his boot caught me in the ribs with an audible crack. The female guard raced back and tried to interfere, but he walled her off, his magic stronger, if only barely.

Blow after blow struck me in the sides, in the arms, in my face, and there was nothing I could do to get away. Bones cracked and blood splattered the ground, but through it all I saw the face of my attacker. How he sensed my weakness and reveled in it. Then the air stirred, filling with a sound much like a whip being cracked, and through the swelling of my eyes, I watched Guillaume's head drop to the ground next to me.

"Get up."

I struggled to rise, and my father's hand latched under my arm, hauling me to my feet.

My lone defender stood wild-eyed. "I tried to stop him, Your Majesty," she pleaded.

"Go find others to replace them," he snarled at her, and she took off running.

It took every ounce of willpower I had not to pass out from the pain as he dragged me through the streets to the palace. They were empty as they only were during curfew, but the faces of those peering out from behind windows filled with dismay when they recognized me.

"What's happened?" I asked, spitting a mouthful of blood.

"Sluag," he said. "Now keep your mouth shut until we're behind closed doors."

He brought me to his office, dropping me unceremoniously on the plush carpets. Going to a tray laden with goodies, he plucked up several linen napkins and a pitcher of water before kneeling next to me and wiping blood off my face.

"That hurts," I complained, flinching away to get into a

better position, the knife tucked into my boot burning against my skin.

"Gives you a bit of a taste of what it's like to be human."

Neither his words or his tone were what I'd expected, and I lifted my head. "You don't seem surprised."

"I'm not." He rinsed the napkin in the water, then held it to the cut on my cheek. "Winter called your debt. Cécile was here and she told me enough. I sent her to tell you to stay put in Trianon, but it would appear she didn't make it in time."

There was never a chance she would.

"Stones and sky, you're bleeding like a human," my father muttered, his jaw tightening. Then in one violent motion, he rose to his feet and threw the pitcher against the wall in an explosion of glass. Going to the cold fireplace, he rested his arms on the mantle, head bowed.

And his back to me.

I inched my fingers down to the hidden knife, moving slowly so as not to catch his attention. I'd known without magic that he'd discount me as a threat, would lower his guard. And now was my chance.

Do it!

My hand closed around the hilt, slowly pulling it free.

"You should've told me about the debt," he said. "I could've bargained with her. Given her what she wanted in exchange for letting you be."

I froze.

"Though I suppose I can't blame you for not trusting me. It was how you were raised." He sighed deeply. "And now the Winter trickster is free to run around the Isle, slaughtering her enemy's people at will with no one to stand in her way."

She wasn't free, but I'd made sure to make it to Trollus before any of his spies could bring word that she was trapped. It wouldn't be long now, though, and as soon as he knew, I was sure he'd see through my plot.

Kill him.

I swallowed, my hand still gripping the hilt. "You could stand in her way. You have all of Trollus at your command."

"I think we both know that's not the case."

I bit the inside of my cheeks, unsure of whether he doubted his capacity or his control.

"Besides," he said. "I can't leave. You aren't the only one who's had to pay the price of a desperate bargain, Tristan."

Even with the curse broken, he was bound to Trollus. Knowing it was so was like the last piece of the puzzle falling into place, explaining why he hadn't taken Trianon, why he hadn't moved to stop Roland and the Duke, and why, given they finally had freedom in their grasp, that he'd locked the citizens of Trollus back in their underground cage. "Who holds this bargain?"

"Your aunt," he said. "She threatened to drown your mother if I didn't give my word never to leave Trollus, and for obvious reasons, I can't kill her to free myself. No one plays the game better than her, and no one is less trusting."

"Can you blame her?" Pain ricocheted through me as I climbed to my feet, using his desk as leverage. "No one forced you to be a tyrant. That was your choice, and these are the consequences."

Laughing, he picked up a bottle of liquor sitting on the mantle and drank from it directly. "You remind me of myself at your age. Idealistic." He took another swallow and grimaced. "So certain you know everything."

"Since obviously I do not, perhaps you might enlighten me." The clock was ticking, my chance to put an end to the man who had haunted my steps all my life growing smaller by the second. But I had to hear him out.

He drained the bottle, then turned to face me. "I hated my father as you hate me, perhaps more so, for he was a far worse creature. Perhaps the worst ever to rule, in that he relished in killing. Though they were bonded, he slaughtered your grandmother with his bare hands in front of the court for crossing him, and if it hurt him, he never once showed it." He paused. "He and Roland were cut from the same cloth."

I'd heard stories of my grandfather, but they were not given much breath. Why should they be when Trollus had to contend with a living and breathing tyrant king.

"Like you, I had a vision of a better Trollus. And as you have your friends and coconspirators, I had mine, your aunt being one of them. We dreamed of abolishing the enslavement of half-bloods, of setting laws that made everyone equals. That, if given the chance, trolls would choose their matches based on character and commonalities, not power. That, if given the chance to love as they wished, the classism of magic would cease to exist." He snorted, then snatched up another bottle. "Hearing it now, it sounds like some sort of comedic nonsense a poet might spout."

I wiped away the blood dripping into my eye as I struggled to come to terms with this vision he was painting.

"Of course, there was a girl." He sat on a chair, the wood creaking. "There always is."

"Lessa's mother."

His chin jerked up and down once. "Vivienne. She belonged to my mother and then to me, and I loved her. And she told me she loved me. That there was no one but me."

Lost in memory, his eyes were distant and unseeing.

Kill him!

But I would've soon as stabbed my own heart as struck him down, because he was telling his story. And his story was my story.

"I was going to change all the laws of Trollus so that I could bond her and make her my queen. And in doing so, I believed I would start our world on a better path. I kept our relationship a secret, and when she became pregnant – as will happen easily with any girl with human blood," he gave me a pointed look, "I hid her in the city until she had Lessa. Until I was ready to act."

"But grandfather found you out?" I asked, fascinated by the notion that my father had not always been infallible. I knew he had killed his own father, but never considered there was a greater reason than a desire for the crown. I was beginning to believe I'd been very much mistaken in that.

"He always knew." A bitter smile crossed his face. "It seems a universal flaw of youth to believe one's elders oblivious to one's undertakings."

I waited silently for him to say more, curiosity making me forget the pain of my battered body.

"I went looking for her one day and could not find her."

I tensed, certain that my grandfather had killed Vivienne to make a point, as my own father had done to the human peddler I'd once been so fond of.

But it was worse.

"Whispers and rumors led me to find her in my father's bedchamber. She was his lover, and had been for some time. It had all been a plot to put me in my place, Vivienne only playing a part, every one of her words a lie. And he laughed in my face, and told me I was a fool for putting my faith in something so weak. And he did not mean just her."

Hatred that was more than a memory filled his eyes, and I wondered if that was how I looked when I spoke of him.

"When I was done, the only way they were able to identify them was by their absence." His jaw tightened. "After that, I turned my back on my foolish dreams, and Trollus learned to fear a new king."

Lies or no lies, Lessa's mother would've had little choice in her actions. When you were property, and especially when you were the property of a king, "no" was not part of your vocabulary, if you valued your life. But I said nothing, because he knew that as well as I, half a lifetime of regret and guilt lining his face in this rare moment of honesty.

"There was no going back after that," he said, meeting my gaze. "At least, not for me. But I knew early where your sympathies resided, and so began over a decade of planning. I would be the people's tyrant so that you could become their savior. Their liberator."

I swayed on my feet, the scratch of my fingernails on the desk barely registering in my ears. "What do you mean?"

A massive concussion shattered the air, and the ground shook, both of us staggering. Righting himself, my father swore. "Stay here."

I caught his sleeve. "Wait, you have to tell me what you meant."

He shoved me back into the office, the door slamming shut, locked in place with magic. "Father, wait," I screamed, but it was to no avail. I knew what that concussion had been: Roland. Too late I remembered Cécile's repeated words of Angoulême's strategy; too late I understood why they planned to go first after my father, who had the might of Trollus at his disposal, rather than me. Because the Duke had seen what I had not: my father would defend my life to the bitter end, whereas I'd stand back and watch him die. I couldn't let that happen. I needed to hear more, needed to understand why he'd done what he'd done.

Picking up a chair, I slammed it against the door, wood splintering and breaking, but the magic holding strong. "Help! Someone open the door."

Nothing.

I spun in a circle, desperate for a way out. But I knew this room well, and there were no windows. No doors. The walls were solid stone and without magic, I wasn't strong enough to break through them. I looked up. The ceiling was polished wood, and that, that I could break.

Ignoring the pain in my body, I snatched up a piece of the broken chair. Leaping onto the desk, I slammed it against the panels until one of them broke, then I used it as a lever to pull free enough boards for me to fit through. Splinters catching and tearing at my clothes, I climbed into the narrow space, wriggling on my belly until I was certain the hallway was beneath me.

Breaking through, I dropped into the ground and started running. "The King?" I shouted at the first troll I came across. "Which way did he go?"

The troll stared at me in astonishment, and I grabbed his shirt, slamming him against the wall. "Which way?"

He pointed, and I took off in that direction.

The halls of the palace were a familiar maze, and I soon guessed his path. Even deprived of my own, I could still feel the weight of his magic, and I pursued it, catching sight of him right as he slammed open the doors to the gardens. "Father!"

He turned at my voice. "Go back."

Instead I pressed forward, grabbing hold of the front of his coat. "Roland's come to kill you."

His eyes bored into mine, then he looked away. "What does it matter? Without magic, they won't follow you. All that I've done…" He shook his head. "It was for nothing."

"It wasn't." I tried and failed to pull him back into the hallway. "If you would just listen."

Then he stiffened, eyes going wide with shock. Fear. Pain. "Tristan–" he gasped, then he collapsed to the floor at my feet.

CHAPTER 35
Cécile

I sank to my heels, bracing a hand against the slick rock of the tunnel. *Deprived of my magic...* It had been the Winter Queen who'd taken it. Who else could accomplish such a feat? And in all likelihood, it was my fault for putting myself in danger. Why else would he step outside the safety of the castle walls?

But why, knowing I was all right, had he continued into Trollus? Was he here to make an alliance with his father? To surrender? Or another reason all together?

I couldn't see Martin's face in the darkness, but his breathing was loud enough for me to reach out and pull him close. "You need to go to the twins," I whispered. "Tell them where to find the Duke – they might be able to defeat him." I swiftly gave instructions to the camp and the signals to use so they'd know he was no foe.

"What about you?"

I gave him a gentle shove down the road. "I'm going after Tristan."

The gate stood open, Guilluame's corpse and one other lying next to it in a pool of blood. Though it had been hours since I'd left the king fighting the sluag, the streets were still empty, the citizens of Trollus bound by curfew.

Pulling up my hood, I kept to the shadows, avoiding the patrols of guards armed with sluag spears. The main gates to the palace were flanked by armed trolls, as were the side entrances. Sitting on my haunches next to one of the towering pillars of the stone tree, I contemplated how I might get inside. Then, from behind the palace, blossomed a familiar glow.

The glass gardens.

Only royals and members of the Artisan's Guild were allowed to light the gardens. The guild members would be subject to curfew, and I sincerely doubted Thibault was in the mood for a whimsical stroll. Which left only one, or rather, two, other candidates. And they might just be willing to help me.

I entered through the hidden gate at the rear that Tristan had once shown me, the glass brilliant with the unearthly beauty of troll-light. I dreamed of them often, but even the limitless bounds of imagination had failed to capture their beauty. It was a place one needed to *be* in order to experience, and though I'd explored them countless times during my time in Trollus, I knew that if I spent the rest of my life walking through them, there would always a new detail to discover. The curve of an unknown flower. The vaulting height of a tree. A dewdrop balanced on the tip of a leaf.

As I searched the paths and courtyards for the Queen and the Duchesse, the waterfall roaring as it toppled from the heights, little memories layered themselves across the present. The places I had lingered, deep in thought. The songs that I had sung. The maze of hedgerows I had walked with Tristan shadowing my steps, both of us deeply aware of the other. Listening. Watching. Wanting. But neither of us daring to hope there might be a chance for us.

My chest ached as I remembered those moments. The enchantment of Trollus. Leaving had been like waking from a dream, and no matter how many nights I slept, I could never find my way back. And even if I did, it would never be the same.

I stopped in my tracks, resting a hand against a tree trunk while I gave the profoundness of that loss its due.

Then I heard them.

The Queen and the Duchesse were arguing; more accurately, the Duchesse was lecturing while her sister protested with soft sounds of dismay.

I crept closer, so focused on the placement of my feet that I did not notice my sleeve catch on a bush.

Snap.

A twig, little more than a filament of glass, broke away. I reached for it, but my hand was too slow and it shattered against the ground.

The faces of both trolls snapped my direction, and I hunched down, holding my breath. Not that there was any point.

Magic wrapped around my waist, lifting me up and over the foliage, depositing me in front of the two women. "Why am I not surprised," Sylvie said, crossing her arms. "We keep sending you away, but back you come."

Queen Matilde's eyes were wide, her full lips slightly parted. "Oh, Cécile, you look dreadful." She shook her head. "This will not do."

My scalp prickled, and seconds later, little bits of black rained to the ground. "Better," she said, slender fingers plucking at one of my shortened curls, which was crimson once more. Pulling a pin from her own hair, she carefully twisted mine back from my face and smiled.

"Can't remember what she had for lunch, but she can do that." Sylvie's face was sour. "Why are you here, Cécile? Thibault sent you to Trianon."

"I didn't go," I said. "I had to come back."

"Why is that?"

"Tristan's here," I blurted out. "He's lost his magic."

"What?" Sylvie barked even as Matilde exclaimed, "Where?" She rotated in a circle, eyes searching the gardens.

"Matilde, stand still!"

I swiftly explained as much as I could, along with my suspicion that it had been Winter who'd taken his power. "He walked in here of his own accord." My eyes were burning, and I blinked furiously. "I think he's given up and surrendered."

Sylvie's eyes lost focus, shifting back and forth as she delved into the problem, the expression eerily reminiscent of Tristan's when he was deep in thought. "No," she said. "He hasn't. But he is about to make a mistake."

The ground shook and I was flung against the corner of a stone bench. I fought the urge to curl up in pain, struggling instead to my feet. "Is it her? Is it Winter?" I gasped.

Magic lifted me up into the air. "Tell me what you see," Sylvie ordered, lifting me higher and higher.

The air was filled with dust mixed with frost, and I coughed, covering my mouth with my sleeve as I peered toward the end of the valley. "There's no one at the gate." Other than the bodies of the guards.

She lowered me so swiftly, I might as well have fallen, my spine shuddering as my heels hit the ground. "Stay here," she said; then to the Queen: "Matilde, find Thibault now. Hurry!"

In a blink, they were gone.

I stared in the direction they'd gone for another heartbeat, then I took off after them.

Keeping up with the troll queen was impossible, but she was heading toward the palace, so I took the shortest way I knew. There was probably nothing I could do to help, but Tristan was in there without any way to protect himself, whereas I still had magic. If Thibault or Matilde would lend their power, I suspected my spells would be just as affective against the Winter Queen as any troll.

"Mother?"

I skidded to a halt just shy of a bend in the hedgerows, my skin breaking out in a cold sweat at the sound of that familiar voice. Pressed my arm to my mouth to muffle my ragged breathing, I squatted down making myself as small as possible.

"Roland!" The Queen's voice was serene and sweet.

"Matilde, no! Matilde!" The Duchesse screamed the warning, but it was too late. A cry of pain cut through my ears, then the rustle of silken skirts and a thud.

Tears streamed down my face, but I knew better than to move. If Roland saw me, I was dead and would be no help to anyone. But if I waited until he was gone, then there was a chance I could save Matilde and Sylvie.

"Cécile?"

I flinched at the Duchesse's voice.

"There is no chance you stayed where I told you to, so you can come out now. Roland is gone."

Mustering my courage, I peered around the corner. The Queen lay on her side, silver eyes blank and unseeing, blood pooling on the white stone beneath her. The hilt of a knife stuck out of her chest, the blade embedded in her heart. Without having seen it, I knew she'd reached for her son with open arms, innocent and unsuspecting.

And he'd killed her. Not because of anything she'd done, but to put an end to his father. To take the throne.

My mind was awash with Tristan's emotion, and I shook my head to clear it as I approached. Sylvie hung limply from her twin's back, but she was alive. For how long, I could not guess. Touching the knife at my waist, I silently contemplated whether it would be possible to separate the two, and if it was, whether I had the mettle to do it.

"No."

I jumped at the coldness in her voice.

"Banish the idea from your thoughts," she said. "Then come and hear me out before I breathe my last."

I knelt next to her, desperate to find Tristan and get him free of Trollus before Roland found him. We could hide, or find a ship that would take us to the continent. *Run and live while everyone else suffers for your mistakes.*

"Thibault is dead," she whispered, and I watched in disbelief as a tear trickled down her cheek.

"You do not know that for sure," I said, taking her hand. "He's strong, it's possible that–"

"No," she said. "It isn't." The air surrounding the hand I held shifted, illusion falling away to reveal blackened bonding marks. "When Thibault and Matilde were bonded, something unexpected happened. We kept it a secret, but the time for that is over."

"I thought you hated him," I said. "That you were helping Tristan with his plot to kill his father."

"I did." She smiled. "And I was. I've hated Thibault since he destroyed our plans over Lessa's fool of a mother. Fought against his decision to bond my sister and made his life a living hell every day since. But over Tristan, we were united. Allies against enemies who would've seen that boy dead a dozen times over and comrades in our efforts to mold him into the man he needed to be."

Like the gardens around us, I could spend a lifetime amongst these creatures and never stop being surprised at their duplicity.

"Don't look at me like that," she whispered before breaking into a ragged cough. "I know Thibault was cruel to his son and that you think me equally so for supporting him, but it was all to protect Tristan. Believing that Thibault was Tristan's enemy stayed the hands of Angoulême and his followers, because they believed Thibault would kill Tristan himself before allowing a sympathizer to take the crown. It was the only way."

She shuddered and I gripped her hand tight, knowing death would come to her in moments.

"But our methods left their scars on him," she said. "And that I regret. Please tell him that he was loved by all his family. That he was all we hoped him to be and more. A true king."

She went still, and I thought it over, but then she stirred. "Cécile?"

"Yes?" I asked, afraid of what more there could be to say.

"What happened to Matilde was Angoulême's doing. Roland may have wielded the blade, but he wept as he was doing it."

She said no more.

Reaching down, I gently brushed her eyelids shut, then the Queen's as well. When I looked up, Lessa, still wearing her Anaïs disguise, was smiling at me.

I jerked the knife out of the Queen's chest, holding it up as I climbed to my feet. It was coated with her blood, but I didn't know if there was enough power in it to bind Lessa or not. Nor was I sure if I could get close enough to find out.

"I ought to just kill you and be done with it," Lessa said, her eyes glittering with amusement at the knife. "But keeping you alive might serve a better purpose. For now."

Run.

But my feet were fused to the ground with magic, and before I could try to throw the knife or work another spell, Lessa threw back her head and screamed, "Help! Someone help! The Queen has been murdered."

CHAPTER 36
Cécile

Beneath Trollus ran a network of sewers. Below that, extensive caverns and vaults where grain and foodstuffs were stored. Underneath that, I discovered, was where the trolls kept their prisoners. That it was devoid of light was a given, but as the guards dragged me deeper into the earth, it seemed darker than the city, than the mines, than even the labyrinth, because it was so very far from any sort of light.

The low-ceilinged tunnels were damp with moisture, the air stale as though no one came down here very often. Or perhaps stale from the countless exhalations of prisoners who would never again see light.

The guards hadn't doubted Lessa's words when they'd come upon us, me holding a knife coated with blood, the troll queen and her conjoined twin sister lying dead at my feet. While most would've forgiven Tristan for killing his father – many even applauding him for it – having his human wife achieve the same results by killing his mother was another matter. At best, it made him a coward, and at worst... Well, the Queen had been well-loved by her people, and the Duchesse, too. Their murderer would not be forgiven.

I couldn't even defend myself or offer up the truth. Lessa had gagged me before anyone arrived on the scene, warning the guards who took me away not to allow me to speak lest I use my witch magic upon them. They'd taken her words to heart – though in truth, I did not need to say a word to work with troll magic – guiding me at arm's length with steel shackles, eyes wary and watching. I might have struggled still, but they were taking me in Tristan's direction, and where he was, I needed to be.

"Put her in here," one of the trolls muttered. His light gleamed against the heavy steel door, which swung open on oiled hinges to reveal mildew covered stone walls of a tiny space. Then he shoved me inside, and all there was to see was blackness. The shackles on my arms clinked, but they were nothing compared to the walls closing in on all sides, the space barely larger than a coffin.

Stay calm! I ordered myself, but I didn't know how I was to do so when I'd been effectively buried alive. Tristan was very close, but what good was that with us both entombed and me gagged? Snot bubbles snapped and splattered against my cheeks as I struggled to breathe through my nose, through my tears, but I couldn't get enough air.

My lungs fluttered like the wings of a sparrow, and I clawed at the liquid magic filling my mouth. But it did no good. I was drowning on my own tears, on my own panic, and my elbows slammed against the walls, tearing my skin and bruising the bone.

"Cécile?"

His voice did as much as a mouthful of air to calm me, and I rested my forehead against the door, my breathing steadying.

"There's a gap at the base of your cell," he said. "Reach down, and you will feel my hand."

I dropped to my knees, scrabbling around until my fingers found his, warm and familiar. Fresh tears threatened, and I bowed my head, pressing my face against our linked hands.

"Say something. Tell me you're all right."

My nails dug into his skin, and I shook my head, strands of my hair brushing against our fingers.

He was silent, then, "They've gagged you? Squeeze once for yes, twice for no."

I squeezed once for yes.

"They told me that you killed my mother and my aunt–" He broke off. "Is it true?"

He didn't want to believe it, I could feel it. But there was doubt there, too, and I couldn't blame him for it. Maybe I'd done it in a desperate attempt to save him, or maybe I'd decided to finally have my revenge. I squeezed twice. *No.*

His relief was staggering, but short lived. "Lessa?" he asked. *No.*

Then reluctantly, "Roland?"

I didn't want to answer, because he already shouldered too much of the blame for his brother's actions.

"Cécile?"

A tear dripped off my nose. *Yes.*

He pulled his hand away from mine, his pain making my teeth ache. I shoved my fingers through the hole, my fingernails scratching against the stone, but my manacle caught on the edge, holding me back. He'd drawn away, pulled in on himself. And as I rested my cheek against the wall, very faintly, I could hear him weeping. In a moment, he'd lost nearly all his living family, the remaining two the perpetrators.

They loved you, I mouthed against the wall, wishing he could hear, though the knowing might make it worse.

"It's my fault." His voice hitched. "Because of me, the gates were left unguarded. They might not have been able to stop him, but they would have slowed him down. Given my father enough time to get to her." A sob tore from his throat. "He knew. That's why he was running to find her, and I stopped him. Stole those precious seconds that might have made a difference."

And I'd sent the Queen and the Duchesse running straight

toward Roland. If I hadn't told them Tristan was in the palace, perhaps they would've stayed hidden in the garden maze for those precious seconds. We were both complicit. But we weren't at fault, and neither was Roland.

I clawed my nails against the stone, snagging and tearing them in an attempt to get his attention. "Stop." Tristan pressed my hand against the ground. I retracted my arm, then turned my hand over and slid it back through, catching hold of him. Flattening his palm, I traced the letters. L.I.S.T.E.N.

Slowly, but methodically, I spelled out my message: *I was there. Spoke to Sylvie before she died.*

His hand stiffened at the mention of his aunt, but I continued. *Angoulême made him do it. Roland wept as he struck the blow.*

Silence.

I saw red even in the darkness, and Tristan said, "I'm going to rip his heart out for this. I'm going to make him pay."

I agreed with the sentiment, but how we would accomplish the act was another matter. Roland might not wish his brother dead, might hate the Duke as much as we did, but he was wholly under Angoulême's control, which made him an unreliable ally, to say the least. Even if he did somehow help us kill the troll who held his leash, the world would be no better off with us having our revenge. He'd be violent and uncontrollable, and without his magic, there would be no way for Tristan to stop him. Try as I might, I could not see a way through.

I squeezed Tristan's fingers tight, refusing to give up, and a shiver ran through my body. It was cold, and growing colder by the second.

She was coming.

CHAPTER 37
Tristan

The walls crackled as the moisture coating them crystallized into frost, the chill biting with every inhalation, my skin burning wherever it was exposed. But even without Winter's familiar calling card, I would've known it was her. The magic she'd taken prickled with familiarity, and I felt almost – almost – as though it would do my bidding if I bent my will to it.

"Be silent, no matter what you hear," I whispered, then I got to my feet, even as I heard a familiar clink of metal coming from Cécile's cell.

The heavy door tore from its hinges, flipping end over end until it smashed against the end of the hallway with a reverberating crash. "I see you've been practicing," I said, inclining my head to the Queen of Winter and praying Marc had bargained well.

She scowled, face fixed in the visage she'd worn when last I'd seen her. Magic slammed me against the rear of my cell, and I forced a groan into a laugh. "Careful now, I'm feeling fragile, and it would do neither of us any good if you were to accidentally kill me."

"What makes you believe it would be an accident?" she hissed, grabbing me by the shirt and jerking me forward until we were separated by mere inches.

"Because you wouldn't have risked coming here if there were

anyone else capable of releasing you from this burden," I said, prying her fingers loose one by one. Physically, I was stronger than her, and that was a very good thing.

Her lip curled. "Take it back. You may consider it a gift."

I straightened my shirt. "No."

Magic flexed in the air, and I held up one hand to stall her. "Not as a gift, but I will take it back in exchange for something from you."

"You have no ground to stand on," she said, lifting her chin. "You either take it or I kill you."

"You give me what I want," I said, "Or you remain bound to this world as surely as any troll." It had been one of the gambles I'd made stepping outside of the safety of the castle walls. One, that couched in her offer of support was the desire to see all my kind dead before my uncle could put us to use. Two, that if I eliminated grounds for an alliance – which she intended to use as a guise for killing off as many trolls as possible – she'd take my magic to do the job herself. Three, that in taking my magic into herself, which was as corrupted by iron as was my flesh, she'd be bound to this world. Corporeal, and vulnerable.

She hesitated, and I added, "Time flows different in Arcadia than it does here. How long have you been gone from your throne? Do your people still owe you their allegiance, or have you been replaced? Have you lost the war?"

Silence. "What is it that you want?"

"Your oath that you and yours will never venture into this world again."

She snorted. "Your boldness undermines your cleverness, troll. Let's see how well you bargain while the witch bleeds."

Winter wrenched open Cécile's cell door; but out of the darkness swung heavy steel shackles, one of them catching the Queen hard across the cheek, slicing it open. Blood poured down the fairy's cheek as Cécile stepped out of her cell, her face tight with focus as she bound the Queen's magic. My magic.

"Witch!" The fairy shrieked, but before she could attack Cécile, I tackled her to the ground, wrapping the manacle chain around her.

"Where are your wolves?" I whispered into her ear. "Where are your dragons and leviathans? Have they abandoned you now when you need them most?"

It was that more than the burning metal around her neck that brought fear to her eyes. The idea that she had been gone too long, and that her desire to be queen of all had rendered her queen of nothing. "You cannot go back while in the possession of my magic," I said. "You are trapped."

Her throat convulsed. "If you take your power back, I'll swear it."

I eased off her throat. "Say it."

"I swear to keep the Winter fey from this world."

I smiled. "Done."

This bargain, much like the first I'd made with her, reverberated through me like a thunderclap. But with it came the sweet ache of power, and almost immediate relief as my multitude of injuries began to heal. Releasing her from the steel wrapped around her neck, I sat back on my haunches.

Her outline blurred, the shape of a woman falling into semi-transparent mist. Then her glamour shifted, and what rose to its feet was a thing of fangs and claws, elongated pupils alien and unreadable. It snarled once, then the world tore and it sprang through the opening, which disappeared in the blink of an eye.

Cécile stood shivering, one arm braced against the wall, the other pressed against her stomach. I removed the magic that had been gagging her. "Are you all right?"

"No." She blinked once, eyes glazed. Then her knees buckled. I caught her, pulling her close even as I knew we couldn't linger. Holding her chased away any lingering need I had for the seeds; made me forget why feeling nothing had ever appealed to me. With her, whether she was in my arms or on the far side of the world, I wasn't alone. Never had that meant more than now.

"That was quick thinking with the spell," I said, needing to break the silence before I broke down. "How did you get free?"

Opening her balled-up fist, she held out a hairpin decorated with a jeweled flower. I recognized it, pain stabbing through me anew. "She fixed my hair just before…" She swallowed hard. "Take it."

It felt like punishment, but I plucked my mother's hairpin from Cécile's palm and placed it in my pocket. One final gift that seemed laden with foresight; because without it, Winter might have come out ahead in our transaction.

"Your aunt left me with some things to tell you," Cécile said, squeezing my hand.

"They will have to wait. We need to get out of Trollus before someone discovers I've recovered my magic." That no one had come down yet was concerning. Marc was supposed to have bargained for the safety of trolls and humans alike before releasing her from the circle, but what if she'd gotten free some other way? What if everyone in Trollus was dead?

I helped Cécile to her feet, then lifted her into the air. She'd been pushed to the point of death and beyond in this past day, and we weren't done yet. I needed her, and that meant conserving her strength. "I can't risk an encounter with Roland within Trollus," I said, cloaking us in illusion and dimming my light. "The city would be destroyed along with everyone in it. We'll need to lure him out to fight, but I don't know how."

"We lure him out by capturing the one who holds his strings."

I risked a glance down at my wife. She was so very pale, skin marked with livid bruises and scratches. What had happened to her in the days that she'd been gone? In the days where I hadn't cared whether she lived or died? One thing was certain: I needed to get her help immediately. "That would be a good plan, but I don't know where Angoulême is."

A faint smile cross her lips. "But I do. He's with your ancestors," she said, then she passed out in my arms.

CHAPTER 38
Cécile

I woke to the smell of wood smoke and roasting meat, my body sore, but the worst of my aches and pains gone.

"She's awake. I'll give you two a moment alone," I heard my gran say, and as I blinked away the stickiness in my eyes, Tristan leaned over me. "How do you feel?"

"Better." I looked around the interior of the cabin. "I don't remember getting here."

"That's because you slept the entire way," he replied, then twisted from side to side, cracking his back. "You're heavier than you look."

I made a face, allowing him to help me upright. "I meant, how did you find the camp?"

"I have my methods," he said, then he kissed me. "Though you might wish I hadn't. Everyone is quite angry about that stunt that you pulled." His lips found mine again, harder this time, his teeth catching my bottom lip. "What were you thinking?"

"What were *you* thinking with that stunt *you* pulled?"

He made a noise that was both agreement and exasperation, then sat next to me on the cot, his arm strong and steady behind my back. I took in his messy hair, torn clothes, and face marked with a streak of soot. His mouth was drawn into a thin line, and I wondered when I'd last seen him smile. Or if he ever would again. How much of the truth did he know about his family? And if he knew nothing, would me telling him do any good?

"Are *you* all right?" I asked.

He inhaled softly, and I knew he was thinking of deflecting my question, but instead he shook his head, a quick jerk from side to side. *Not all right.*

"Your aunt," I said. "She told me things about your father–"

"I can't," he interrupted. "Not now. I just... I don't want to think about it. Him. Them."

My heart ached along with his, knowing full well what it felt like to lose a parent. My mother might have died years ago, but I hadn't known that until Anushka revealed the truth. The pain had been fresh and horrible, and how much worse would it have been if I'd lost my father, too. Or my gran?

"I'm sorry," I whispered, then twisted around so that my knees were on either side of him. Wrapping my arms around his neck, I pulled him close, feeling his breath warm against my collarbone. I carefully pulled through the tangles in his hair with my fingers while I waited to see if he wanted to talk, knowing better than to press him. He knew that I felt his hurt, and maybe that was enough.

His hand slipped under the bottom of my shirt, palm hot against the small of my back, his other hand tangling in my hair. Clinging to me as though I were the strong one.

And maybe I was.

"I wanted him dead," he said, his voice muffled. "I planned for it."

He had. It seemed like a hundred years ago that we'd stood in the stables in Trollus and I'd blackmailed him into telling me the truth in exchange for the return of the plans for the stone tree. Looking back, he seemed so much younger, so convinced of his emotional fortitude because it had never been tested. Not really. And now, whatever naiveté he might have once possessed was gone, burned away by pain and fear, loss and guilt. No longer a boy and a prince, but a man and, whether he liked it or not, a king.

Which I supposed, whether I liked it or not, made me a queen.

"You didn't plan for this," I said. "Angoulême did. And we need to make him pay for what he's done." I leaned back so that we were eye to eye. "With Roland controlling Trollus, the Duke will believe we're on the run. That he's hunting us. But he's wrong."

I felt Tristan's anger chase away his grief, and he lifted me up and set me back on the cot. "I'll get the others."

I retrieved the steaming cup my gran had left for me, and, moments later, Tristan returned with the twins, along with my father and Jérôme.

"You going to live?" my father asked, and when I nodded, he added, "Good. I wouldn't want you to die before I had the chance to wallop you like the idiot child you are."

"You should let me do it, Louis," Victoria said, crossing her arms. "It will hurt more."

"I—"

"Shut-up, Cécile," Victoria said. "I'm not interested in hearing your excuses. You took advantage of our trust and ran off without so much as leaving a note to say where you'd gone. We thought Winter had caught you. Or the Duke. Then we tracked your horse to the labyrinth just in time to watch it collapse. Do you know what it was like for us watching the sky for Marc's signal that Tristan was dead or near to it because you'd gotten yourself killed?"

I licked my lips and glanced at Tristan, but the look in his eyes told me I was on my own in this. "I know. I'm sorry."

"Sorry?" Both Victoria's eyebrows rose. "You think sorry is going to make up for leaving us to watch your grandmother weep for fear of what had become of you? Not even close, Cécile. You're going to have to earn our forgiveness."

"I understand," I said, knowing better than to ask how I

might accomplish that. Just as I knew better than to try to justify my actions. What I'd learned had been worth the risk, but that didn't mean I was exempt from the consequences of my actions.

Chris came running in then, bending over as he struggled to catch his breath. "Came back as soon as I heard Cécile was here." His eyes landed on Tristan, and his face broke into a grin. "Well, if it isn't the prettiest prince to ever walk the Isle. So glad you could finally join us."

"Necessity," Tristan replied. "As you can see, my attire has been woefully neglected since my half-trained manservant abandoned me to a greater cause."

Chris's face turned bright red, then he laughed and slung an arm around Tristan's shoulder. "How fortunate that you make even rags look good, Your Highness."

"It's Your Majesty, now. Although I suppose Roland might contest my claim." Tristan's tone was light, but Chris seemed to sense that congratulations were not in order.

"Don't let it go to your head," he said, taking a swig of a wine skin before passing it to Tristan. "I've trouble enough finding hats to fit your ego as it is."

Then they all turned expectantly to me. "What's the plan?" I asked. "When do we leave?"

"As soon as you tell us where we're going," Tristan responded.

Unease prickled over my skin. "Didn't Martin tell you…" I trailed off.

"Martin isn't here," Tristan said, then turned to Vincent and Victoria, who both shook their heads.

"He was with me when we learned what had happened to you," I said, setting aside my cup. "He was supposed to come here and tell you where Angoulême's hiding – your family's tombs," I added, glancing at Tristan. "I gave him directions to find the twins and told him the signals to use."

"I don't know this Martin fellow," Chris said. "But given he's never been outside of Trollus, there is every possibility he's wandering around lost in the woods."

"Or that he's run afoul of someone he shouldn't have, and they know our location," Vincent said, scratching his arm. "We may need to move our camp."

They all argued about where Martin might be and what he might be doing, but I barely heard them, my ears full of a strange ringing.

Tristan touched my arm. "Cécile?"

My mouth was dry. "He was in love with Élise."

Tristan hissed softly between his teeth, and everyone went silent.

"I promised him revenge," I said. "That you would see Angoulême dead for what he did to her."

"And in discovering I'd lost my magic, he likely believes he's the only one left to deliver that revenge." Tristan rattled off a string of profanity. "We need to go. Now. Cécile, you are sure this is where the Duke is hiding?"

I explained how Martin and I had come to the conclusion based on Lessa's words.

Victoria rubbed her chin, eyes on the map Chris had spread flat. "Makes sense. The tombs are deep in the mountains and are easily defended."

"And difficult to reach, as I recall." Tristan pressed a gloved finger against the map. "One needs magic – or significant climbing skills – to reach them. It isn't a place you just stumble upon. Chris, can you guide us there?"

My friend nodded. "I'll ready the supplies. Who's going?"

"Us three and you," Tristan replied, then he chewed on his bottom lip.

I was about to voice exactly what I thought about being left behind, when he added, "And Cécile."

My gran made a noise of protest that was seconded by my father. "She's dead on her feet already. You trying to kill her, boy?"

"We'll all be dead if we don't succeed in this," Tristan said, his voice betraying none of the guilt my father's accusation had instigated. "It would be one thing if merely killing the Duke was an option, but we need to capture him. To use him to lure Roland out of Trollus to a place where I can engage him without fear of casualties. And our success may depend on Cécile's power."

"Then I'm coming, too," my gran said. "I'm not powerless myself."

Tristan nodded absently. There was already a plan forming in his mind. I could see it; could feel it. And there was some comfort in knowing that. I should've known that Martin had no intention of sitting idly – that he would've gone after the Duke himself. But I'd been so caught up in my concern for Tristan that I'd been blind to anything but my own plight. I prayed we'd catch Martin before we reached the tombs, or that he'd change his mind and come back. And though it pained me to do so, I prayed that if he managed to reach the Duke, that he'd fail in his quest. Because if Angoulême was killed, Roland would be free to do what he wanted.

And all the world would burn.

CHAPTER 39
Tristan

"What is with you trolls and mountains?" Chris muttered, rubbing his hands together to warm them.

"We like impressive things," I said, resting my elbows on the rocky outcropping. Dawn was upon us, and, just then, the sun crested the horizon, illuminating the faces of two towering statues of a king and queen seated on thrones. Though time had worn the stone, the crown resting on the king's brow was deeply familiar to me from the countless times I'd seen it on my father's head.

Chris whistled through his teeth. "Relatives of yours?"

I nodded. "They were the first. He was the brother of the Summer King, and both were immortal until the iron bound them to this world. Even then, they lived and ruled for many hundreds of years before succumbing."

"And the pass leading to the tombs runs between them?"

"Yes," I said. "Give the sun a few more moments, and we'll see it."

The line of golden light slowly edged its way down the statues, revealing the queen's elaborate jewelry, the king's embroidered coat, a scepter resting across his knees, and a blade across hers. And then it revealed something else.

"What is that?" Chris asked, leaning forward.

It was a bundle of fabric suspended across the mouth of the ravine between the two statues, the loose ends of the material flapping in the breeze. Whatever was contained within it was large, and my skin crawled. "Something," I murmured, "that we were meant to find. Stay close."

I shielded us from sight and from any form of attack as we moved across the open stretch, the ground still dark until the sun rose a little higher. There was only one set of footprints, but Chris insisted on poking the ground in front of us with his walking stick. "Ain't falling for my own trick," he muttered.

I didn't argue. Despite the frigid temperature, sweat was trickling down his brow, and there was no missing the staccato beat of his heart. If doing something eased his nerves, so much the better.

The bundle swayed on a strong gust of wind, droplets raining down from the soaked fabric. My eyes followed the drips as the sun crested the mountain behind us, bathing our path with light. Beneath the bundle was a circle of crimson, and as the breeze reversed, the metallic tang of blood filled my nostrils.

"God in heaven," Chris whispered, and I debated sending him back to camp and out of harm's way. Except with Angoulême, Lessa, and Roland still alive, was anywhere safe? Chris knew the risks, but he'd agreed to come anyway. He wouldn't thank me for sending him away.

"Whoever it is can't have been dead long," Chris said, stopping just shy of the circle of blood. "Doesn't take long for a body to freeze in this weather."

I knew who it was, and, catching a slight tremble of motion from the bundle, I knew he wasn't dead. "This is either a warning, a trap, or both," I said. "Be ready."

Slicing through the magic suspending the drenched bundle, I lowered it to the snow, the fabric falling open as I relinquished my hold, limbs spilling out with it.

Chris staggered away and retched into the snow. I wanted

to do the same, but instead I swallowed the burning bile and approached the dying troll. "Martin?"

The librarian didn't answer, his open eyes twitching, but unseeing. Unconscious. Which was a small mercy, because what had been done to him was a testament to what even a lesser troll could endure. But there was no coming back. Not from this.

Kneeling next to him, I pulled out a knife. A blow to the heart would end his suffering. I owed him that. I lifted the blade, then his eyes snapped into focus. "No!"

I lowered my arm. "Martin, you don't want to survive this."

His gaze was full of the knowledge of what had been done to him, but still he said, "Not yet. Not until Angoulême is dead." He shifted awkwardly in the snow, back arching and head twisting from side to side in a futile struggle to move. "He has to pay for what he did to her."

"He will," I said. "I promise he'll pay for it." The air pulsed slightly with the power of my oath, and he settled back, eyes on me. "Let me help you," I said.

"No," Martin whispered. "Not until he's dead. I need to see him dead."

I exhaled softly, knowing I couldn't deny such a request, then turned to Chris, who was still on his hands and knees. "I need you to take him to Cécile's grandmother. He shouldn't be that heavy without–" I broke off as Chris blanched. But then he nodded.

"Cauterize them," Martin whispered. "I don't want to bleed out while I wait."

For the first time in my life, my magic faltered. Trying again to raise heat, I swallowed hard as it failed again.

"Cécile's braver than you," Martin said around clenched teeth. "She wouldn't flinch."

"I know." Then fire burned in the palm of my hand, and the stench of scorched blood filled the air. Martin screamed once, then fainted, and when I was finished, I vomited in the snow.

"Go," I said to Chris, and without looking to see if he complied, I followed the trail of Martin's blood into the ravine.

The walls rose up to either side of me, cut sheer by a stream that had run this way since before trolls walked this world. At first, the rock was unadorned, but as I rounded the first bend, the carvings began. Princes and princesses, dukes and duchesses, their expressions austere and eerily similar to my own. Many of them I recognized, but as I drew closer, the elements had washed away all but the suggestions of faces. It didn't matter: they were my family. All of them. And Angoulême had no right to be in this place.

The ravine snaked its way between the two mountains, abruptly opening into a wide circular space, with a third peak at its far side. At the center lay a small lake frozen solid, and all around rose statues of the kings and queens from before the Fall. Their eyes were set with glass that had once been filled with troll-fire, and it seemed they were all watching me, fixing me with silent scrutiny. The entire space hummed with magic, the ground coated with it and the air so thick with it that it seemed scarcely breathable.

But there was no sign of life.

Maybe he's gone, a little voice whispered my head. *Maybe you're too late.*

But I didn't think I was. The tombs were the most defensible place on the Isle, and Angoulême could hide within them long enough for Roland and Lessa to arrive. Little did he know, we planned to be long gone by the time they got here. When I went up against my brother, it would be in a place of my choosing.

On my terms.

I walked up to the edge of the lake and stared across. Twin falls poured down the mountain's face, and between them stood a door twice my height and carved of solid stone. It was closed.

I eyed the track of footprints and blood leading around the right half of the lake, then at the untouched snow around the left. With little tendrils of magic, I searched the statues for anyone who might be hidden behind their bulky stone shapes, and opened my senses to any troll of power who might be near, but it was impossible to tell when the air was teeming with so much latent magic.

Which was very likely their intent.

The shield encircling me was as strong as any I'd ever used, but it gave me little comfort. Angoulême was clever, and underestimating him might see me dead. I knew something would happen, but not what. And not when. And not where.

Exhaling softly, I stepped onto the frozen surface of the lake and began my way toward the door. I was about halfway across when I felt the surge of magic as it resolved toward its purpose. I started to run, but it was too late.

The lake exploded around me in liquid fire, and the world fell out from beneath me.

The weight of the magic shielding my body dragged me down into the depths of the lake, bubbles from the boiling water obscuring my vision as I descended further from the surface.

Clever bastard.

Lessening my shield enough for buoyancy to pull me back up put me at risk of cooking alive, and it left me vulnerable to whatever attacks Angoulême had planned for when I resurfaced.

I lashed out with ropes of magic, blindly aiming for one of the statues, but they slammed against a shield at the surface of the lake, the impact driving me further into the depths. I struck out again, harder, but I had no leverage, and the motion sent my sphere tumbling, disorienting me until it slammed against the lake bed. Bracing against the ground, I flung the full force of my power at the shield, destroying it with explosion that made the earth tremble.

My ropes of power swung through the air, searching for an

anchor, but Angoulême knocked at them with his own power, preventing them from finding purchase. I fought blindly, earning a concussive blast each time the magics collided.

Louder.

While my ropes continued to flail above, I turned my attention to the rock beneath my feet, channeling heat into the earth until it glowed brilliant red, the water boiling and turning to steam in a violent blast. I launched out of the lake under the cover of the white cloud of mist, landing in a crouch on the edge of the now dry lake.

A whistling razor of power sank into my shield, then another and another, all coming from different directions. Pulling out my sword, I coated the steel with magic and listened, swinging hard, not just deflecting, but destroying the invisible weapons with explosions of silver sparks.

Then I turned on the door.

"Come out, come out," I crooned, slipping strands of magic through the cracks to magnify my voice to a deafening level. Lifting a hand, I scratched my finger through the air, mimicking the magic I used to claw at the door. The sound was horrible, and with a smile, I repeated the gesture. Then I punched out with my fist, and a giant crack formed in the granite. Again, and a large piece split off, smashing as it hit the ground.

But I couldn't draw this out much longer. He knew I was toying with him.

"I'd rather not destroy the last piece of our history remaining outside of Trollus," I said, walking forward until I stood a few paces from the entrance. "Perhaps you might do the honorable thing and come out rather than hiding in yet another hole."

"I think not, Your Highness." The Duke's voice filtered out on threads of magic, and if he feared his imminent demise, his tone did not betray it. "I'm quite comfortable where I am. Did you find my gift, by the way? Why you bothered sending such a weakling was beyond me – especially one who knew so much."

Who could say what the librarian had told him under torture? But two could play at that game. "I haven't seen the man in months, and I most certainly didn't send him to do my dirty work. He was here to settle a different score. You are not a popular troll, Angoulême."

Silence.

"Curious how I found you? I'll tell you," I said, not waiting for an answer. "It was straight from Lessa's lips." I adjusted the sleeves of my coat. "My sister is a double-crossing liar, Your Grace, and yet you've left her in charge of your puppet prince. It's unlike you to be so trusting, but perhaps trust is a privilege you reserve for those who warm your bed."

All I could hear was the whistle of the wind, and a bead of sweat trickled down my spine. What if he suspected our plan? What if even now, he was setting a trap? But then he spoke. "You've always been over fond of your own voice, *Tristan*."

"We all have our faults." I let the smile fall from my face. "She had you fooled for a time, though, didn't she? Made you believe she was Anaïs, which I'm sure was infuriating. But she convinced you of the merit of letting the ruse play out, revealed a long game beyond what you'd ever imagined."

Staring at the cracked granite, I let down the walls between me and the hurt my friend's name always conjured. "You know it was Lessa who killed Anaïs, not my father. Not even on his orders, though I'm sure she said otherwise. Still trust her?" I paused to let that sink in. "You're a fool if you do. She's clever, and willing to go further than either of us to get what she wants."

"She lived in my home her entire life, you blathering fool," Angoulême snarled. "Do you think I don't understand how her little mind works? How to dangle the carrot? How to use her like a tool?"

The only time the Duke lost his temper was when he was not in control. "As you say, Your Grace, your family *owned* her for most of her life. Used her as a servant, and, I think, as your whore. How long do you think she'll suffer you to live once she is queen?"

"She's no fool. She knows she needs me to control Roland."

I drew on my power, letting it seep through the cracks in the granite, knowing how it would prickle and burn on his skin. "And yet courtesy of my dearest sister, here I am."

They had to be inside by now. I could feel Cécile moving, her nerves and anticipation. But was she ready? If I stalled any longer, Angoulême would know I was up to something, and that would put everything in jeopardy.

Sighing, I polished the last remaining button on my coat. "Enough of this, Your Grace. You know Roland won't make it in time, so quit the stalling."

A chuckle rolled through the mountains. "No, I don't suppose he will be arriving *here* anytime soon. But I trust you're clever enough to understand the consequences of killing me and letting the boy off his leash, and that you will act accordingly. I've taken my own precautions – if you try to force your way in, everyone inside – including me – will die."

Including Cécile and my closest friends.

"Unless you've grown wings," he continued, "by the time you made it back to the coast, all you'll find is a city full of corpses."

Unease snaked down my spine as I parsed his words. "Neither you nor Roland wish to see Trollus destroyed."

"No," Angoulême said, his voice full of mockery. "But then again, Roland isn't in Trollus." He laughed, and I heard the tap tap of his cane against the stone floor of the tomb as he retreated into his depths. "I suggest, Your Highness, that you start running now."

CHAPTER 40
Cécile

The twins' mining skills had come in handy, as they'd easily drilled a tunnel into the rear of the tombs under the cover of Tristan's attack.

"Where did they put the bodies?" I asked, running a finger over the dusty statue lying prone on an altar of carved marble and glass. My finger left a streak of gleaming gold in its wake, and I bent low over the figure's face, marveling at the level of detail, from the realistic swell of the troll's lips to the slight creases at the corners of his sightless diamond eyes.

"That *is* the body," Victoria replied, smiling slightly as I recoiled, shoving my offending hand into my pocket. "They dip them in liquid gold after they die."

"Still?" For some reason, the notion horrified me: being encased in metal for all of eternity.

"Maybe that's why Thibault ate so much in his later years," Vincent said, coming back from his assessment of the piece of stone sealing the room. "He wanted to ensure his final resting place was worth the most."

Victoria laughed, but I remained silent. Thibault had been a villain, but he deserved respect. "Do not speak ill of the dead," I said, but my words were drowned out by a series of percussive blasts.

Vincent took advantage of the noise to shift the stone blocking the entrance, and then he cautiously eased out before stepping back in and nodding.

Sandwiched between Vincent and Victoria, I stepped out into the corridor, taking in what I could of our surroundings. I'd expected it to be dark and close, but much like the chamber we'd just left, the ceilings were high and painted with brilliant depictions of both trolls and fairies alike. The floors were dusty, but they were as smooth as polished tile, and railings inlaid with golden vines ran up both sides of the hallways.

Though Tristan had plumbed the depths of his seemingly endless store of knowledge, all he'd been able to tell us was that the tombs were a vast multilevel maze of chambers and corridors that were illuminated with natural light through the use of tiny shafts and mirrors placed just so. More mirrors sat above the golden railings, and though we were encased in as much rock as we ever were in Trollus, the halls practically glowed with sunlight.

Dusty and faded, the tombs remained beautiful. And entirely wasted, I thought, on the dead.

"This way," Vincent muttered, eyeing the compass in his hand. The Duke would be engaged with fighting Tristan at the entrance, so that's where we needed to go. Magic coating our feet to muffle the sound, we ran as swiftly as we dared, passing great stone slabs blocking the tombs of the royalty of old, names and carved likeness marking who was interred within.

"Come out, come out," a voice thundered through the corridors, followed with a horrifying scratching.

Panic flooded my veins, and turning, I went to run. And collided with Victoria. "It's Tristan," she said, wincing. "Aggressive use of acoustics, but I'm sure that's purposeful. Though in irritating the Duke, he's likely to render the three of us deaf."

We crept forward more slowly, listening to the one-sided

conversation, Tristan doing his best to bait Angoulême. To keep him interested.

But of the Duke's responses, we could hear nothing.

Until we did. "Unless you've grown wings, by the time you made it back to the coast, all you'll find is a city full of corpses."

Vincent held up a hand, and I extracted the vial of blood I needed to perform the spell and handed it to him. Leaning forward, I peered around my friend's bulk. We were at the top of a sprawling curved staircase, which, from what I could see, was one of three winding down to a vaulted foyer lit with dozens of troll-lights. Angoulême stood in front of a great set of doors, one of which was cracked. He stood alone in a pool of blood and gore. Which didn't feel at all right. Where were his followers?

"Neither you nor Roland wish to see Trollus destroyed," Tristan said.

"No," Angoulême replied. "But then again, Roland isn't in Trollus." He laughed, tapping the tip of his cane against the floor, and I swore I heard the same sound come from somewhere else. "I suggest, Your Highness, that you start running now."

I was still looking around for the other source of the tapping when Vincent stepped out onto the staircase to get the angle right for a throw. He made it down three steps, then the stone exploded beneath him.

Victoria jerked me backwards, magic shielding us against the rain of razor sharp shards of rock, but it did nothing to stop her terrified scream from piercing my ears. "Vincent! Vincent!"

We both scrambled toward the shattered ledge, and leaned over, peering down into the dust. Vincent lay in a pile of rubble beneath us.

And Angoulême was gone.

CHAPTER 41
Cécile

"Vincent! No, please, no." Tears cut tracks through the dust coating Victoria's face as she moved to leap off the ledge.

I grabbed her arm, heaving with all my might. "Be careful! There might be more traps, and we won't be able to help him if we set them off and kill ourselves."

For a heartbeat, I thought she meant to shrug me off and jump, but instead she scrubbed a gloved hand across her face and nodded. Lashing magic around a pillar, she flung out her hand and a glowing ladder uncoiled into the air, tumbling down to hang above her brother. She descended with impressive speed, and though I knew it cost her to do so, hesitated just above the rubble, her magic carefully testing for any hidden pitfalls before she stepped onto the ground.

I scuttled down after her, my heart sinking at the look on her face as I found my balance on the shattered staircase. Vincent's eyes were blank and unseeing, the pale stone beneath his head drenched with blood. Part of me refused to believe it was him: the twins were invincible, untouchable. Not... this. Vincent had known what he was doing – had been shielded and wary. And yet...

Gasping, panicked breath filled my ears, and it took me a moment to realize it was my own. *Keep yourself together,*

I silently screamed, clenching my hands so tightly my fingers ached.

"Cécile?" The plea in Victoria's voice cut me to the core, and I knew if he died that she would not last long. Their bond was natural, not magical, but it ran just as deep. Deeper.

Swallowing hard, I said, "I'll try," even as I knew the delay in our pursuit of the Duke would carry a price. That to save one life, I was putting many more at risk. But that was the choice I'd always make.

Tucking the vial into my pocket, I pulled off my gloves and pressed one palm to the pool of blood and the other to my friend's cheek. Closing my eyes, I delved into the alien magic, feeling it curl and rise into my fingers. But it was faltering, fading. And even as I pulled, I knew it was hopeless. Knew he was too far gone.

"Damn it!" Grabbing Victoria's arm, I pulled out my knife and sliced it across her sleeve, cutting through fabric and flesh. Hot blood ran across my fingers, the magic within it eerily similar to that which I had just touched.

No, not similar. The same.

Victoria sagged against me, and my fragile control slipped and a sob tore from my throat. "I'll get Tristan," I said, knowing he was just beyond the door. "He'll be able to help."

"No." Victoria pulled me back down. "Angoulême has the whole place rigged. If you open the doors, this room will collapse. You need to go – you can't let him get away."

"Cécile?" Tristan's voice filled the room, and I stumbled to my feet. "Can he hear me?" I asked Victoria. She gave a weak nod, and I moved over to the door, careful not to touch it lest I set off the magic.

"Tristan, the twins are hurt and Angoulême's escaped," I said, scanning the two remaining staircases leading up, and the one large one that lead down. The Duke we'd seen standing in the foyer had been an illusion, a projection of some sort. But I'd heard the echo of his cane tapping. He'd been close. Which way had he gone?

"How bad?"

I glanced back at the twins, Vincent unmoving and his sister slumped next to him. "They're dying."

His jolt of anguish sent a fresh crop of tears down my face. "Move back, Cécile. I'm going to break the door."

"No!" I shouted the word, and it echoed through the cavernous room. "Victoria said it's rigged to collapse.

"Stay where you are," he shouted. "I'll come in the back."

Retreating back to my friends, I pulled the vial of blood out of my pocket and tilted it from side to side, watching the liquid move. Then I dropped to my knees next to them.

"Go after Angoulême, Cécile." Victoria lifted her face. "If there was ever time for one of your mad risky schemes, this is it. If he gets out of the tombs somehow, Tristan won't be able to find him. He's too clever. Far more clever than we ever gave him credit for." Her eyes went to the vial in my hand. "You have what you need to stop him, but you need to be quick about it."

"Yes, I do," I said, then I closed my fist on the glass. It shattered, and Tristan's magic came to my call. Slapping my hand against Vincent's cheek, I shoved the magic into him, praying it would know what to do. Praying that it would be enough.

It was like watching a flower bloom. As I stared, it seemed as though nothing was happening, but when I blinked, his injuries had healed a little more, the gruesome wound to his skull sealing over until only the mess of blood in his black hair indicated he'd been hurt at all. His breathing steadied, and I withdrew my hand, wiping it on my trousers. "Follow when you can."

Victoria squeezed Vincent's hand, then stood. "I'm coming with you."

"He'll expect that," I said. "Which is why you're staying with Vincent. I have a plan." Moving to the center of the foyer,

I dropped a rock, listening to how the sound bounced off the walls. Moving to the left, I dropped another rock. Then another. I knew acoustics. And I knew which way Angoulême had gone.

The lower levels were filled with the crypts of lesser Montignys: princes and princesses, lords and ladies of various ranks, but I paid them no mind as I ran, following the tracks in the dust as I was sure the Duke expected me to do. This was a trap.

And it was set for me.

But Angoulême wouldn't kill me, because he needed me as a hostage to get past Tristan and the twins. Which was fine, because for my plan to work, I needed to get close.

Gripping my knife tight, I used my other hand to muffle my false sobs as I minced forward, carefully peering around each corner before I proceeded forward. It was much darker on this level, long expanses of blackness stretching between each of the clever little skylights. My heart thundered in my chest as I made my way further and further into the mountain. What if I'd been wrong about the direction he'd gone? What if he'd looped back to dispatch the twins while they were weak?

I stepped past a slab of rock blocking the entrance to a crypt, and magic lashed around my waist, jerking me toward the hard surface. I shrieked, certain I was about to be dashed to pieces, but then I passed through the illusion and was slammed against the floor between two altars, burning ropes pinning my wrists and ankles to the floor. The blow knocked the air from my lungs, but as I was gasping for breath, the first thing I noticed was the smell of unwashed body. Then Angoulême was in my face, his eyes wild and hair disheveled.

"Stupid, blubbering fool!" he hissed, his breath vile.

I turned my head, sobbing, "You killed my friends. You killed them." The crypt was littered with clutter, rotting scraps of food in a corner and the stench of waste. He'd been living in here. Hiding in here.

Alone.

"They deserved it." He plucked the knife from my clenched fist, tossing it out into the corridor. "Foolish half-blood-loving idiots. Just like you. You'll deserve it when I finally slit your throat. Now where is it? Where is it?"

His hands roughly searched my body, tearing at my clothes and bruising my skin, leaving not a square inch unscathed. I cringed and wept. "Where is what?"

"The blood!" Drops of spittle sprayed across my face. "I know you have it, you filthy witch."

"It broke," I sniveled. "It spilled. Look at my hands."

He launched himself back and away, watching me like I was some sort of venomous snake. Then he snatched up a wine skin and poured the contents over my palms, washing away all traces of Tristan's magic. Only then did he relax, sitting on his haunches, silver eyes fixed on me. "Where is he?"

"Outside." Snot bubbled around my nose, and his lip turned up with disgust. As though he were one to talk. From the smell, he hadn't washed since the day he left Trollus. Seeing him this way was unnerving, all the polished veneer gone, a strange fearful madness in its place. "He'll kill you," I whispered. "He'll kill you for this."

He twitched, ever so slightly. "Oh, I doubt that, Cécile. There are consequences to my death, and now that I have his precious little peach, he'll do nothing at all. You, you, you!" He was on his knees over me. "You are such a wondrous creature, because you make him weak. You make him stupid. You'll be the death of him."

I shook my head and looked away. "No."

"Yes. Now, up-up. Time to go." He dragged me to my feet, his cane still firmly gripped in one hand. He didn't need it – he had no infirmity – and it wasn't a weapon. But he always had it as he walked sedately, carefully, through Trollus. I marked his high collar, his hands gloved with thick leather. Nothing but his face exposed.

"Where is everyone?" I struggled futilely against his magic.

"There's no one here but you and me." His smile was all teeth. "Unlike Tristan, I do not put my trust in weaklings."

He'd cracked, I realized. A lifetime of deception, of suspicion, of not being able to trust a single soul, had finally gotten to him alone in this place of the dead. "Except Lessa," I said. "She told us where to find you."

He twitched again. "Lies." And in one smooth motion, he flipped me over his shoulder. "We are leaving, now."

I bit down on the inside of my cheeks, hard, and then on my tongue. My mouth filled with the metallic taste of blood.

"You're lucky you didn't trigger one of my traps like your clown," he said. "I've spent a lifetime coming up with the best ways to maim."

I said nothing, keeping my mouth closed, slowly filling with blood.

"They are everywhere, as your friend Martin knows."

The glee in his tone filled me with fury. Angoulême hurt people – hurt my friends – not just to accomplish what he wanted, but because he enjoyed it. He was sick and twisted, and he needed to be stopped.

Fury running hot through my veins, and I twisted my body, biting down hard on his neck, my blood flowing into the wound as I tore out a chunk of flesh. He howled and flung me, my body rolling and bouncing across the floor. I cried out in pain, but before he could attack, I shouted, "You kill me, you bleed to death, Angoulême."

He froze, hand clapped to the wound on his neck, blood flowing between his fingers. My aim had been good. Lethal.

"Just like Pénélope," I said, ignoring the screaming pain of my body as I pushed onto my knees. "You're afflicted. Even the tiniest of wounds is a labor to heal, and that is no tiny injury. Especially given it is full of my nasty, iron-filled human blood." I grinned, feeling the crimson droplets running down my chin.

"You. Need. Me."

He hissed and reached for me, and I recoiled, falling backwards. I heard him shout just before my elbow impacted and something burst hot beneath it. Magic coated my skin as the air filled with fire. It was only for a second, then it was gone, and I could not see.

And I could not breathe.

There was no air. My chest heaved as my lungs dragged in mouthful after mouthful of nothingness. Hands snatched me up, and I was moving, but I didn't care.

I couldn't breathe.

I couldn't breathe.

I couldn't...

CHAPTER 42
Cécile

I opened my eyes, blinking away the bits of frost on my lashes, droplets running in cold little rivulets down my cheeks. The night sky loomed above me, vast, unending, and empty. I frowned as I considered the last, the notion of it troubling me with its wrongness. "Where are the stars?"

"We see other worlds in a different way."

The voice startled me, and I rolled onto my hands and knees, sinking deep into powdery snow that sucked the heat from my hands. I lifted my face. "Where am I?"

Tristan's many times great-uncle, the King of Summer, smiled at me, but the radiance he'd exuded the first time we met was nowhere to be seen. "You know."

I did. A blast of wind, icier than was ever felt in my world, raked at my hair. "Winter."

He nodded once, gesturing outwards. There was no source of illumination that I could see, but everything around glowed with an unearthly and pearlescent light. Massive peaks encircled the barren plain on which we stood, their tips capped with white like a frosted crown. Snowflakes rose instead of fell, dancing upward into the void above, and as I turned my head, my stomach clenched.

Dizziness swept through me as I stared at the palace in the

distance, identical to that the Queen had built in Trianon in everything but size. A river of ice flowed through its center, massive burgs rolling and smashing against each other as they traveled. It was the only sign of motion. The only sign of life.

"Why am I here?" I asked.

"Because I once gave you a name."

I flinched; and, because I was afraid of what he might demand of me, I asked instead, "Why now?"

"The opportunity presented itself."

No answer. I licked my lips. They were smooth and unchapped beneath my tongue, and my hair hung in a long braid over my shoulder. I tugged at its tip, choosing to focus on this insignificant detail rather than the impossible setting surrounding me.

"You are as you imagine yourself to be," he said, answering my unspoken question.

"Because it's a dream," I mused. "Or am I really here?"

"Much can happen in the space between two heartbeats." Clasping my arm, he pulled me to my feet. An orb appeared in his hand, and he held it out to me. "Look."

The orb was warm and moist against my palm, and I cringed as a lid peeled back to reveal an eye. It blinked again, and ignoring my disgust, he guided my hand closer to my face. "Look."

I stared into the elongated pupil, and suddenly, I was far above the ground. Soaring. Swooping. Flying. Beneath me raged a battle unlike anything I'd ever seen. A wave of gold and green crashed against a wall of frosted blackness, a chaos of creatures that defied description: man and beast, and everything in between. Fighting, warring, as far as the eye could see. It was dawn and dusk; the ebb and flow of the seasons. But as I circled above, there was no mistaking that the battle line was moving. That the dawn was being pushed back.

"Your world lured my people from me," he said into my ear.

"The iron bound them, and the witch locked them away, whole bloodlines lost. I would have them back."

I lowered my hand, swaying as my vision was once again my own. "That's impossible. The trolls are mortal – they cannot pass between worlds. And if there was a way to change that, they'd have found it."

The orb disappeared, replaced by a book that was deeply familiar to me. "I lost this," I said, letting the cover fall open. "It's at the bottom of the lake."

"Do you still need it?"

I didn't. Not really. It had been in my possession long enough that I knew nearly all of the spells by heart. Well enough to know that none of them could do what he wanted.

"It will take someone or something more knowledgeable and powerful than I am to accomplish this task," I pleaded, knowing what it meant to be dealt an impossible request. "I'm only a human witch."

"You limit yourself," he said. "Sometimes, one must become the unimaginable."

I shook my head. "You ask too much."

"Your debt has been called due, Cécile de Montigny," he said, my name ringing in my ears like a bell. "I will have all my people back in Arcadia, and you will make it happen."

And before I could press him as to how I might accomplish such a feat, my body was wrenched back into blackness.

"Breathe, you cursed weakling of a human!"

Sunlight burned into my retinas, and I heaved a mouthful of air into my lungs before knocking Angoulême's hands away from my chest so that I could roll over and heave my guts out onto the damp earth. Shoving aside all thought of Summer, I propped myself up on one elbow, the water soaking into my sleeve warm, mist rising up in a ghostly cloud that partially obscured the broken statues surrounding the muddy lakebed.

The Duke was crouched next to me, blood still pouring from the circular wound on his neck.

"Heal this," he snarled, "or on my last breath, I'll command Roland to destroy the world and everyone you love."

"You could've asked nicely," I whispered, my throat raw. Before he could respond, I slapped my hand against the wound, took hold of his magic, and bent it to my will. It was formidable, greater than all I'd used save that of Anaïs and Tristan, but it struggled at the task. Halting. Fluttering. Resisting. But slowly the injury closed beneath my hand.

He slumped, taking several measured breaths before fumbling about in the mud for his cane. What for a troll of his power should have been nothing had drained him to exhaustion. On what must have been sheer willpower alone, he rose to his feet, then reached down and jerked me up. "We're going."

"I don't think so."

Angoulême turned, and Tristan's fist caught him square in the face, sending him sprawling back to land unconscious in a puddle.

Tristan lowered his arm, his breath coming in swift pants as though he'd been running hard. He squeezed his eyes shut, and when he opened them, they were gleaming liquid bright. I stumbled the few paces between us, collapsing into his arms. We stood there in silence, the mist collecting in little beads on our faces, the weight of what we'd accomplished rendering us speechless. We'd caught Angoulême. But now...

"Roland's in either Trianon or Courville, I don't know which." Tristan turned his head in the direction of the coast, though it was impossible to see anything from where we stood. The cities were in opposite directions, and if we chose wrong, the chances of us making it to the other in time to save it were slim. *Stones and sky,* I thought, *there's little enough hope of us making it in time if we choose right.*

My sense of accomplishment fell away as I turned back to

the already stirring Duke. Even lying there in the mud, bound with Tristan's magic and cut off from his power, he still had the upper hand. And as his silver eyes flickered open and met mine, I knew he knew it.

"Did you know," Angoulême said, "that Roland wept when I told him you would have to die for him to be king? The same when I told him he would have to kill your father, which is why I sent him after Matilde instead. Too much of a chance he'd hesitate and Thibault would finally grow the stones to put an end to him." A cruel smile grew on his face. "For all that he knows I cannot lie, he refuses to believe you'll hurt him. The innocence of childhood, I suppose."

It was the worst thing he could have said. His jaw bulged as Tristan jammed magic between his teeth to shut him up before encasing him in a black box, probably as much to protect him as to closet him away. Then he twisted away from me and strode over to one of the broken statues. He took one deep breath, then another. Then in a blur of motion, he punched the stone, a piece breaking off even as he swore and doubled over.

I watched in silence, knowing what it felt like to prefer the rush of physical pain to the relentless and inescapable press of emotional anguish.

"This is why, Cécile," he shouted, rounding on me. "This is why I didn't want the curse broken. Because this is my life now – running up and down this blasted Isle trying to keep my people from harming yours. Roland will be the first I have to put down, but not the last. He probably won't even be the last child I have to kill. How long until it drives me mad; or worse, how long until I start to like it?"

Grabbing both sides of his head, he howled, the frustration and torment in it making me step back a pace. "Tell me the solution, Cécile. Give me a solution that doesn't see half my people dead at my hand."

I licked my dry and split lips, praying it hadn't been a dream.

Praying that it was possible, and that I'd find a way, and that this wasn't just another false hope. And when I was done with praying, I met Tristan's desperate gaze, and said, "We send them back where they belong. Back to Arcadia."

CHAPTER 43
Tristan

"How?" I demanded, the audacity of Cécile's suggestion temporarily cooling my temper. "Do you not think if such a thing were possible, someone would have figured it out in the thousands of years we've been trapped here?"

Cécile shrugged. "You spent five hundred years searching for Anushka, and I was the one who found her."

"Technically, she found you," I pointed out. "And what, pray tell, has motivated this particular notion?"

Cécile paled slightly, and my skin prickled with apprehension. But before she could explain, the twins walked out of the shattered doors of the tombs. Their faces were drawn, Vincent's hair matted with blood and Victoria's trousers soaked with it.

"Are you all right?" I asked. I'd felt the pull on my magic while I'd been scrambling around the mountain and suspected what Cécile had done.

"We're alive," Victoria responded. "That Angoulême?"

I nodded, more interested in my friend's demeanor than my prisoner. I opened my mouth to press her further, but she gave me a slight shake of her head. *Later.*

"He can't hear us, can he?" Cécile was chewing on the edge of her thumb, then remembered what her hands were coated in, made a face and spit into the dirt.

"No." But the Duke was very much awake, and there was no way to know what he was ordering my brother to do. Nor any way of stopping him, short of knocking him out again. Which I was sorely tempted to do.

"The Summer King called my debt."

All thought of the Roland and the Duke fell away, and I rounded on Cécile. "What?"

"I was there, in the in-between-space – Arcadia," she said. "He told me that Winter has been slowly gaining territory, and he blames it on so many of his people being trapped in this world. A loss of lines he called it." She shrugged one shoulder, but it made sense to me. A good many powerful fey had been trapped along with my many-times great-grandfather, and the loss would have compounded over the centuries. It also explained Winter's actions: why she'd believed we were a threat and why she had been so desperate to destroy my people. She'd known exactly what my uncle had been up to.

"He told me he wants his people back, and that I'm the one who is going to make that happen." She started to chew on her thumb again, and I recognized it as a tick she'd adopted when under my father's compulsion.

"Did he tell you how?" I asked, wary of pushing her.

"No, I came back before he could," she said, and I saw a fresh droplet of crimson appear where she'd bitten through her skin. I caught hold of her hands, holding them away from her mouth.

"But he wouldn't have asked me to do it if it weren't possible, right?" Her blue eyes were wide, bright, and I felt the edge of fear slicing at both our minds. She remembered what it was like to be under compulsion, and with Aiden, she'd seen what it meant to fail.

If my uncle were truly desperate to bolster his host, potentially sacrificing the life of a human girl would mean little to him. Would mean nothing to him. "He's not one to squander a debt," I said, and any guilt I felt at the half-truth was vanquished by the relieved slump of her shoulders. Yet still, I couldn't help but ask, "Do you have an idea of how you might proceed? Or how long it will take?"

She shook her head, then met my gaze. "I'm not sure I'll figure it out in time to save Roland."

It had been foolish to hope, even for a minute. And even with this great revelation, this great possibly that Cécile had unearthed, nothing had changed. I had to kill my brother. A child, who, though he might be a monster, was also very much a victim of his family's failure to protect him. How different would he have been if we had kept him, if I'd made more of an effort to see him, to teach him to control his proclivities? Maybe it wouldn't have made a difference. But maybe it would've changed everything.

I scrubbed a hand through my hair, thinking. Our plan to capture Angoulême and use him to lure Roland to a place of our choosing had been predicated upon Roland being in Trollus, which I was certain neither of them had any desire to destroy. But if we pushed the Duke too hard with Roland in one of the human cities, he might have the boy raze it out of spite.

Think.

Think.

But as hard as I bent my mind to a strategy that would stop Roland with the fewest casualties, it kept twisting its way back to finding a way to subdue him. If I could just keep him in check long enough for Cécile to find a way to send him back to Arcadia...

You don't even know if there is such a way.

How many lives will you risk to keep your conscience clear?

I swore, curbing the desire to drop the magic around the Duke and beat him to death just to ease some of the tension singing through me. "If Roland had attacked either Trianon or Courville, Marc would have signaled for assistance."

"You think he was bluffing?" Cécile asked.

I shook my head. "No, of a certainty, Roland is in one of the cities. But I do not think Angoulême's ordered him to attack just yet."

Cécile's brow furrowed, but then she nodded. "He's keeping that card up his sleeve; we harm him, he sends Roland on a killing spree."

"Likely," I agreed. "But also, all setting Roland loose on one of the cities would accomplish is drawing me out to confront my brother, which would put his puppet king at risk. I think he's keeping to his original plan."

"Building an army," Cécile said. "Stacking his cards, so that when it comes time for him to make his move, he can be assured of victory."

"Which we are going to let him do," I said, watching as Cécile's eyes widened. "As it buys us time." My attention drifted to the twins, neither of whom seemed to be listening. Vincent was staring off into the distance, and Victoria was watching her brother with a jaw so tight her teeth were likely in danger of cracking.

"What's wrong?" I demanded. "Victoria?"

Her shoulders twitched. "Noth–" The lie stuck in her throat. Cécile came around me, arm outstretched. "Vincent?"

"Leave him be!" Victoria knocked her hand away, and Cécile gasped, more in surprise than in pain. "But he's better," she whispered. "I used Tristan's magic. The wound healed."

"Vincent?" I felt Victoria's magic burning with the heat of her distress, and I pushed Cécile behind me. "Vincent, answer me."

He didn't respond, didn't even seem to hear. Brushing aside Victoria's hand, I stepped in front of the friend who'd been like a brother to me. Who'd guarded my back, supported my plans, and made me laugh even in the moments when all seemed lost. "Look at me," I said, and when he did not, I forced his chin down until his eyes met mine.

There was nothing in them.

Vincent was gone.

CHAPTER 44
Cécile

Never in my life had I felt like a greater failure.

I sat in the sled with the bound form of my enemy, wishing I could tear open the wound I'd so casually healed and watch him slowly bleed to death. To make him pay for what he'd done.

To make him pay for what I'd failed to fix.

Tristan ran on silent feet behind me, and the twins before, Vincent mindlessly following his sister's guiding hand. Angoulême hadn't just ended one life when he'd detonated that staircase, he'd ruined two, because there was no life for Victoria without her brother. Part of me wondered if they'd have been better off if I'd let them die.

"Chris took Martin back to camp," Tristan said, and I jumped. It was the first thing he'd said since we departed the tombs.

"His body, you mean?"

He shook his head. "He was alive when they left, but Cécile..." I turned in my seat in time to see him swallow, his throat convulsing as though what he had to say made him sick. "Angoulême dismembered him."

All the blood rushed away from my skin. Martin, poor dear Martin, who'd wanted nothing more than to bury himself in books until that fateful day I'd walked into the library looking for a way to break a curse.

"Don't," Tristan said. "It's not your fault. He made his choices, and he has to live with the consequences, just as we do."

"Will they grow back?" I whispered. The idea of it made my stomach twist, but the trolls could recuperate from so many things.

"No."

Recuperate from almost anything. Except for dismemberment. And injuries to the brain.

And iron.

I chewed absently on my thumb, my mind going to the task the Summer King had set me. Of a surety, iron was the problem, and, to a lesser extent, gold. They were all fascinated by it, every one of them known to extract a gold coin from a pocket to play with while they were deep in thought. It was what had kept those ancient fey in this world long enough for the iron to infect them. To infiltrate their bodies. To steal their immortality.

Infect.

I frowned, trying to think of the iron as a disease that could be healed, but it felt all wrong. The metallic taste of blood filled my mouth, the skin on my thumb torn open. "Stones and sky," I muttered, spitting into the snow and then sitting on my hands.

"Camp's ahead," Tristan said. "Victoria, wait here with the sled, and..." He grimaced, then gave me a look that said *don't let anything go wrong while I'm gone.* As if I could stop Victoria if she decided to have her vengeance.

Tristan trotted off toward the camp, magic falling away to reveal a campfire and a single figure. I recognized Chris's sturdy frame, his hand going to the pistol at his side, then relaxing as Tristan's light flickered in the predetermined signal. Their heads bent together, one fair and one dark, and it dawned on me that they'd become friends.

The snow crunched as Victoria approached, and I tensed. "Untwist your knickers," she said, sitting down in the snow next to the sled. "I haven't had enough time to think of creative ways to hurt him, so he's safe for now."

Angry shouts burst from the camp, Martin's voice and Tristan's. "You might have to get in line," I said, resting my chin on my knees, my eyelids heavy even as I knew there'd be little rest in the coming days.

We both regarded Angoulême, Tristan's black box of magic having been replaced with fetters that blocked him from sight and sound. He shifted, testing his limits, and my skin prickled with unease. I'd spent so much time fighting against him, watching him hurt those I cared about, that he'd taken on almost monolithic proportions in my mind. It was difficult to reconcile that with the slight troll lying helpless at my feet, his fine clothing dirty and ragged at the cuffs, one boot half pulled off his foot. His strength was in his mind, his genius; and, as he turned his head to me, nostrils flaring slightly, I had to fight the urge to recoil.

He wasn't helpless. He was a snake waiting for an opportune time to strike.

"I can't remember why I'm fighting this fight."

Victoria's gaze had left the Duke and was now on her brother, who stood stock still in the snow. Rather than saying anything, I slipped my hand into hers and squeezed it hard.

"At first, it was fun," she said. "A way to alleviate the grinding tedium of Trollus with secret meetings, codes, and plans to overthrow a tyrant. We liked the idea of changing our world, of making it better; we knew the risks, but… Following Tristan has a way of making one feel invincible. Even when we were breaking you out of Trollus, and I knew half-bloods were dying, it didn't sink in that this fight was going to cost me."

I gave a little nod, knowing what she meant.

"Even when the King separated us and it was such misery, I believed it was only for a time. That Tristan would come up with a plan and we'd rally." She sniffed and wiped her nose with the back of her sleeve. "Then he told us that Anaïs was dead – that Lessa was posing as her – and it hit me that nothing we could do, or Tristan could do, would bring her back. Death is final. There is no coming back from it. And since then, no matter how hard we fight, no matter what we accomplish, those who matter most to us keep falling. It seems that even if by some miracle we win, *I* will have lost."

I wanted to tell her not to give up hope, that maybe there was a way to help Vincent. That to give up now would mean Angoulême had won. That people were counting on her, and her fight would make a difference to them. But it all sounded sour in my mind – false assurances and empty platitudes – and I knew none of it was what she wanted to hear. "What do you want to do?"

"I want to be done." Fat tears rolled down her cheeks, and she wiped them away with a vicious swipe. "You should've let us die."

"No, I shouldn't have." Climbing out of the sled, I took hold of the rope on the front. "As you said, death is final. But where there is life, there is hope." Tugging hard, I dragged the cause of all our plight into camp.

My gran had a steaming cup of tea ready for me as I stepped into the firelight, and I gratefully accepted it as I handed off the rope to Tristan. "Where's Martin?"

"In the tent." Tristan rubbed at one temple. "I'd leave him be. He's angry that Angoulême is still alive."

"Aren't we all." But the fact remained that the librarian was a wealth of knowledge, and right now, I needed him. Motioning for my gran to follow, I ducked under the canvas.

"Thank you," I said, taking a seat on top of a rough wool blanket.

"For what?" Martin's eyes were closed, but the muscles of his jaw were working back and forth as though he intended to grind his teeth to dust. I was thankful, because I felt my face lose its color at the sight of his injuries. Both arms were gone at the shoulder, and his legs, judging from where the blanket fell flat against the ground, had been removed just above the knee.

"Helping me catch Angoulême."

Martin's eyelids snapped open, silver gaze full of fury. The air around us warmed, and I felt Tristan come closer, ready to step in if things got out of hand. "Bad enough," he said, "that you went back on your word to kill him, but must you also mock me?"

"I'm not mocking you," I said. "You said once that you'd see him bleed out like his daughter. At first, I thought you meant Anaïs, but then it occurred to me in the tombs that you meant Pénélope. That Angoulême had the same affliction as her." I swiftly explained what had happened.

"You bit him?" Martin shook his head, then accepted a mouthful of tea from my gran. "You know I can do it myself," he said to her, the cup lifting out of her hand and floating in the air.

"Gives me purpose," she said, taking hold of the handle and pulling it back. "And what's a life without purpose?"

"What indeed." He stared at the blanket where the rest of his legs should've been. "I never saw any proof that Angoulême was afflicted," he said. "But a number of years ago, several volumes of research on the condition went missing from the library, and there was a rumor that circulated amongst the librarians that someone from the peerage had paid for them to be destroyed. After Lady Pénélope's affliction became known, my curiosity was piqued, and I delved into the matter. Of a surety, the girls' mother was no more than a carrier if she was able to bear two children, which, based on my research of other inherited conditions, lead me to believe the Duke was a victim of the ailment.

"I thought you never speculated," I said, realizing that I'd staked everything on an unproven notion.

"It was a well-researched hypothesis," he said, accepting another mouthful of tea. "Which you subsequently proved to be correct."

"Right," I said, wishing my cup was filled with something stronger. "I need your help with something else now." I explained my meeting with the Summer King, and his belief that the trolls could somehow be brought back to their homeland.

"Fascinating," Martin breathed, leaning back on the bags stacked behind him, lost in thought. "There are very old manuscripts within the library recording the accounts of the fey who lost their immortality. Many spoke of a growing difficulty in passing between worlds, that it became physically painful for them to do so. Some took it as a warning and left, never to come back, but some couldn't help themselves and remained. The change happened swiftly and to nearly everyone at once; only a few were able to flee back to Arcadia, the rest no longer even possessing the ability to open paths. It was as though our link to our homeland had been severed."

"What did they do?" I asked

"It was a panic, of course," Martin replied. "They knew it was iron that was holding them back, but not how to rid themselves of it. Many tried starving themselves and forgoing water; others attempted to bleed themselves dry, believing they could remove the contaminant that way. There were casualties, but when they realized that they'd started aging, that their magic had begun to change, that they were no longer immortal, they tried anyway. Those ancient fey were still long-lived by our standards – hundreds of years – but with each passing generation, lifespans grew shorter. Now they are no better than the average human. In a few hundred years, perhaps we'll live and die in the space of a handful of decades." He sighed. "There have been some who have postulated that it is this world's way of getting rid of that which does not belong, but that strikes me as fancifulness."

"It's a poison to you," my gran said thoughtfully, tapping an index finger against one tooth. "One that is compounding over the generations. Has it caused trouble other than mortality?"

Poison.

"Birth defects; madness; and, as is the case with the Duke, hemophilia," Martin said. "Though some of it might be caused by inbreeding, particularly amongst the aristocracy."

Gran wrinkled her nose. "Vile habit. And what of those with mixed blood: human and troll? Are they similarly afflicted?"

Martin shook his head. "There isn't a single case of an afflicted half-blood on record; and for the thousands of years our kinds have intermingled, the life expectancy of half-bloods has remained constant. Injuries inflicted with steel weapons on half-bloods heal at approximately the same rate as those inflicted by other metals. If not for the marked decrease in power, the injection of human blood into our lines might have been a viable method of adapting ourselves to this world."

I heard everything he said, but my mind was all for the word *poison.* "Gran," I said. "How do you cure poisoning in humans? With magic, that is?"

"Depends," she said. "Some poisons run their course quickly, and the magic cures the damage that has been done to the body. With others, the toxin lingers or builds, and the magic is used to draw it out of the body, which sometimes does more harm than good. It's painful, and always more magic is required to heal the damage."

"That's it. The latter," I said, my mind racing. "Do you know a spell?"

She nodded. "The best requires *lobelia*, but there will be none of that found in the dead of winter, so we will have to use alternatives. Regardless, it's what needs doing afterward that's the difficult part. But," she eyed Martin, "you've told me time and again that the earth's magic is ineffective on full-blooded trolls."

"It is." But what Martin had said about the earth using iron to rid itself of what didn't belong had struck a chord. "A witch's magic won't work on them because they are not of this world," I said. "But the iron is. What if the spell could be used to draw it out?"

"Surely it's been tried?" Gran asked Martin, who shook his head. "Not that I've ever heard. Or if it has, it certainly didn't work. "

Excitement flooded through me, chasing away the cold and exhaustion. "It won't hurt to try."

Gran hissed softly between her teeth. "It will hurt. For better or worse, the iron is part of them now, has infiltrated every part of their bodies, even their magic. You'll be tearing them apart to get it out."

"And putting them back together with their own power," I finished. There was a perfect symmetry to the idea. It felt right. "I want to try it."

"Then you'll need a test subject," Martin said. "I propose that subject be me."

I hesitated. He'd been through so much, and the thought of causing him more pain made my stomach sour. "Are you sure?"

His smile was more of a grimace, but he nodded. "A life without purpose is no life at all. The fight to make our world a place worth living was everything to Élise, but she didn't get to see it through. I'll do this for her."

CHAPTER 45
Tristan

"All that effort to keep him from taking control of the islanders, and now you're just going to let him have them?" Chris jabbed a stick into the fire, sending a cloud of sparks up into the air. "What a waste of effort."

"It wasn't a waste." I winced as a slight breeze blew smoke into my eyes, making them water and sting. Chris had a strong sense of fair play running through him, and he'd insisted if the rest of them had to take smoke to the face, so did I. "Your saving Courville was never a possibility, so in that, nothing's changed. And they'll only be bound to him for as long as he's alive, which won't be for much longer."

"Unless he kills you," Chris said. "And then everything will go to shit anyway."

"Thank you for your vote of confidence."

"You've got enough of that," he replied. "I consider it my duty to keep it in check."

"Noted." Picking up a stick, I jabbed the fire, hoping the smoke would switch directions. Instead, I was rewarded with a cloud to the face.

Chris laughed and threw on another log. "So you're sure he's in Courville?"

"Reasonably. Marc and the half-bloods are holding the

perimeter at Trianon. It would be nothing for Roland to force his way past, but they'd know it, and Marc would have signaled us." My eyes went to Angoulême, who I'd left in the sled a few feet away. "He knows I won't attack Roland while he's surrounded by so many humans."

"We could always put him on a spit over this fire and see how long he lasts before calling his pet troll to come save him."

"Tempting," I muttered. "But what would be the chances of him leaving Courville unscathed in his departure? There has to be a better way to lure him out."

"And here I thought you were some sort of strategic genius."

I grunted. "So is he."

Snow crunched, and Cécile approached the fire, eyed the damp ground and then perched on my knee. Extracting the stick from my hand, she nudged the burning wood a few times, and the smoke switched directions. Chris scowled and I smiled, pulling her closer.

"I think we've figured it out," she said, and I sat up straight, almost toppling her to the ground. "Are you serious?"

She nodded. "Martin's volunteered to be my test subject. I think he's the best choice, for… for obvious reasons, but I know we've few enough trolls on our side that you might not be willing to let him go."

Cécile was right about that. I rested my chin on her shoulder, staring into the flames. Sentiments aside, the loss of Vincent was a major blow, especially as it had rendered Victoria unreliable. I didn't dare pull Marc away from Trianon, which meant that my arsenal was a group of armed farmers and a maimed librarian with only middling power at his disposal. If Cécile's plan worked, Martin's magic would almost certainly change: I'd be down a weapon and up a fairy with a new set of powers he had no idea how to use. Not that there wasn't potential in that, but was it worth the risk?

"Waiting to try it on one of the half-bloods in Trianon would be better," I said. Cécile's expression didn't change, but there was no missing the flash of disgust.

"We discussed that," she said, pushing away my arm and climbing to her feet. "If I were to attempt this on a human, it would kill them as surely as a knife to the heart. We believe it would do much the same to most half-bloods, if not all." Her arms crossed, she swiftly explained the premise of the spell. "I will very nearly have to kill him to cure him."

"You might, in fact, kill him," I said. "We'll have gained nothing and lost another member of our force."

"And what would you have gained killing him on that mountain top?"

Chris whistled through his teeth. "I'll leave you two to this little chat." He rose and swiftly left the fire's circle of light. I waited until he was gone before saying, "That would've been mercy, Cécile. You weren't there. You didn't see him bleeding on the ground, his limbs scattered about him like chopped wood."

Her intake of breath was sharp, and she closed her eyes for a moment. "He doesn't need mercy, Tristan, he needs a victory. He couldn't help Élise, he couldn't stop Angoulême, and now what? Do we strap him to a horse and send him galloping into battle where in all likelihood he won't make a damn lick of difference? This could be something. It could be the solution."

"To what?" I demanded. "To my moral dilemma over killing my brother?"

"No," she shouted. "To our mistake!"

I froze, not entirely believing what I was hearing.

"I was wrong," she said. "You were right about not breaking the curse and a fool for letting me convince you otherwise. Maybe we might make it work for our lifetime if we rule with an iron fist, but what then? There will always be more Angoulêmes, and God help us, more Rolands, and what will happen with us not there to stop them? So many have already died because of the choices we made, and this might be the chance to make things as right as they can be. To save both your kind and mine."

She scrubbed a hand across her face, leaving a smear of blood and grime. "Your kind doesn't belong here, and with God as my witness, I'll send every troll back. And if it's what you want, I'll send you along with them." Then she turned on her heel and stormed into the darkened woods.

My boots seemed fixed to the ground as I watched her retreating form. Of all the things I'd expected to hear her say, that wasn't one of them. Always, always, she was the optimist, and to hear her give up on our dream, to say that our fight was hopeless... It made it true.

Your kind doesn't belong here.

If she was right, if the spell worked, then what she was offering was a solution beyond what I could ever have hoped for. Not only a way to save both our kinds and keep blood off our hands, but for me, it was a chance to see my people thrive. They'd be immortal once more, no longer afflicted with iron-wrought maladies, or fearful of what the cursed metal would do to their children.

Your kind.

It would be a freedom so much greater than just release from Trollus. The lands of endless summer would be theirs again, along with countless other worlds and endless years to explore them. It would be the greatest gift I could give them – the ability to return home.

You.

You don't belong here.

The cold seemed to bite through my clothing, the wind blowing through the trees a mournful howl. On numb feet, I slowly followed her tracks into the woods.

I found her sitting on a dry patch beneath a fir tree, face buried in her knees, shoulders shaking. "If it's what Martin wants, do it," I said, swallowing the tightness in my throat. "And if it works, I'll do what I can to see every other full-blooded troll goes with him."

"Every?" Her voice was soft.

"I think most will clamor for the opportunity."

"Will you?"

I thought of her sharp words, the guilt and the blame. What I had done and left undone, and all the blood on my hands. Our hands. I knew she would forgive me for my failures, because that was her way. But would she ever forgive herself? If I stayed, would I not always be a constant reminder of how she'd forsaken her own kind, however temporarily, for me? Would it be better if I left? Would it help her forget?

"This is all speculation," I said. "Neither of us know if your spell will work."

It was the worst of silences, but I felt too cowardly to ask if her heart had veered so far in the opposite direction that she now wanted me gone with all the rest of my kind. And I feared her silence was reluctance to ask it of me.

"Do you have everything you need for your spell to do it tonight?" I asked, needing the moment to end. "One way or another, I need to leave at first light."

"Gran was gathering what we needed," she said, getting to her feet and wiping her face with a sleeve. "She should be done by now."

Cécile started back to camp, and I knew I needed to say it now. "Cécile–"

She stopped in her tracks.

"Given the choice between one lifetime spent with you or a thousand without, I will always choose you." I took a deep breath. "That is, if you still want me."

She didn't turn, kept her back to me and didn't answer. But this was what made the bond between us worth every risk – she didn't need to say anything at all. Slowly, she stretched her arm back, palm open, and I took it.

CHAPTER 46

Cécile

"Do you smell that?" I asked as we approached the camp.

Tristan sniffed. "Smells like *outside.*"

"Like summer," I said, hurrying my step. And then stopped dead.

The camp we'd left behind had been all snow and mud, but now it was a lush oasis of greenery. Grass as high as my knee carpeted the ground, bushes were thick with leaves, and wildflowers painted the clearing in a myriad of colors.

We approached Gran and Chris, who stood near a bunch of lavender flowers.

"Always such a fondness for pretty things, Christophe," Tristan said. "Were you planning to leave some on my pillow?"

"What I planned to leave on your pillow didn't smell half so nice."

Ignoring their banter, Gran took hold of my arm. "Whole clearing took to bloom after you two scampered off to have your spat." She jerked her chin at the flower. "*Lobelia.*"

"That's certainly no coincidence." I plucked one of the blossoms. "Shall we?"

"You're sure you want to do this?" I asked Martin, tucking the blanket around him. "It will not be pleasant."

"Can't be any worse than what he did to me." We'd brought

him out of the tent and laid him on the grass, but his eyes had been on the Duke the whole time.

"Stay back," I said to Tristan and Chris. "The last thing we need is you getting caught up in this." Victoria stood a little further on, Vincent sitting on the ground at her feet, fingers plucking at the grass, and I waited for her nod before I turned back to Martin and my grandmother.

It took a bit of time to create the potion, Gran murmuring instructions as I worked, but when it was finished, I wished it had taken longer. If it didn't work, not only would I be back to square one, who knew what state Martin would be in?

I started pouring the basin of liquid at his forehead, moving slowly down his body, until I reached the stumps of his legs. The potion sat suspended in a gleaming line, trembling with each of his nervous breaths. Picking up the cast-iron pan, I touched fingers to either side of the liquid on his forehead, and murmured the incantation. The potion spilled in two sheets to either side, flowing like twin waterfalls. At first, it seemed as though nothing was happening, that it was nothing more than an interesting trick to entertain the eye. Then all at once, gravity seemed to double in strength, dragging me down.

And Martin began to scream.

The potion turned pink, then bright red as the spell tore apart his skin, his eyes, his insides, rending him as it took back what belonged to the earth.

Tears streamed down my face. I wanted to stop. Needed to stop. But it was too late. The potion thickened into a metallic slurry that pooled on the ground.

Then it was done.

The twin waterfalls ceased their flow, and I changed my focus, catching hold of his magic and bending it to my will, forcing it to heal him. The gruesome carnage faded, but his chest was still.

"Come on, Martin," I screamed, slamming my hands down on his chest. "Breathe!" My fists struck him again, then again, but as I flung them down the fourth time, instead of hitting flesh, they sank along with his clothing into earth beneath him.

"Stones and sky!" I jerked my arms back so hard I toppled onto my bottom, watching as his misty figure drifted and swirled, then finally coalesced into the librarian I knew and loved.

He blinked at me.

"Martin?" I bent closer. "Can you hear me? Are you all right? How do you feel?"

His lips parted and his eyes shifted back and forth. "There are no words for this, Cécile. Not in any language."

It was only then that I realized he was whole once more. "You are as you imagine yourself to be," I breathed, so painfully happy that I'd fixed my friend that it took me a moment to realize I felt no relief of my promise. Martin was free from iron and fey once more, but there was something more that needed to be done. Something that I'd missed.

"Tristan," I said, turning. "I think I..." But the words died on my lips, because I found myself face to face not with Tristan, but with Victoria. And before she even spoke, I knew what she would ask.

CHAPTER 47
Tristan

"You fixed him," Victoria said to Cécile, her voice strange and breathy. Desperate. "You made him better."

I knew where this was going, and judging from the look on Cécile's face, so did she.

"Victoria, no," I said, catching hold of her arm to draw her back.

In a blur of fury, she spun, her fist connecting with my face in a burst of pain. *She'd hit me.* I touched my lip, then looked at the blood on my fingers, trying to understand how we'd gotten to this point. How instead of untrussing Angoulême and dealing with him, I was fighting with my closest friends.

"It's not up to you, Tristan. Not this time."

"Can we please discuss this rationally," I said as Cécile crept away on her hands and knees. But before she got more than a few paces, magic lashed around her leg, jerking her back. Her grandmother grabbed her hands, but Cécile brushed her away. "Go," she said. "Get out of the way." And when the old woman didn't listen, to Martin: "Take her."

His brows furrowed, then his misty form solidified. Snatching up the fragile woman, he bolted for the trees. Chris remained, crouched low to the earth, pistol in hand. He was no more likely to leave with Cécile in danger than I was.

"Let her go." I circled, trying to get closer to Cécile, but Victoria pivoted, keeping between us. I didn't want to believe she'd hurt her, but Victoria was mad with grief, and that made anyone unpredictable.

"You owe me this," she said. "You owe Vincent. Let Cécile fix him."

"She can't. Not yet."

"Why?"

Against my will, my eyes flicked to Cécile then back. "You damn well know why not."

Victoria laughed, and the sound of it made me cringe with its unfamiliarity. Not only had Angoulême stolen Vincent from us, he'd taken Victoria, too. Destroyed her spark, her humor, her spirit, and left a bitter angry girl in his wake. "Because you still have a use for us? Because you don't want to give up any of your tools?"

"Don't," I snarled, remembering how Lessa had lobbed the very same insult at me when I still believed she was Anaïs. "You bloody well know how much he means to me. His loss hurts more than just you."

"He's not lost," she shrieked, and Cécile winced, clutching at the magic wrapped around her ankle. But she caught my eye and shook her head. *I'm fine.* Which was all well and good until Victoria lost her temper and accidentally snapped her leg in two.

"How can you say that?" I couldn't keep the edge from my voice. "I've looked in his eyes, Victoria. He's not there!"

"You don't know that."

"But what if I'm right?" I demanded. "What if Cécile strips away the iron and his mortal form and there's nothing left? Think of what that will that do to you." *I couldn't lose her, too.*

"Think of what *this* is doing to me!"

"At least you're alive," I said, putting voice to my thoughts. "Be grateful for that."

It was the wrong thing to say. The grass smoldered and burst into flame, and the magic holding Cécile whipped her body through the air like a rag doll.

"You're hurting her," I shouted, slicing through the rope holding Cécile even as my magic rose to counter Victoria's attack. Our powers collided with a thunderclap, snow falling from trees for miles as the ground shuddered. But I'd used too much power – far more than I'd intended – and Victoria was launched through the air, landing heavily on her back on the far side of the clearing.

Cécile landed on the ground, the grass not doing as much as I'd hoped to cushion her fall, but already she was rolling to her feet, shouting at me to leave Victoria alone.

Victoria was struggling against my power, her voice a maelstrom of blistering oaths. "Enough," I shouted at her, furious that she was making me do this. "If you have any loyalty left in you, you will stand down."

But my words were drowned out by a roar, and something slammed into me, knocking me from my feet. Fists pummeled my face as we rolled into the trees, but I didn't fight back, because it was Vincent. Vincent, who had come to the aid of his sister.

Victoria had scrambled to her feet and in a swift motion caught hold of her brother's arms. The roaring ceased, his broad shoulders heaving with each breath he took. And although his eyes were still blank, for the first time, I had hope.

"This is something," I said to Victoria. "You were right – he's still with us."

"Forgive me," she whispered. "I was disloyal."

I shook my head. "You've never been disloyal a day in your life. I know Vincent comes first for you, just as you do for him. If what you really want is for the spell to be performed on him now, I won't stand in your way." My eyes tracked to Cécile, who was chewing her bottom lip.

"The spell's not complete," she said. "There's more to it, but

I don't know what."

"She's right." Martin had returned, his form shifting from transparent to opaque, the effect dizzying. "I've read enough to know that I should sense Arcadia, but I don't. Changed as I am, I'm not sure I could go back."

"But you're still whole," I said. "Which makes it more than a partial victory." I turned back to Victoria, who was holding tight to her brother's hand. "What do you want to do?"

"We'll see this through," she said, squaring her shoulders. "The spell will wait."

That was loyalty, pure and true. Where would I be without my friends? What would I be? And not just the twins and Marc, but Cécile, Chris, and Sabine. My nature was to be distrustful, but not with them. And it wasn't a weakness.

Angoulême lay unmoving next to the fire where we'd left him, and I considered the state in which we'd found him. Alone and half mad, and not, I thought, from the solitude. It was the lack of control. He trusted no one. Not his mother, nor his followers, and certainly not Roland. The one exception seemed to be Lessa, whom he'd left to execute his plans. Only I didn't believe for a second that he'd put his faith in my duplicitous sister without certain controls.

"He's forced her into some sort of promise," I muttered, knowing in my heart she wouldn't have sworn to anything except under duress. Which, in its own way, would make him trust her less, because he'd know she'd be looking for ways to get out from under his control.

I was certain I'd rattled his confidence in her with the knowledge that she'd lied about Anaïs's death, but what if we undermined it further? What would he do if he suspected she'd double-crossed him? What would he do if he thought she'd altered his plans?

"I'm glad of your decision," I said to Victoria, my mind whirling. "I need you and your magic to take over Angoulême's containment. And I need you to do a poor job of it."

Victoria lifted one eyebrow. "Why is that?"

"Because I need you two to help me play a trick."

CHAPTER 48
Cécile

"I don't like this strategy," I said, wrapping my arms around Tristan's neck to steady my nerves. I was used to being on stage, but never before had lives depended on my performance. And we were trying to fool a master of duplicity. "I don't trust Lessa – her only loyalty is to herself. Already she's gone back on her word. They were supposed to remain in Trollus."

"I don't trust her, either," Tristan responded. "But we know she likes to play both sides until she's certain who will land on top. Angoulême was a fool to believe she'd be content under his control. Lessa isn't Roland."

"No, she isn't," I said. "At least Roland cares for you in his strange fashion. Lessa only sees you as a means to an end. Once we've cured Roland, she'll try to kill you. Or me. Again."

"Likely," he said, his voice cheerful. "But we don't really have a choice. As long as Roland remains surrounded by humans, I can't take him by force without risking casualties. And frankly, I'm not sure I could subdue him without killing him. Your spell took the iron from Martin and fixed him – I want that chance for Roland. And if we can cure his madness, then there's nothing to stop us from killing Angoulême."

My stomach clenched at his admission, scripted though it was. Just because he wanted to save Roland didn't mean it was part of our plan.

"What if it's a trap?" I asked, readying myself to lie. "What if she hasn't given Roland the potion? What if we get there and I try to work the spell to cure him, and nothing happens. We'll be caught in a battle in the middle of Courville."

"It's possible," Tristan admitted. "But from her own lips, she doesn't want Roland to be King."

This was the crux of our plan: to create doubt in Angoulême's mind of Lessa's loyalty, but not certainty that she'd switched sides, because all he'd do then was have Roland kill her.

"You're going to have to give up something," I said. "She's not going to let us near Roland without concessions, and we only have so much time before the potion passes through his system. And once it's gone, we aren't going to get another chance."

"The plan will work." His voice took on a slightly irritated edge.

"Don't get mad at me for worrying," I snapped. "You were the one who was so confident that capturing Angoulême in the tombs would go off without a hitch and look what happened. Vincent's a mindless shell, and Victoria's a grieving mess."

Silence.

"A low blow, Cécile." The fury in his voice made my skin burn, and I stepped back despite knowing it was an act. "You'd do well to remember that it's to save *your* kind that I have to do this at all. That it's *my* friends and people who are suffering to ensure their survival."

I flinched, because his words were the cold truth.

"I'm going to finish packing up, and then we're leaving," he said. "Courville is a long ways from here."

I waited until he'd gone to the far side of the clearing, then, whirling, I stormed around the fire and kicked Angoulême in the ribs. "I hate you," I snarled. "This is your fault!"

The snow crunched as someone ran up behind me, then Chris

lifted me off my feet and pulled me back. "Cécile, don't!"

"Why not?" I demanded. "He deserves it a thousand times over for what he did to Vincent. And to Victoria."

"Because he's bound and helpless, that's why." Chris's words sounded rehearsed, and I prayed the Duke didn't notice.

"He's not helpless." I slumped on a stump next to the fire, every inch of me tense with having the Duke in such close proximity. Especially knowing that Victoria's magic was slowly unraveling. Knowing that he could hear me. "Do you think Tristan would be treating him with kid gloves if he was helpless? Would be negotiating with that backstabbing whore?"

"Easy," Chris replied, sitting across from me. "Tristan knows what he's doing. He'll make the deal, and in a matter of days, Roland will be cured and the Duke will be dead. The war will be over."

"But at what cost?" I blew my nose on a handkerchief. "Do you know what deal Lessa offered him before? That he set me aside and take her, pretending to be Anaïs, as his wife. Her allegiance in exchange for him making her queen."

"That's revolting." The disgust in Chris's voice wasn't feigned. "Wait, you don't actually think that he'd…"

I stared into the fire for a long time before saying, "No. He'll never forgive Lessa for killing Anaïs or her part in killing his parents, but he will string her along if it means defeating Angoulême." My eyes burned from the smoke. "Where is Victoria? She's supposed to be keeping an eye on him."

"Off trying to get Vincent to speak, I expect," Chris said. "God in heaven, but I feel for her."

"I do too," I said, "but she needs to stay focused. I doubt Angoulême is out of tricks just yet."

"Cécile." Tristan came up behind me. "It's time to go."

We said our goodbyes to our friends; then we left the camp. Once we were out of earshot, Tristan stopped. "He knows Victoria is distracted by Vincent, so he shouldn't suspect that we're allowing him to escape."

I nodded, wishing there were fewer uncertainties.

"Even if he's not entirely convinced Lessa turned on him, he'll still call Roland out of Courville and her reach until he's sure. All I have to do is follow him, and then…"

"Kill your brother."

He sighed and looked away. "Yes."

I stood on my tiptoes and kissed him hard, trying to keep my trepidation in check. "Please be careful."

"I love you," he said; then he disappeared into the night.

I crept back on silent feet to the tent where Gran and Martin sat silently watching. Taking a seat next to them, I turned off the lamp, and together, we waited.

The fire burned low, Chris occasionally prodding it with a stick and sending bursts of sparks in the air. The wind howled softly, and faintly, but clearly, I heard Victoria's voice. "Please, Vincent. Say something, anything."

She cajoled him gently, reminding him of stories of their past, but of Vincent, I heard nothing.

The blanket overtop Angoulême's sled stirred, the motion imperceptible enough that I would've missed it if I hadn't be watching for this very moment. The edge of the blanket lifted, and I almost imagined I could see the Duke's silver eyes peering out from the shadows. My gran gave a soft cough as one does in one's sleep, and a few minutes later, Chris rested his head in his hands, shoulders slumping with apparent exhaustion.

I clenched my teeth, desperately afraid as the blanket stirred again. *Be brave, be brave, be brave,* I silently chanted, even as our prisoner extracted himself from what he believed was a neglected cage of magic. My eyes caught a faint distortion in the air, then the blanket settled down, taking on the shape of a prone man, though I knew nothing lay beneath.

Sweat prickled on my skin as I waited for the Duke to make his move. He could kill Chris where he sat before Victoria could make it back to camp. Tristan was long gone, making his way down to the coast. We were banking on Angoulême's cowardice.

My pulse hammered in my ears, and I took hold of my grandmother's hand, squeezing it hard.

Then the distortion moved, making its way swiftly toward the trees. Martin touched my shoulder, then his form turned misty and he ran on silent feet into the night, returning some time later with a smile on his face.

The Duke had taken the bait.

CHAPTER 49
Tristan

Our ruse had worked, instilling enough doubt in Angoulême's mind about Lessa's loyalty that he was willing to risk coming out in the open rather than jeopardizing his puppet prince. Tracking him in the fresh snow was easy, and he set a brisk pace towards Courville. Our entire strategy was dependent on him calling Roland out of the city in order to hide him while Cécile's "potion" wore off, and I prayed that it worked. I did not know what I'd do if it didn't.

We ran through the night and into the dawn, and I felt no small amount of relief when his tracks broke off the Ocean Road and moved down towards the beach. I crept slowly, relying on stealth rather than illusion so that they'd be less likely to sense my power.

I reached a clearing, and stopped in my tracks at the sight of Angoulême. But it was Lessa, not Roland, who approached and my stomach clenched. This wasn't the plan.

"What are you doing here?" she demanded.

"So surprised," Angoulême said. "Is that because you believed me captured or dead?"

Her eyes widened. "Why should I believe such a thing?"

"Because you sent Tristan after me. Betrayed me." *So he had believed.*

"I did no such thing," she retorted. "I've followed every step of your plan. That's why we're here – we're on our way to take Trianon. You told Roland it was time."

My stomach clenched at that news, but now wasn't the time to think about the other city. She'd said we, and that had to mean Roland. He was nearby. He had to be. And that meant I would have my chance to kill him with no fear of human casualties.

"One of the conditions of you keeping my daughter's face was that you never lied to me," he snarled at her. "You gave your word. Or does your human blood allow you to break that as well? Are all your promises lies?"

"I'm not lying," she shouted. "What more must I do to make you trust me?"

I crouched in the trees, debating whether I should remain watching them on the chance Roland would arrive, or to go looking for him myself. It would be only a few moments more before Angoulême would suspect I'd duped him, and the first thing he'd do is warn my brother.

I scanned the terrain for any sign of motion, sending out delicate filaments of magic as I searched my surroundings for a source of power strong enough to be Roland.

Then my hackles rose.

Slowly, I turned my head, my eyes going up the slope until they came to rest on Roland.

He smiled. "Hello, Tristan."

Attack, attack, my mind screamed, but I stayed frozen in place as he trotted down the slope toward me. I braced for a blow, but all he said was, "What are you doing here?"

I swallowed hard. "Looking for you."

He cocked his head. "To kill me?"

Yes. "I don't want to hurt you," I said. "You're my brother."

Instead of answering, he sat cross-legged on the ground next to me. "I hate him."

I risked a glance down at the arguing pair. "The Duke?"

Roland nodded, and his eyes welled up liquid bright. "He takes away my possessions. Makes me do things I don't wish to do."

"Like what?" My mind was scrambling. I'd come here to kill him, and in this moment, it would be so easy. He sat watching the Duke, entirely trusting that I would not harm him. But it was this very weakness that would not allow me to strike.

"He took mother." His eyes flicked up to me as though trying to judge how much I knew before admitting his own guilt.

"He took her from me, too," I said.

Roland picked at a leaf, chewing at his bottom lip. "He says that to be king, I'll have to kill you, too. That it's the only way." He looked up at me. "But I don't want to."

"What do you want?" When was the last time I'd had a conversation with him alone? When was the last time I'd tried – really tried – talking to him?

"For you to tell the Duke that you don't want to be king. That you want me to rule. Then maybe…" He sighed, pressing his hand to his head in a way that was familiar. The Duke had bound him so tightly, by name, by promises, that Roland could barely think. How much worse was his madness, his violence, because of Angoulême's manipulation? Was it possible that once he was released from it all, that he'd be a normal little boy?

I hesitated, knowing that I was walking on dangerous ground, that the wrong thing said might trigger him. But the risk was worth it if it supported the kernel of hope growing in my heart. "If you were king and able to do anything you wished, what would you do, Roland?"

He rested his chin on one small fist, expression dreamy. "I would paint the world red."

Foolish hope.

I rested my hands on his shoulders. They were bony, as scrawny as mine had been at that age, his unkempt hair brushing against his coat. *One quick twist, and it will be over. He won't even feel it.* My fingers twitched, but he didn't seem to notice, entirely lost in his daydream.

Do it, you coward!

I reached for his head, hating myself. Hating and knowing I'd never forgive myself for this.

"There they are!" He sat up straight, jostling my hands away as he pointed. "Look, Tristan. Look at all the humans."

Dread filled my stomach with ice as my gaze jumped from the forested slope, to the beach below, and then to the open water.

"Yes, Tristan. Look at all those humans." Angoulême's voice drifted up the slope. Cutting. Cruel. "Roland, kill him."

My brother whispered one word before his body went stiff, power manifesting with vicious heat: "Run."

CHAPTER 50
Cécile

"It looks like a sheet of fabric being torn from the middle out," I said, throwing another log on the fire and giving Martin an encouraging nod. "Or a piece of paper."

"Your analogy is not becoming any more helpful with repeating," he replied, scowling and plucking at the air. "I feel so useless. I should be able to feel the press of Arcadia against this world, but I feel nothing."

And I felt no relief to the press of my promise to the Summer King. It was as though, despite removing the iron from Martin, despite making him fey once more, that I'd accomplished nothing. Because he could not go back to Arcadia, and that, ultimately, was what the fairy king wanted. There was another piece. Something that I was missing. But what?

"You aren't useless," I said, holding my hands over the flames. "Without your bravery, we wouldn't even know removing iron from trolls was possible. It's just that there's another step in the process that we haven't figured out yet. But we will."

And hopefully soon. Beyond fulfilling my promise, there'd be advantages to having someone with fey magic on our side. In fact, I couldn't stop thinking about all the advantages we'd gain as we sat around the fire waiting for Tristan to save the world. Or die trying.

Chris had finally lost patience and gone hunting, Victoria had somehow convinced Vincent to chop wood, much to the detriment of the forest, and my gran was busy gathering what plant life hadn't been razed by troll-fire. The only thing I could think to do to keep my mind off Tristan was to help Martin, but all it had amounted to was frustration.

"You'd know if something was wrong," the librarian said, focusing on solidifying his form so that he could pat me on the arm.

I got to my feet and began to pace, tension singing through me from head to toe. Everything *wasn't* fine. Tristan was in the thick of it, and the constant bombardment was making me physically ill. I'd wretched up everything I'd eaten for breakfast, and now I was dizzy and tired.

A deep sense of reluctance filled my core and my mouth tasted abruptly sour. I shoved one of the mint leaves Gran had given me into my mouth and chewed furiously.

Then a jolt of panic hit me and I staggered, Victoria catching hold of my arm. "Something's happened," I said. "Something's not right."

In the distance, explosions of bright color filled the sky and Victoria swore. "That's Marc. Trianon's under attack."

Chris ran into camp right as the earth began to tremble. "Earthshake," Chris shouted, but as I was thrown to the ground, I knew that wasn't it. Trees toppled as the intensity increased, and my ears popped with the sound of an enormous thunderclap.

I pushed up on my hands and knees in time to see Chris point and say, "God in heaven, what is that?" A white cloud of mist roared toward us like an ocean wave, and as it passed over our heads, a wall of heat hit my face, turning what snow remained on the trees to water.

"Is Roland attacking Trianon?" my gran asked, her face pale.

"Wrong way," Chris said, helping me up, both of us swaying

as the ground shook again. "That cloud came from the direction of Triaucourt." His eyes went to mine and I nodded, trying to keep my fear in check. "Tristan's fighting Roland."

I grasped Martin's shoulders. "You need to figure out your fey magic, we need to see what's happening."

"I can't! I don't know how." There were tears on his face, but I didn't care, because Tristan was in trouble, and I didn't know how I could help him. "Try harder," I screamed.

He shoved me away, and I fell into Chris's arms. "I can't!" he shouted. "You might have cured me, but you didn't fix the problem, because I can't go back. I can't feel the press of the worlds. There is no connection."

Can't feel… No connection.

I struggled out of Chris's grasp. "The Élixir," I demanded. "Where is it?"

Martin blinked at me, then fumbled at his robes. "It's gone," he said. "It's not here."

My heart was racing, Tristan's panic mixing with my own. "Did Angoulême take it? Think!"

"I don't know, I don't know." He tore at the pockets of his robes, and I swore. Because the robes weren't real – they were a manifestation of his magic. His real robes lay in a heap in the tent. I only prayed the vial was with it.

I sprinted across the camp, stumbling as the ground shuddered, falling through the tent flaps to land on my knees. Martin's blood-stained clothing was in a heap in the corner, and I rifled through it.

"Please be here, please be here," I muttered. Then my fingers brushed against something cold, and I jerked the vial free from the fabric.

I threw myself out of the tent and nearly collided with Martin. "Drink it," I said. "Now."

"But why?"

I was shaking, my fear so intense I barely kept control over my body. "It binds. That's what the magic does. Not just hearts and emotions, but worlds. Drink it – drink it now."

Snatching the vial out of my hand, he tore open the stopper and poured the contents down his throat. The noise of the battle faded into white noise as I watched him. As I waited. "Did it work?"

Instead of answering, he slashed one hand through the air, tearing a hole in the world's fabric.

A sense of relief filled me, but it was short-lived.

The view through the portal was of Trianon, and all of us forgot the battle being waged between Tristan and his brother.

"Stones and bloody sky," Chris whispered.

The walls of Trianon still held, and I could see the half-bloods standing atop them, but that wasn't the source of our horror. Surrounding the city was a teeming horde of people some thirty feet deep – more at the gate – every one of them fighting to get inside. They were pushing and shoving, some crawling over heads and shoulders while others were on their hands and knees, digging into the earth. There were bodies on the ground, some still, some writhing in pain, but man, woman, or child, no one stopped to help.

"What are they so afraid of to behave this way?" Martin asked.

"They are the islanders who were forced to swear loyalty to Roland," I said, icy sweat dribbling down my spine. "He's commanded them to breach the walls."

Chris picked up a rock and threw it against a tree, staggering as the ground trembled again. "This wasn't supposed to be their plan," he shouted. "We were supposed to have time. Roland was supposed to march with them. If we'd known, if I'd known–" He broke off, dropping to his knees and burying his face in his hands.

"More and more keep arriving," Victoria said, pushing me out of her way so that she could get a better view. "Where are they all coming from?"

"Does it matter?" I demanded.

"Yes." She waved her hand through Martin's misty form. "Earn your salt, fey, and go do some reconnaissance."

Martin crawled through the small opening and disappeared.

"Victoria," I whispered, my tone causing her to look at me sharply. It was taking every ounce of control I had to keep from breaking down, from letting everyone know just how dire the situation was. I stared into her silver eyes: *he's not winning.*

Her jaw tightened and she gave a slight nod. Then Martin reappeared. "There's a highway of magic stretched between Courville and a beach just outside of Trianon," he said, squeezing back through the hole. "It's covered in skiffs filled with humans – hundreds of them!"

"Of humans?" Chris demanded.

Martin shook his head, eyes wild. "Hundreds of skiffs."

Which meant thousands of people out over open water entirely at Roland's mercy. Once again we'd underestimated Angoulême's ingenuity: he hadn't fallen into our trap. We'd fallen into his.

CHAPTER 51
Tristan

I ran like I had never before. Roland's magic hammered against my shields, knocking me to my knees and leveling the forest, leaving nothing but smoking ruins and steam.

I couldn't kill him, not with a city full of civilians balanced precariously on his magic.

I couldn't flee, not without risking him dumping half of them into the ocean to lure me back.

There was no option but for me to engage. I kept to the coast, sending out feelers of magic deep into the water to test the steadiness of Roland's bridge. It was solid. That's why he'd been sighted standing on the beach: not because he'd been fascinated with the water, but because he'd been building, preparing, for this moment. Holding up those thousands of people was costing him nothing, but if he dropped them and I had to catch them, it would cost me everything.

Cutting down onto the sand, I risked a glance out to sea and confirmed my hope. The skiffs were moving, propelled by a dozen or so trolls that no doubt had been responsible for forcing the people into the wooden craft in the first place. All I had to do was keep him engaged until they were across. Never mind that it might take them hours.

Skidding to a halt, I turned, waiting for Roland to cusp the hill so that I could launch an attack of my own.

His short legs were pumping hard as he came into sight, tear-streaked face a twisted mixture of wrath and desperation, and never in my life had I hated Angoulême more. Who did this to a child? Who used an eight year-old boy as a tool to slaughter their enemies, especially when said enemies were the boy's own family members?

But conflicted or not, Roland didn't hesitate to attack. Our powers collided with thunderclaps that shook the earth, explosions of heat melting snow for miles around. His strategy was nearly as mindless as my mother's had been, but as with her, his total disregard for his own safety or the destruction he was causing allowed him to channel more power into his offensive.

Not that it should matter: he was eight. A child. A decade from realizing the potential of his power.

He struck again, and my magic shuddered violently. Again, and my heel slipped. Again, and I had to take a step backward or risk falling.

A wicked little smile blossomed on his face, and fear twisted up my spine like a snake. Contrary to popular opinion, I was not the most powerful troll living.

Not even close.

CHAPTER 52
Cécile

Fallen straight into Angoulême's trap, and there was nothing we could do about it. This battle would be over in a matter of moments, and we were hours away. Tristan was on his own. Marc, Sabine, and all our friends in Trianon were on their own. There was nothing I could do to help.

"What are our options?" I asked, staring down at my boots. Melted snow was pooling around them, seeping in to chill my toes, but I couldn't be bothered to move.

"If I travel light, I might be able to make it in time to do some good," Victoria said.

I knew what travel light meant – without me. "Go," I said. "Take Vincent. Run."

"Cécile…"

"It's not a request," I snapped. "It's a command. Go. Now."

In a heartbeat, they were gone, leaving me alone with Chris and my grandmother.

"We always knew it would come down to a battle between trolls," Chris said, taking my hand. "We've done what we can. Now we wait to see who wins."

But his words were clipped, the muscles in his jaw standing out against his skin. Passiveness sat about as well with him as it did with me.

And it sat not at all well with my gran. "Enough of this defeatism," she snapped. "Those are human beings surrounding Trianon and some of them are hurt. Which we can do something about. Pack your bag, Cécile. Chris, you saddle those horses, and be quick about it."

We both gaped at her, but when she picked up a stick in a way that made it appear alarming like a switch, we scuttled in opposite directions to do her bidding.

"Where is Martin?" I asked, shoving my things into my satchel.

"Left while you two were whinging," Gran replied, carefully packing the *lobelia* she'd gathered. "Said he was going to help."

I didn't know what he thought he could accomplish, but I said nothing. If he'd stayed, I could well imagine myself frozen in place, watching through a tiny portal while Tristan was slaughtered by his brother. Which did no good for anyone.

I stood and Gran moved with me, catching the front of my shirt and pulling me close. "No matter what happens to that boy, don't you think about lying down to die, do you hear me?"

It was too easy to remember what it had felt like; the moment the sluag venom had pulled him away from me and all my will to live had vanished in an instant. How the cold press of the guillotine had felt like mercy.

"Do you hear me?" She jerked me closer with surprising strength for her frail frame. "It's not just your life anymore."

She was right. Tristan not surviving this encounter did not excuse me from the fight. I had a responsibility and a duty to keep going until the bitter end, and my ability to do so wouldn't come from a spell or potion, but from force of will. "I hear you," I said, lifting my chin. "Now let's ride."

But as we turned to the horses, a shriek filled the skies over our heads. A sound like an eagle, but far, far bigger. The horses went wild, tearing free from their pickets and galloping into the trees. The moment I looked up, I wanted to do the same, because cutting across the sky was a dragon.

"I thought Tristan said they couldn't come back," Chris shouted as we ran to the trees.

"He did." Gran stumbled, and I hauled her up, risking a glance back as I did. The dragon had landed in the clearing, golden scales glittering in the sunlight. And I recognized it.

"Winter," I breathed. "The Winter fey can't come back."

Letting go of her arm, I retreated to the clearing.

"Are you mad?" Chris dragged me backwards.

"Let me go," I said, and his arms fell away.

My pulse roared in my ears as I approached the dragon, my eyes flitting between its enormous claws and teeth the length of my hand. It snorted, and a gout of steam rose into the air. "Are you Melusina?" I asked, flinching as it lowered its massive head until it was only a few feet from my chest. Emerald eyes gleamed and it huffed out another breath that smelled of sulfur and flame.

"Cécile!" Chris hissed my name from behind a tree as though the slender trunk would protect him from the enormous beast.

"There's a statue of it... of her in Trollus," I said. "She's a Summer dragon." I reached out a hand and, though it was probably not prudent to do so, pressed it against the creature's hide. Her scales were hard as steel, but through them, I felt the same sort of preternatural heat the trolls exuded. "Are you here to help us?"

Melusina eyed me, then inclined her great head.

"Can you take us to Trianon?" I asked, terrified and excited at the prospect.

Wings snapped out with a crack, then tucked against the dragon's body as she lowered her bulk to the ground.

"I think we're going to need some rope," I said.

I spent the bulk of the journey with my eyes squeezed shut and my face pressed between my gran's shoulder blades. It wasn't until Chris poked me in the side that I risked a glance downward. The sight of the hundreds of islanders surrounding the walls was as alarming as the distance from which I was seeing them. Gran had seemed confident we'd be able to help, but watching people desperately climb over one another in an attempt to breach the wall, I didn't see how.

Nor did I see any hope for the citizens of Courville, who were packed into skiffs across the open water of the bay, the other city only barely visible in the distance. The skiffs appeared to be floating on thin air, but I could see where the surf broke against the magic, froth and foam soaking those it supported.

Melusina circled the city, and the three of us all gazed down the coast of the bay, past Trollus, to where Tristan and Roland still warred. The earth was razed for miles in either direction, clouds of black smoke filling the air, broken by the occasional gout of fire or steam.

"Land us on the castle tower," I shouted at the dragon, my stomach rising into my throat as she plunged. The castle grounds teemed with soldiers running frantically to their posts, hands gesturing skyward; and as we dropped, a cloaked figure stepped out onto one of the towers, concealed face tracking our progress. It was Marc.

But my elation was short-lived. Melusina shrieked and pulled up as the air charged, all of us sliding to one side, barely holding on.

"Marc," I called. "Marc, it's us!"

The dragon screamed again, then dived, and I was sure we were done for. That Marc had pulled her from the sky. Then her wings snapped wide, and my spine cracked as she pulled up, hovering above the tower. With birdlike delicacy, she carefully took hold of the battlements and closed her wings to her side.

"Cécile?" Marc demanded.

"Get us down!"

I rested on the icy stone of the tower to regain my equilibrium before staggering to the edge to look out over the water. The magic road trembled and shook, countless people falling into the sea. Swimming. Drowning. "We need to help them," I said, and no sooner were the words out of my mouth then the ground shook.

And all the skiffs plunged to the water.

CHAPTER 53
Tristan

My plan to let Roland hammer away at my shields for the next hour vanished out from under me. I wouldn't last another ten minutes.

Blocking his next blow, I dived into the woods, rolling behind a pile of boulders. The air whistled, an invisible blade slicing through the trees so cleanly that they didn't topple, remaining upright until a gust of wind sent them falling like a series of dominos. A line of glowing red bisected the boulder next to me, molten rock dripping from where it was severed mere inches above my head.

I pushed out a wave of heat, lighting the forest on fire, and set a barrier above to hold in the smoke. Under the choking cover, I ran blind, tripping over rocks and debris even as I ducked under Roland's attacks, using magic only when needed, conserving my strength. But I couldn't keep it up for long. Angoulême would realize I was buying time for the citizens of Courville to get across and would start drowning them or worse to lure me out.

Killing Roland might be possible. He was more powerful, but I had years more training. Except there was every chance he'd rip the magic bridge out from under their feet in his death throes. I might be able to catch them, but I'd still have Lessa and the Duke to contend with. My only other option was to find

Angoulême, kill him, and pray Roland wouldn't turn to violence the second he was freed.

They were terrible plans, every one.

A massive tree, roots and all, flew over my head, crashing into the foliage where it was soon joined by another. Yet another hit home against my shield, exploding in a spray of splinters. Over my shoulder, I saw Roland had given up pursuit for the moment and was instead standing on top of an abandoned stone building lobbing everything in sight my direction. It was the chance I needed. Obscuring myself with magic and smoke, I sent an illusion of me running off in one direction while I turned back to where I'd last seen Angoulême and Lessa. The trick would only last as long as it took for Roland to land one of his projectiles, so I had to make every second count.

They were gone by the time I reached the clearing, but I'd expected that. Keeping myself concealed, I looked for tracks, but the heat of the battle had turned the ground to a slushy mess.

"Where are you?" I snarled, eyeing my surroundings. He'd need somewhere he could see the action without being exposed to the fallout of the battle. Somewhere nearby.

But there was nothing. The ground was rolling, but none of the slopes were high enough to give him the vantage he needed. Turning in a circle, I glanced out at Roland's bridge, and noticed an old lighthouse sitting on a cluster of rocks about a hundred yards from shore. The roof was caved-in, but it was still tall enough to provide the vantage the Duke needed.

Sure enough, a shadow passed one of the narrow windows. *Clever. But not clever enough.*

Smiling, I walked down to the edge of the sand and built an invisible bridge of my own over to the tiny island.

It was harder to hide oneself in the brilliant sunlight of midday, but only someone watching carefully would see the distortion in the air caused by my illusion as it crossed over the water. And the ruckus Roland was causing as he searched for me was a substantial distraction.

Swiftly across the bridge. Up onto the rocks. The rotten wooden door at the base was slightly ajar, but one gentle touch...

The island and everything on it disappeared in a pillar of white-hot heat that seemed to stretch up to the sun itself.

Stepping back into the shadows of the forest, I knelt down. And I waited for them to come ensure that I was dead.

Moments later a hooded figure stepped out of the trees, arms crossed beneath the cloak that dangled to his heels. Part of me wanted to see the Duke's face – for him to know it was me who had ended him. But enough was at risk without theatrics, and vengeance was vengeance.

Magic honed as sharp as a razor flew from my hand, blood spraying as it sliced the Duke's neck in two. The hooded head toppled even as the body slumped to the ground, rolling end over end until it stopped next to my feet, face up.

It wasn't Angoulême.

Which meant he was still in control of my brother. And there was one very easy way for him to test as to whether I was still alive.

Swearing, I threw all the magic I had toward the ocean, and prayed it would be enough.

CHAPTER 54
Cécile

Dismay echoed from the lips of everyone on the tower, followed by a collective sigh of relief as the skiffs were caught just above the waterline, visible fingers of magic grasping and clawing at the wood to keep them upright and steady.

Marc swore. "That has to be Tristan holding them, but it isn't sustainable."

There was no missing what he meant. What had been a straight and steady bridge over the water was now little more than a floating dock, waves pummeling both magic and skiffs, sending them swaying back and forth.

Chris rounded on Melusina, who remained perched on the edge of the tower. "Will you take me closer?" She ruffled her wings and then dropped a shoulder for him to climb on, barely waiting for him to hook his feet into the ropes before taking off.

The door slammed open and Tips clattered out on his crutch. "Are you seeing this?" he asked, his eyes widening at the sight of me.

"Can you hold the wall?" Marc demanded.

Tips nodded. "For now, anyway. Might not have to for much longer – they're killing each other out there. Countless injured or dead."

"I'll try to think of something," I said. "Are there trolls amongst them?"

"No, not yet," he said. "Though I expect it's only a matter of time – this human shield of theirs won't do much good if they're all dead."

"I'll think of something," I repeated, though I had no idea what I could do that would help in time.

"Pray to your god that these people aren't oath sworn to Roland," Marc said, bracing himself against the stone. "Because I'm bringing them to shore."

We stood mutely as Marc plucked skiff after skiff off the failing bridge, dropping them on the beach. But people still over the water were climbing from their craft, trying to run toward shore. They slipped on the slick surface of the magic, unable to keep their balance as it bucked and plunged, sending them tumbling into the water.

"Idiots," Marc shouted, but his voice was full of desperation, not anger, as he abandoned the skiffs on the bridge to save those who'd fallen in the water.

It was impossible to look away, especially knowing that Tristan's power was beginning to fail. His panic was thick in my mind, as was his fear. There were still countless skiffs out there, and even more people in the water, but there was no more time.

"Hurry, Marc," I pleaded, knowing he was doing the best he could. "He can't last much longer."

"Cécile?"

I turned in time to see Sabine running toward me, Souris at her heels, barking like mad. I caught her and we went down in a heap. "Thank God you're here," she said, tears smearing against my cheeks. "We don't know what to do. It's madness outside the walls: they're all so afraid, but they can't seem to help themselves. So many people are dead or hurt, but no one knows what they'll do if we let them in."

Gran was leaning against the wall next to Marc. "I'd say we put them to sleep or in a trance like you did in Revigny, but we haven't the supplies for so much potion, and even if we did, I've no notion how we'd get them to drink it."

"Compulsion?" Marc asked, his voice strained. "Roland's oath is a weak method of control – it might be that you can overcome it for a time."

The very idea was overwhelming. I'd compelled a handful of people simultaneously, but it took an incredible amount of focus on each individual, and I'd never been able to sustain it for long. "I don't think I can," I said, explaining why.

Grim silence filled the tower as we all came to terms with the idea that we might not be able to do anything. That the survival of those people was entirely dependent on whether Tristan persevered.

"What about a song?" Sabine asked, and when I raised both eyebrows in askance, she added, "I saw your mother, I mean Anushka, do it at the masque. So did Tristan. When she sang, it seemed as though everyone was in a trance. No one moved – they barely seemed to breathe."

But that had been Anushka, a witch who'd been honing her craft for five centuries. What she had been capable of and what I was capable of were two very different things. Still, the idea resonated with me, and the more I thought about how it might work, the more I believed it was possible. To focus on the song as sort of a spell. Not to compel, but to... mesmerize?

"It won't hurt to try," Sabine said, squeezing my hand.

I nodded slowly. "Marc, could you amplify my voice enough that everyone could hear without stopping what you're doing?" I had no intention of sacrificing those at sea to save those outside the wall.

"Yes," he said, then tapped a gloved finger against his chin. "We'll have to muffle the ears of any human we don't want affected, half-bloods, too."

"Marie might still have rowan, which would work just as well. I'll go find her," Sabine said, helping me up before she departed.

My gaze went to the open sea. "I won't be able to do this forever, Marc. What is it that we can hope to accomplish?"

"I'll go out and help as many injured as I can," Gran said before he could respond. "I'll see if Sabine can get me the materials I need."

"Speak to Lady Marie," Marc said. "She'll be able to help you faster. Tell her I sent you. And find Joss – she could be of use."

It was only the two of us and the dog left on the tower. "Marc?" I asked again.

In a rare move, he pulled his hood back, revealing his disfigurement in its entirety. It struck me then that if I removed the iron from him, he wouldn't have to look like that anymore. That is, if he didn't want to. Part of me was certain that even given the chance, he'd remain the same.

"We'll be buying time for Tristan," he said. "That's all."

"And if he falls?" Even saying it hurt; as did the idea that there would be more for me to do if he did.

Marc was quiet, and I swore I could hear the screams of those outside the walls. "We can run," he said. "Take those who matter to us and get far away, regroup, then try again another day. Or not."

His eyes met mine, straight on, without a flinch. I wasn't sure if he'd ever done that before. What had changed?

"Or we fight," he said. "To the bitter end. Try to rally Trollus against Roland and Angoulême. Roland isn't invincible and Angoulême isn't infallible. There are more ways to end them than pure strength of magic alone."

"You'd make a good ruler," I said, having thought it for a long time but never voiced it.

"Maybe during times of peace," he said. "But to effect change, to rally people to risk everything, that requires a more ambitious and charismatic individual than I'll ever be. Either way, I hope we'll never have to find out." Then he waited, because I hadn't answered his question.

"We fight," I said. "Until the bitter end."

Sabine returned to the tower top. "Tips says they're ready," she said. "The half-bloods have blocked their ears with magic, and Fred's men still had their rowan from the night of the masque." She went to stand next to Marc, and it was not lost on me that she stood near enough to him that their elbows brushed. It made me wonder if Marc was ready, or even capable, of moving on from Pénélope, or if Sabine was pining for a young man who had nothing left to give. Either way, it was not my place to interfere, and given we might all be marching toward the end, what would be the point?

Sabine handed me a skin of warm lemon water, and I drank deeply, then ran through a series of exercises to warm up my neglected voice. She started to stuff her ears with wool, but Marc turned from his task and gently pushed her hands down. "Better not to take chances with you."

Sabine touched the side of her face, and I knew she was feeling the warm press of magic protecting her from my spell.

Turning so they wouldn't see the tears burning in my eyes, I took a deep breath, and then I sang. I chose a lullaby my mother – my real mother, not Anushka – had sung to me when I was a little girl, focusing my will into the lyrics and their sentiment. *Be calm.*

My voice filtered away from the tower and was caught with the threads of Marc's magic, which carried it out across the city, over the wall, and into the fields and hills beyond.

Be still.

Power filtered up from the earth, through the stones of the castle, and into my feet. Wind soared in from the sea, carrying mist that tasted like salt on my lips. The magic felt pure, wiping away the tarnish of the blood magic I'd used, the troll magic I'd stolen, and making me feel clean. It was a gift.

The horde of islanders outside the walls lost its erratic,

desperate violence. People stopped pushing, stopped fighting, their arms falling limply to their sides as they listened.

"It's working," Marc said. "Don't stop."

So I sang, repeating the lullaby like a soothing mantra, watching as my people sat down in the snow and the mud; and though it was too distant for me to see their faces, I knew they were transfixed. Mesmerized. There was motion amongst them now, Fred's men, my gran, and whomever else they'd chosen to help, moving amongst the horde, pulling out the injured and doing what they could to help them.

But it was not sustainable. Exhaustion was tugging at my limbs, and my lungs burned, the melody beginning to rasp in my throat. *Hurry, Tristan,* I silently pleaded.

The bridge blinked out.

I screamed, despite myself. Screamed, because hundreds of innocents were about to drown, were about to die. Men and women who'd done nothing to deserve this fate. Children who'd never had a chance to live.

Then skiffs were rising out of the water and moving toward land. Fingers of magic beyond number plucking people out of the surf and bringing them to safety.

Melusina swooped over our heads. "It's Trollus. The magic's coming from Trollus," Chris shouted. "There's hundreds of trolls on the beach bringing them in."

Martin, I thought, knowing that was where the librarian must have gone for help. And that so many had been willing to give it meant I hadn't been wrong to break the curse. They deserved their freedom, and right now, they were proving it.

"Can you see Tristan?" Marc shouted, and Chris shook his head. "They're on the beach, but she won't go close to them. I'll try again."

Then it happened.

I felt the air ripple, then everything rocked with a thunderous boom. My song faltered, and I struggled to keep focus, seeing the horde stir. The air pulsed again, but instead of a boom, it sounded like a thousand mirrors shattering.

Then I was falling.

Tristan was falling.

Marc's hands were reaching for me, catching me, but it didn't matter. "No," I whispered, but his magic was still tangled in my voice and the word rippled across Trianon. "Please, no."

CHAPTER 55
Tristan

My magic skated over the sea, stretching in a long strip beneath Roland's bridge, reaching both ends just before his magic vanished and the whole mess of humans and skiffs dropped on my flimsy replacement. There'd been no time to brace it against the sea floor, and the weight jerked me to my knees, dragging me forward and sending Damia's, the Dowager Duchesse d'Angoulême's, head rolling off into the brush.

I skidded on hands and knees toward the surf, my wrists trembling as I tried to find enough leverage to keep those thousands of people from plunging to their deaths. An icy wave struck me in the face, but I managed to turn and stop my slide with my heels, edging backwards as I sank a series of pillars into the ocean depths to hold the bridge up.

But it wasn't enough.

Water hammered the length of it, the strength of the sea dragging my bridge back and forth, waves cresting to push at the skiffs, forcing me to grab them with fingers of magic to keep them in place. But for all my efforts, there were overturned craft in the water. It wouldn't be long until bodies washed up on the shore.

And Roland was coming.

Get up, I ordered myself, staggering to my feet. I could feel the weight on the Trianon end lightening; the familiar brush of Marc's magic as he lifted the skiffs off the bridge. But he wasn't moving quickly enough. Not even close.

I couldn't run. If Roland got between me and the bridge, it would be child's play for him to cut the flows holding it up. This was where I would make my stand.

It wasn't long before my brother stepped out of the trees, Angoulême at his side. Roland's eyes looked dead, but the Duke's were full of fury. He knelt next to his mother's body and touched her cheek, and any thought I might've had that he'd set her up to die was chased away.

"If Cécile survives your death, I'm going to find her and make her wish she hadn't," he hissed, rising to his feet. He shoved Roland hard between the shoulders. "Kill him and take the crown. Make yourself King of Trollus and ruler of the Isle of Light."

The words acted like a trigger, delight washing across my brother's face. Then he attacked.

The first blow made my shield shudder; the second radiated through my limbs, making my body ache. I couldn't do both, couldn't hold all those lives out of the water while holding back my brother. *One more*, I told myself, *one more, and you'll have done all you can.*

The impact sent me staggering, and the magic behind me collapsed. I swore I could hear the screams of the drowning over the pounding of the waves.

Roland laughed, and magic whirled toward me like a storm. I braced, putting all the might I had at my disposal into a counterblow. The strength that had held up Forsaken Mountain. That had quelled my enemies. That had allowed me to walk through fire and ice unscathed.

It was not enough.

CHAPTER 56
Cécile

Hands were on me, Sabine's and Marc's, trying to hold me steady, but I pushed them away and fell against the wall, my fingernails digging into the stone. Drawing in a deep breath, I tried to sing, but it came out raspy and jarring. Snatching up the water skin, I guzzled the contents even as the horde began to shift and move, many of the people climbing to their feet, the injured struggling against those trying to help them.

I began the lullaby again, but the magic was faulty and impure, the islanders not reverting to that blissful calm, but swaying and twitching with collective unease.

"Is he dead?" Marc demanded, his hand gripping my arm hard enough to leave bruises.

I shook my head, tears falling from my face with the motion.

"Hurt or unconscious?"

I nodded, but those terms didn't encapsulate all of what I was feeling. Unconscious, hurt, and... drained.

"Shit!" He was across the tower to the door in an instant. "Get all of ours back inside the wall," he ordered the half-blood messenger Tips had left behind. "Now. Hurry." Then he set off a series of lights, which were answered by flashing on the wall.

Chris swooped over top of us. "I saw Roland," he shouted. "He's sitting alone in a field. But I couldn't find Tristan."

Bile burned in my throat, and I tried and failed to tune him out.

"And we've got more trouble coming our way," he shouted as Melusina circled. "Dozens of Angoulême's followers are coming this way, fast."

"How do you know they're his?" Marc asked. "They could be from Trollus."

"Because I recognize the troll leading them," Chris replied. "It's Comtesse Báthory. They'll be here in a half-hour, tops."

So much for Roland killing her.

The dragon landed on the tower, and Chris climbed off. "You need to find him," Marc said. "Go and look."

"I don't know how," my friend said, his eyes welling up. "The water is full of bodies."

I felt sick, but the song kept flowing.

"Victoria and Vincent will be out there as well; look to them for help," Marc said.

"I'll try," Chris said, then he inexplicably snatched Souris up and stuffed him in his coat before leaping onto the dragon's back.

Lights flickered in a pattern on the wall. "Everyone's inside," Marc said, then his hands fell on my shoulders. "Stop singing."

I stiffened, risking my focus to turn and look at him.

"Better they think Tristan's dead," he said. "And if he was, you wouldn't have the focus for magic."

Stopping felt like abandoning all those out there, but I knew he was right. We'd done what we could for them, and now we needed to prepare for the attack. I let the song trail off, turning to the center of the tower so I wouldn't have to witness the reemergence of their madness. Then I took a deep breath. "We need to go down to the wall and see what we can do to prepare."

Marc had raced ahead to warn Fred and his men of what was coming. Sabine and I followed on horseback, her clinging to my waist as we raced through the empty streets. Windows and doors were boarded shut, but there was no missing the fearful eyes peering through the cracks or the tension singing through all of Trianon. They knew what was coming.

On the wall, it was even worse. The half-bloods were arrayed at equal intervals, holding up their piece of the patchwork barrier, but their faces were drawn, hands resting against the stone for balance, a few even on their knees as if the effort of standing was beyond them. The expressions of the human soldiers were even worse. Some sat staring blankly at nothing; others wept openly; more still were muttering prayers for divine protection which were barely audible over the cries of the horde below.

I glanced through an arrow slit, and immediately wished I had not. "Let us in, let us in," they screamed when they caught sight of my face, a mass of them surging forward with renewed effort. Clawing, grasping, pushing, and shoving – not a one of them seemed without injury, and the ground at the base of the wall was drenched with blood and bodies. Had that hour of respite done them any good, or had I only prolonged their anguish?

Turning away, I hurried to where Marc stood. Fred and Joss kneeling at his feet, in my brother's arms a still, silver-haired form. "No," I shrieked, sprinting toward them. "Gran!"

But even as I fell to my knees, I knew it was too late.

"We were out there helping the children." I looked up and saw Lady Marie standing next to Marc. I hadn't recognized her in the plain homespun she wore, her hair pulled back in a tight braid. "She was healing those who needed it, and I was giving a sleeping draught to them so they wouldn't rejoin the mob when your spell broke and…" Her voice cracked. "She had just finished healing a little girl, and she collapsed. There was nothing I could do."

A sob tore out of my chest, and I staggered over to an arrow slit and looked out. Sure enough, beyond the horde lay a long row of small forms, their faces still with the peace of sleep. "Bring them in," I choked out, refusing to see them trampled or injured when the battle began. Refusing for my gran's last act to be a waste.

No one moved.

"Bring them in," I screamed.

Marc nodded, and I watched as tender ropes of magic wrapped around the children, lifting them over the madness made of their parents and relatives, and deposited them gently on the ground inside the dubious safety of the wall. He turned to Sabine, but she was already moving. "I'll get them somewhere safe," she said.

"I have more of the potion," Marie said, touching my shoulder. "If you'll let me bring more of the children in, I can give it to them and treat their injuries."

She was asking my permission, I realized. Like I was the ruler instead of her. "Do it."

Nodding once, she turned and called, "Zoé!"

The half-blood girl who had once been my maid appeared, and the two hurried around the bend in the wall, their heads together as they conferred.

I gently kissed my gran's forehead, pulled her cloak over her face, and then I said, "How do you think this is going to go?"

"They know I'm in here," Marc replied, staring out over the hills and fields as though he could see our enemy coming. "They know hundreds of half-bloods, many of whom possess a fair amount of power, are in here." His jaw flexed. "Angoulême built this army for a reason – I believe they'll disguise themselves and join the horde, break down sections of the wall and get inside the city hidden within the flow of humans. After that..." He shook his head.

"But you'd be able to pick them out of a crowd, wouldn't you?" Fred asked. "Feel their power, or however that works?"

"Yes," Marc said. "But they'll be hemmed in by civilians on

all sides. Attacking them without harming dozens of innocents would be next to impossible. And even if that was a sacrifice we were willing to make, we don't have the power to fight them all."

"Can we get word to Trollus?" I asked, wishing there was a way for me to contact Martin. "The trolls there helped those on the water – maybe they'd be willing to help here."

"We can send a half-blood," Marc replied. "But even if they'd be willing, I'm not sure they'd make it in time."

Fred was staring through the arrow slit down at the screaming islanders, not seeming to be paying attention to anything we said. I jabbed him in the ribs with a finger. "Suggestions?"

He nodded slowly, and in a tone that was alarmingly similar to one I often employed, he said, "I think I have a plan."

CHAPTER 57
Cécile

It was deathly quiet on the wall, every half-blood in Trianon grim faced as they held their portion of magic reinforcing the stone. Down below, almost every soldier Fred had at his disposal stood armed to the teeth, waiting. Ready to fight the moment the wall was breached.

Almost every soldier.

I paced up and down the narrow walkway, stopping to peer carefully through an arrow slit from time to time to see if I could pick out a familiar face in the horde below.

Under Marc's watchful eye, several of Tips's crew had carefully opened the tunnel they'd dug to get under the city wall when they first arrived, allowing Fred and a hundred of his most trusted men to leave Trianon undetected. Dressed in civilian clothes with cloaks to cover their weapons, they'd joined the mass of islanders trying to push their way through the wall, mimicking their wails and mannerisms. Waiting.

"Please go back to the castle, Cécile," Marc said. "Sabine, Marie, and Joss could use your help, and there is nothing you can do here."

The women had taken cartloads of sleeping children back to the castle, and it was true that many were injured and needed a witch's touch. But I couldn't bear to leave. "My brother's out there," I whispered. *I'm afraid of losing him, too.*

"I can't spare anyone to stand guard over you."

"Then don't," I said. "I know the risks, and I'm not helpless." I pulled open my coat to reveal a pair of pistols and a set of blades. "Besides, the castle will be the first place they look for me."

Out of the corner of my eye, I saw him shake his head, but he voiced no further argument.

"Let us in, let us in." I tried not to hear, not to listen, but sweat had already soaked through my shirt despite the chill of the air.

Marc hissed through his teeth. "Báthory."

"Where?"

"The woman in the red cloak. I'd recognize that strut anywhere." His hand went to the pommel of the sword at his waist, as though that would be his first line of attack. "There's another. And another." Careful to keep out of sight, he pointed out the approaching trolls. All of them wore hooded cloaks that obscured their faces, and other than Báthory, all were doing a fair job of imitating the motions of their human shield. Moving at a speed that would not attract attention, they joined the mob of humans, carefully pushing their way forward until they were hemmed in by islanders on all sides.

"Mark them." His order rippled softly down the line of half-bloods, those known to have a deft touch lighting the faintest of sparks behind the heads of the enemy trolls. If I hadn't been watching, I wouldn't even have noticed, and I prayed it was enough to guide Fred's men to their targets.

Sure enough, men began to move slowly toward the trolls, carefully, making it appear as though those around them were pushing them in that particular direction.

"Come on," Marc hissed. "Get into position."

And it was then I picked Fred out of the crowd, only a few feet away from Báthory now. "No," I moaned, my hands turning to ice. "Not her."

But he was right behind her, now pressed up against her, the troll not even noticing amidst the bumping and jostling of limbs and bodies.

"Brace yourself," Marc said, and a heartbeat later, a horn blared and everything turned to chaos. Pistols fired and then men surged at their targets, steel blades in their hands. I saw a dozen trolls or more go down, but Báthory was not one of them. One hand pressed over the spurting hole the bullet had left when it exited her chest, she screamed and spun, catching Fred's blade as it descended and wrenching it from his hand. Plucking it from the air, she sliced with a speed no human possessed, catching him on the arm. He went down, the crowd falling over him, and I screamed his name.

"Báthory," Marc shouted, then he was over the wall, landing amongst the humans, who even in their stupor seemed to know enough to move. The air charged, magic smashing against magic; then the Comtesse was flying through the air, landing some distance away. Marc sprinted after her, sword in hand, and with a cruel slice, separated her head from her neck.

But none of that mattered. Not caring about the risk, I hung half over the wall, searching for Fred amongst the teeming mass. "Fred," I screamed again. "Marc, find him!"

His silver eyes searched with no more success than mine, but before he could do more, stone shattered and a section of the wall collapsed. Shaking his head at me, he ran in the direction of the breach.

I didn't know what to do. Even if I didn't break both my legs jumping from this height, I was likely to be crushed by those beneath, most of whom were significantly larger than I was. But my brother was down there. My brother.

There was only one thing I could do, and if it gave away that I was alive, that Tristan was alive, then so be it.

I began to sing.

The islanders stilled, then sank down into the mud, their

faces serene as they listened. I searched amongst them for my brother, relief crashing through me as I saw him struggle out from under the limbs of a pair of men, then drag himself away from the crush of humanity. His arm was bleeding profusely, but he was alive.

For now.

Because amongst the seated humans, there stood several cloaked figures who were unaffected by my magic. Not all of Angoulême's followers had been killed. Not even close.

As one, they attacked, hammering against the half-bloods' shields, and when those fell, the thick rock beneath. Sections of the wall crumbled or were blown inwards, and everywhere, everywhere, there was screaming. Great pieces of stone fell on the islanders below, their serene faces never registering fear as they were crushed, maimed, and killed. The soldiers behind me fought valiantly against the trolls who strolled in through the breaks in the wall, stepping on fallen humans like they were cobbles of a paved street. I hazarded a glance back and saw Marc fighting amongst them, but he was only one against dozens.

"Drop the wall and fight," Tips roared, and the half-bloods fell into teams, sprinting down stairs and leaping off the walkway into the fray. Some threw themselves at the full-blooded trolls with no regard for their own lives, while others defended the human soldiers as they withdrew or regrouped. Some of the trolls fell, but only at incredible cost of life. We could not win this.

My voice was the only thing keeping the islanders out of the battle, but it felt like I was doing nothing. Pulling out one of my pistols, I leveled it at a troll wielding twin maces formed of magic that shattered bodies with each swing. If he was fighting like that, his shields were down. Finishing a verse, I aimed and fired, the bullet passing straight through his shoulder. He bellowed and spun around, eyes searching for the culprit.

And landing on me.

I fired with my other pistol, but he brushed the bullet aside, expression feral as he slashed an arm sideways. Half-bloods and human soldiers flung themselves at him, but it was too late, the air was already rippling with magic. Turning to the wall, I lunged toward a break in the parapet, and toppled over the edge.

I clenched my teeth for the impact, ready to start singing no matter how many bones I broke, because if I didn't, the resurgence of the mob would trample me to death.

But the impact never came.

Instead, arms broke my fall, a familiar face appearing in my line of sight.

"I've been looking for you," Martin said, winding his way through the islanders as they stirred. He started to say something else, but his voice was drowned out by the blare of a horn. Not the horn Angoulême's followers had used in their attack, but the great horn of Trollus. It blared again, then I caught sight of movement in the trees and trolls broke into the open, sprinting our direction. Hundreds of them.

"I brought reinforcements," Martin said. "Now let's get out of the way."

The citizens of Trollus descended on Trianon, some stopping to pluck the oath-sworn islanders up, drawing them back and holding them steady, while others leapt though the breaches in the wall, attacking Angoulême's followers. They showed them no mercy, ripping them to pieces, and once the soldiers and half-bloods realized they were allies, not enemies, they roared a rallying cry. Not long after, it turned to cheers of victory.

The battle was over, and against all the odds, we had won.

But not without cost.

CHAPTER 58
Cécile

The rows of bodies seemed to go on forever.

A drop of sweat dripped into my eye, and I wiped a grimy hand across my forehead, not caring that I'd probably left a streak of blood, dirt, and worse behind. The soldier before me was breathing steadily, his chest now a network of scars rather than open wounds, but what was saving one compared to the hundreds who'd died because of my choices, my actions?

I sat back on my haunches, watching yet another cartload of sleeping islanders trundle past, headed to the prison, which had been deemed the only safe place to keep them. Except for the children – Marie had insisted they all be brought to the castle, where she'd enlisted several of the newly arrived trolls to watch over them in case any woke.

But it was a stopgap. Asleep, they could neither eat nor drink, and we hadn't the resources to tend to each individual as we had with Aiden. The young lord remained under my spell – and Zoé's watchful eye – his mother insisting he remain so until we'd won the day. And if we lost, well… It wouldn't matter at that point if the King's compulsion had destroyed his mind or not.

"Is Tristan still unconscious?" Marc knelt next to me, handing me a steaming tin cup.

I nodded, trying not to let my fear show. Too easily, I

conjured up Vincent's face, devoid of all that made him him, and wondered if the same had happened to Tristan. Whether he lay somewhere, alone, with a head injury so traumatic that even his seemingly endless power hadn't been able to overcome it. After all, his power hadn't been able to help Vincent.

"Victoria and Chris are looking," Marc said. "They'll find him."

"I should go." My eyes burned, but I was so drained, it felt like there were no tears left to spill. "I could find him."

"If that's what you want."

His tone was careful, and I knew it was his way of saying that to do so would be a mistake. "Just say what you're thinking, Marc," I muttered, knowing I shouldn't be sharp with him. That Trianon wasn't in total chaos was all thanks to him and Tips. The injured were being cared for, the dead put to rest, and the walls rebuilt, and though the city had been through hell and back, there was no sense of hopelessness.

The sound of trolls and humans hard at work fell away, and Marc pulled forward his hood to conceal his lips from sharp eyes. "No one knows that Roland defeated Tristan yet," he said. "And for now, we need to keep it that way. Trollus has chosen to rally behind him, but if they knew the truth…"

"That might change," I finished for him.

He nodded. "Angoulême likely saw how Trollus helped the people of Courville who were on those skiffs, and he'll know what that means, so he will be eager to inform them of Tristan's demise – that their chosen one is, to his knowledge, a dead man."

"So what do you think he'll do?"

Marc's eyes went distant as he thought. "The news of Tristan's death would throw Trollus and Trianon into chaos. The humans would have lost their protector, and the trolls would be faced with the decision of whether to accept Roland or rally behind a new candidate as king or queen. The latter will cause infighting that will lead to even more upheaval until someone lands on top. He'll want to attack now rather than risk fighting a new, unified front."

"If we find Tristan, won't they fight for him?"

Marc blew out a breath between his teeth, the expression in his unblinking eyes answering my question, and sickness burned the back of my throat. Whether Trollus remained loyal would depend on what state Tristan was in, and as it was, there was no chance he'd be recovered by the time Roland and Angoulême arrived to attack.

"Of a surety, some of the Duke's followers survived the battle, and they'll be running to meet him with the news that not only are you alive, you're well enough to perform magic, which will make him suspect Tristan survived the battle with his brother."

"Will that keep him from attacking?"

He shook his head. "I think it will only cause him to move faster – to strike before Tristan has the chance to recover."

"Surely we can hold against him," I said. "We've hundreds of trolls here, plus all the half-bloods and human soldiers."

"But at what cost?" Marc asked. "Angoulême will walk up to the gates and inform everyone in straight terms that Roland has defeated his brother. He will give them a chance to capitulate or face Roland's wrath. What do you think they'll choose?"

"Then what?" I snapped, my temper fraying. "What do you suggest we do? As I see it, our only hope is to find Tristan and see if I can help him recover. If he were here, if the trolls could see him, then maybe…" It would still be another battle. Hundreds, maybe thousands of lives lost, with no certainty of victory. Was surrender the better option? Was it inevitable?

"We have one advantage," Marc said. "For a few hours more, Angoulême believes you both are dead. His guard will be lowered."

I threw up my hands in frustration. "So? It isn't as though Tristan is capable of doing anything about it."

"I'm not talking about Tristan," Marc said. "I'm talking about you."

CHAPTER 59
Cécile

We crouched in a copse of trees, twilight upon us. Melusina had delivered Marc, Sabine, and me to the location an hour ago, but we'd waited for the twins to join us before making our move. It had killed me to ask Martin pull them away from their search for Tristan, but Marc couldn't handle Angoulême and Lessa on his own.

He's still alive, I reminded myself. *Chris is looking for him – he'll find him.*

"We're running out of time," Marc muttered, sitting back on his haunches to reveal the portal Martin had made. We were waiting for Roland to be alone, but thus far, he'd been unaccommodating. And it wouldn't be long before the survivors of our victory at Trianon would arrive with word that I was still alive.

"We could intercept them," Victoria said, absently braiding her long black hair as she watched Roland. "Can't talk if they're dead."

"Risky," Marc replied. "We don't know who survived – you'd have no idea of who you were going up against." His jaw tightened. "But I don't see as we have a choice. Go, and we'll send Martin for you when we move."

If we moved. I sighed, pulling my hood further forward to keep my ears warm.

"He looks so sad," Sabine said, leaning against me as we watched the twins disappear into the darkness, Vincent following at his sister's heels.

I glanced at her. "Roland?"

She nodded, and I fought the urge to regale her with stories of the many ways Tristan's brother had harmed people, including me. Truthfully, she was right. Roland sat across a crackling fire from Angoulême and Lessa, his chin resting on his knees as he stared into the flames. Neither of his companions made any attempt to engage in conversation, and the human soldiers and servants in their camp gave them wide berth.

"He's been made to do things he didn't wish to do," I said. "That's why he's upset. Not because he feels badly for the hurt he's caused."

"A broken child," Sabine said. "But still just a child."

That thought in our minds, we all sat in silence watching the trio.

"Stones and sky, Roland," Marc muttered. "Go take a piss or something."

"This isn't working," I said. "We need to find another way to lure him away from his minders."

"What if we sent him a message," Sabine said. "A note."

"How?" Marc asked. "It isn't as though any of us can traipse in there and deliver it."

"Why not?" Sabine asked, and I immediately shook my head, seeing the direction this was going. "It's too dangerous, Sabine. He's too dangerous." I looked to Marc for agreement, but instead his gaze was thoughtful.

"What are you thinking?" he asked.

She shrugged. "I smell cooking, and a growing boy's got to eat."

"I should be the one doing this," I muttered as we approached the group of servants working around the cook fire.

"No, you shouldn't," she replied. "From what I've heard, the

Duke is wise to all our tricks and he's not so much a fool to have completely lowered his guard. If any of them were to sense the magic of your disguise, you'd be done. Tristan would be done. And I don't really care to fight the rest of this war without you."

I couldn't argue with her logic.

Two of the cooks looked up at our approach, and we both smiled. "She's going to serve His Majesty his dinner tonight," I said, a breeze drifting through the camp as I forced power into my words. "You've both known her for years. Me, you never saw."

Moving at a sedate pace that wouldn't attract attention, I retreated into the woods to where Marc and Martin waited, their eyes on the portal.

"Here she comes," Martin whispered, and we all watched in silence. If it went badly, there was nothing we'd be able to do to help her.

Sabine and two other women approached the three trolls, trays of steaming food carefully balanced in their hands. She dropped into a curtsey, and the other two followed suit, dishes rattling against each other.

"Idiots don't know the first thing about serving royalty," Lessa muttered.

"Perhaps you might instruct them, my lady," Roland said. "Given your own expertise in the matter." There was a sly edge to his voice that reminded me of his brother, but I shook away the thought.

"He knows she isn't Anaïs," Marc murmured, and I nodded. Knew, and wasn't entirely pleased about the deception.

"Check them," Angoulême said, his tone sour. Indeed, for one who, in his mind, had won a victory a lifetime in the making, he seemed of a poor temper.

Roland glanced at Sabine, then turned back to the fire. "They are who they are. Human. No magic."

"Are you sure?"

Roland slowly lifted his chin to meet the Duke's gaze, and the hatred in his eyes was like nothing I'd ever seen. A wrath inhuman in its magnitude. "By all means, Your Grace, please check for yourself. Or perhaps have *the lady* check them, given she excels with disguises. Or at least thinks she does." His eyes shifted to his half-sister, eyeing her up as though wondering how she'd look without her skin.

Lessa licked her lips nervously, and shifted a few inches away. But Angoulême seemed unperturbed. "Do not test me, boy," he snapped, jerking the tray from one of the women's hands and slamming it on the ground.

Noticeably trembling, Sabine approached Roland, and I took hold of Marc's hand, squeezing it hard to keep my fear in check.

"Your Majesty," she whispered, dropping into another curtsey, then carefully setting the tray in front of him, her body obscuring Angoulême and Lessa's view. Then she slowly lifted her face to meet his eyes and I held my breath. *Please don't hurt her.*

Roland's head tilted ever so slightly, expression considering. Then his eyes flicked to the scrap of paper Sabine carefully dropped onto his tray.

Please. Please.

"Thank you," he said, his smile revealing too many teeth to be comforting. Then magic plucked up the scrap, he glanced at the words, and it disappeared in a smokeless puff of flame. "It smells delightful."

Sabine curtseyed a third time, then retreated with the other women back to the distant cook fire. Roland watched her go, then began eating, showing no interest in divulging the existence or the contents of my note to his master. He finished his meal and rose to his feet. "Excuse me."

"Where are you going?" Angoulême demanded.

Roland stopped in his tracks, and even from the distance where we watched, I felt the ground tremble. "You've made it quite clear, Your Grace, that I'm responsible for dirtying my hands for you, but I did not realize that you intended to reciprocate."

Marc snorted out a laugh. "Madness aside, he's got a Montigny tongue on him."

Angoulême scowled. "Don't be long."

"That's hard to predict," Roland replied, strolling off into the woods.

"You pushed him too hard," Lessa hissed once he was out of earshot. "He hates you. And you heard him – he knows who I am."

"What of it?" The Duke broke the roll on his plate into tiny pieces, eating none of them. "He is under my control and no threat to you or me."

"Is he?" Lessa shoved aside her untouched tray. "If he looks hard enough, he'll find a way around your commands. Around his promises. There is always a way around."

"Speaking from experience?"

Lessa recoiled, then leaned forward, catching at the Duke's sleeve. "My family cast me aside," she whispered. "Yours took me in. Gave me everything and taught me everything. Do not let Tristan and Cécile's lies turn you against me – you know I'm loyal. And they're dead." She reached up to touch his cheek and he slapped her hand away violently.

"Not while you're wearing her face."

Lowering her arm, Lessa glanced around, then let Anaïs's face melt away to reveal her own. "Anaïs was loyal to Tristan, not to you," she said. "I killed her because she was a traitor."

"You killed her to further your own ends," Angoulême snarled. "Anaïs was my child, and you slaughtered her. Then you lied to me about it." He leaned closer. "Lied like a cursed human."

Lessa crouched in on herself, realizing, I thought, that she'd made a mistake in killing Anaïs. That Angoulême had cared more for his daughter than he'd let on, and that it was only his unwillingness to disrupt his plans that kept him from having his revenge. But that might not always be the case.

"I'll give you another," she said. "And once our child is strong enough to hold the throne, we can be rid of Roland."

Angoulême's anger fell away, and he stroked a finger down her cheek. "I can't help but admire your ambition, darling. Your willingness to see your entire family dead in your pursuit of the crown." He leaned forward and whispered something in her ear, her face growing still. Then he sat back. "You promised to love me. Remember that."

"I love you," Lessa whispered. "I always have."

"His cruelty really does know no bounds," Marc murmured, and I moved away from the portal, unwilling to watch any more of this abuse. Never would I have thought to have cause to feel sympathy for Lessa, but to be forced to love that monster? I sighed.

Then Martin spoke. "Roland's gone some distance from the camp. He's waiting."

"You ready for this, Cécile?" Marc asked.

My pulse was loud in my ears, my ice-cold hands drenched with sweat, but I nodded at Martin and the world tore open to reveal the monster with whom I needed to form an alliance.

Hissing in surprise, Roland leapt back and swiped at the tear, but his magic passed through it as though the opening wasn't there.

"This is fey magic," I said to him. "You cannot attack it."

The violence fell away from him, and he tried again to pluck at the edges of the tear before giving up and acknowledging me. "Why aren't you dead?"

"It's not for lack of your master trying," I said, crossing my arms.

"I am King," Roland replied, his face twisting. "I have no…" His throat choked off the lie, and I could all but feel his fury.

"What is it you want, human?"

"Revenge." I hesitated, terrified of saying something that would trigger one of the traps the Duke had placed in the boy's mind. "Angoulême has taken everything from me, just as he has taken everything from you."

"He gave me the crown, just as he said he would."

"Has he?" I asked, then before he could respond, "For your brother's sake, will you hear me out?"

"Tristan cares not what I do." Roland said, eyes going to his boots. "He's dead."

It was no answer, but I knew I had him – that he'd listen. "I know the Duke forced you to kill your parents and your aunt," I said. "And to... attack your brother." I bit the insides of my cheeks. "He has your name and he controls what you do."

The barest hint of a nod.

"How can you truly be king if you are controlled by another?" I asked. "He is only using you for your power, Roland. To eliminate any who are strong enough to contest him."

Silence.

"You know that is Lessa pretending to be Anaïs? That he betrothed you to his lover who is also your half-sister, and if that were not awful enough, he intends to cuckold you and pretend the child is yours. And when that child is strong enough to hold the throne, he intends to kill you and your sister so that there are no Montignys left. So that there are none alive more powerful than him."

"What is it you would have me do?" Roland's voice was acidic. "As you say, *he* is the one in control."

I lifted my chin, forcing myself to hold his gaze. It was like staring into the eyes of a viper. "So you would live the rest of your life under his thumb, as his puppet, until he decides to do you in?"

Roland's jaw tightened.

"What if there was another way?" I asked, before his temper

snapped. "What if we could make it so that he could no longer use you as his weapon?"

"How?"

I swiftly explained to him how my spell worked. "You would be immortal," I said. "Your powers would be the same as your great ancestor, the King of Summer, and you'd be able to travel to worlds beyond counting."

For all he was mad, Roland wasn't stupid. I didn't dare mention that if he went through with our scheme, that Angoulême wouldn't last long in the land of the living: Marc was certain the Duke would have set triggers in the boy's mind to attack anyone who threatened his master. I didn't have to say anything – Roland knew as well as anyone that Angoulême had many enemies who would take advantage of his vulnerability.

"If I did this, I'd be king of nothing," he eventually said.

My hands shook as I debated my response, then I crossed my fingers and said, "You're already king of nothing. Angoulême rules. But you can take that away from him, if you want."

"How do I know this isn't a trick," he said. "How do I know you aren't lying, and that this isn't an elaborate scheme to try to kill me?"

I nodded at Martin, who stepped through the tear. "She's telling the truth, Your Majesty," the librarian said. "Cécile took the iron from me, and now I can travel back to Arcadia. She will do the same for you, if you wish it."

"Why?" Roland demanded of me. "I've harmed you. Killed your kind. And I..." His throat convulsed. "I killed my brother, to whom you were bonded."

"And I hate you for it," I said. "But you are Tristan's brother, and he loved you for all your faults. For him, I will do this."

Roland stared at me for a long time, seeing but not, and then he nodded. "Come meet me here and do the spell now, *he* will notice if I am gone for much longer. Come alone, and Cécile..."

"Yes?" I was so afraid. So terribly afraid.

"Mind your words. If you say the wrong thing, it will not go well for you."

Following Martin's directions, I walked on silent feet through the darkened woods, my body twitching at every rustle in the blackness. Marc was watching, but he couldn't come close for fear of Roland sensing him, his primary goal to prevent Angoulême or Lessa coming upon us mid-spell. Martin had gone to update the twins, and they were to retreat if they could and engage with Angoulême's camp when the rest of his followers arrived.

"Breathe," I told myself. "Just breathe."

Then magic had me by the hair and I was hurtling through the trees, branches lashing at my body as I passed. I tried to scream, but my jaw was locked shut, invisible rope twisting around my wrists and ankles. I landed heavily in a pile of snow, then small hands were on me, ripping through my pockets and tearing at my clothes before shoving me aside to inspect my bag.

Roland appeared in my line of sight, and smiled. "Can't be too careful – I know all about your spells."

My jaw was released from his grip, and I whimpered, curling in on myself.

"Did that hurt?" His breath was hot on my ear.

"Yes."

He laughed softly, then sat cross-legged next to me. "Good. Now get up and get started. If he comes, I won't be able to stop him from killing you. He made me promise to leave you to him, if we found you alive."

I pushed up onto my hands and knees, extracting the flask containing my premixed potion. His eyes tracked my every move. "If this doesn't work, I won't be happy," he warned.

"It will work." I swallowed hard. "If you would remove your coat and shirt and lay on the ground, Your Majesty. "

He obliged, the snow immediately melting to form a pool around his overheated skin.

"It will be painful," I warned.

"I don't feel pain," he said, then his eyes flicked to me. "I feel nothing."

"Then let's begin." I poured the potion, and drew upon all the power the world had to offer.

CHAPTER 60
Tristan

I drifted just outside the threshold of consciousness, aware. But not.

It was cold. I was cold. Numb.

Bodies jostled against me, dead limbs clutching and grabbing. Faces full of accusation. They dragged me deeper and deeper until I couldn't breathe. The weight of a thousand corpses, a thousand victims, pressing down on my chest.

Get off, I screamed at them. *I tried. Did everything I could.*

The dead do not listen. The dead cannot hear.

I reached for the flame that was my magic, clawed at it with desperate fingers. But instead of burning bright, it guttered. Faltered. Blackness tugged me away from consciousness, further and further until it was only a distant gleam. But something wouldn't let me go.

A sound, sharp and repetitious. Familiar.

"Tristan!" A voice I knew well. "Don't you dare be dead, you stupid pretty-faced troll!"

Then the weight was pushed off my chest, the bodies shoved away, and hands, warm with the heat of life, were pulling me out of the cold.

I opened my eyes.

CHAPTER 61
Cécile

Roland opened his eyes and sat up, staring at one misty hand as though he couldn't believe it was his own.

"Roland," I said. "Are you all right?"

His form solidified, and I eased back, ready to run if I had to. Just because he couldn't harm me with magic any longer didn't mean he wasn't capable of ripping out my throat. "Roland?" I repeated.

He lifted his head, and I sensed in the moment that his eyes met mine that his madness was gone. That in removing the iron from his body, I'd stripped away the poison twisting his mind. "I'm sorry it hurt," I said, gently touching his hand.

He flinched, and I wondered how long it had been since someone had comforted him, if they ever had. If he had even wanted it. Then warm fingers clutched at mine, his chin trembled, and I knew the pain of the spell was nothing compared to what he was feeling now. How much terror had he caused in his young life? How many had died at his hands? His parents and his aunt, and, in his mind, his brother. Worse, how much emotional neglect had he suffered at Angoulême's hands? His iron madness had been what drove him to commit all those atrocities, but now it was gone. And he was going to have to find a way to live with what he'd done.

A sob racked through his shoulders, and in a movement almost too fast to see, he curled up in a little ball, my fingers clutched painfully tight in one of his hands. In the same moment, I felt Tristan regain consciousness and relief thundered through my heart.

"Roland, Tristan's alive," I said. "He's all right."

He went still, then peered up at me with hope. Then his gaze flicked over my shoulder, and in a blur of speed, he slammed into me, knocking me flat on my back. I struggled against him, convinced that I'd been wrong about his madness being gone, when a wave of heat washed over our heads.

"You little human bitch," Angoulême snarled. "What have you done?"

"Cured him," I shouted, allowing Roland to pull me to my feet. He stepped between me and the Duke, and I wondered if he knew his powers had changed. "Good luck using him now, you abusive coward."

"Cured him?" The Duke's hands were balled into fists as he stalked toward us. "Cured him? You've ruined him – now he is nothing. He is worth nothing!"

Roland flinched, but stood his ground.

"Feeling brave, are we, you miserable little wretch?" Angoulême lifted a hand, face twisted with fury. "Let's see how long that lasts."

The air filled with fire, but instead of incinerating us, it blasted around a shield of magic. Marc stepped into the clearing. "It's over, Angoulême," he said. "Surrender."

The Duke spat in the dirt at Marc's feet. "We've been through this before, you broken fool. You can't defeat me."

"Perhaps it's time we put that to the test."

Angoulême laughed. "Kill her, boy."

Roland stiffened. Slowly, he turned to face me, and I saw tears were running down his face. "I'm sorry, Cécile," he said. "I must obey." Then he lunged.

Stars burst in my eyes even as I heard explosions punctuating the air as Angoulême and Marc fought. Magic ripped Roland off me, tossing him into some bushes, but he was back in a flash, body turning to mist as he ran through Marc's defenses, solidifying just before he struck. I rolled, his fists striking the earth where my head had been seconds before.

But he was on me in an instant, fingers clawing and bruising my legs as he clamored up my body, reaching for my throat. Then Martin appeared out of nowhere, wrapping his arms around Roland's waist, and pulling him off me. Prying open the boy's lips, he emptied a handful of gleaming blue liquid into Roland's mouth and let go of him. Roland stood gaping at him for a heartbeat, then a tear opened in the world and Martin stepped through, dragging the troll prince with him.

But I wasn't out of danger yet.

Angoulême and Marc battled on, magic flaring bright with concussive blasts that made my ears ring. Swaths of trees were leveled while others were reduced to a smoking ruin. And beyond, I could see the twins had brought the battle to the camp to keep Angoulême's people from helping their master. Ignoring the aching pain of my body, I rolled behind a boulder, keeping my head down as I watched.

For all of the Duke's bluster, it seemed an even match, both dripping sweat as they dodged and attacked. But like Pénélope, Angoulême had spent his life avoiding any chance of injury, and that sedentarism had come with a cost. His breath came in great winded gasps, and he began to trip and stumble as he dodged Marc's blows.

"Come on," I whispered. "Come on."

Then he fell, landing on his side in the mess of blood the spell on Roland had left behind. He struggled backwards, barely deflecting Marc's next attack.

"There's a long list of people who wanted this honor," Marc said, pulling out a sword. "I hope they forgive me for taking it myself."

"No!" The scream sounded like breaking glass, and Marc barely turned in time to block Lessa's blow. She wore her own face, and it was coated with blood, her hair a tangled mess, and her clothes torn. She attacked with a mad ferocity, not giving Marc a moment's respite.

Which was why he didn't see Angoulême move, or the knife that appeared in his hand.

But I did. And I also saw that his face was smeared with Roland's blood, blood that was steeped with all the iron I'd pulled from the boy's body. I reached for the power, for the magic, and said, "Bind the light."

Angoulême froze, then his silver eyes tracked through the smoke and darkness to land on the rock where I was hidden. Giving one passing glance to ensure Marc was engaged with Lessa, he climbed to his feet and started toward me, knife in hand. "I think you've played your last card, little bird."

I scuttled backwards, the smoldering ground burning the palms of my hand.

"I'm going to take my time with you," he said with a smile. "Who do you think it was who taught Roland all his tricks?"

I whimpered, feeling my pants dampen and hating myself for it. I was supposed to be brave, was supposed to see this through, no matter what the cost. But I'd been afraid of him from the moment we'd met, and that, that hadn't changed.

Then a roar filled the air, and fire brighter than the sun filled the sky. A massive form with wings passed over me, and I curled into a ball, closing my eyes against the heat. I felt rather than heard the thud of something landing next to me, and then Tristan was there, smothering the flames eating at my clothing. His face was carved with shadows, his clothes torn and crusted with salt. But he was alive, and he was here.

"Are you all right?" he asked.

I wasn't, but I nodded anyway. "Angoulême? Where is he?"

Tristan's eyes searched our surroundings, then he shook his

head. "I don't see him."

"His magic is bound," I said. "Find him, and kill him."

"But Roland–"

"Is cured," I said. "Now go before Angoulême finds somewhere to wash off the blood."

His eyes lit up in a way I hadn't seen in a very long time, and he kissed me. "Be safe," he said, then was gone.

With the exception of the crackling of the burning woods, the night had gone eerily quiet. Holding my shirt over my mouth in an attempt to block the worst of the smoke, I began to search for my friends. I found Sabine first, and Chris, who had Souris tucked into his coat. But of Marc and the twins, there was no sign.

"How did you find him?" I asked, allowing Sabine to pack snow against my blistered palms.

"I didn't," Chris said. "His little rat dog friend did. He was half dead under one of those skiffs and surrounded by bodies, but the damn thing has nose like a bloodhound." He took hold of my shoulder. "But he's burnt out, Cécile. I don't think he could create so much as a ball of light if his life depended on it."

And I'd just sent him after Angoulême.

"You two find Marc or the twins. I have to find him," I said, starting off in the direction he'd gone. To myself, I said, "If the Duke breaks my spell, Tristan won't have a chance."

"And what a shame that would be," Lessa said, stepping into my path.

CHAPTER 62
Tristan

It occurred to me as I sprinted through the woods without enough magic to keep the burning ground from singing my boots that I was making a mistake. That I should retreat and regroup, give my power a chance to recover itself, and then come up with a clever strategy for catching Angoulême.

But I was done with clever strategies.

Done with relying on deception and duplicity, bluffs and illusion, to capture my enemies and win my battles. I wanted a fight, and if it was to be bare knuckles, so much the better.

But in order for there to be a chance of that happening, I had to catch Angoulême before he could wash off Roland's blood and with it, Cécile's spell. And knowing that would be his goal, I headed in the direction of the river I'd seen from Melusina's back.

My lungs choked on the ash in the air, my body screaming under the strain of being pushed so hard after it had already endured so much. Sparks bit at my skin, burned holes in my already torn clothes, but I ignored the pain and pushed on, jumping over fallen trees and pools of grey sludge, finally reaching the edge of the forest fire.

Angoulême crouched in the center of the clearing, coat and shirt in a heap beside him, hands full of the snow he was using to scrub the blood off his skin. Swearing silently, I put on a burst of speed. He looked up, and I slammed into him, our combined weight sending us tumbling through the clearing and down a steep slope.

We crashed up against trees and rocks, bushes cutting and slicing as we rolled into the gully to land with a crack on the frozen stream. The ice fractured, and we dropped, freezing water flooding over my head. Staggering to my feet, I dragged him out and threw him against a tree, the trunk cracking with the impact.

At first I thought he was choking on the water he'd inhaled, then I realized he was laughing. Climbing out of the stream, I stalked toward him even as he rose to his feet, one hand pressed to his side. "Feeling a little burned out, are we, Your Highness?"

"I don't need magic to kill you," I said, and struck. He ducked and rolled, coming up swinging, and then we were fighting in earnest. Fists and feet flew, both of us landing blows. I was the better fighter – had trained with Marc, Anaïs, and the twins since I was a child – whereas he'd disdained of combat in order to hide his affliction. But I was burned out, my movements sluggish, and my healing slow. And he knew it – staying on the defense. Wearing me down. And with each spare second, he used handfuls of snow to wipe away Cécile's spell.

I had to end this now, or he'd regain his magic and I'd be done.

Without warning, he turned and sprinted up the slope, the gully sharpening and turning into a ravine that carved back into the foothills. My breath came in labored gasps as I struggled to keep pace, refusing to let him get away to fight another day. We'd been at this game of Guerre for far too long, and it was time it came to an end.

Cutting through a copse of trees, I saw him once again on his knees in the snow, water beading on his skin where it had melted. Snatching up a rock, I dived into him, nearly sending us both over the edge. Then magic snatched hold of my body and flung me hard.

I smashed into the forest, taking a tree down with me. And his laughter followed.

"Once again, you have erred, boy," he said, watching me rise with glittering eyes. "And so ends the reign of the fabled Montignys."

I leaned one hand against a broken tree trunk. "I'm afraid you are mistaken, Your Grace." Then I held up the sharp piece of rock in my hand, one edge coated with crimson.

His eyes widened, and then he felt it. The warm flood of blood from the severed artery at his neck coating his chest and running down to pool at his feet. His magic manifested and struck, but the blow was weak and glancing. He tried again, but his power faltered, and he dropped to his knees.

I walked over to stand in front of him. "Checkmate." I said, and the light fled from his eyes and he fell to the ground at my feet.

My enemy was dead. But instead of triumph, all I felt was numb, because his death did nothing to bring back all of those I'd lost. An empty victory.

"Well done, little brother, well done."

I jerked up from Angoulême's body to see Lessa standing on the opposite side of the gorge, holding Cécile in front of her by the hair.

"Let her go, Lessa," I said, searching for a way to get across and coming up with nothing. My magic was flickering, but it wasn't strong enough to hold my weight, and a fall from this height might well kill me.

"Oh, I fully intend to let her go now that you've disposed of my master for me." She spit into the ravine, her face full of hatred. And yet she'd fooled Angoulême for years, made him think she loved him and was loyal. It made the lie that I had lived seem like nothing. Like child's play.

"I finally made it to the top," she said. "Everyone who stood in my way is dead, or is about to be dead, and I am ready to take my throne."

"Take it," I said, my heart skipping as she leaned Cécile over the edge. "You can have it, just let her go."

She laughed. "Easy for you to give up, when you know you're planning on sending all our people back." She jerked hard on Cécile's hair, eliciting a cry of pain. "I saw what she did to Roland, but it won't work for me, will it? Cursed human blood, always holding me back. You'd make me queen of nothing, witch."

"Lessa, please." If I could just buy enough time for my magic to strengthen, maybe there'd be something I could do to stop her.

"I offered you the chance to rule with me, Tristan," she said. "And when you turned me down, I told you I'd make you pay."

There was a flash of motion behind Lessa, Marc, running toward her, face barely recognizable though the burns.

But he was too late.

"Goodbye, brother," Lessa said, and she let go of Cécile.

She screamed, and I flung out all the magic I had at my disposal, a slender rope wrapping around her waist. Her weight hit, and it felt like my body was being jerked apart. But the magic was just strong enough to hold her tiny form. Out of my periphery, I saw Lessa and Marc falling, but there was nothing I could do.

My eyes burning with pain, I dragged Cécile up. "I've got you," I said, pulling her close. "I won't let you fall." Our enemies were dead, but looking over her shaking shoulder at the two bodies at the base of the ravine, I knew we had not won.

We found a goat track and picked our way down to the base of the ravine, climbing over the frozen creek and slippery rocks until we found our friends. Chris stood sentry over Lessa's body.

"She's dead," he said. "Very dead."

I didn't care. All that mattered was the still form next to her.

Sabine knelt on the ground next to Marc, her face streaked with tears and his hand clutched in hers. Blood was pooling around her knees, but that wasn't the worst of it.

"Is he...?" I found I couldn't say it.

She shook her head, and I saw that his chest was still moving. His hood had fallen back to reveal his face, and I wanted to pull it forward again. Not for the reasons he'd always worn it, but to hide the silent plea in his eyes. A dull ache filled me, and for a moment, it felt like I'd been the one to fall. Like I was the one who couldn't move. Couldn't breathe.

"Alive! Thank the stars," Cécile said. "I can do this. I can fix this. I just need..." She eyed me wildly, then caught sight of the twins limping up the creek bed toward us. "Victoria, hurry," she shouted. "I need you."

"No," I said, taking hold of her upper arms and drawing her back.

"What do you mean, no?" she demanded, twisting to look up at me.

"No magic. No spells," I said. "Leave him be."

"But he'll die!"

I didn't answer, only held her steady and away from my cousin, my best friend. Victoria was on her knees next to him, shoulders shaking as she wept, but when she lifted her head, her eyes were full of understanding.

Cécile was thrashing in my arms. "You can't do this, Tristan. You can't let him die. Please let me help him."

But she wouldn't be helping him. For my own sake, not his, I'd forced him to live when Pénélope had died. I wouldn't do it again. This was his decision, and he'd made it. Whether I agreed didn't matter. It wasn't my choice.

"Please," Cécile whispered, but she ceased struggling. And she wasn't speaking to me. "Marc, please don't leave us. We need you. *I* need you."

His gaze shifted to hers, and whatever she saw there made her shoulders slump. She nodded once, then stepped away from me. Then taking a deep breath, she sang. It was the lament she'd sung for Élise, and it echoed hauntingly through the ravine and up into the night sky. Sabine and Victoria moved back, and I dropped to my knees and took my friend's hand.

His heart was faltering, his breathing ragged and uneven. It would not be long. But what could I say in the space of moment that would do justice to the troll who'd been like an older brother to me? What was I without him? What would I become without him? The world and fate and the stars had given him nothing. Had stolen away almost everything that had mattered to him. And yet despite all he had endured, he was twice the man I'd ever be. If the world were just and fair, I would be the one lying broken on the rocks.

But the world was not just. And it most certainly wasn't fair.

Say something. I clenched my teeth, desperately searching for the words that would convey how much he meant to me. How badly losing him would hurt. How much I didn't want to let go. Then he caught my eye, and I knew I didn't have to say anything all. And in the knowing, I was able to speak. "I hope you find her," I said, my voice cracking as I clenched his hand tight.

The light in his eyes glowed bright for that last faltering heartbeat, then burned out.

Marc was gone.

CHAPTER 63
Cécile

It took time for me to forgive Tristan, and even longer to understand the choice he'd made, though I never really accepted it. Marc's loss was a hurt that was felt by many, and whenever I saw Sabine sitting alone, face marked with grief, my anger flared anew, because there had been a chance. A chance for life, for love, for a future, and now...

I did not know the extent of the relationship between the two of them. How far their sentiment for each other went or whether it had been acknowledged. Sabine never said, and I knew better to ask. Whatever had happened was hers to share. Or not. But I knew he'd left a mark on her soul that would not soon fade, if it ever did.

There are some who'd say she hadn't known him long enough to be so affected. I knew better. There are a rare few in this world with the power to touch the hearts of all those they meet, but Marc was one of them. He'd been my first friend in Trollus, and not a day went by that I wasn't stricken with an anguish so intense it stole my breath. For Marc. And for everyone else who'd fallen.

The endless tasks demanding my attention helped take my mind off all our friends who had been lost in the battle I'd started. There were countless injured humans who needed a witch's skill, and Marie dedicated herself to tracking down witches across the Isle who could help, personally guaranteeing their safety. The time of witch burnings was over.

And so was the time of the trolls. Day after day, I worked my magic on the full-bloods, sending them off into Arcadia through a tear that always appeared at the opportune moment, the trolls stepping through wide-eyed and never looking back. I enlisted some of the other witches to help, because once the flow started, it seemed no one intended to give me a moment's respite, even to sleep.

Tristan worked tirelessly to rebuild that which had been destroyed, opening the Trollus coffers to import the food, grain, and supplies that the Isle needed to replace what had been burned. He frequently rode about on a wagon with Chris, distributing the goods to those who needed them, returning filthy, but in high spirits, to the suite of rooms we'd once again taken command of in the Hôtel de Crillon. Those nights we made up for all the time we'd been apart, lying tangled in each other's arms until dawn, and our respective duties, dragged us out into the sunlight.

Still, there were times I'd start awake in a cold sweat, convinced that Angoulême had returned, and that we were once again at war. Tristan, too, suffered dreams. Lying awake next to him, I could feel the grief and guilt that plagued his mind, though he refused to speak of them in the morning. Neither of us, I thought, were quite willing to believe we were to be given the chance to live the life we'd dreamed. That we could be together and that no one would have to pay the price of our happiness. But as the days turned into weeks, I dared to hope. And I think Tristan did, too.

We both should've known better.

"Are you sure you're ready for this?" I asked. "It does hurt, you know."

"You mean all those screams coming from your laboratory weren't of ecstasy?" Victoria asked, leaning back in her chair and putting her boots on my workstation, which, no matter how many times it was scrubbed, remained stained dark with troll blood. "That's ominous."

I glanced over at Vincent, who sat in the opposite chair, and a ghost of a smile crossed his lips. He still hadn't spoken, but his eyes were no longer expressionless, and when Victoria, Tristan, or I spoke to him, he listened intently. It was impossible to say whether my spell would cure him, as his affliction was not the result of the iron poisoning his blood. But it was hard not to be hopeful.

Tristan and I had offered Victoria the chance to be first of those I worked my magic on to send back, but she'd refused, and had instead taken on the responsibility of gathering up the few full-bloods who were reluctant to take their place on my workbench, either for fear of the pain or because their madness did not allow them to understand the opportunity it presented. All had been cured of their iron affliction, although many who had physical deformities maintained their outward appearance by choice, walking through the tear into Arcadia in the same form in which they'd lived their lives.

The three trolls standing in my presence were all who remained in this world.

"You aren't getting soft, are you?" Tristan asked, punching Victoria in the shoulder and then dodging Vincent's fist. "I never took you for a coward."

Their banter drifted to my ears as I prepared the potion, trying not to let my emotions get the better of me. I'd lost so many of those I loved already, and though the twins were hardly dying – I would be making them immortal – it felt much the same. The Summer King wasn't taking any chances with losing his people to this world a second time, which meant none of the trolls I cured would be able to come back. I'd never see the twins again. A tear ran down my cheek, and I brushed it aside before anyone noticed.

Tristan had gone walking with them earlier today, all the tears and goodbyes accomplished already. They were trying to maintain their levity now, but it was strained. With grief, yes, but also with an anxious sort of hope, because we did not know how the spell would affect Vincent.

"There's only one way to find out, Cécile," Victoria said, seeming to read my thoughts. Another tear fell, but I nodded. "I'm ready."

My worktable was too small for the both of them, and given the connected nature of their power, I believed I needed to perform the spell on both of them at the same time. While Tristan dragged the table out of the way, the twins came over to me, each of them taking one of my hands. "You've been a good friend," Victoria said. "And a mad accomplice. We'll miss you dearly, you know that?"

"Likewise." I wiped my nose with a handkerchief. "The world will seem a much duller place without you two, and infinitely less alliterative."

Vincent smiled, and I knew it was time. They lay next to each other on the floor, Tristan standing in the shadows of a corner, his face revealing none of his anxiety. He gave me a slight nod, and I began.

Neither twin made so much as a peep as the blood began to rise from their skin, grimaces the only sign of the intense pain they were feeling. Sweat beaded on my forehead, and though it was cowardly, I closed my eyes. I felt it the moment they changed, my hands falling into nothingness. Victoria would still be there, but would Vincent? Was there enough left of his mind to maintain his existence without a mortal body holding it together?

No one spoke, and with my heart in my throat, I opened my eyes.

Victoria sat in front of me, her eyes wide as she watched the mist of Vincent's form fade and drift. "Please," she whispered.

"Please don't leave me, brother."

A hand gripped mine, and I cast a sideways glance at Tristan, who was kneeling with me in the twins' blood. "Come on, Vincent," he said. "You can do this."

I held my breath, and then slowly, improbably, Vincent solidified. He turned his head to his sister. "Victoria?"

A sob tore from her lips, and she flung her arms around her brother's shoulders. Tristan's hand relaxed against mine, and it wasn't until I felt the dull ache in my fingers that I realized how tightly he'd been holding it. Vincent was himself again, but the moment was bittersweet, because we were still losing them.

Reluctantly, I handed the twins the last of my store of Élixir, watching sadly as they drank it.

A tear opened behind them, the smell of summer filling my laboratory.

"We have to go," Victoria said. "He's calling us." They rose. "Goodbye, my friends," she said, then to me, "Thank you."

I nodded, holding Tristan's hand tight. And then the twins were gone.

We were both were silent for a long time, then Tristan said, "Get cleaned up, and then let's go for a ride. There is something I need to do."

Tristan's horsemanship had improved in the time he'd spent with Chris, and he rode with almost reckless speed, trusting that I'd keep up. He kept to the Ocean Road, slowing to a trot just before we reached the bridge spanning the rock fall. Sliding off his horse, he waited until I was on the ground and silently tied up our mounts. Then he took my hand, and led me down to the entrance to Trollus.

I hadn't been back since Tristan and I had fled, but he had. Often. The magic holding up the mountain was his once more, the Builder's Guild all departed to Arcadia. The stone tree, which Thibault had very nearly completed for him, was hidden in the darkness of the cavern.

"Would you like to see?" he asked, brushing a bit of dirt from his sleeve.

I shrugged, turning to examine a fountain that I'd always admired so that he wouldn't see the smile on my face. "I suppose."

He was silent for a moment, then he laughed. "It's almost as though you know me."

"Almost." I sat on the edge of the fountain, tipping my head back to watch as the magical tree illuminated, its light revealing the stone structure Tristan had dedicated so many years of his life to create.

"It's lovely," I murmured, wondering if trolls were even capable of building something that was otherwise. Slender pillars and elegant arches filled the cavern, and it seemed impossible such a graceful structure was capable of holding so much weight.

"Care to see if it works?" Tristan asked.

I blanched, but before I could speak, the light of the tree blinked out. The groan of shifting rock filled the cavern as the rocks settled, and I clutched at Tristan's arm.

"It feels as though you doubt me," he said, squeezing my hand and sending a hundred balls of light up toward the ceiling to replace the light of the tree. Little rainbows of color danced in the mist of the waterfall, and slowly, very slowly, I relaxed. "You're mad."

He grinned. "Runs in the family."

I let him lead me toward the palace, the silence of the city seeming strange. "There's no one here."

Tristan shook his head. "None of the half-bloods cared to stay, and everyone else…" He lifted one shoulder, face reflecting the sorrow of his heart.

All his people were gone. For as much as the half-bloods shared some of the same blood, they were not the same. And not for the first time, I wondered if he'd be lonely. If all the humans he'd come to know and care for would be enough to replace what he'd lost.

We meandered through the palace, that beautiful structure full of the work of artists with skill the world might never know again, our boots thudding against tiles that inexplicably remained polished to a high shine. Our travels ended at his rooms – our rooms – as I'd known they would, and I sank into the sumptuous covers while I watched him carefully pack certain items into a bag. A few books. A rolled up painting. Miniatures of his mother and aunt. A ring. A broken blade.

As he walked by the closet doors, he shoved them open to reveal the dozens of elaborate gowns I'd worn during my time here. "Put on your favorite."

I raised one eyebrow. "Why?"

"Why not?"

There was something about the tenseness in his shoulders that told me not to argue. And with his assistance, I donned an emerald velvet evening gown, my fingers brushing against the familiar fabric. With the ease of someone who'd spent a lifetime surrounded by wealth, he plucked matching jewels from the box, brushing aside my hair to fasten them around my neck.

"Take anything else you want," he said, seeming not to notice when I shook my head.

We moved on, making our way to the throne room. He led me between the statues lining the walls, their eyes brightening with magic as we passed, then dropped my arm to go to enormous golden throne, where he sat. "I'm going to abdicate."

"Pardon?" It was the last thing I'd expected him to say. "To whom?"

"Aiden."

I frowned, disliking the choice. When we'd returned to Trianon, I'd woken him from his sleep, only to discover that he'd been mostly aware the entire time. That he'd remained sane was a miracle, the only sign of his tribulations the haunted expression he wore when he thought no one was looking. Zoé had watched over him for most of his ordeal, and he remained as attached to her as though all their time together had been waking. More than attached, and Zoé seemed inclined to be more forgiving than I was of the mistakes he'd made.

"This is an Isle of humans," he said. "It makes no sense for me to rule. And besides, I was thinking we might travel for a time. See the continent. The world."

As if I could begrudge him that.

"Besides," he said. "If he turns out to be dreadful, I can always take it back." Unhooking the crown that had been left on the back of the throne, most likely by his father, he tucked it in his bag. "There's one more thing we have to fetch."

And it was fitting that it was in the glass gardens. Though no doubt he knew the exact location of what he wanted, he led me on a meandering route through the maze of glowing foliage. We crossed the place where his mother and aunt had been slaughtered, but, mercifully, someone had cleaned up the mess, and I said nothing. Eventually we ended up next to the small fountain where, through the tear in the fabric of the world, dripped the Élixir de la Lune. The fountain was almost empty, depleted from all the trolls I'd sent back to Arcadia. "Planning on taking another wife?" I asked, as he carefully filled a small vial.

"I can barely keep track of the one I have." He lifted the glass cylinder and sniffed at it before stoppering it. "I've a promise to fulfill." He gave no further explanation, and I followed him out of the gardens and down to the river, where he turned in a slow circle as though drinking the city in.

"The time of the trolls is over," he said, though it seemed the explanation was more for his benefit than mine. "To the half-bloods this place is nothing more than a broken cage – none will ever willingly live here again. And I do not wish to see it taken by those who care only for its riches, who would steal the gold, the art, the knowledge, and use it for their advantage."

"What do you propose?" I asked, my chest aching with a pain I couldn't explain.

"It's a tomb," he said. "And it's time it was sealed."

Gripping my hand, he led me down the river toward the gates, and as we walked, I felt the heat of magic manifesting. When we were almost at the River Road, the roar of falling rock shattered my ears. Twisting to look over my shoulder, I watched as column after column collapsed, the rock of Forsaken Mountain falling from the sky to smash into the city below. Elysium disappeared, then the library, then the palace. The glass gardens – so many long years of labor – destroyed in a moment. Tears flooded down my cheeks, but Tristan didn't look back.

Not once.

Instead he drew me into the tunnel of the road, his magic stalling the collapse of the mountain until we stood on the beach, sunlight on our faces. Then he turned back to look at the rock slide that had given him so much purpose and nodded once.

Trollus was gone.

I'd returned to my laboratory to pack what things I wanted while Tristan had gone to the castle to give Aiden the keys to the kingdom and to deliver the Élixir to Zoé to use as she wished. I sang as I packed, thinking about the plans we'd made on our ride back to Trianon. The places we'd go. The things we'd see.

"You're beautiful when you smile like that."

I turned to see Tristan leaning against the door frame, coat unbuttoned and shirt loose at the throat. His hair was longer than he usually kept it, inky black where it brushed against the white of his collar. Silver eyes unearthly bright and beautiful, and for the first time that I'd known him, free of concern.

"Like what?" I asked.

"Like you're happy."

"Then expect to see it often," I said, crossing the room. "Because I am."

Wrapping my arms around his neck, I rose on my tiptoes and kissed him, relishing the feel of his lips against mine. The heat his touch sent racing through my veins.

"I love you," he murmured into my ear, the warmth of his breath making my body ache. I parted my lips to respond in kind, when the smell of summer washed across my face. I turned in his arms in time to the tear open wide, and the King of Summer stepped into our world.

"Your Majesty," Tristan said, and to my surprise, he stepped away from me and bowed low.

I stood my ground, goosebumps rising to my skin despite the balmy temperature of the room.

The King inclined his head, then turned his attention to me. "You owed me a debt, Cécile de Montigny."

I lifted my chin. "And I have paid it. You have your people back."

His head tilted, and I found I had to look away, my eyes burning as though I were staring at the sun. "Not all of them."

"You cannot have the half-bloods," I said, catching hold of the fabric of my gown and clenching it tight. "They belong as much here as they do there, more so, in fact. If I tried to take the iron from their flesh, they'd die."

"Not them," he said. "Their magic and that of all those born to them I will bind by name."

"Then…" I closed my eyes. I couldn't breathe.

"No," Tristan said, and the word sounded torn from his throat. "I will not go."

The Summer King's words rang through my mind: *Your debt has been called due, Cécile de Montigny. I will have all my people back, and you will make it happen.*

All.

All.

"Please." Tristan dropped to his knees. "I'll do anything. Promise anything. Bind my magic, take it away, I don't care. Just don't make me leave her."

The fairy said nothing. He didn't need to. The weight of my debt was enough.

My body moved, picking up the pouch of *lobelia* and then the basin, my hand mechanically preparing the potion even as sobs tore from my chest.

"Cécile, don't." Tristan jerked the basin out of my hands and tossed it aside with a clatter. "Please don't do this."

"I have to."

The pouch burst into flames in my hands, the flowers incinerated but my hands untouched. "Fight it," he pleaded.

But it was like stopping an ocean tide. A hurricane wind. The sands of time. It could not be done. Flowers burst up through the floorboards, the reek of *lobelia* filling the air, cloying and horrible. Tristan tore at them, the petals turning to ash at his touch, but more sprang up in their place.

"Tristanthysium," the King said. "Abide."

His fury made my mind scream in pain, but he could not deny his name, especially when uttered by the one who had given it to him. Tristan dropped to his knees in front of me, and I flung my arms around him, refusing to let go.

But it was for naught.

The spell tore from me, magic rising from all directions to take back what belonged to this world. I wrenched the iron from his veins, feeling his pain as though it were my own even as I forced his magic to heal the damage I was causing. And when it was done, I was holding on to nothing.

He was mist, and the tears running down his face disappeared the moment they left his skin. But that did not stop the King from closing a hand on his shoulder. He handed Tristan a vial, waited until he'd drained the contents, then drew him back toward the tear. Back and back.

"Tristan, I love you," I said.

Then he was gone.

They found me in a carpet of flowers, my anguish uncontrollable. Voices. Questions. Hands lifting me up and carrying me out. A tonic forced down my throat, and then nothing.

Even when the tonic wore off, I clung to that nothing.

Because I'd lost everything.

Days passed.

It wasn't fair.

They took me home to the farm; to a familiar bed. Familiar sheets.

We'd fought so hard.

Joss and Sabine took turns forcing food down my throat.

We'd won.

I could still feel him, distant, but there. But not here.

We'd been happy.

Days passed.

Then one morning, I got up. On weak knees, I dressed in an old gown of homespun and tied back my hair. The kitchen was empty, so I went out into the yard and into the barn where I found my sister working. Her eyes widened at the sight of me, but she said nothing until I picked up a pitch fork and started mucking a stall.

Setting aside her shovel, she came over and gently pried it from my hands, meeting my gaze. "It will be a fall baby."

"Yes," I said, a tear running down the side of my nose.

"Gran knew, you know. She told me before she died."

I bowed my head, not able to speak.

"Maybe he…" She hesitated, and I caught her hands, cutting

off the thought. "Just give me something to do. Something to keep me busy."

Joss nodded, but she didn't give me back the pitchfork. Instead she said, "Perhaps you ought to do what you do best."

For a moment, I wanted to refuse. To tell her that it was not in me to seek respite in something that had once given me pleasure. But Tristan wouldn't have wanted that. And I found that I didn't either.

So I sang.

CHAPTER 64
Tristan

And I listened.

Time was different here, and it seemed I spent days with that song in my ears, sitting in silence while I watched through a fissure I'd torn between our worlds. It was all I'd done since my uncle had forced me here against my will, and if I had my way, it would be all I'd ever do.

Vines sprung from the earth, twisting up a web of green and brown, obscuring my view. I scowled, and turned. "Cécile's pregnant. You must let me go back."

"Must?" As always, his voice was amused. As though I were some minor curiosity providing a few moments of entertainment. "I fail to see why?"

"She did what you asked," I snarled, tearing the vines away only for them to spring forth anew. "You have the lost bloodlines back in Arcadia, are gaining the ground you lost, are driving Winter from worlds frozen for millennia, and all because of Cécile. Yet you punish her for it."

He cocked his head. "Do I?"

Questions answered with more questions. The fey were irritating, and he was the worst of all. I stared down at my hands, at the golden marks painted across my knuckles. Were they really still there, or were they only a reflection of what

I wanted to be?

No, I decided. *They were there.* I could still feel her – a whisper of presence in my mind.

"There are worlds beyond count for you to explore, and yet you'd waste your time watching this mortal life?" he asked. "Why?"

"Because it is my life," I whispered, forcing the vines to grow apart so that I could see once more.

Cécile remained on the farm in the care of her family and Sabine, her cheeks regaining their color even as her stomach took on a noticeable curve. Visitors came and went. Tips, whom Aiden had taken on as an advisor, came often, keeping her informed of the developments of the Isle as though she were queen. Marie and Zoé, whom Aiden was now courting, arrived with bolts of silk and velvet from the continent, regaling her with gossip from the city. Chris, who had returned to his father's farm, took her riding often. And when she grew too large to do so comfortably, on carriage rides up and down the coast, Souris sitting at their feet. Everyone came together for her eighteenth birthday, the farmhouse filled to the brim with those who loved her.

For all of them, she smiled.

For all of them, she laughed.

For all of them, she pretended.

Only when she was alone, in the darkest hours of the night, did she unleash the hurt, curling in on herself. Soaking the pillow with tears. Muffling her sobs with a quilt. Every time it tore me apart, filled me fury, and sent me in pursuit of my uncle, where I begged, pleaded, and raged that he allow me to go back.

The answer was always the same.

Childbirth was not easy for her. Two days of pain, Sabine and Josette's eyes filled with the fear that they would lose her, the marks on my fingers tarnishing and blackening at the tips as she labored and bled.

Then our son was born.

From the lands of endless summer, I watched the arrival of this small half-blood boy who would never know me, but whom I already loved above all things. So caught up was I in examining his perfect little features, that at first I didn't feel the flux of power as a portal formed between our two worlds. Noticed only when the room filled with a warm glow and my uncle stepped into the room.

Cécile lost her mind, throwing herself from the blood soaked bed and crawling between him and our child. "You cannot have him, too," she screamed. "You cannot take him."

He bent down to say something in her ear; then, ignoring her pleas, his insubstantial form passed through her so that he could bend over the wailing infant and whisper a name in his ear. A command, binding him from using his magic before he ever knew he had it.

Then he was gone, leaving Cécile to clutch our son to her chest, all the anger, pain, and fear she'd pent up over the months unleashing in a torrent.

I tore into his court, my fury splintering into countless nasty creatures that clawed and bit, scattering all those present until my uncle's creations rose to battle with them. Monsters made of fear and thought multiplying and attacking. We stood in the center of a war of nightmares, and in countless worlds, the seas rose high and the winds raged.

And finally, his temper snapped.

"You do not belong there," he snarled, a storm of wind and heat, thunder and lightning punctuating his words. Claws caught me by the throat and hurled me to the ground, defeated.

"You could have told her that I love her," I said into the dirt. "You could have told her that I can see her. Hear her."

A scaled foot tipped with bloody claws dug into the ground next to my face. "And what would knowing do for her?" he said, shape blurring and shifting into a human form. "How well would she live her life knowing you were constantly looking over her shoulder?"

"It might be some small comfort."

"For her? Or for you?"

They were wise words. Not that I listened, the stubbornness that was my best and worst ally pushing me back to my portal to watch the life I longed for. The life that should've been mine.

Cécile, by contrast, lived.

With Sabine and our son, who'd eventually informed her his name was Alexandre, in tow, she moved back to Trianon, where she met with the banker, Bouchard, about taking the reins of the businesses she'd inherited from Anushka, the foremost of which was the Trianon Opera House. She took control of it with characteristic ferocity, ruthlessly firing those who stood in the way of her vision, while hiring the best and brightest stars, who she paid exorbitantly, or in her words, "Precisely what they're worth."

It took several months of work to repair the damage done to the opera house while it had housed refugees, and I smiled every time she muttered, "It's your cursed gold that's paying to fix this, Tristan."

And on opening night, she took to the stage in front of a sold out crowd. I opened a portal in Bouchard's box, watching over his shoulder as she sang her heart out.

She did not stop there, investing in opportunities with a keen eye for business that I wouldn't have expected from her. For Sabine, she provided the funds for a dress shop, and my coconspirator swiftly became the most in demand designer in Trianon, her creations worn by nobility and songstresses alike. After much argument, she convinced Chris to accept the gold needed to import stock from the continent, and he spent his days surrounded by horses and Souris's growing number of progeny.

When all was settled as she wanted it, Cécile toured the continent, singing on every great stage and becoming as famous for her voice as she was for her role in the events that had taken place on the Isle, which had become legendary throughout the known world. And with her, she always brought our son, raining affection on him even as she castigated him for all the less desirable traits he'd inherited from me.

He was a clever boy, dark-haired and slight, and constantly getting into trouble. As he grew older, he took liberal advantage of his fame and good looks, and kissed half the girls in Trianon before Aiden and Zoé's daughter took a liking to him, thus ensuring he never looked twice at another girl ever again.

Time passed, and Cécile lived it well. But it was a mortal life.

And all mortal lives must come to an end.

CHAPTER 65
Tristan

It came on slowly, and then very quickly.

A chill caught on a ship coming back from the continent. Then a cough that took hold of her during auditions, causing her to excuse herself lest she disturb the young performers. "Just a tickle in the throat. Nothing that a cup of tea won't cure," she assured her assistants.

But it hadn't. Not a cup, nor a pot, nor all the potions and tonics on the Isle had any affect, and before I knew it, the cough had moved into her chest. A deep rasping thing that drained her, leaving her weak and frail. Blackness began to creep up the bonding marks on my hands, and I knew.

"Let a witch see to you," Sabine had said, but Cécile only shook her head. "You can't heal age," and then, "I want to go home."

The farmhouse in Goshawk's Hollow was the domain of her sister, now, their father long since passed, and Fred a senior officer in Aiden's army. Joss and her husband had a legion of children, and even a few grandchildren, and the home had been expanded to accommodate. They kept a room there for Cécile, and it was in that bed they lay her, almost too weak to speak.

"Someone needs to send for Alex," Sabine said to Chris, who had come as soon as he'd heard. "She isn't going to last much longer."

Though I'd known it was coming, the words were a blow.

For many years, I'd been wondering how this moment would go. Whether, now that I was immortal, her death still had the power to kill me. Whether I wanted it to. Or not. And in the wondering, an idea had come to me, little pieces of a lifelong puzzle falling into place. That idea had blossomed and grown, and turned into the wickedest of all things: hope.

Closing the tear, I made my way to the hedge maze that stretched higher than I could see, meandering through the paths that changed depending on his mood, allowing only those whom he cared to see through to the center. The maze opened up into a clearing, at the middle of which lay a lake of molten fire, its surface heaving and shifting, the air above it shimmering with heat. The sun.

"She's dying," I said, and the lake settled, my reflection appearing on the smooth surface. "Will you let me see her through?"

An enormous tear opened in front of me, and with a bittersweet ache in my heart, I stepped back into the world of my birth.

The opening was in a field on the de Troyes farm, and I stood motionless for a moment, savoring the crisp scent of pine on the spring breeze that still had the bite of winter. Icicles dangled from under the eaves of the barn, drip-dripping into the barrels beneath them with a sound like music. The sun overhead was warm on my back, and I stopped to pat the head of the dog sitting on the front porch before adjusting my cuffs and knocking at the door.

It swung open to reveal Chris standing in the front entry. He'd grown sturdier with age, crow's feet marking the corners of his blue eyes, but his blonde hair was untouched by grey. He stared at me for a long moment, then said, "You pretty-faced troll bastard. How dare you show up looking like you haven't aged a day when the rest of us had to go and get old."

A grin – the first in longer than I cared to admit – pulled up the corners of my mouth. "I've missed your compliments. No one else phrases them quite like you do."

"Did I hear you say…" Sabine pushed past Chris, then clapped a hand over her mouth. "Stones and sky," she whispered. "Is it really you?"

Not waiting for an answer, she flung her arms around my neck. "Oh, Tristan. Cécile, she's…"

"I know," I said. "That's why I'm here." Her eyes met mine, and she gave a slow nod of understanding.

They led me inside, where Joss stood next to the same scarred wooden table she'd once sat me at. Without saying a word, she lifted my hand, tears flooding down her cheeks at the sight of my blackened bonding marks. "I'd thought maybe…" She scrubbed a hand across her face, wiping away the damp. "It's good that you're here – it will mean everything to her."

Sabine took my arm at the elbow. "She hid it well, but we all knew she never recovered from losing you," she said. "And of a surety, she never stopped loving you. Not for a moment."

My chest tightened, and for a second, it hurt to breathe. "She never lost me."

Boots clattered down the stairs, and my son stepped into the kitchen. "Aunt Joss–" he started to say, then froze, his inability to use his own magic doing nothing to dampen the sense of mine.

"Alex, this is–"

"I know who he is," Alex said. "I've seen his portraits, and even if I hadn't… Well, I do own a mirror."

"The ego does not fall far from the tree," Chris said, but I ignored him, knowing well what my son's wit was hiding.

"If you're here, then…" Alex looked away, jaw tightening as he struggled to contain his emotions, wiping a hand across eyes that were more blue than grey. *So like his mother.*

I nodded, confirming his fears. But what was there for me to say in this short moment when I was allowed in this world? I'd watched him born, watched him grow from a boy into a man under his mother's guiding eye. I *knew* him, but to Alexandre, I was a stranger. Little more to him than the sum of the stories told about me. He was older than I'd been when I left – than how I appeared to him now – somewhat shorter, but filled out by his adult years and hours spent training with his uncle. Though he was everything I could have wanted in a child, sentiment between us would be awkward and strange.

But neither could I leave having said nothing. I was not my father.

"When you are playing cards," I said, "you might consider losing from time to time. Especially when you're playing against your Uncle Fred. He takes great offense to cheating, and he's starting to become suspicious."

His eyes widened, then he crossed his arms. "I don't cheat."

I laughed. "All trolls cheat at cards – it's in your blood. The lying on the other hand, that came from your mother." Clapping him once on the shoulder, I started up the stairs, goodbyes seeming unwarranted now that they knew I could see them when I wanted.

Her labored breathing filled my ears before I even entered the room, and for a long time, I stood with my hand on the handle, searching for the courage I needed.

"I know you're there." Her voice was weak, but familiar. "So quit skulking, and come in."

Smiling, I opened the door.

Thirty years had come and gone, but even though illness had rendered her frail, she was as beautiful as she'd been at seventeen. Her crimson hair had grown long again, and it hung in a thick braid over one shoulder. The scar on her cheek had faded into a thin white line that was fiercely lovely, and the faint creases near her eyes spoke more to character than age.

But none of that mattered, because her blue gaze was filled with pain, fluid rattling in her lungs, and her heartbeat weak. It would not be long now.

"I've been waiting for you," she whispered as I sat next to her on the bed, taking her hand. "But I was starting to think you wouldn't come. That you didn't..."

Twin tears rolled down her cheeks, and mindful of her fragile state, I pulled her close. "I told you once that I'd love you until the day I took my last breath, and that is true now as it was then. But how did you know..."

"He told me," she said, her breath ragged against my throat. "When Alex was born, he told me that I'd see you in the end."

And how many times had I accused my uncle of being heartless and cruel?

A rash of coughing took her, and I held her slender form through it, fear building in my chest as her heart stuttered. She was dying. Cécile was dying.

"It hurts."

My eyes burned. "It will be over soon."

Cécile took one last breath, and then her heart stilled.

The pain was incredible, like I was being gutted, my chest ripped in two. The silken thread of our bond stretched and frayed, but I clung to it, held on. Refused to let go.

Please, was the only thought in my mind as I tore open a path to Arcadia and stepped through.

CHAPTER 66
Cécile

The air was warm and humid with the taste of a lurking summer storm. The sweet scent of some unknown flowers filled my nose, and against my cheek, I felt the press of a linen shirt, the skin beneath burning with unnatural heat. And a heartbeat in my ear that was as steady and familiar as my own.

"A dream," I whispered, because I'd lost track over the years of how often I'd lost myself in his arms, only to be torn awake and find myself in an empty bed.

"Not a dream," Tristan said, and I lifted my face to gaze into silver eyes, his face exquisite and unchanged.

"Then I'm…?"

He nodded, the hand pressing against the small of my back warm through the silk of my sapphire dress. My body, I noticed, had reverted to a state it had not seen in decades. *You are as you imagine yourself to be.*

"How?" I asked, casting my gaze around at the lush green of Arcadia, the landscape shifting and changing and full of strange life. "I'm human." And I knew better than most how much iron ran through my veins.

"A human body cannot pass between worlds," he said, "but a human soul, it turns out, suffers no such impediments. That's how my uncle was able to bring you here before, however temporarily."

"Much can happen in the time between two heartbeats," I said, repeating what the King of Summer had told me while we stood in the heart of Winter.

"Or when a heart beats no more," Tristan said. "Our bond was what kept your soul from going... elsewhere, but–" He cleared his throat, looking over my head. "It could be broken, if that's what you want."

I stood on my tiptoes and kissed him, drinking in the taste of him even as I banished that foolish thought from his mind. I could've kissed him for another lifetime and still not had my fill, but I lowered down onto the soles of my feet. "Is Marc..."

He shook his head, and even though the wound was old, the pain seemed fresh again. "But the twins, Martin, Roland – they're here and well. I'll take you to see them."

I bit the insides of my cheeks, afraid to ask my next question, but knowing that I had to. "How long can I stay?"

A smile curved his cheeks. "Forever."

My eyes burned and I shook my head slowly, letting the sweetness of that singular word sink into my heart. "Why didn't you bring me sooner?"

He tucked a curl of hair behind my ear, then cupped my cheek with his palm. "Would you have wanted to miss it?"

Instinctively, I knew what he meant: my life. All the places I'd gone, things I'd seen, people I'd known and loved. A thousand accomplishments, mine and those of my family and friends. My son, growing from a tiny baby into a man of whom I was immensely proud. *My* life, which should've been *our* life together. "No," I whispered. "I wouldn't have wanted to miss a minute of it. And I'm so sorry you had to."

"I didn't." He kissed my lips. "At least, not entirely. There are some advantages of being able to see all."

My chest ached as I imagined him watching all those long years. The depth of his love and loyalty to me, to our son, to our friends, that he'd not turned away and forgotten. "I wish they knew. Alex... He'll take my death hard." And though he was a man grown, it was hard for me to accept leaving him.

"Sabine suspects," Tristan said. "She'll know what to say. To him, and to the rest of them."

It was as though the last of my burdens had been lifted, and I took a deep breath and savored it, knowing that I'd done all I could for those I loved best. For those I'd left behind. Their lives were theirs to live. As was mine. "Tristan..."

"Yes?" His face betrayed none of the nervousness I knew to be roiling through him.

"You say you saw all?" I cocked one eyebrow, then smiled as I felt his nerves turn to faint embarrassment. "As I recall, some things are better..." I paused, giving him a slow smile, "face to face."

"I could not agree more," he replied, embarrassment turning into something far better. Then his arms were around me, his lips on mine, and the feel of them – of him – was infinitely sweeter than memory.

Pulling him down onto grass like velvet, I lost myself in him. In the love that had consumed me for so much of my life. A love that I'd feared would always be colored with the bittersweet tarnish of loss. An echo of a song. But now, against all hope, that love was polished clean and new as it had been in those first days we'd fallen.

My mortal life was over.

But our immortal life had just begun.

Acknowledgments

I've faced a unique set of challenges with the writing of each of my novels, but one constant has been carving time out of each day to put words on the page. Never, however, has that been more difficult than the six months I spent plucking *Warrior Witch* from this sleep-deprived, new mother's mind. With great certainty, I can say that this novel would be a half-finished mess of words on the page without the support of my family. An enormous amount of thanks must go to my parents, Carol and Steve, for providing endless hours of babysitting, and to my mother-in-law, Pat, for swooping in during those moments when I was falling asleep on my feet. Most especially, I must thank my other half, Spencer, for waking up at 5am everyday so that I didn't have to, and for ensuring that I ate more than just pizza and granola bars.

Gratitude, as always, must go to my utterly amazing agent, Tamar Rydzinski, who always goes above and beyond the call of duty. A big thanks to intern Rachael for her summarization skills, and to Laura Dail, for always being an enormous support. To my publishing team at Angry Robot: Phil, Marc, Mike, Penny, and Caroline, thank you so much for all the hard work you've done to ensure the success of my novels.

Thanks goes to Donna, for getting me out of my pyjamas

and out of the house, and to Carleen and Gena for texting me things that had nothing to do with novels so that I remembered there was a world outside my writing cave. Lots of love to my brother, Nick – you are the consummate salesman and I owe you one.

Last, but not least, I must express a huge amount of gratitude to the book-bloggers and reviewers who have been such an enormous support to me and my novels, but most particularly to Melissa (@StolenSongbird) who picked up my social media slack while I was struggling to finish this novel. And the biggest thanks of all goes to the readers who have stuck with me through to the end – I hope you loved every minute of it.